BADGER
TO THE BONE

Also by Shelly Laurenston

BADGER TO THE BONE

The Honey Badgers Chronicles

SHELLY LAURENSTON

KENSINGTON BOOKS
www.kensingtonbooks.com

KENSINGTON BOOKS are published by

Kensington Publishing Corp.
119 West 40th Street
New York, NY 10018

All Kensington titles, imprints, and distributed lines are available at special quantity discounts for bulk purchases for sales promotion, premiums, fund-raising, educational, or institutional use.

Special book excerpts or customized printings can also be created to fit specific needs. For details, write or phone the office of the Kensington Sales Manager: Kensington Publishing Corp., 119 West 40th Street, New York, NY 10018. Attn. Sales Department. Phone: 1-800-221-2647.

Kensington and the K logo Reg. U.S. Pat. & TM Off.

ISBN-13: 978-1-4967-1442-8 (ebook)
ISBN-10: 1-4967-1442-3 (ebook)

Kensington Electronic Edition: April 2020

ISBN-13: 978-1-4967-1440-4
ISBN-10: 1-4967-1440-7

First Kensington Trade Paperback Printing: April 2020

10 9 8 7 6 5 4 3 2 1

Printed in the United States of America

Thanks to my California family for inspiring my honey badger sisters and teaching me about true loyalty. I love you guys!

A nose, both cheekbones, and an upper jaw broken by the force of a ball. A twisted arm cracked from the pressure, then a shoulder. A kneecap destroyed by one kick. A lower jaw cracked by a fist. A trachea crushed by another fist.

A circle formed, preventing the prey from running.

Charles Taylor knew he had to intervene, but he was fascinated. What he shouldn't be, though, was surprised. Their team had just won the Girls' High School Basketball State Championship. Because if it was one thing they knew how to do, it was how to be a team.

Finally, he stepped out from beside the tree. One of the prey reached out for him, begging him with tear-filled eyes for help.

Charles, instead, looked at the predators and they all stared back, waiting for him to yell, to chastise, until one happily waved at him.

"Hi, Pop-Pop," his granddaughter greeted with a wide grin, one eye bruised and swelling. Her lip and jaw doing the same. Marks on her throat suggesting she had been choked first. He glanced down at the men, parts of them so badly broken they couldn't get up. Several, however, attempted to drag themselves away. One was faster than the others, but before he could get very far, one of the teammates stepped in front of him.

She, like his granddaughter, was a little thing. Deceptively small and innocent looking . . . except for the broad shoulders and thighs. And the eyes. Their eyes betrayed what they were. What his granddaughter was, but only because Max was not his blood. He'd adopted her the same way he'd adopted her younger sister—with absolutely no state or federal involvement and no legal paperwork. But their kind didn't often do things like the full-humans who surrounded them. When his blood-related granddaughter had come to his Pack-owned home, she'd brought her half-sisters with her and all three had become his concern. His responsibility. His problem.

And, to be quite honest . . . his entertainment. Because where the three of them went—whether together or apart—trouble didn't simply follow. It nested inside them like a parasite. The trio were the Typhoid Marys of trouble.

So he had no idea how these men had gotten on the bad side of his granddaughter Max and her teammates, but he also knew that Max Yang didn't attack without reason. Honey badgers never did. But God help you if you attacked them, because they never stopped. They never would stop. No matter how much bigger their enemy, how much stronger, how much faster. Badgers never stopped.

Unless, of course, one offered them something better.

"Your sister is making breakfast. You better get home."

"Breakfast?" She looked at her watch. "Little late."

"She calls it brunch, but when waffles are involved, it's breakfast. Or dinner. It's never brunch."

She shrugged those brawny shoulders of hers and looked at her teammates. It was a Saturday but the boys' basketball team had been given a parade for their championship win. The girls, however, who'd rocked the state championship as only a group of badgers could, had not been rewarded with such spirit. So the ladies had gone to the parade in their team uniforms and, knowing them as he did, had probably started a lot of shit because they had gotten no respect from their own school. The school they'd played and won for.

Although the whole team was great, it was these five who had led them to glory and who probably got the most attention. And, most likely, the attention of these men.

Charles knew the broken men on the ground. They didn't live in his little town but they drove through it when they were on their drug runs, their American-made motorcycles making rumbling noises that just upset those in his Pack.

These men usually didn't mess with the residents but maybe it had been too hard to resist five young women in matching, bright yellow basketball jerseys and shorts walking down the street. Maybe that had bothered them or enticed them, but when they didn't get the response they wanted, they'd hurt Charles's granddaughter.

And that's why they were crumpled into screaming piles five feet into Charles's territory.

"Up for waffles?" Max asked and the four other girls nodded.

"But we should clean up," one of them said, a basketball under her arm, her badger gaze locked on her cursing and sobbing prey. "It's always good to be tidy."

"None of that," Charles replied, immediately knowing these girls weren't discussing washing their hands. "You five will not be doing any *cleaning up* of anything."

"Well, you shouldn't do it," Max debated. "You're getting old."

"It's like you *want* a paw-slap."

Another raised her hand to silence them, her head turning, eyes closing. She lifted her nose to the air. Sniffed.

"They're coming," she finally announced, her voice ominous.

Charles immediately knew who "they" were, and it wasn't his Pack. It wasn't more humans. It was a Clan. Not *the* Klan, of course, with a *k*. The Klan had come onto their territory once, back in his father's time to put a stop to the "mixed-race utopia going on over there" . . . and were never seen again. But a Clan with a capital *C*.

Hyenas. They'd moved into the farm next door to Charles's Pack a few years back. Thankfully, neither side gave the other much trouble, but a fight this close to territorial lines could cause all sorts of problems if not handled correctly. Especially since one of these basketball players was the half-sister of some of the hyena adults. Although her badger genes overrode anything else inside her, giving her full-on honey badger traits, the Clan still believed her to be their "property." The way they believed all the male hyenas were *their* property. At least, she would be until she turned eighteen. Unless she was at basketball practice, the hyenas didn't take kindly to her hanging out with her honey badger teammates outside of school.

Charles didn't hesitate. "All of you go to the Pack house. Now."

"We're not leaving you here alone," Max informed him.

Charles wasn't worried. Not when he had the perfect distractions right in front of him, still trying to drag their broken bodies away. A few had already crossed territorial lines and if there was one thing this particular Clan hated more than howling wolves . . . it was human men.

"You'll do what I tell you," Charles insisted.

"But—"

"While you're under my roof, Max MacKilligan—"

"Oh, God." Brown eyes rolled dramatically. "Not the speech."

"Move your asses," he ordered the girls, before adding, "or I can go get your sister and she can—"

Four of the girls abruptly sprinted off toward the Pack house before Charles had the chance to finish his threat, but Max stood there, smirking at him.

"That was beneath you," she told him.

"Was it, though?"

Max laughed and started off. But before she could disappear into the surrounding woods, Charles told her, "The new Alpha female has been making some noise about you and your sisters."

Max stopped, but didn't turn around. But he could see her shoulders tighten. Just a bit, but enough.

"I don't want Charlie to hear about it," he went on. "She's got enough on her plate right now. There's some bidding war going on between universities that want your baby sister. Charlie is trying to deal with all that without a lawyer. This will just stress her out even—"

"I've got it," Max said, but she wasn't standing where she had been. She'd already disappeared into the trees.

★   ★   ★

"Hi, Betsey."

Betsey froze; that voice whispering in her ear. She hadn't lived in the Pack house for years. She only came home for major holidays and one week during the summer. Otherwise, she stayed as far away from the Pack as possible. Not because they were cruel to her. They really hadn't been. But as a hybrid, she hadn't really been accepted either. Tolerated? Yes. Accepted? No.

So she only came when necessary. Like this weekend. It was her mother's birthday on Sunday. And Betsey did what she always did when she came here . . . stayed out of everyone's way; kept to the shadows. It wasn't hard. No one was ever looking for her except her mother, and no one would care when she left Monday morning.

Yet things had been different since she'd arrived Friday night. She knew why, too. It was them. The MacKilligan sisters. She remembered when they'd first arrived. Alone and dirty, they'd managed to secure a spot at the house despite the strong Alpha who always made it clear that he loathed hybrids of any kind. But they'd gotten him out and Betsey had never seen the man again. She used to think that had been down to their grandfather. He'd been so angry that day . . .

But a few years later, out of nowhere, their ex-Alpha had reappeared, very much alive. According to her mother, he'd immediately started making noises, causing problems, had rounded up some lone wolves to create a makeshift Pack in the hope of reclaiming what he still thought was his. It had gotten so bad that Charles and his Beta had traveled to Milwaukee to meet with the Smith Pack to ask them to help back up the much smaller Pack, something he did *not* want to do. But Charles had always been willing to make sacrifices to protect his Pack; especially with his two adopted granddaughters still under eighteen.

Betsey happened to be back the weekend he'd headed off for that meeting and, about thirty minutes after Charles left, his eldest and middle granddaughters had walked out the front door without a word to anyone. They returned the next day; bruised, bloody, and carrying an actual dog puppy they'd found on the road. They didn't say a word to anyone, simply went upstairs, took showers, and spent the rest of the day training their new puppy. They'd weirdly named him Karris, which she didn't find out until much later was after a character from the movie *The Exorcist.*

At the ages of sixteen and fifteen, it wasn't really strange that kids with their only guardian out of the house would disappear overnight. One would assume they'd been off drinking beers with their friends. But Betsey suspected otherwise and was then certain when she'd found out that their ex-Alpha and his small Pack of wolves had suddenly disappeared. No one had any idea where they were or when they'd be back, but Betsey knew they'd never "be back." Whatever Charlie and Max had done, they'd made sure that their ex-Alpha would never return again to bother their grandfather. The disappearance didn't disturb Betsey as much as the girls' lack of concern about it. Shouldn't they be showing signs of PTSD or remorse for what they'd been forced to do? But nope. They'd instead focused on their adorable, disturbingly named puppy and went on with their lives as if nothing had happened. Thereby proving what Betsey had known since the girls first arrived at the Pack house: they were killers. Not simply predators. All shifters were predators. But at least the first two were hard-core killers. Shifters who could do what needed to be done without losing sleep or needing recovery time.

So hearing Max, of all people, whisper in her ear nearly made Betsey wet herself. She didn't but almost.

Even worse, Betsey had been caught eavesdropping as she liked to do when she came home. Since no one paid any attention to her, it was easy enough.

Max leaned over a bit, looking into the sunken living room. Betsey was going to slink away, but Max had put her hand on Betsey's nearby forearm. It seemed innocent. As if she'd just reached out for balance. But Betsey knew better about that, too. Knew that the badger was just keeping her in place so she couldn't warn anyone.

"If we try to force them out now," the Beta female explained to the Pack's new Alpha female in that sunken living room, "you are definitely going to have a problem with the oldest."

"That's Charlie, right? Charles's granddaughter."

"Charles thinks of all three as his granddaughters."

"Sure, sure. I understand that."

The new Alpha female wasn't Charles's mate. He'd lost his mate a long time ago and had never replaced her. But the females still needed someone to lead them and this one had come in from Ohio less than three months ago. She was tolerable, Betsey supposed, but she was making the same mistake as all the other Alpha females who'd come to the Pack in the last few years: trying to push out the MacKilligan girls.

Not that Betsey blamed her, but still. These three were not like Betsey and her hybrid friends. Half wolf and half black bear, Betsey entertained herself with soccer balls and tough rubber toys that were used for pit bulls; she made sure that all her meat-and-vegetable meals were smothered in quality honey; and, if she wasn't paying attention, she tended to howl along with ambulance sirens. Normally not a big problem . . . except she'd just started medical school and would eventually be doing her residency at a hospital. With ambulances. That had sirens.

Awkward.

But the MacKilligan girls? They were different from everything. Even the middle one, whose parents were both honey badgers.

Like now. Instead of glaring into that room the way Charlie would, pissed off and annoyed that these females were having this discussion without them, Max glanced at Betsey with that freakish grin of hers. Betsey never knew how to read that smile. Was it happiness? Delusion? A neurological tic? She didn't know. She just wanted it far away from her.

The conversation in the living room faded away and Betsey heard the Alpha tell the other females to get something to eat. Charlie was cooking breakfast and everything smelled delicious. But Betsey wasn't about to make any sudden moves. Not yet.

"Come in, Max," the Alpha said from the other room.

Still smiling, Max winked at Betsey before she stepped in front of the big opening that led to the living room. With her hands behind her back and one sneakered foot resting on the other, she stood on the top step. She looked adorable. Innocent even. But again . . . Betsey knew better.

"Come, come," the Alpha said. Her voice sounded friendly. Not the fake friendly either, but truly friendly. That didn't really mean anything, though. Betsey had been pummeled by a librarian once. A six-four grizzly female that she'd accidentally startled in the stacks. So "friendly" didn't mean the same to their kind as it did to the full-humans.

"I guess you heard, huh, Max?"

"I heard a little. Yes."

Unable to help herself—curiosity being her main weakness, damn her bear genes!—Betsey leaned over so she could peek around the corner. Max now stood in front of the imposing Alpha female. Big shouldered and slim-hipped, with gray and brown hair, she towered over the tiny badger.

"You understand, don't you? Why you can't stay? It's nothing personal, I swear. We just have to protect our pups, and your younger sister, with her recent mood swings, puts our pups in danger. You understand that, right?"

"I understand," Max replied . . . still smiling.

The Alpha leaned over, patted Max's shoulder. "Don't worry. I'll tell Charlie myself. And I promise, we will not just send you out into the world alone. We'll arrange something for you. Something safe. Okay?" With a soft, sincere smile, she turned to go, but Max's voice stopped her.

"Oh, I'm sorry. I wasn't giving you permission to tell my big sister that our baby sister is too much of a freak to stay here among your boring, useless, stable pups." Max was still smiling and Betsey knew that wasn't a good sign. Not a good sign *at all.* "She's under enough stress and I don't want to add to it. And other than snarling at your pups every once in a while, Stevie isn't a threat to anyone here. She just needs quiet sometimes. The howling wears on her nerves, which isn't exactly surprising when you understand that she is almost positive that she knows when the world will end—during our lifetime due to climate change and a coalition of dictators turning on each other."

The Alpha faced her again, attempted to remain calm. "I don't see how that's our—"

"Both my sisters need to be here right now. It keeps them calm. It keeps them . . . I won't say 'happy' since neither is what you'd call happy. But they're not hysterical either, which is great. I mean, the reality is that the three of us won't be here much longer. Any day now I'm expecting Stevie to get a call from one of these big universities with an invitation to work at some fancy lab where she can get some more degrees and hopefully prevent the end of the earth as we know it. You just have to wait a little longer."

"I'm sorry, Max"—and the Alpha did seem truly sad—"but that's just not going to work for our Pack. I'm sure you and Charlie will understand that."

Still smiling and with a sweet laugh, Max said, "Oh, you misunderstand again. This isn't a discussion. I'm actually telling you that if you upset either or both of my sisters, I'll kill you and, possibly, anything you might remotely love."

And still she smiled.

As with most wolves under threat, the Alpha's softness disappeared in a blink, replaced by hard, animalistic rage. "What . . . what the fuck did you say to me?"

"I know I was clear and concise. Because I don't have to beat around the bush. You see, I'm trained. Trained to kill. Not maim. Not harm. Not disable enough to give me time to get away. But to kill. And, quite honestly . . . I'm really fucking good at it. I have to be, because it's up to me and Charlie to protect Stevie. She has great work to do. She has a world to save and she can't do that if she's making meth for a Peruvian drug lord. And Charlie . . ." Max let out a long sigh before her smile returned. "She has the weight of the world on her shoulders. All she cares about is keeping Stevie from being captured and used by the government or drug lords or whoever else my father has tried to sell her to. She has had so much stress in her young life that it shocks me she has not gotten an ulcer. Yet. So we trained, Charlie and me. To protect our sister—our family. Because the three of us and our grandfather are all we've got. Which is why, of course, we couldn't join the military. Great training but a little too limited and restrictive for our needs. And me getting up at five a.m. every day with some dude yelling at me? Yeah. That wouldn't last long. So our neighbor . . . a few farms over . . . former Marine, former Navy SEAL, former Black Ops. He taught us everything he knows. All we had to do was take care of his cats when he did mercenary jobs. And I fucking hate cats. But I did it." She stepped closer to the Alpha female and, based on the expression the wolf shifter now wore, she finally understood what she was truly facing. Not some poor girls with no one to care for them. No, she was dealing with something else. Something brutal and untamed, with no feeling for anyone they didn't consider "family."

"So let me be clear that when I say I'll kill you . . . I mean it." Her grin widened. "I'll kill you and have you buried before the sun rises. It'll be like you never existed," she added with a laugh. "So, yeahhhhh. You're going to let us stay here. You're not going to bother Charlie. You're definitely not going to say anything to Stevie. And if you even *hint* to my baby sister that she's in any way unstable or mentally unwell . . . I'll dismember you while you're still breathing. And, in case you're concerned, because it seems like you'd be concerned—you're clearly very caring—I won't miss a lick of sleep or have any PTSD over it. Your screams will mean nothing to me, because I won't give a fuck. Why? Because I'm a cunt. I'm a raving, raging cunt. At least that's how my last boyfriend described me as the EMT guys were shoving him into that ambulance." She clapped her hands together. "So we understand each other, right? We never have to have this conversation again?"

Without meeting Max's eyes, the Alpha shook her head. "No. We won't have to discuss this again."

Max let out a relieved sigh. "That's great. Really. But don't worry. I promise you, we're going to be out of here in another month or two. As soon as we hear from one of the many universities trying to woo Stevie to their campus but definitely *after* I graduate since Charlie's made it a personal goal for herself that I get my high school diploma. The things she worries about, I swear!"

Betsey scrambled back to her spot against the wall. She couldn't hear Max moving, but her scent became stronger as she neared the stairs that led to the hallway.

Max came up the stairs, entered the hallway, and headed down toward the kitchen. But when she was right in front of Betsey, she stopped. Slowly Max turned her head toward Betsey, then raised her forefinger to her lips. "Shhhhh," she said, as she had the first time Betsey had met her.

"Max!" Charlie barked, coming down the hallway toward them. "If you want to eat, you better get to the kitchen. That ravening horde of yours is devouring everything I made."

"Do you mean my basketball team?"

"Whatever," Charlie tossed over her shoulder as she headed up the main stairs toward the second floor.

Smiling, Max walked off, leaving Betsey to slide down to the floor, resting her chin on her raised knees and staring blindly ahead at the wall in front of her.

After a few minutes, her mother stepped in front of her. "Honey? Are you okay?"

"Yeah," she lied. "I'm fine." She licked her lips and added, "But your next birthday . . . you're coming to Chicago to visit *me*."

chapter ONE

Nine years later . . .

Max MacKilligan didn't see it coming. For once. But how could she when she'd been so focused on the white kidnap van and her ice cream cone? It wasn't until her psychotic cousin grabbed her from behind and yanked her deep into the alley that she realized the bitch had been standing behind her.

Flung to the ground, her ice cream tossed off somewhere, Max didn't even have time to put her arms up to protect her face before she was hit again and again. First with a fist and then . . . ? A crowbar?

Christ! What was *with* this woman? Why did her cousin hate her so much? This was the *second* time she'd tried to kill Max. The second time she'd come after Max *specifically*. Not even sending someone else to do the job, but coming herself. Why did the bitch have it in for her? Max didn't even know Mairi MacKilligan personally. She was from the Scottish side of their family and even the American side barely recognized Max and her two sisters. Until recently, the Scottish had paid them absolutely no mind.

Maybe this was a hate crime. Maybe Mairi just hated Asians. Max was half Chinese. Honestly, Max really didn't know. Usually people had to get to know Max MacKilligan before they started hating her.

But then Mairi screamed and Max was able to look up in time to see that her cousin had been shot several times in the chest and stomach by a long-range rifle. She praised her solid decision not to do all this alone and scrambled to her feet, ignoring the pain in her face and skull from where her cousin had cracked her with that damn crowbar.

Of course, this beating of one cousin by another was pretty meaningless. Because Mairi and Max were honey badgers. Gunshots to the chest and stomach . . . ? That didn't kill their kind. Crowbars to the head? Nope. That wouldn't kill their kind either. It took much more than any of that to actually do serious damage to a MacKilligan.

Still, Max was on a mission here, so she moved with purpose, scrambling over her cousin and charging out of the alley, across the busy Leiden street, and directly into the plain white van that held the men hired to kidnap her.

When Max hit the inside of that vehicle she looked at the men, expecting a sense of urgency about their job. But all they did was gawk at her. Like idiots. What were they doing? Didn't they have a kidnapping to perform?

She waited another few seconds until she saw her cousin, bleeding from all her gunshot wounds, stumble out of the alley. Max didn't have time to wait for these men to get their shit together.

"Go!" she ordered them, pulling the black hood over her head. "*Go! Go! Go!*"

Mairi MacKilligan stood on the corner and watched the white van speed off. People ran up to her, speaking to her in some fuckin' language she didn't understand, attempting to help her. As if she had time for any of that. She wasn't like these people. Boring, useless full-humans. Easily destroyed by the slightest shot to the body. So, no. Mairi didn't need an ambulance and Christ knew she didn't need the fuckin' coppers.

So, she turned away from all those panicked people and headed down the street to her car. Her phone vibrated in her pocket and she stopped long enough to answer.

"What?" she demanded, slapping away the people still attempting to help her.

"Bosses want you back," a male voice ordered. "Our people will pick you up at the airstrip."

The call disconnected. Not even a time given! Idiots!

"Fuck, fuck, fuck!" she raged, realizing she had to get back to Rome right away. She had to get to that fuckin' airstrip before her twin aunts' hired men came looking for her. Mairi wasn't supposed to be here. She wasn't supposed to be going after her cousin.

But she really hated that bitch, and nothing would make her feel better about life and the world in general than seeing the little twat dead.

The black hood came off and he saw her for the first time.

This was her? This tiny woman with purple hair and a few bruises on her face? *She* was the reason an entire unit of ex-military had been hired to snatch her off the Netherland streets?

He didn't understand why they were here. Why they'd grabbed *this* girl. Especially when their jobs mostly consisted of wiping out small villages at the behest of cold-blooded warlords. But the man who'd hired them wanted her, and he wanted her alive, although he didn't seem to care how she was treated in the interim. Again, strange. Usually the ones who made these kinds of orders had very specific requests—whether to treat the victim as a princess or to manhandle her for some sort of petty revenge—but this guy had been beyond vague. The only thing he'd been specific about? To not trust her. To use metal cuffs and make sure they were tight. And not to ever let her "off the leash." Usually kidnap victims were so terrified and panicked that they could be released from bondage after a few days. They never tried to make a run for it, always assuming their rich families would pay the ransom demand.

This girl, though . . . she was *literally* a nobody.

Crouched in front of her, he brushed her hair off her face, and dark brown eyes locked on him. He didn't see panic in those eyes, though. Didn't see fear; despite the fact the kidnappers were all wearing black balaclavas to cover their faces.

Her unconcerned gaze looked the group over, studying

them. Patowski, standing behind him, said, "If I were you, little girl, I would just stay quiet and wait until this is over. Don't give us a problem and you'll be just fine."

One of the men turned on more lights in the private airport hangar and Zé took in the bruises on her face. The blood dripping down her swollen chin from her damaged lip.

Anger welled up inside him. An anger he'd been well known for when he was a U.S. Marine. His anger and, as one fellow Marine put it, "your sense of annoyance at the very presence of most human beings," had gotten him some nicknames that should have insulted him more than they did. "Lord Unhappiness" was a personal favorite and "Colonel Fussy-Bottom" was another that almost made him smile. But the one his former teammates used the most was "Captain Destructo."

Seeing this girl's face made him feel very Captain Destructo.

Assuming he knew who had done this, he stood and pushed the kid, Anderson. Although Anderson had gotten an honorable discharge from the Marines, Zé could sense that was only by the skin of his teeth. He was sure the kid had wanted to stay but the Marines had wanted him out. And seeing the way the boy enjoyed hurting others, Zé wasn't exactly surprised. Why the team leader had picked Anderson for this job, Zé would never understand, but he wasn't close enough to anyone to find out. Maybe it was simply because the kid would do anything they told him to. Anderson didn't have much of a moral compass.

Zé snarled at the kid. "What did you do to her?"

Anderson's eyes widened and he shook his head. "Nothing."

"Don't lie to me. What did you do?"

"Nothing! One second she was disappearing into an alley and a few seconds later, she was charging into the van."

Zé frowned, confused. "She what?"

"I'm telling you what happened."

"It wasn't him," a female voice announced, and they all looked down at her. Once the hood had been removed, she'd been sitting there, gagged, her arms handcuffed behind her back. Now the handcuffs and gag were on the floor, and her free hands were briefly scratching her scalp.

Pointing at her face, she said, "This was courtesy of my cousin. I guess she followed me here, to the Netherlands. The woman is obsessed with me."

She opened her swelling mouth wide and immediately winced at the pain, placing her hand against her jaw.

"It's not like *I* was the one who left her in prison all those years," she muttered. "Why is she coming after me?"

"Get me an icepack," Zé ordered Anderson before crouching in front of her.

She raised an eyebrow at him. "Trying to make me feel safe there, green eyes?"

"Not particularly, no."

She laughed at that but abruptly stopped, frowned, and then out of goddamn nowhere, she leaned in to him and pressed her nose against his neck. And Zé could be wrong, but it seemed like she was . . . sniffing him?

Zé froze, wondering what the fuck was happening. It was over in less than five seconds, but in that brief time, this tiny woman had managed to completely disturb him. And it didn't help that when she leaned away again, she asked, "What are *you* doing here?"

He had no idea what that meant, but it didn't matter. The other men heard it and their attention was immediately on him.

Confused, Zé admitted, "I don't know what you mean."

"You have to know what I mean. What are *you* doing here"—her gaze bounced from man to man for a moment— "with *them*?"

Christ, this idiot was going to get them both killed.

Zé tried again. "Lady, I don't know you. And you can't even see my face."

"No. But I can smell you. And, of course, you don't know me . . . but you *know* me."

Now just annoyed, Zé snapped, "What the fuck does that even mean?"

"You know exactly what it means." She frowned in confusion and her head tilted to the side. "Oh, my God," she said softly, her eyes widening, "you honestly don't know."

"Don't know what?"

Zé felt the muzzle of a semiauto pressed against the back of his neck.

"Yeah," Patowski growled, "he doesn't know what?"

"He doesn't know what he is, and I wouldn't do that if I were you."

"What he is?"

"Uh-huh." She nodded, smiled. "He's a cat."

Which was weird enough, but then to illustrate this comment, she lifted her hands, curled her fingers like they were claws, and made what could only be called a "rowrrr" sound.

A moment before, the barrel against his neck had been pressing down hard, but now it loosened and Patowski asked, "*What?*"

"You know. Kitty. He's a kitty-cat." She shrugged. "Well . . . actually . . . he's a jungle cat, I think. Cats definitely aren't my thing, but he's not a lion or a tiger. *Those* are scents I'm well acquainted with."

The gun moved away from his neck and Zé stood.

"Oh, boy," Patowski sighed, removing the balaclava and revealing his face. A move that didn't bode well for this woman. And when all the others did the same . . .

Uh-oh.

But Zé also understood their reaction because this woman was clearly insane. He needed to save her, but she was insane, which would only make his job that much harder. He'd thought he'd be dealing with some scared-to-death rich girl that he could move around as needed while he got her out of here and took down Patowski's operation at the same time. That was his current assignment. Look, he knew from personal experience that leaving the military life behind was not easy. Civilian life had many challenges and none of the camaraderie most of these men had been used to. But to simply forget about the laws of the land so one could make a few bucks by kidnapping, murdering, or doing anything else someone with cash asked one to do was a shitty life decision in Zé's estimation.

As a former Marine himself, Zé knew there were better choices to be made. He'd made them—why couldn't these guys?

But this kind of mission was a lot easier when the victim one was trying to save was a bit more . . . pliable. This tiny woman might be too crazy to be pliable.

Zé pulled off his own balaclava and looked down at her. And she smiled back. A wide, breathtaking smile that made no sense in the current situation. Was, in fact, *miles* from sense.

"Let's get the cuffs back on her," Patowski softly suggested to Zé, something Zé was not about to do. But he didn't have a chance to do anything.

Picking at something on her thumb, she said, "That's not gonna happen."

Patowski, known for his short fuse, glared down at her. "Pardon?"

Zé quickly raised his hand, hoping to cut off the man's anger, and again crouched in front of her. "Look—"

She placed her forefinger against her lips. "Shhhhh."

Annoyed—Zé hated when people shushed him—he asked, "Why should I?"

"Because we both know you don't belong here. At first, I thought, 'Why is this dude hanging around a bunch of'"— she stuck her tongue out and made a "bleh" sound—"'full-humans?' No offense, but . . ." she said to the other men before sticking out her tongue again and making that "bleh" sound. "But then I realized you don't belong with them at all." Her smile grew wide. "You're an infiltrator."

The men all stared at him, and although she was absolutely right, he still had to ask these idiots, "Are you really taking the girl who thinks I'm a cat seriously? *Really?*"

They exchanged confused glances.

"Look, you guys," she said, smiling at them, "I'm here for one reason. I need *you* to tell me where Devon Martin is."

Zé glanced at Patowski. "Our benefactor," Patowski replied.

"Yeah. Your benefactor, but my pain in the ass. He keeps sending people after me, and I need it to stop. I've got too much going on right now." She began to count off on her fingers. "I've got my sisters to deal with, the crazy cousin who did this to my face, the twin aunts who blew up my uncles on their plane, and now my uncles have moved into our house and I've *got* to fix that."

"Your blown-up uncles live with you?" Zé asked.

"Of course they do. They don't want to go back to Scotland until they figure out what's going on, but . . . a bomb on a plane? Whose bright idea was it to do that? Everyone knows you can't kill honey badgers just by blowing up the plane they're on," she scoffed.

"Your uncles are honey badgers?"

"Well, so am I."

"Of course you are." Zé sighed.

"Okay, we're done," Patowski said, and Zé knew he meant it. But before he could move, Patowski motioned to Anderson and Anderson took the butt of his pistol and bashed the woman on the side of the head. It was an unnecessarily hard hit. She should have dropped instantly. She didn't.

"Owwwwwww!" she whined. Then, in retaliation, she punched Anderson in the nuts.

He roared in pain and anger, bending over before wrapping his hand around her throat and squeezing the life from her.

Gasping for air, her hands swinging out wildly, she locked her gaze on Zé.

"Let her go!" Zé bellowed at Anderson. When the kid didn't, Zé shot up and turned to Patowski. "Now! Let her go!"

"She's right about you," Patowski guessed, his gaze sizing the taller man up, "isn't she?"

Instead of stopping Anderson from killing the woman, the other men began to slowly move toward Zé, but when they heard it, everyone froze.

When they heard her laughing.

Zé looked down. She was no longer in the chair, but on the floor, on her back, with Anderson's hand tight around her throat. But she was no longer struggling to breathe. She was laughing.

Frustrated and snarling, Anderson tightened his grip but . . . she only laughed harder.

Then Zé saw it. It was just a flash. Just a moment. But for a brief second, she moved her head so the bright lights hit her eyes—and they changed, becoming glassy and reflective. Like a dog's standing under a streetlight.

"Fuck," was all he got out before the knife she'd been hiding under her long-sleeve tee appeared. Gripping it tight, she rammed it into Anderson's throat, hitting him directly in the artery.

Shaking, squealing, and pissing himself, Anderson released her and stumbled back, trying to stop the spouting blood with his hands.

She got to her feet, her gaze locked on Zé. Another teammate went to grab her, but without moving her gaze from Zé, she brought her blade up, back, and across, cutting the guy's throat from ear to ear.

Then it hit him. This was not some crazy girl who happened to get her desperate hands on a knife. This . . . this was a well-trained killer. And staring at him, that well-trained killer put her blood-covered forefinger to her lips and said, "Shhhhh."

It had all been so simple. Or so she'd *thought.*

Allow herself to be kidnapped by Devon's men, go with them to a secondary location—risky but necessary in this particular case—meet Devon or, if he wasn't with the mercenaries, find out where he was, track Devon down, kill Devon.

This was *not* a complicated plan. And it should have had her back home in no time, her elder sister none the wiser.

But the cat . . . the cat had thrown her off. She hadn't expected to find a shifter here among all these shitty full-humans. Then, even more confusing, he was clearly here for some *other* reason. Not just to make some easy cash and damn whoever might get killed in the process.

When she'd realized there was a shifter among the group,

she'd moved quickly to get him out of the way. Unlike the full-humans, a cat would know how to neutralize her kind quick, before Max could make a move. But his reactions? His confusion? He sincerely thought she was delusional.

Then it hit her: he really wanted to help.

Max was not a cat person, normally. Big or little, she wasn't a fan. But she knew this guy was trying to help her. He didn't belong with these full-humans: ex-military who turned from a life of good works and heroic risks to brutal mercenary work and murder for profit. But the cat . . . he was here to stop them.

How did she know? He had that look. Her mother called it, "The good-guy look. You have to watch out for them, honey. For those good guys," she used to tell eight-year-old Max. "Your gut will tell you what they are; then just look in their eyes. You'll see it in their eyes, and you'll be able to spot them a mile away. They're the ones who'll get in the way of your taking what you want. Don't let them."

And this cat had that "good-guy look." But what really had Max concerned about this guy was the fact that he didn't know what he was. Just as her twin aunts hadn't known they were honey badgers for decades, he didn't know he was a jungle cat, and that put him at a great disadvantage among these killers. If he didn't know what he was, he didn't know the level of his power. He didn't know what he could do. He didn't know he could unleash fangs and claws and tear these useless full-humans apart. He didn't know any of that, which meant Max had to protect him.

Her mother hadn't taught her that. Her big sister had. Charlie, whether she meant to or not, had that "good-guy look," too. She cared about others. She didn't want "innocents" caught in the cross fire of any fight and, if they were caught, she wanted to make sure they didn't end up getting killed. It was one of the main reasons she was such an awesome shooter. The last thing Charlie ever wanted to do was to accidentally kill someone who didn't deserve it.

Although Max's desire to protect innocents wasn't as intense as Charlie's or Stevie's, she still felt a sense of responsibility.

Especially to a fellow shifter. Max could have easily dug her way out of this hangar in seconds and disappeared into the surrounding territory, out of real danger. But if she did that, she couldn't bring the cat with her.

So she would stay. And she would help.

Of course, Max's idea of "help" was . . . well . . .

Max wrapped her hand around the gun raised behind her, easily pushed away the strong arm holding it, and rammed her blade into the throat of the shocked mercenary gawking at her.

Gunshots rang out from another mercenary and Max grabbed the cat by his Kevlar vest and yanked him to the ground. She landed on top of him and grinned down into his shocked face.

"Who's a cutie kitty?" she asked, loving his appalled expression. "Who is? You are!" She then slapped her hand over his face so she could lever herself up. She threw her blade at the shooter, nailing him in the throat.

More shooting now from different directions and the cat rolled them over so he was on top. He already had his semiauto out and immediately began firing, pushing Max under a large nearby table at the same time.

It was cute. How he was trying to protect her.

The poor guy! He was like an adorable kitten. Just so weak and defenseless he might as well be a full-human.

A sexy, Latin full-human.

His seemingly black hair was cut in jagged layers that kept falling into his face, the ends nearly reaching his shoulders. And his eyes were a bright green that she assumed would turn gold should he ever learn to shift to his true form. The shape of his eyes was definitely like a cat's, too, as was his flat and wide nose. Just like a cat muzzle.

In other words . . . *how could he not know he was a cat?* How could no one have guessed? The man was a walking, talking jungle cat in human form! And it boggled Max's mind that absolutely no one he'd previously known was a shifter or had pointed out the fact to him. Especially if he'd once been in the military. Tons of shifters joined the military and worked for the government. Max had been actively recruited by the CIA for years before she was even eighteen, but Charlie had put the kibosh on that. Unsure of what her big sister had done to discourage that interest—the CIA was not an organization that was usually put off by an easily stressed eighteen-year-old who loathed her father and had been fired from Dairy Queen once because she'd put a mouthy patron in a headlock—Max came to realize that organizations like the CIA, the FBI, or the military weren't for her. They were too regimented. Too cautious. You had to take orders. Max hated taking orders from anyone but Charlie.

Just ask Stevie. If Stevie gave her an order, Max went out of her way to do the exact opposite or, at the very least, to let Stevie believe she'd done the exact opposite. Just to piss the kid off. And that was her sister. Imagine if some guy she didn't know, who had never saved her life and thought he was in charge simply because of his rank, tried to give her orders . . .

Nope, nope. The regimented life was not for Max. She needed at least the *illusion* that she was free to do what she wanted. That was important to her, even if it was a lie.

Getting to one knee, the cat raised his weapon and shot. Men went down, one after another, hit either in the head or face, each careful shot avoiding the protective vests altogether.

Max was impressed. She'd only ever seen her sister handle a gun that well. Charlie was still better, but that was because no one matched her skill level.

"We need to get out of here," the cat told her, and Max saw from her spot under the table that more men were running toward the hangar from outside, automatic weapons already drawn.

She looked around while the cat continued to fire, stopping only to reload. She saw a door that led to offices in the back of the hangar. If she could get the cat back there, they could wait it out until her backup arrived. Because—as she'd learned from her sister a long time ago—she always had backup.

As Max started to pull herself out from under the table, she saw that one of the shooters was smarter than the others. Instead of trying to hit the cat with a spray of bullets, he aimed above the table and hit the chains that held one of the long fluorescent lights above their heads. The cat turned, ready to shoot the mercenary, but the light crashed down, ramming him in the back of the head, knocking him down and out.

The mercenary ran forward and re-aimed, about to shoot the cat at point-blank range. Max, now out from under the table—but without her knife—charged forward and launched herself at the shooter. Slamming into him, she dug her claws into his shoulders and took him to the floor with one hit. She unleashed her fangs and bit into the side of his neck, ripping out his artery in one move.

When she got to her feet, she spit the blood and flesh into the face of the closest mercenary, shocking him long enough for her to snatch his military-grade knife from its holster. She cut that one's throat and dashed to the next closest. That one opened fire and Max dropped to her knees so that she slid across the smooth floor and into his legs. She shoved the blade into one of his thighs, opening the artery buried there.

When he dropped, she grabbed his body and used it as a shield against the fresh round of gunfire sprayed exactly where she was kneeling.

But a stray bullet grazed her leg and, at that point, Max got a little angry. Because if she got shot, she'd have to explain to Charlie how that happened. She could dismiss lacerations and bruises, but not bullet wounds. Those she couldn't explain away, which meant that now she'd have to get very nasty . . .

The agony in his head blinded him, made him sick. Zé couldn't believe how painful it was. He felt weak, confused. He just wanted to go to sleep. But he knew he had to help . . . somebody. For some reason. It was all a bit sketchy, but he didn't have the time or ability to figure out why he was doing what he felt he needed to do; he just knew he had to do it. Now. Something.

Yeah, he was confused, but . . . oh well.

Zé turned over and began to drag himself out from under

the debris. He lifted his head, blinked hard once . . . twice . . .
Then he watched as a pretty Asian woman launched herself
into several armed men who had been firing directly at her.
And, as she moved through the air, she changed from a woman
into a . . . rat? Was that a giant rat? Like the capybara? No. He
didn't think so. He'd grown up in the South Bronx. He knew
a rat when he saw one, and that was definitely not a rat. But it
wasn't a woman either. Whatever it was, though, it was pissed,
tearing into those men with claws and fangs and absolutely
zero pity.

Still holding his . . . um . . . uh . . . what were these called
again? Oh. Yeah! His gun! Still holding his gun, Zé raised the
weapon to shoot the other men who, after a moment of stunned
screaming, launched themselves at the . . . thing? Yeah. The
thing that was attacking their teammates.

But Zé didn't get to pull the trigger before more of those giant not-rat things showed up. They joined the attack, dragging
the men to the ground, ripping them apart. Body parts and
blood flew. Men, begging for their lives, screaming in panic
and fear, were dragged across the floor in front of Zé.

At that point he didn't know whether to shoot, ask questions, or just go back to sleep. He was thinking sleep when a
Latina woman he didn't recognize stepped in front of him. She
was armed with a very expensive automatic weapon. She gazed
down at him with cold, dark eyes before raising the gun and
aiming it at his head.

It didn't occur to Zé that she was about to blow his brains
out because he wasn't sure about anything at the moment. But
by the time he realized what was about to happen, a voice said,
"No, Streep! Not him!"

The Asian woman reappeared, only now she was naked and
covered in blood. She stood next to the Latina, smiled down at
him. "That's my kitty cat. You can't shoot my kitty cat."

"Wait . . . is this that Denmark Syndrome thing?"

"It's *Stockholm* syndrome, Einstein, and no. He's not with
these guys. He tried to protect me."

The Latina sneered down at him. "Good job."

The Asian woman crouched in front of him, gently took his gun away, then stroked her hand over his head. "Don't worry, kitty cat, we'll take care of you. You just get some sleep."

He wanted to tell her that she shouldn't take him from the scene. That, for some reason, he needed to stay . . .

But he was just so sleepy and his head hurt so bad and he was sure if he didn't go to sleep, he'd vomit instead and he really didn't want to do that so . . . yeah . . . sleep.

The cat's head dropped and he was out cold. Max felt his forehead. He was already slipping into what shifters called "the fever." It helped seriously injured shifters heal if they weren't killed outright. At least that's what she'd heard. Max had never had the fever and, according to Charlie, none of the three MacKilligan siblings could get the fever, no matter how badly they'd been hurt and, of course, that anomaly was their father's fault. Their father and his fucked-up genes.

The rest of Max's teammates now stood around her: Streep, Tock, Mads, and Nelle. The most loyal bunch of outstanding ladies Max had ever known. They'd played basketball together since junior high. But their relationship had always been more than mere teammates. All five were honey badgers in a land of wolves, bears, and cats; most of them had family issues beyond "Daddy works too much and Mom is always in a yoga class"; just in general, they simply didn't fit in with anyone. Not with other badgers. Not with other shifters. Not with other people. But they fit each other for some strange reason and that made all the difference.

Max had realized, even as a young teen, that if these girls were going to be part of her life, they would need to know how to protect themselves. How to fight, how to hurt, how to destroy. As honey badgers, they had a natural instinct for all that but Max had always agreed with Charlie: just being shifters wasn't always enough. Especially when it came to protecting their baby sister. So Max and Charlie had learned how to protect themselves when human, too. They learned how to use guns and knives as well as hand-to-hand combat. And what

Max had learned, she'd taught to her teammates. She simply didn't tell Charlie about it.

In fact, when it came to her teammates, Max didn't tell Charlie about a lot of things. Not only because she knew her sister would freak out, but because her teammates begged her not to say anything. They were terrified of her sister. They'd never understood how dangerous Stevie was, but despite Charlie's inability to shift and her calm demeanor when it came to outsiders, Streep, Tock, Mads, and Nelle all managed to agree on this one thing:

That Charlie MacKilligan was the most terrifying being on the planet.

Max didn't see it. She knew her sister was a dangerous woman but so were Max and Stevie, and the four honey badgers weren't scared of them. As honey badgers, they weren't scared by anyone . . . except Charlie.

In the end, it didn't matter. Keeping her four teammates in the background worked out fine. Charlie had enough to worry about without adding Streep, Tock, Mads, and Nelle to the mix. And, thankfully, her teammates picked up shooting and fighting as easily and as well as Max had. So if Charlie couldn't be her backup, she knew her four friends would. Like now. They'd saved her from her psychotic cousin in the alley, followed her here, and now they were stepping in to help with this mess. What a great team.

"Who is that?" Nelle asked.

"Max's kidnapper," Streep replied. "But she plans to make him her boyfriend."

Max stood and faced her. Streep wasn't her real name. Her real name was Cass Gonzalez. They called her Streep after the actress, because when Streep was on the court, she was the queen of the dramatic moment. God forbid some player lightly bumped into her when their team desperately needed a foul. Streep would hit the ground with such drama and hysterics that the refs became worried she was having a seizure . . . or a nervous breakdown.

Nelle sniffed the air. "He's a cat? What's a cat doing with these full-humans?"

Gong "Nelle" Zhao's family came from Hong Kong. They'd had to move to the States when the shifter division of the Chinese government cracked down on the criminal activity of honey badgers. Thankfully Nelle's father had seen the writing on the wall. He got his family out before the Zhaos could end up on the wrong side of criminal charges, and he got out with the family money, making the Zhaos extremely wealthy. Nelle—pronounced "Nell"—picked that nickname for reasons unknown. But she was a style guru in the middle of Wisconsin. Max never did find out how her wealthy family had ended up in their town but she'd always been grateful. Nelle was a hell of a power forward and an even better diamond connoisseur. Skills Max needed to deploy on occasion.

Tock pointed at her watch. "We've got exactly three minutes to bury these men and get the fuck out of here." She tapped the timepiece. "Tick-tock."

Yeah. Emily "Tock" Lepstein-Jackson got her nickname for obvious reasons.

Mads, having shifted back to human but still naked, didn't say anything, just kept spitting blood on the floor. And Mads didn't have a nickname. Mads was her name. Her mother had given it to her at birth. No one knew why and no one asked. Mads didn't like a lot of questions.

"You want to take him with us?" Nelle asked, tossing her white-blond hair over her shoulder. She'd been bleaching her hair that color since her sister had told her she didn't look good as a blonde.

"I can't leave him here. Poor, helpless little kitten that he is."

Streep frowned. "Why do you keep talking about him like that?"

"Because he doesn't know that he's a shifter. He's clueless."

"How is that your problem?"

"It became my problem when he shoved me under the table to protect me. So we're taking him."

Max reached down and grabbed an arm. Three of her team-mates grabbed the other arm and legs and hefted him up. Nelle picked up the tossed-aside clothes of those who had shifted so they could put them back on when they were in the helicopter.

As they headed toward the exit, Mads stopped. "What *is* that?"

"What's what?"

Mads's head tilted to one side, then the other. Although genetically she was all honey badger, her mother was hyena, which seemed to have given her extra-sensitive hearing the rest of them would never possess.

She finally looked down at the cat. "It's him." She leaned in, again tilting her head one way, then another. Mads finally reached over to the arm Max held and yanked the cat's big, heavy watch off his wrist. She tossed what was probably a fifty-grand accessory aside like it was a used tissue and again they began to move, quickly heading out of the hangar to the heli-copter waiting to take them to another private airfield where Nelle's private plane waited for them.

"What was that?" Tock asked Mads.

"No idea, but the sound was irritating the hell out of me."

With Mads's magnified hearing, it could have been sim-ply the moving of the watch hands that irritated her, but Max couldn't help but glance back at the watch and wonder . . .

Amelia Kamatsu entered the hangar with her team. They had their automatic weapons loaded and ready, moving as a unit as they charged in. But they stopped after a few seconds, freezing in their steps.

"Holy shit," one of her men muttered behind her.

"Keep your focus," she ordered. "Clear the hangar."

"Seriously?"

"Just do it!"

And they did. Moving around and over the bodies that lit-tered the room. The murderous men they had been assigned to take down were lying in pools of their own blood, their weapons beside them or close by. But only a few of them had been killed with a gun. Most had either slit throats, strategically opened veins on inside thighs or, from what she could tell with a quick look, torn-out throats by . . . ? She didn't know. The wounds were so jagged, maybe someone had used a piece of glass or torn metal.

Despite the evidence, she knew this had not been a sloppy rage killing. It was something else. Something she wasn't sure she'd ever seen before. At least not with well-trained soldiers who knew how to protect themselves; who lived lives of protective paranoia.

Once the hangar and offices had been cleared, they all returned to the hangar.

"Anything?" she demanded.

One of her team held up a watch. "Just this," she said.

Amelia let out a pained sigh. That was Zé's watch, which had a carefully installed GPS system inside it so that they could track him wherever he might be. Now that he was no longer wearing it, she had no idea where her friend and teammate had been taken.

"What do you want us to do?" another teammate asked.

"Find him. I don't care what hole someone may have stuffed him into; I want Zé Vargas found."

chapter TWO

Zé woke up and stared at the slightly cracked ceiling. He stared at it because it wasn't that far from him. At first, he thought someone had shoved him inside a tiny hole to wait until his country's enemies came in to torture him into telling military secrets. But then he realized that there was way too much light in this "dungeon" for it to actually *be* a dungeon. Usually torturers didn't let a guy see the sun.

So he turned away from the slightly cracked ceiling and toward the light, and that's when he knew. He was in a house. A very boring house, to be honest, but definitely a house. The boring dining room of a boring house, to be specific. The blinds were open on the long windows, letting in all that excessive sunlight, which immediately made Zé feel a little better. He still didn't know where he was, but he definitely felt better about things.

Lifting his arm, Zé reached for the ceiling to see how far away it was. When he still had a few more feet to go before he could touch it, he sat up. He didn't move quickly, though. The back of his head hurt too much for any speed, but when he explored his scalp with his fingers, he didn't feel any wounds or major damage. And that was strange, wasn't it? Because he was pretty sure he'd gotten hit in the back of the head.

Hadn't he? He couldn't remember exactly.

"Fuck," Zé sighed, glancing down. Not sure what was happening to him. That's when he saw them. Three pairs of eyes, staring at him. Just staring.

"What?" he asked and the three dogs' heads tilted to the side. "What are you staring at?"

Not surprisingly they didn't reply, so Zé focused on how he would get down from where he was—on this china cabinet? How the hell did he get on a china cabinet?—without breaking his neck.

As he studied the distance to the nearest windowsill and the dining room table, debating which could hold his weight, two men appeared from another room. They were both ridiculously large and tall and . . . twins? They had to be. They looked exactly alike. Especially the way they loped by, both eating delicious-looking buns.

As they passed, their heads turned toward him and, as one, they both nodded and kept going. As if a nearly naked man on top of a china cabinet was something one saw every day.

A few moments later, Zé heard female voices coming from behind him and, seconds after, two women appeared. One was blond and white; slight, with barely any meat on her. She was barefoot and wearing a very loose sundress. The other was Asian, short but powerfully built. Her hair was dyed purple and she wore jeans and a pair of bright orange Converse basketball sneakers.

Zé narrowed his gaze on the Asian woman. He knew her! From . . . from . . . ? Somewhere! He knew her from somewhere!

"Answer me," the blonde insisted.

"No."

"Answer me."

"No."

"Answer me."

The purple-haired woman stopped and spun to face the blonde. The pair stared hard at each other. Then, abruptly, they bent a little at the knees and . . . hissed? Did they really? Did two grown women just hiss at each other nowadays? Was this due to the damage of social media?

Zé rubbed his eyes. Looked again. Did he also see fangs? Why did he think he saw fangs? That was crazy, right? Human beings didn't have actual fangs. Especially mouths full of fangs. Not vampire fangs but an entire *mouth* of fangs.

"Do not bare fangs at each other!" a female voice yelled from another room. "I mean it," she added after another second. "Don't make me come out there."

The two women relaxed until the blonde pushed again, "Just tell me."

Rolling her eyes, the other began to turn away but she spotted the three dogs staring up at Zé. She dramatically gestured to them with both arms.

"Again?" she demanded. "First the cat, now this?"

"The cat is your fault."

"That cat starts it."

The blonde pointed at the dogs. "What are they staring at?"

Both women looked right at Zé. They gazed at him for several moments, their mouths open.

The blonde was the first to speak, turning to the other woman and demanding, "Why won't you just tell me where you've been?"

"I don't have to tell you anything!" she snapped, walking away; the blonde followed.

Which, Zé had to admit, wasn't what he expected. Were they not going to question a nearly naked man sitting on top of their china cabinet? If nothing else, he expected them to at least help him down. But they went off, still arguing.

When the arguing became louder, another woman appeared beside the china cabinet. This one was taller and African American. Her curly brown hair reached to large shoulders that fairly burst out of the red sleeveless T-shirt she wore. And the cutoff shorts nicely showed her long brown legs. But those *huge* feet . . . eesh. He'd hate to get kicked with those.

She faced in the direction the bickering voices came from and Zé assumed she was about to yell at the pair again, but she caught sight of the dogs first.

"Hello, you guys," she greeted. "And who is your little friend here?"

The smallest dog, at about fifteen or twenty pounds, ran up to her, sniffed her bare feet, then went up on its hind legs, front paws waving wildly.

Grinning, she picked the dog up and cuddled it close. Something Zé wouldn't do because that dog didn't look like it had been bathed in ages. The thing was probably infested with fleas and ticks but the woman didn't seem to care.

"You are just so cute!" she cooed at the dog. "Are you just visiting?"

"Do you really expect it to answer?" Zé had to ask. Because he'd never understood people who actually spoke to dogs.

Still holding the animal, she looked up at Zé. "What are you doing?" she asked instead of answering him.

"Honestly, I have no idea."

She let out a breath, briefly closing her eyes. Then, with a very healthy bellow, "*Max!*"

"It's not my fault!" was the reply.

"I swear . . ." the woman muttered before she yelled out again, "Who is this person on the china cabinet?"

"That's a cat," was yelled back. "I rescued him!"

"I thought we agreed. No more strays!"

"Are you keeping that dog I see you holding?"

"He . . ." She lifted the dog with both hands, confirmed its lower bits, and finished with, "*He* is just visiting."

"Well, so is the cat!"

Rolling her eyes, the woman looked at Zé again. "I'm Charlie," she said.

"Zé."

"Hi, Zé. Do you need help getting down from there?"

"Yes. I thought maybe I could make it to the dining table but it's got that glass top . . ."

"Yeah. Don't do that." She frowned a little. "Are you naked, Zé?"

"Except for this towel . . . yes. Not sure how I got this way, though."

"Let's not think about it. You just stay there—I'll be right back." She put the dog down and went back the way she'd come. When she returned, the dogs were still staring at him and now she had the two large men with her.

"I'm getting cats out of trees now?" one of the men asked Charlie.

"That's a cabinet and yes. Could you please get him down from there?"

"How did he get up there in the first place?"

"Why do you ask me questions we both know I don't have the answers to? Why are you making this difficult? Is it because he's naked?"

"Well, that's not helping."

"So you want *me* to help him down while he's naked?"

"No, no," the man hurriedly replied, stepping closer to the cabinet with what Zé assumed was his twin.

"All right . . . come on," the man said to Zé. But Zé couldn't stop staring at the pair. He really hadn't noticed exactly how tall they were. Now that they were standing so close he realized they were taller than the cabinet he was on. Like two giants.

"Are you going to move or what?" the man barked at Zé, which just annoyed Zé.

It annoyed him a lot, which was why he ordered, "Carry me," and held his arms out for them to do so. It was something he used to say to his grandfather when he was little. And, on more than one occasion, he still said it to his grandfather because it annoyed the man and Zé was at least six inches taller. Which was why he was saying it now—to annoy.

And annoy it did.

"That's it," the man growled. "I'm leaving."

"Help him down," Charlie insisted, laughing.

"This is why I hate cats." He glared at Zé. "*All* cats."

"That's fascinating. Really." Zé still held out his arms and each giant grabbed him by a forearm and roughly hauled him off the cabinet, dropping him to the ground from a higher distance than seemed necessary. But Zé managed not to fall on his ass and instead simply wrapped the towel he'd had over him around his waist.

Zé was a tall man. Six-two since he'd turned thirteen. But for the first time since he'd done a little protection job for the NBA playoffs, he felt short. Almost tiny. Especially when these two glared down at him in mutual dislike.

"Problem?" Zé asked. He knew he probably shouldn't start trouble but he was from the South Bronx. On his street, he had never been known to back down from a fight. Especially when people insisted on annoying him. And these two were annoying him.

Having picked up that nasty dog again, Charlie yelled over her shoulder, "Max, you better get in here if you don't want your cat to get his ass kicked."

"Calm down. Everyone calm down." The one they called Max rushed in and quickly stepped between Zé and the twins. "It's not his fault," she explained, which Zé didn't understand. True, he was being kind of an asshole but he hadn't actually done anything to warrant an "it's not his fault" statement. "He doesn't know what he is," she . . . whispered. Why was she whispering?

"I don't?" Zé asked.

"I told you that you don't," she replied, looking over her shoulder at him.

"And . . . what am I not aware of?"

"That you're a cat."

It all came back to him then. Everything that had happened at the hangar. Everything that had happened with her. Everything that she had done.

"Oh, God," he said, stepping back and colliding with the cabinet, "it's you. The crazy woman they kidnapped."

All of Charlie's good humor left so quickly, it was like it had been yanked out of her. Continuing to hold that dog, she locked her dark eyes on Max and growled, "What kidnapping?"

Max now glared at Zé. "Now ya see? Ya got me in trouble."

"Sorry. Let me fix that for you." Zé faced Charlie. "Don't

blame . . . Max, is it? Yes. Don't blame Max for being kid-napped. Although her abductors did tell me that she *threw* her-self into their kidnap van and let them whisk her away from the streets of Leiden."

"Leiden?" the blonde called out before she ran into the room. "Leiden? That's in the Netherlands. Why were you in the Netherlands, Max? *What were you doing in the Netherlands?*"

Zé looked down into the now-*glowering* face of Max and he smiled. "See? All fixed."

And this was why Max hated cats!

Tricky, evil, fur-licking cats!

Now here she was, in the kitchen, her sisters grilling her like a steak about something she'd already forgotten. Life was too short to get all wound up about who kidnapped whom and who had shot whom and why a woman might willingly dive headfirst into the van of her kidnappers!

Her sisters were so goddamn obsessive! Max didn't obsess about anything but good honey and liquor flavored with snake venom. Those were the important things in life. Everything else was a waste of her energy. But there was no way out of it now, and all because of that damn cat!

"*I don't understand you!*" Charlie raved.

"The Netherlands are nice this time of year," Stevie rhap-sodized.

"You put yourself in danger and for what?"

"You should have told me you were going to the Neth-erlands. I have a few scientist friends over there. And several conductors who would have let you stay at their homes. Really nice homes, too."

"It's like you're trying to die. Are you? Are you trying to die? Are you depressed and I don't know? Is life meaningless to you? Do you think you'd be better off dead?"

"Did you at least bring me a *bitterballen*? They're delicious. My favorite snack when I visit. Did you bring me any?"

Max raised a finger. "Could you excuse me a minute?"

She pushed the kitchen chair back and walked out of the

room. She went through the long hallway, through the dining room, up the stairs to the second floor. She went down that hallway until she reached Berg and Dag, standing outside one of the unused bedrooms. She stopped to untie her right high-top, pulled it off, and threw it through the doorway so that it collided with the back of the cat's big head!

"Owwww!" The cat, who'd been busy putting on a pair of jeans loaned to him by one of the Dunns, spun around to face her, his hand rubbing the back of his head. "What was that for?"

"*Because you deserve it!*" she spit out between clenched teeth.

With only one sneaker on, she walked back through the house until she reached the kitchen and sat down at the table again.

"So where were we?" she asked her sisters.

"The beauty of the Netherlands!"

"Your stupidity and/or suicidal tendencies."

"Why do you guys have jeans that fit me?" Zé asked the men, who were at least seven inches taller than he and ridiculously wide.

"Those jeans belong to the wolverine," Berg muttered. "He's only six feet but he wears his jeans long. We figured they'd fit you."

"You have The Wolverine living here?"

"Not *The* Wolverine. *A* wolverine."

"He doesn't know," the other brother replied. His name was Dag, which was a weird name. "Remember?"

"How does anyone not know?" the first brother asked.

"Charlie's twin aunts didn't know. That's why they're pissed now and trying to kill the whole family."

"What are you all talking about?" Zé finally asked.

"Don't worry your pretty little kitten head about it."

Zé had no response to such a weird put-down, so he simply picked up Max's orange Converse high-tops and walked out of the room.

Following the sound of female voices, he ended up in the

kitchen. The rest of the house was rather run-down, so he had to stop a minute in the doorway to gaze in wonder at all the stainless steel appliances. Very nice and they appeared brand-new.

"Hey," Charlie greeted, her smile warm. "How are you feeling?"

"Better. Now that I'm on the ground and wearing pants. Head still hurts, though."

"That's because you were hit with a steel light fixture. Crushed the back of your skull." Max glanced back at him. "It's still healing."

"My crushed skull is still . . . healing?" He stared at her. Just stared.

"What's unclear?" she finally asked.

"That sentence seemed logical to you, considering most crushed skulls don't heal in . . . what? Two, three days?"

"Yesterday, actually."

"So, my tragically crushed skull almost healed overnight? Again, what seems logical to you?"

"See what I mean?" she said to her sister, tossing up her hands.

The little blonde pushed away from the table and came to Zé's side. "Here. You sit down." She led him back to her chair. "Coffee?"

"That would be great."

"Since my sister has no apparent breeding and doesn't know how to properly introduce people to each other—"

"Because suddenly you're incapable of introducing yourself?" Max snapped.

"—I'm Stevie."

She placed a mug filled with coffee in front of him.

"Zezé Vargas. Accent over the last *E*. But everybody calls me Zé." He glanced around at the three completely different women. "Sisters?" He let his gaze bounce to each one until he settled on Charlie. They were the two brownest people in the room.

She chuckled. "*Half*-sisters. Same useless, worthless bastard of a father; different mothers."

That made more sense.

"And where am I exactly?"

"Did you tell him anything, Max?"

"How is this my—"

"You're in Queens, New York," Charlie said, not letting her sister finish.

"Great. I'm originally from the South Bronx. So being in Queens is good. That works for me."

"Would you like a cinnamon bun?" Charlie asked.

Zé shrugged. "Sure."

"You didn't offer *me* a cinnamon bun," Max complained.

"No buns for *liars*!" Charlie ended on a bellow before placing a plate with two delicious-looking cinnamon buns in front of him and returning to her seat.

Stevie sat in the only other empty seat and smiled at him. That's what they all had in common. Their smiles.

"I didn't lie," Max insisted. "I just didn't tell you anything."

Charlie held her hand up, palm out. She didn't even look at her sister but at Zé.

"Why don't *you* tell us what happened yesterday, Zé?"

"You don't have to tell her anything," Max cut in.

She sat catty-corner from him, so he leaned in and whispered to her, "Would it be better for you if I said nothing?"

She grinned at him. "Yes."

Zé leaned back and looked at Charlie. "I'll tell ya anything you want to know!"

Max's grin faded. "You are such a cat."

"What was my sister doing there?"

"She had been kidnapped. These men are ex-military, now mercenaries. We've been tracking them for months now—Zimbabwe, Ukraine, Pakistan, the Sudan. We weren't even sure they'd take this job since it seemed so small compared to their usual work. But the man who hired them paid a lot."

"What man?"

"Don't know him and I only heard one name. Not sure if it's first or last. Devon."

Charlie closed her eyes and clenched her jaw before demanding, "*You went after Devon?*"

Sighing loudly, Max replied, "I figured if I could find him, I could kill him, and we could be done with all that. We've got so much else to worry about right now."

"The homicidal twin aunts?" Zé asked.

Stevie frowned. "How do you know about that?"

"Those genetic anomalies you have roaming around mentioned something about it."

Charlie tapped the table. "So did you find Devon or not?"

"Unfortunately I did not track him down."

"Why not?"

Max shrugged. "Things got a little out of hand."

"She killed everybody," Zé offered before biting into one of the cinnamon rolls. It was the most delicious thing he'd ever had. He pointed at it. "This is amazing. Did you buy this or bake it yourself?"

"She baked it herself, and I didn't kill everybody . . ." Max brushed nonexistent lint off her T-shirt.

"But?" Charlie pushed.

"Just most of them."

"So the rest saw you and got away?"

"I think her friends got the rest," Zé said, a flash of memory flitting through his still-aching brain.

But as soon as the words left his mouth, Zé knew things were about to turn very ugly between the women.

"Friends?" Charlie demanded. "What fucking friends?" Her dark eyes narrowed dangerously and she exploded. "*That idiot!*"

Max immediately raised her hands. "It wasn't Dutch! It wasn't Dutch!"

"Who's Dutch?" Zé asked Stevie.

"Max's best friend since junior high."

"Then who, Max?" Charlie pushed, hard. "*Who* are these friends he's talking about?"

"He got hit in the head. I'm surprised he remembers anything."

Charlie motioned to Zé. "With that hard head? Cats fall from the top of redwoods and their heads are just fine. Now tell me."

"So is it LSD all of you are taking?" Zé asked Stevie. "Or something new? I've heard bath salts can be a real problem."

Stevie crinkled her nose at him. "You are so cute!"

"It was my basketball team," Max finally admitted, causing everyone to stare at her.

"Your basketball team?" Charlie asked. "What basketball team?"

"My team. The one I played with in junior high and high school. We made it to the championships?"

Stevie nodded, apparently knowing exactly who her sister was talking about, but Charlie just continued to stare, her face completely blank.

"Remember?" Max gently pushed. "Tock? Mads? Nelle? Streep?"

"Meryl Streep?"

"Meryl Streep?" Max repeated. "You really think *Meryl Streep* is helping me to take down a bunch of mercenaries *and* helped the team get to the championships?"

"I don't know what secret life you have!"

"*Well, it's not one that involves Meryl Streep!*"

"All right!" Stevie yelled before she let out a breath. "*I* know her basketball team, Charlie. I know them."

"You do? They exist?"

"Yes, they exist. And, honestly, I must say if it wasn't us with Max, watching her back, I know that those four can do the job without a problem."

"Does any of that make this situation better?"

Stevie shook her head. "No."

And again Max threw up her hands. "What are you doing to me, woman?"

"Helping?"

★　★　★

"You know what?" Max said, deciding to end this. "We've got bigger issues than whether I—"

"Slaughtered a bunch of people?"

Max glowered at the cat before finishing with "—found Devon."

"Like what?" Charlie asked, appearing extremely angry. Max knew that expression on her sister's face. Knew what it meant. Her sister hated when Max went off to "do something stupid." And "stupid" to Charlie was anything that involved violence but didn't involve her as Max's backup.

Fair enough. Charlie was awesome backup. Max would enter any dangerous situation if her sister was with her, but Charlie had enough shit to worry about on a daily basis. Why would Max add to that when Devon wasn't her sisters' problem? He was Max's problem and only because her mother was still in prison and unable to deal with him on her own. Because Devon refused to believe that Max's mother didn't have the money from their last heist together. The heist that Freddy MacKilligan had managed to fuck up as only Freddy could.

If anyone had that money, it had probably been her father, but Max was sure he'd spent it or lost it a long time ago. Probably months or days even after the heist had ended with Devon and her mother in prison.

Devon didn't want to hear any of that, though. He was convinced Renny Yang had his money and believed that Max was his way of getting it back.

Luckily, Max didn't mind proving him wrong. But until she'd dealt with Devon properly, she'd have to find a way to distract Charlie from getting involved. And there was only one way to do that—with lunacy.

"Like our guest here," Max replied, gesturing to the cat with a sweep of her hand. "Poor kitty doesn't know he's a kitty. He thinks he's a boring full-human with no skills. We can't let him continue to go through his life in such a sad, pathetic way."

Her sisters focused on Vargas, but the cat was busy downing the last of those cinnamon buns. He was mid-chew when he realized they were all watching him, crumbs covering his mouth, green eyes bouncing from one woman to the other.

"Wha?" he asked around his food.

"We're here to teach you about our ways," Max informed him.

"No thank you." He swallowed, took a sip of coffee. "I'm fine in my reality."

"But your reality is wrong."

"Is it? Or is my reality simply drug free?"

Max heard Stevie snort but she fought the urge to slap her sister on the back of the head.

"I don't know how to tell you this, but you need to accept the fact that you are a—"

"Cat. I'm a cat, according to you. In other words"—he pointed at the kitchen window near the stove—"I'm like him."

Max looked and immediately picked up a spoon and hurled it at the window. The feral cat that she hated didn't run, though, but simply hissed at her. Bastard!

"Is that any way to treat my kind?" Vargas asked, smirking.

"That is not your kind, idiot," Max snarled. She was fed up with this. "You're like us. A shifter. Your DNA is a combination of human and . . ." She gestured with her hand around his face. ". . . some kind of big cat."

"Wait. I can tell." Stevie ran around the table to Vargas's side. She lifted strands of his hair and leaned in close, studying them. Vargas motioned to his empty plate. "Any more of these?"

Without a word of complaint, Charlie picked up his plate and went to where she had a large platter filled with cinnamon rolls. She brought back five for the cat.

"You're just giving him food now?" Max asked.

"He's a guest."

"But I don't get any?"

"You're a liar."

When Max focused on Vargas, he smiled around the big bite of roll he now had in his mouth.

"Jaguar!" Stevie announced, triumphant. "He's a jaguar." She returned to her seat. "It took a second because leopards have similar markings but if you *really* look, you can tell the difference. And he's definitely jaguar. A black jaguar." She winked at him. "Kind of rare."

"*What is happening?*" Max demanded. Why were her sisters being so nice to someone who was being so . . . cat? He couldn't be more cat if he was lounging in a tree with a gazelle carcass.

"Look," Vargas said, wiping his mouth with a paper towel, "I appreciate you guys living in this fantasy universe. And I get it. The world is terrifying right now; it's easier to pretend that you have special mutant powers. But I live in reality and no one has special mutant powers. And that's okay. It's okay to be normal. Be proud of your normalness. Be proud of who you are."

Deciding this wasn't worth the effort, Max was about to get up from the table and show Vargas out. She'd call him a car. She had the app on her phone. She'd send him back to the full-humans he seemed most comfortable with, and she'd go back to her life as a MacKilligan. It was for the best.

That was the plan. Until Shen Li, Stevie's boyfriend, came in through the back door. He'd been outside, hanging upside down from a tree, eating bamboo. This was after he'd had a morning swim . . . in his panda form. That was also the way he'd entered the kitchen. In his panda form. He easily opened the screen door, came up the stairs into the kitchen. In his panda form, he was a healthy size, easy to see from where Vargas was sitting.

And Vargas did see him. His expression didn't change; it stayed artfully blank, but his bright green-eyed gaze was locked on the panda as Shen went up on his hind legs, used his nose to open one of the cabinets, and used his paw to knock down a few bamboo roots. He picked one up in his mouth, lumbered over to Stevie's chair, and with nothing more than a thought, shifted from panda to human. He took the bamboo from his mouth so he could lean down and kiss the top of Stevie's head.

"I'm going up to take a shower. I'll be down in a few."

"Shen," Max said, gesturing to their "guest," "this is Zé. Zé, this is Shen."

Shen nodded. "Hi, dude."

"Hi . . ." Vargas cleared his throat. "Hi."

Then, bless him, Shen put the bamboo back in his mouth, shifted back to panda, and lumbered his way out of their kitchen on all fours.

Silently, the three sisters watched Vargas. Watched . . . and waited.

After a minute, he glanced at his nearly empty mug and announced, "So you drugged the coffee, then."

Max threw up her hands and pushed away from the table. "I'm out."

chapter THREE

Mairi MacKilligan got off the helicopter and walked away from it, keeping her body low so her head didn't get chopped off. One of the few, *true* ways that one could kill a honey badger.

She made her way to the upper deck where the Guerra twins were sunning themselves. She cringed when she saw their oiled skin, wondering how they could believe for a moment they wouldn't get skin cancer one day. It was like looking at roasting sausages.

Before she reached them, however, one of their many bodyguards stopped her. Without a word, he demanded her weapons. She removed her guns and knives and piled them on the table provided for just that purpose. One of the men then came toward her to search her thoroughly but as soon as she looked at him, the man—a foot taller and two hundred pounds heavier than she—stumbled to a stop and looked at the one in charge. None of these men wanted to touch her. They were all full-human and probably didn't understand their intense fear and distrust of a woman they didn't know, but instinct in mammals was a valuable thing.

With a wave of his hand, the one in charge motioned her through and she walked across the deck. Several bodyguards stood behind the chair where Aunt Celestina was stretched out. Aunt Caterina was already coming toward her, so Mairi stopped and spread her arms wide.

"Hello, dearest Aun—" she began but the brutal slap across

her face stopped the remainder of Mairi's greeting. She froze where she stood, the sound of that slap still echoing across the ocean surrounding them.

"*How hard is it,*" Aunt Rina thundered at her, "*to kill one man?*"

"It depends on the man, don't it, Auntie?" She smirked. "That Grigori Rasputin—they stabbed him . . . but it didn't kill him. Fed him cyanide . . . still he kept going. Took three shots to take him down but only because they hit him in the right spot. If they hadn't, he'd probably be runnin' around Russia right now, givin' that Putin a hard time. Which is what I told you about good ol' Uncle Will, but you didn't listen, did ya? Blow him up, ya said. Take out his sons, too, ya said. Didn't listen to me and now . . . he knows you're after him. They all do, and the MacKilligans won't let you or me get near him again."

Aunt Tina took a sip of some fruity-looking drink before calmly asking, "And why do you keep focusing on that little one?" She put her drink down, took a few grapes from a bowl. "We know you were in the Netherlands when she was."

"And how do you know that, Auntie?"

Now Tina smirked. While Rina was nothing but raw rage and hatred, her twin was the cold plotter. Together, they were a dangerous pair because they had nothing but money and time.

"I'll never understand you two," Mairi admitted. "You could be anywhere, doing anything, but instead you focus on a family that could not care less about either of you." It was true: Mairi's granddad was like most of the MacKilligan men, fucking anything that walked and had a pussy. But the MacKilligan male honey badger didn't like the single life. So no matter how many girlfriends he might keep, he always chose a mate as mean and as vicious as he could find. Sometimes she was another honey badger, sometimes a full-human. And no matter who he fucked on the side, who he lied to about divorce and children, who he promised "forever" to, it didn't matter. Because at the end of the day, the mate the MacKilligan male had chosen was the one he stayed loyal to until the end.

"Your father—me granddad—would have never left our

grandmum for your mum and he never would have claimed you two as his own," she told them frankly. "Not ever. So I don't see why either of you are sweatin' about it."

"He didn't have a problem claiming his American children."

There was truth to that. But, in Granddad's defense, he'd bred those children through the meanest and most vicious honey badger female he could find in the States. He had wed both women. Just not legally. But what was a badger to do with all those stupid laws that prevented him from being married to two women at the same time? Of course, Granddad's tragic end came when those two females found out about each other. That's when they lured poor old Granddad to some place in Paris to plan a heist—and he never came back. The pair, however, did return. They met with the uncles, split up the available funds between the two families, and the American returned to her cubs in the States while Grandmum returned home. It was never discussed again; it was never analyzed or thought about. It was the risk a male took when he tried to have more than one honey badger mate.

"Well, choosing to acknowledge his American cubs over you . . . that was different, wasn't it? That was because he *loved* their mum."

This time the blow to Mairi's face came from a fist. Impressive, when she thought about those ridiculous nails her aunts filed so that they resembled actual claws. Considering they both had claws naturally, it seemed excessive.

"You piece of shit," Rina spit out in her Italian accent, "you do what we tell you."

"We're not paying for you to go after that Asian one," Tina said.

Ah, yes. The Asian one. The one who thought she was so special. So smart. So much better than the rest of them. At least the other two knew their place among the MacKilligan clan. Knew exactly where they belonged. But Max Yang thought she was unique. Blessed. She was none of those things, and Mairi was committed to showing her cousin exactly that.

A commitment Mairi was not going to be dissuaded from no matter what her aunts ordered.

"Well . . . I won't get near Uncle Will," Mairi responded. "Not now. His sons will make sure of that."

"You focus on Freddy," Tina said, standing up. She pulled at the bottom of her gold bikini, digging it out of her ass. Classy! "He still has our money."

"Don't you mean Uncle Will's money?"

"He lost it. Now it's ours."

"Everyone wants Uncle Freddy," she reminded them.

Rina leaned in close to her and growled, "Find him. Or the money stops and then we start—on you. Understand?"

"Perfectly."

In their matching gold bikinis and six-inch designer heels, the twins stomped off. Guards followed them and the one who had asked for Mairi's weapons stepped in beside her. He gestured to the exit that would take her back to the little table and the helicopter that would fly her to the private airstrip and the private plane that would whisk her back to the States.

But before she followed the armed guard, she took a moment to look over the super yacht. She could still feel where Rina had hit her. Could still hear the ringing in her ears from her condescending tone. But that was okay. She didn't mind. Not now. Not when she had much bigger, long-term plans.

Mairi grinned as she took in the beauty of this yacht that would, one day . . . one day soon . . . be *all* hers.

Zé sat down on the couch in the living room, but the back of his foot struck something under it and he reached down and grabbed the object.

When he'd fished it out, he immediately realized it was a sneaker. A sneaker that required him to hold it up with two hands. A sneaker that was the biggest he'd ever seen. Did the NBA stay here on weekends or something? Because who else had feet this big? This thing was Shaq sized.

"It's a Viking boat," he muttered. "It's a shoe the size of a goddamn Viking boat."

He tossed the sneaker down and leaned back, but he kept leaning until he was lying flat, staring up at the ceiling. Zé sat up and examined the couch. It was also enormous.

He was not a small man. He was six-two, nearly two-hundred-and-sixty. He used to play football in school. Could have gotten a scholarship to play ball in college but, just to irritate his grandfather, he joined the Marines instead, pissing the old man off. Because they both knew he could have easily gone pro. He used to be that good. But despite knowing other players who were way bigger than he was, he'd never gone to their houses and found couches this size—although he was sure many of them would have appreciated something so comfortable.

Zé shook his head. No, no. He was letting those crazy women get into his head. He was letting them convince him of something that was just *not* possible. There was no way what they were saying . . . no way he could be . . . no way there was even a chance that . . .

Resting his elbows on his knees, he dropped his chin on his raised fists and simply sat there. Staring across the room at a TV that wasn't turned on.

He had no idea how long he sat there like that before the back of his head itched. Without really thinking, he reached around and scratched his scalp. That's when he felt it. Just under the skin. Small pieces of bone . . . moving into place. He jerked his hand away and immediately noticed his headache was abruptly gone.

What was happening? What the hell was happening?

He heard a door open at the front of the house and five men walked into the living room. They didn't look at him and Zé didn't speak. One older man seemed to lead the others, strutting in front of them. They weren't tall like the brown-haired men he'd spoken to earlier but they were stocky and powerfully built. He could see their muscles under their suit jackets. He also heard accents as they spoke to each other. Scottish. Or Irish. He'd always had trouble catching the difference.

They'd barely made it to the far side of the living room when Stevie rushed in. She held her hands up but the men simply walked around her. She blinked in surprise at being ignored as if she wasn't even standing there and she ran around to block them again. This time stretching out her arms wide and yelping, "No!"

This time the men did stop and stare at her.

"Dear sweet niece," said the older man, "a lovely sight as always."

"Hello, Uncle Will. Uh . . . I thought you guys had left. For good."

"Why would we do that? Charlie said we were welcome to stay."

"She was lying. She's a vicious little liar. She lies and lies—we can't stop her."

"Now, we all know that's not true, dearest girl. I'm sure if I talk to her—"

"*No!*" Stevie barked again, her hands pressed against her uncle's chest specifically to keep him from moving forward. She forced a smile. "My sister has a lot on her mind right now."

"That's too bad. You know what?" her uncle suddenly announced, smiling. "She should take a break. Maybe go spend some time with that grizzly of hers. I'll suggest it to her."

Stevie stood her ground. "You want *her* to leave that house? *That's* your plan?"

"Do you have a better one?"

"Anything's better!"

"Awww, now, Stevie. Don't be unfair. You know I only want the best for your sister."

"Since when?"

"Come on," the man pushed. "We'll tell her together."

"We're not telling her anything. You're just leaving. I've got a lot of work to do and all of you are nothing but distractions that I'm beginning to loathe."

"Oh, so it's *you* that wants us out, is it?" He smiled and even though Zé saw nothing that actually said, "Hello there, I can change into some kind of large jungle animal," the smile did scream "predator!"

"Well," her uncle went on with that grin spreading across his face, "that changes everything, doesn't it?"

Stevie's left eye twitched at his words. Zé could see it from across the room. It was so dramatic even he felt the need to inject himself into the situation, but he never had the chance.

"What's up?" Max asked as she walked into the room. She'd changed into long, blue basketball shorts, a matching tank top, and blue high-top Converse. Her purple hair was in two ponytails and she had a red, white, and blue basketball tucked under her arm. This placement was necessary so that she could hold a large jar of honey in one hand and spoon said honey into her mouth with the other.

Christ. Who wanted to eat that much honey? She ate it like she was eating ice cream.

"Just havin' a little chat with your baby sister here before I go and get me a nice cuppa."

"Nice cuppa what?"

The Scots—or Irish . . . whatever—all looked at her, their lips curled in disgust. Were they not clear on where they were? They were in America! Where one has cups of coffee! The only tea drinkers around these parts were those gentrifying bastards in Brooklyn. Not real Americans!

"I'm telling them to leave," Stevie said, finally lowering her arms so she could cross them and tuck her hands under her pits. It was a weird visual. She seemed a little old to pose like that. Even when annoyed.

"Why?" Max asked. "We love having them here."

"See?" the uncle said, grinning again.

"Yeah. They can stay as long as they want. Right, guys?"

The men gave a little cheer at Max's words and she handed over her jar of honey. One of the younger males took it and eagerly scooped spoonfuls into his mouth. Why? Honey was an additive! A condiment! It was not to be used as a self-contained treat!

With her hands free, Max began to dribble the basketball. She didn't do a fast dribble. Just one annoying bounce at a time. It was . . . methodical, the way she dribbled that ball. One bounce. Two beats. Another bounce. Two beats. Another bounce. Two beats. Yeah. It was methodical. Or, at least, that's how it felt. It felt methodical . . . almost planned. Which was ridiculous, right? He'd been around a lot of basketball players in his old neighborhood and high school, still played some pickup games when he spent a weekend with his grandfather, and if there was a ball in someone's hand, they always bounced it repeatedly, as fast as they could because it was a ball in their hands. They didn't even think about it. They just did it. No matter how much bouncing that ball annoyed Zé.

And God, did it annoy Zé. Then and now!

It was a habit he found so annoying that on more than one occasion, he had snatched a ball from some bouncing offender, only to slam it back into the man's face. Why? Because he needed to learn! Sadly, his grandfather had been forced several times over the years to explain to some pissed-off neighbor from down the block that "it was a total accident. You know what a fumble-fingers my grandson is. Aren't you, idiot?"

"Yes, sir. I'm a fumble-fingers."

The memory almost made him smile except that the bouncing was really starting to irritate him. It was, he also quickly noticed, annoying Stevie.

He could tell when she carefully placed her middle and forefingers against both sides of her head, making small circles at the temples, before asking, "So you're *not* leaving?"

"Oh, we'll leave. Eventually. You know, still trying to find out who blew us up. That's kind of our priority right now."

"We know who blew you up. It was the half-sisters who hate you!"

"Who can say?"

"I can!"

"Dearest niece, I understand how it is. Sometimes you just have to throw your own kin out into the cold night."

"It's *summer*," Stevie bit out between clenched teeth, that left eye twitching again. "And it's morning." She glanced at her sister. "Could you stop doing that, please?"

She didn't snap that request. But there was a tone there that Zé didn't want to examine too closely. A tone that would make him aware he'd want to stop bouncing that ball.

But not Max. Not the crazy woman who took on ex-military like she was pranking a bunch of junior high nerds. No. She just smiled. That smile he remembered so well from the other night. She smiled and she just kept going.

"You don't understand," Stevie continued. "I have a lot of things going on right now. I've got a ballet to write—"

"Isn't that cute?" her uncle said to the burly men with him. And there went that eye twitch again.

"—a lab to set up—"

"Oh, are you doing the science thing again? Good for you, lass. Good for you. Bet you could do well with that sort of thing . . . if you just tried. You know, put your mind to it. Focused on it."

"—and my boyfriend's parents to meet."

"Is that the Oriental bloke we saw around here?"

Oooh. There went that nasty twitch again and now it was getting . . . intense.

"The word is *not* Oriental. It's Asian or, if you want to be specific, Chinese. My boyfriend is Chinese American."

"You can barely tell," the uncle said. "His English is really good. Like he was born here."

"He *was*—" She managed to cut herself off, but Stevie's fingers had now curled into fists.

"Please stop dribbling that ball," she asked Max again before she said to her uncle, "So what I'm saying is, I'm sure you'd be much more comfortable in a hotel—"

"A hotel? I don't know about that. We're so low on cash right now, ya know . . . after what your father did and all."

Stevie slowly blew out a breath, then said, "I can pay to put you up in a hotel for a bit."

"That's real kind of ya, darlin'. Real kind indeed. But we can't just go anywhere, now can we? After someone tried to kill us."

"What hotel would you like?" she asked.

"For us? It would need to be the Kingston Arms, now wouldn't it?'

The Kingston Arms? Was this asshole kidding? The Kingston Arms was expensive. Seriously, blindingly expensive. It made staying at the Ritz Carlton seem like hanging out at a Motel 6 off I-95.

"Well . . . that's a problem," Stevie said as she tried to slap the basketball away from a still-dribbling Max, "since—the last I heard—the Scottish MacKilligans have been *banned* from the Kingston Arms. *All* Kingston Arms. Even the ones in Africa and Asia."

"Maybe because they kept calling the Asians 'Orientals,'" Max suggested, making Zé snort just a little.

"That wasn't what happened," the uncle argued. "And Africa? How could we be banned from some African Kingston Arms? That's not a country I'd even go to. Isn't that right, lads?"

When the men agreed as if even suggesting such a thing was the real offense here, Stevie threw up her hands and snarled. "Africa is a continent, you dimwits! You've been banned from all the Kingston Arms that are in the many countries on the *continent* of Africa."

"Country or continent—"

"*Continent!*"

"—being banned from Africa was not the fault of the MacKilligans." His head bopped from side to side before he added, "But Asia . . . that was definitely our fault. But not Africa. It was our enemies who got us banned from Africa. That was *other* badgers who used our name."

"I don't care! You need to go! *And you*—" she suddenly bellowed, turning to face her sister, "—*need to stop dribbling that goddamn ball!*"

But Max didn't stop; she simply began dribbling the ball back and forth between her legs. Zé had to admit, though, she had solid technique.

The uncle, however, didn't seem to be aware of anything but getting what he wanted.

"Look, niece," her uncle began again, "we'd go if we could. Truly we would. We don't like being in your way. But where would we go? What would we do? So for now, at least, here we'll stay. And I'm sure with a heart as big as yours, you'll be happy to let us stay, now won't she, lads?"

The burly men heartily agreed, their condescending smirks annoying Zé so much, he thought about hurling that Viking boat of a sneaker across the room in the hopes of destroying them all the way the Vikings did to those monks in 793 AD. But before he could make that move, Stevie abruptly reached over to one of the men and grabbed something off his belt.

Zé watched in shock as Stevie expertly flicked open what turned out to be a butterfly knife—an edge weapon that was not remotely legal in New York. He jumped up, ready to step in before she did something she would regret the rest of her life—although he understood it; he wanted to stab that pushy uncle himself. Dude was annoying. But before anyone could make a move, Stevie snatched the basketball from her sister mid-bounce and rammed the blade into it.

Then she did it again. And again. Then a whole bunch more times. All while staring her sister right in the eyes.

Finally, when she stopped, she hysterically screamed in Max's face, "*I told you to stop playing with that fucking ball!*"

With that, Stevie shoved the deflated ball back into Max's hands, the knife still sticking out of it, and stormed out of the room.

There was a long moment of silence until the uncle said, "That girl should be locked up."

Max pulled out the knife, expertly flicked it closed, and handed it back to one of the other men. "Really?"

"I don't mean in a prison."

"Oh, I understand what you mean. You're talking about a

mental hospital. A loony bin, where the crazies go. Do you really think this is about her being annoyed by you? No. It's about Charlie."

"Charlie told us we could stay."

"I'm sure she did. Charlie's a good person. But she has a very low threshold for other people's bullshit. She puts up with it from me and Stevie but you're not us. You're *them*. And Stevie's brain is so advanced, she can look minutes, days, weeks, months, *years* ahead. She can see that, one day, you're going to do something so stupid and so uncaring that you piss off Charlie. Piss her off so much that she'll kill all of you. She'll kill all of you and not care, even though Charlie cares about everything and everyone. But you'll push her so far that—boom!—over the edge she'll go and you boys will be dead and it will be civil war among the MacKilligans. So Stevie is trying to prevent an outcome she sees as clearly as she saw the formula for the *minor* nuclear explosion she caused that time."

As the men simply stared at her, Max smiled. "Even worse, once the war starts . . . well, that's when *I* will have to step in. And I'll be forced to do what I do so goddamn well. You wouldn't want that, would you? Me, completely wiping out the entire Scottish MacKilligan bloodline because . . . ya know . . . I can."

The smile turned to a grin and that grin grew wide. It wasn't a sadistic smile, though. That's what was kind of terrifying about it. It was a pure, happy smile. As if she was at a child's first birthday party.

"So, to prevent what my adorable baby sister clearly sees," she went on, "I strongly suggest you make a few calls, pack up your shit, and move over to the Kingston Arms. I'm sure they will take you if you give them our name, promise not to steal anything, and pay much more than anyone in the history of the universe. I know you're cheap," she quickly added when her uncle began to argue.

"I ain't!"

"Oh . . . you is. And we all know it. Right, lads?" she asked the men accompanying her uncle. Their reply was to look down at the floor and not say anything. "See? They know. We all know you're cheap. But that's okay. You're just going to suck it up and pay that tab! Willingly . . . and with love."

"Now listen to me—"

She held up the deflated ball right in front of her uncle's face. "What I did with this poor basketball is just one of the many ways I know how to irritate her. You should know that over the years, I've discovered *thousands* of ways to irritate Stevie MacKilligan. You could almost say it's been a lifetime project of mine. Do you want to stick around while I make her even crazier? Or do you just want to get the fuck out?" Still grinning. How could she say all that and still keep smiling? How could she not be angry on some level? But she wasn't. Zé knew anger, and she wasn't angry. Not even a little. "Because I can promise you that my sister can go from slightly hysterical to destroyer of entire worlds in a nanosecond. Can't she, Dougie?" She looked directly at one of the men and, after a brief staring contest, he nodded. "Remember what happened in the Bronx that time, Dougie? Remember what Stevie did there?" She winked at him and crinkled her nose up at the same time. It was adorable and horrifying. "Oh, yeah. You remember."

"She's right, Da," Dougie said with his gaze fixed to the floor. "We should just go."

"See? Dougie knows. Because I can promise you, I have practically an entire garage filled with basketballs and I can bounce them *all* day. I love basketball!" she cheered.

With a growl, her uncle pushed past her, and the burly men followed him out of the room.

"I'll call you guys a car!" She waved at the men's retreating backs. "It was great having you, though!" Then she added in the same happy tone, "But don't ever come back!"

"So what happened in the Bronx?"

He sat on her couch, bare chested and shoeless. His mostly

black hair was a mess, falling over his eyes, but the green glared at her from across the room. He was a very handsome man but stubborn. One of those guys who believed the things right in front of him and nothing else.

"Nothing," she lied. "Why?"

"Because whatever happened scared your uncle and his burly friends."

"Those burly friends were his sons."

"All of them?"

"He has more children. The MacKilligans like to breed. They're like rats that way."

"But honey badgers."

"Yes." She came across the room and plopped down on the couch. She loved this couch. It was huge! Her entire basketball team could sleep on this thing at the same time. Even the subs. "So how are you feeling?" she asked, sitting cross-legged.

"Much better. Whatever you gave me is wearing off."

Max rolled her eyes. "I didn't give you anything. I saved your life."

"Uh-huh."

"If it was drug related, what you saw in the kitchen would be known only by you . . . but I know you saw a giant panda."

He blinked and she shrugged.

"Drug-induced delusions are usually particular to the person experiencing them."

"How do you know that?"

"My sister is a scientist and she talks about that shit all the time. Besides, I did a whole paper in high school on the experiments the government ran on soldiers in the sixties and seventies."

"Why?"

"I was curious. And my teacher rejected the paper I did on serial killers. I don't know why. It was very detailed. I clearly did my research. But the next thing I knew, I was talking to the school shrink."

"That doesn't exactly shock me."

"Did you have to talk to the school shrink?"

"No."

"Lucky you."

"In my school, they were just glad I wasn't selling drugs to the freshmen."

"Where did you grow up?"

"Here. South Bronx. With my grandfather. And you?" he asked after a moment, but she got the feeling he was just asking to be polite. He didn't really want to know. He wasn't even looking at her when he asked the question. But that didn't bother Max. She liked his indifference. She'd discovered that men who wanted to find out everything about you in the first five seconds were the same ones you had to eventually get restraining orders against.

"I was born in Detroit. Lived with my mom until she got busted for a jewelry heist in Bulgaria. Charlie's mom took me in, and I lived in Connecticut with Charlie, her mom, and eventually Stevie until Charlie's mom was murdered. Then me, Charlie, and Stevie hiked to Wisconsin, where Charlie's grandfather took us into his Pack. We stayed there until both me and Charlie graduated high school. Stevie went to Oxford at fourteen to work in a lab there, doing something with physics or whatever. I never asked exactly what she was doing because I didn't care. But we did go with her to England and that was okay. We had a nice time and Oxford paid for it. But when she turned eighteen, me and Charlie had to make our own way financially. We still kept an eye on her, though, because if we didn't, Dad tended to sell her to drug dealers so she could make their drugs."

He was finally looking at her now. Staring at her with wide eyes.

"Oh, and just a side note . . ." She lowered her voice a bit in case Charlie was anywhere within hearing range. She had excellent hearing. "Any time my father is mentioned, Charlie goes off on a whole thing about how much she hates him. Just let her rant. I mean, it's all true. She *hates* him. Not that thing in books and movies where she loves-him-but-hates-him either. It's just pure hate. But it makes sense, when you think about it. Her mother was murdered and my mom is in prison *because* of our father. Although, I should clarify, he didn't actually *kill* her mother and the Bulgarian cops put my mom in prison. But the men who killed her mother were looking for our dad, and he was part of the crew that *my* mom got busted with and he left her there with the rest of the gang to be picked up by the cops. Actually," she added, realizing, "the reason Devon is trying to kidnap me is because he got out of prison and whatever loot they kept from the heist that the cops didn't find . . . he wants it back, thinking my mom has it, but she doesn't. But he *thinks* he can get my mom to tell him by kidnapping me and maybe sending her a finger or whatever. Honestly . . . I'm thinking if there was any loot left, my dad probably grabbed it, but I'm sure he's lost it all by now. Probably to women and gambling . . . and liquor. And very bad Ponzi schemes. My dad is the worst criminal," she admitted.

He was still just staring at her, so she asked, "So what made you join the Marines?"

"No, no," he quickly cut in. "No. Just no."

"No what?"

"Whatever crazy story you just told me—"

"All true."

"Sure it was."

"Who'd make that shit up? Well," she reasoned, "maybe Stephen King. But then it would involve murderous clowns or haunted hotels or . . . the end of the world. Have you read *The Stand*?"

"Is this how Manson worked?"

"Manson who?"

"*Charles* Manson. Did he just vomit up incredibly weird stories while convincing nubile young girls that they had special powers that allowed them to shift into things?"

"Shifting isn't a special power."

"It's not?"

"No," Max admitted. "Our kind is no different from full-humans. We're just better."

"How is that not different?"

"Look, there are a lot of reasons there are shifters. Most involve ancient magic and ancient people, but whatever happened back then, it eventually led to a genetic—"

"Defect?"

Max had been talking with her hands, as she liked to do. But when he said that, she dropped her hands into her lap.

"Seriously?" she asked.

"What?"

"Being a shifter isn't a defect or a superpower. It just is. We are just what we are."

"And no one knows?"

"*We* know. Those we love, some of whom are full-human, know. But our kind has spent centuries making sure that we are never found out so that full-humans don't turn us into their personal guard dogs or do Mengele-like tests on us in an attempt to steal our genetic gifts."

Vargas frowned. "What are you talking about?"

"Don't you get it? In order to protect our kind we've got people everywhere, we've infiltrated everything."

"So, you're saying . . . your people are in our government."

"We're in *all* governments. We have to be. How else do you think we protect our kind?"

"How high up . . . ?"

"As high as we can get." His eyes narrowed and she guessed what he was thinking. "Hello? Teddy Roosevelt?" His eyes narrowed even more. "*The* Teddy Roosevelt?" His lips pursed in disbelief. "Oh, come on! The Teddy Bear? In fact . . . Eleanor Roosevelt was one of us, too, but not FDR."

"And how did that happen?"

"Bloodlines. He was a *distant* cousin of Teddy's. Like a fifth cousin or something. And it's MacKilligan lore that our family is very distantly connected to—"

"Braveheart or Robert the Bruce?" he asked, now sounding bored and unimpressed.

"Neither. Those two were full-human. I'm talking about the Black Douglas. Distantly, of course. Because we're honey badgers and the Black Douglas was a wolf."

"Okay," he said, slapping his hands against his thighs. "We're done. I can't hear any more of this craziness. I just can't. I'm not a cat. You're not a badger—and why anyone would *want* to be that, I do not know—"

"We're hard to kill, that's why."

He sighed and then went on. "And I just can't do this anymore. Plus, I can't stop thinking about who can fit *this goddamn sneaker!*" he said, reaching down and retrieving one of the triplets' shoes from next to the couch. The boys tended to leave their shit everywhere, while their sister was much tidier.

"So, what I'm going to do," he said, standing up, "is get a shirt, borrow your cell phone to call a car, and get back to my non-crazy life."

She could tell he meant it, too. He was going to push everything he'd experienced in the last twenty-four hours from his mind as only a cat could. Because when cats didn't like something, they simply pretended it didn't exist. And that's what he was going to do. Pretend that she didn't exist, her sisters didn't exist, and that none of this had ever happened.

But as always in the world of shifters . . . the bears came in and fucked all that shit up.

It was kind of cute, too. The Dunn triplets did it sometimes, when they thought no one was looking. In their grizzly forms, they marched through the house humming "The Bare Necessities" from that old Disney movie.

The three of them, in a line, lumbered through the living room with their big grizzly heads swinging, all three thousand pounds marching along . . . and humming.

Humming "The Bare Necessities" song.

Vargas watched them go by in silence. When they'd made it out of the room, Max expected him to grab the phone she had in the pocket of her basketball shorts but he just . . . walked out. Not out of the house, but upstairs. She could hear his bare feet slowly slapping against each step.

A few seconds later, a calm but concerned Stevie returned to the living room and pointed in the direction of the stairs. Her furrowed brow silently asked Max what had happened.

And all Max could do was cringe. "I think I broke him."

chapter FOUR

She noticed the Mercedes idling in the middle of the road outside the church. She didn't approach the vehicle, simply watched. Hoped that no one inside had spotted her near this tree. She'd been planning to sleep for a few hours but if she were noticed . . .

But no one stepped out of the car. The driver didn't do anything but sit there. He was waiting for someone; she just didn't know who. She could only hope that whoever was coming wouldn't be a problem. That they wouldn't notice her.

She'd been on her own for a couple of years now, since she'd run away from the orphanage. She did better on her own as long as she stayed away from the city and lived in the woods. She loved the woods. Felt at home. For once. But, like the animals she befriended and that befriended her, she knew to stay away from men. There were men in the woods, sometimes, but she knew how to climb. Knew how to blend into her surroundings. Knew how to disappear if she had to. Just like the foxes and wolves that roamed the forests she lived in.

She didn't move, not even to pull the hood of her coat over her head. Simply watched and waited.

It was a few feet to her left that she heard it. Something coming up from the ground. Scratching at the earth beneath. It took some time for the thing to dig its way through but it finally broke to the surface.

She almost gasped, but slapped a hand over her mouth before she released the sound.

A human hand with a claw on each finger punched its way through the last bit of dirt and forest debris. A few seconds later another hand came through. Arms stretched out and the hands landed hard on the earth nearby. With a grunt, a human pulled itself free. And did it with ease. The struggle was minor, the body wiggling free until a woman stood in the forest. She did an all-over shake that got most of the dirt off her and ran her hands through her short hair. She wiped her face with human fingers, the claws gone. She used those same hands to brush off her clothes before heading toward the car.

When she got close to the vehicle, the trunk was remotely opened and another woman came out from the driver's side. This one was meticulously dressed in a black suit and high-heeled shoes. The women stopped long enough to stare at each other and then the driver pointed at the trunk.

Clothes were quickly changed, the old ones tossed into the forest. Then, in new jeans and a black T-shirt, the digger threw herself into the other's arms.

"Are you all right?" the driver finally asked in English. Her accent . . . it was American. Easy to identify because she'd watched a lot of TV in the orphanage and had seen many American TV shows.

"I'm fine. I'm fine." The digger stepped away from the other. The digger also spoke American English. "They kept me separated from the others and mostly shackled. For their own protection, they said." She shrugged. "The guards kept disappearing. I'm not sure how that happened and neither were they."

The driver laughed. "I see you haven't changed."

"Why would I? Prison is easy once you figure out who the players are . . . and kill them."

The driver nodded toward the car. "We don't have much time before they come after you."

The digger snorted. "I doubt they'll come after me. As long as I stay out of Bulgaria, I'm sure they'll be glad to see the back of me. Besides . . . I've got something to fix. I can't let anyone get in the way of that."

"The aunts don't understand why we didn't do this sooner."

"She was *safe* when I was in. So it was worth staying. But now . . . now he's got a three-million bounty on her head. I either stop him or he gets her. I'm not going to let him get her."

"Even with all those MacKilligan resources, Max couldn't find him. What makes you think that you can?"

"Because I've fucked him," she said matter-of-factly.

"That doesn't mean you know him better than anyone else."

"I know him well enough. I'll find him."

"Then let's get you home." The driver placed her hand behind the other's head and pulled her close until their foreheads touched. They stayed like that for a long but powerful moment.

Then something changed. They must have sensed they were being watched. Slowly, they looked in the direction of the tree she'd been silently sitting against. And she knew that these two women saw her even though she was in utter darkness.

They, however, stood in the light that came from the nearby church. And what she saw told her two things about these women. One was that they were both Asian and probably related. They had the same noses and jaws. And second, they weren't human. The light reflected off their eyes the way it did the wolves and foxes in the forests. Her mother, when she still lived, used to tell her about people like this. People who were only "a little" human. Her mother had told her they were dangerous. Deadly, in fact. Because they were more animal than human.

Yet after living in the forests for so long, she'd also learned that most animals were only dangerous when hungry or startled. Since the digger had just gotten out of prison, she'd probably want something more filling than a scrawny girl who hadn't eaten in two days. And neither the digger nor the driver had been startled.

They watched her for several seconds until the digger put her forefinger to her lips and said, "Shhhhh."

Grinning, the digger winked and went around to the passenger side of the car. The driver got in her side. Doors were slammed closed, the engine revved, and they sped off. Disappearing into the night and leaving her alone with her beloved forests and the animals in it.

She was guessing the digger was right, though, about someone coming for her. No one would be looking for the digger. No one would dare.

Charlie pulled the stray out of the bathtub and quickly wrapped him in a big towel. She gasped when the dog wiggled his way out of the towel and fell to the floor, but laughed when he turned on the towel and grabbed it with his fangs, desperately tugging one way, then the other.

"Do not rip my towel," she warned. When she heard it tear, she quickly released it. The dog stopped tugging once there was no longer any resistance, then shook all over, water flying everywhere.

Charlie laughed harder, holding up another towel to keep from getting drenched. Then he stopped, spun around, and charged out the door. Charlie slid quickly across the floor on her knees, diving on the dog and again wrapping him up in the towel. They wrestled on the bedroom floor outside her bathroom until the dog began to lick her face.

Yeah. She was keeping this dog. Not that Berg would like that. He barely tolerated Benny, who had been his dog before he'd met Charlie. As part wolf, Charlie shouldn't be much of a dog fan either, but she'd discovered long ago that she was definitely a dog person. She just liked them.

Pulling the dog into her lap, Charlie noticed Vargas for the first time. He was sitting on the floor with his back against the wall, forearms resting on his raised knees.

And he was staring. Blankly.

Good Lord, what had Max done to the poor guy?

"Hi, Zé. You okay?"

"You had bears walking through your living room," he said, still gazing at the wall behind the bed Charlie shared with Berg. "I was going to warn you to get out while you still could because you were so nice to me earlier and I didn't want you to be eaten, but then I saw the size of your bed . . . and this." He held up one of Berg's sneakers. "I kept thinking, 'What could fit a shoe like this? What kind of being?' Then I realized . . . a bear."

Charlie didn't have the heart to tell him there were bigger bears than Berg and his brother and sister. Bears that wore bigger shoes. Tiny, their landlord, had three older brothers who were several inches bigger and wore size twenty-four shoes. One of Tiny's sisters had restrained a carjacker once by yanking the man out of the car, throwing him to the ground, and stepping on him with her giant foot until the cops came. All of Tiny's siblings and cousins called him "Tiny"—and he was six-nine!

But Charlie knew that poor Zé wasn't ready to hear any of that yet. She was sure Max had already freaked the guy out. She was really good at that. Really good at terrorizing people without actually meaning to. Well . . . at least sometimes she didn't mean to. Other times, she absolutely meant to. It really depended on Max's mood.

Charlie got off the floor and sat down on the bed, facing Zé. She still held the dog in her arms.

"I know this is hard for you. All these years you thought you were just a guy, but you're not."

That green gaze moved from the wall to Charlie. "So you're one, too?"

"Yeah. All three of us are. Actually . . . everyone on this street is."

His eyes narrowed a bit. "Then do it," he ordered. "Become whatever it is you become."

Charlie shrugged. "Can't. Due to fucked-up genetics provided by my idiot father, I can't shift to wolf or honey badger."

"Of course you can't."

"I can only do this . . ."

Charlie unleashed her fangs and roared. Zé jerked, his back and head hitting the wall behind him; the dog in her lap yelped and ran to the bathroom. He spun around so that his butt ended up slamming the door closed.

Retracting her fangs, Charlie focused on Zé and grimaced. "Ooops. I really didn't mean to scare him."

"Did you mean to scare me?" Zé demanded. "Because you did!"

"You kidnapped a cat?"

Max glared across the yard at her best friend, Dutch Alexander. They'd been friends since Max had met Dutch in junior high.

"I did not kidnap a cat."

"You borrowed one?"

"Very funny."

He moved closer and she continued to dribble the basketball she was holding. She'd set up a basketball hoop by their garage. It wasn't for practice so much as something to do with her hands. That's all basketball had ever been for her: something to do with her hands. You know . . . something other than punching someone in the gut or slashing someone's face with her claws.

"Do you not understand what you've done?" Dutch demanded.

"Of course I do. I saved his life, thank you very much. And, even more impressive, I've taken the time to explain to him that he's one of us. That he's a shifter."

"You saved his life? So he's alive?"

"Of course he's alive."

"What do you mean, 'of course'? You left a shitload of bodies back there."

"So?"

"It was the Netherlands. One of those countries where they care about that sort of thing."

"I don't see what the big deal is."

"Your cat works for our government. They think he's dead and they're looking to nail the ones who killed him."

"But he's not dead. He's in the house."

Dutch took a step back, tossing his head dramatically. "*He's here?*"

"First off, you need to calm down."

"No, first off, you need to get him out of your house, and make sure he forgets that you ever existed."

"Except I'm unforgettable."

"I see," Dutch said, shaking his head.

"You see what?"

"You're trying to make me insane. You're trying to make my life harder than it already is."

"Why do you always accuse me of that?"

"Because you always are!"

"Dude, it's okay. He's fine. He got hit on the head pretty bad, but he's one of us. So he's recovered quite nicely. I don't see what you're freaking out about."

"What am I freaking out about? How about your sister?"

Max lined up her ball and made the shot. It went in and bounced back over to her like a well-trained dog.

"What does Charlie have to do with anything?" She assumed he'd meant Charlie since Dutch and Stevie had always gotten along like a house on fire. Whereas, Charlie always seemed to want to *set* Dutch on fire.

"Max, they know it was you. You and Nelle and the others."

"Who knows?"

"Who do you think?"

"So, the Group." The shifter-only protection organization that Dutch had worked for since graduating college.

"Right. And Katzenhaus. *And* BPC."

"BPC?"

"The Bear Preservation Council."

"Oh, yeah. Them." She shrugged her shoulders. "So what if they know?"

"You and your girlfriends left a trail of bodies in one of the countries that we are close friends with. To those organizations, that just means you're off your chain."

"I'm off my what?"

"That you're out of control. And if you're out of control,

they're going to want one of two things: either to make you join the Group, so they can put your out-of-control-ness to good use; or to put you down because you can't be trusted."

"Well, that seems unfair!"

"I repeat: *You left a trail of bodies in the Netherlands!*"

"Stop yelling at me. And my plan wasn't to leave a trail of bodies anywhere. They shot first. I just reacted." She continued to dribble the ball. "So what now?"

"Has your rescue cat called anyone? Maybe tried to make contact with his team? Which, I feel I should point out, is his *full-human* team."

Max rolled her eyes at the wolverine dramatics. "I don't think so. But he's only been up for a few hours."

"You mean, he's just sitting in the house? Alone?"

"I had to convince him first that he wasn't all that human and then . . ."

Dutch cringed, clearly already concerned with what she was about to say. "And then what?"

"And then he saw the bears . . . as bears."

"What bears? Oh, God!" He quickly caught on. "Not the Dunns!"

"Well . . ."

"You can't show a first-time adult shifter the grizzlies! It would freak anyone out! The Dunns are huge!"

"How was I to know that they'd come wandering through the house in their bear forms first thing in the morning? When the sun comes up, they're usually human again."

"Did he run? Because I would run."

"No. He just wandered upstairs. Charlie was up there, so I figured she could deal with him."

"Charlie knows he's here? And she's not freaking out?"

"Actually, she likes him," Max replied.

"*Seriously?*" Frustrated, Dutch threw his hands into the air. "She likes a stranger-cat but just the sight of me makes her a psychotic—"

"Why are *you* here?" Charlie suddenly demanded, walking over to them from the back of the house.

"How you wound me," Dutch muttered, turning away.

Charlie snatched the basketball from Max's hands. "And you need to get inside and help that cat."

"I did what I was supposed to do: I told him what he is. He just didn't want to listen."

"He's finally listening and now I believe he's having a mini-breakdown."

"How am I supposed to help him with that?"

"By doing *anything*? You brought him here, Max. You told him the truth. Now you have to deal with the repercussions of those actions."

Max rolled her eyes, blew out a breath, and leaned far back in a general show of frustration.

"What did you think was going to happen?" Charlie asked. "That you were just going to tell him he could shift into a giant cat and he would be, 'Oh. Okay. Thanks for the info. I'll go out and live my life now'? Did you really think that would happen?"

"Yes! I did! I didn't think I'd actually have to—"

"Care?"

Max shrugged.

"Get your ass in there," Charlie ordered, "and deal with this. *Now.*"

With a whining sigh that Max knew she wouldn't tolerate from anyone else, she started toward the house. Only stopping to glance back so she could watch her sister react to Dutch's presence by throwing the basketball at him with as much strength as she could muster—which was a lot.

"*Owwwwwwwwwwwwwwwwwwwww!*" the wolverine howled, grabbing his side and rubbing it while pacing in circles. "*What did I do?*"

"*You exist!*"

chapter FIVE

Stevie entered the kitchen just as Max walked in from the backyard. They stopped and stared at each other for a moment before looking at the kitchen table.

Max's rescued cat was sitting slumped over the table, his muscular arms hanging limply at his sides.

"Is he dead?" Max asked, not appearing as concerned as Stevie felt she should be. Max was the one who'd brought him to their house. She was the one who'd taken it upon herself to tell him that he wasn't nearly as human as he thought he was. So, in Stevie's estimation, her sister should be much more concerned about the well-being of her rescue!

"If you're concerned," Stevie suggested, "you should check."

"You check."

"*Max!*" she spit out in a harsh whisper.

"If he's dead, I don't know why you're whispering."

Stevie changed her eye color to the bright gold her shifter form had. She wasn't about to shift. Not in the house. Especially now that she'd begun to worry her shifted form might be getting bigger. Much to her continuing happiness, however, she had complete control of her animal rage. Still, Max insisted on worrying about whether Stevie was taking her meds or not—of course she was!—so just the eye change alone was enough to get Max to—

"Fine!" Max reached across the table to press her fingers against Zé's neck to check his pulse, but before she could touch him, she jumped back and yelped. Blood dripped down her arm.

"*Goddammit!*"

From Zé's lap, the feral cat that lurked around their backyard popped her head up and bared her fangs at Max.

"Don't hiss at me, you little fucker," Max warned, angrily swiping at the bloody wounds the little beast had caused.

The feral cat scrambled up onto the table and onto Zé's head. With her front paws on the back of his head and her back paws resting on his shoulders, she arched her body and her battered, furry tail became big and fluffy.

"If I were you," Stevie softly suggested, "I'd move away from Zé. Because that feral cat does not like you."

"You know, this is all *your* fault."

"How is this *my* fault?" Stevie wanted to know.

"Because you insist on feeding this thing! Now we can't get rid of it."

"*Do you want her to starve?*"

"*Yes!*"

Stevie, without thinking, leaned over and pushed Max. Max, of course, pushed her back. It was something they'd been doing since . . . let's see . . . oh, yes! The day they'd met.

Poor Carlie. She'd welcomed Stevie into her home for what was supposed to be a day-long playdate with her unknown half-sisters. Instantly, Stevie had hit it off with Carlie's eldest, Charlie. But then she'd met Max and was immediately left alone with her while mother and daughter had gone to the kitchen for cookies and milk. In that moment, Max hadn't actually done anything to Stevie. She hadn't touched her or said anything or even stuck her tongue out at her. But Stevie just hadn't liked the way her new half-sister had stared at her. She hadn't liked it at all. So she'd reached up and pushed Max's shoulders. Max had responded by pushing her back. And that's when Stevie had snapped. She'd pulled back her tiny fist, filled with fingers that were currently insured for half-a-million dollars because of her musical career, and punched the older, taller, *meaner* girl in the nose. When all Stevie got back was a grin . . . she knew she was dead.

Seconds later, Carlie and Charlie had found the pair rolling around the tiny backyard of their Connecticut mobile home. It had rained earlier in the day so they were both covered in mud and blood. Stevie had only been six at the time, had already been deemed a musical prodigy, performing solo piano and violin concerts at the Met in New York City to sold-out audiences. She'd already learned that all those feelings she had roiling around her gut were to be repressed. They were to be beaten down, ignored, kept away from the light of day. Being around Max, however, had brought out everything Stevie's family had, up to that day, told her to keep under wraps. Carlie—dear, sweet, loving Carlie—had tried everything to stop the girls from fighting, but she was too nice. A sweet, motherly wolf who had immediately come to adore the Siberian tiger–honey badger hybrid prodigy who was in a nasty fistfight with the other girl who'd been dumped on her for no other reason than that Carlie was just too damn nice. Unable to get the two girls under control herself, Carlie had left it up to her daughter. Charlie, always up for a challenge, had gotten Stevie and Max to stop fighting by grabbing them by the extra skin at the back of their necks and twisting with all the strength she had.

The pain had been so horrible, Stevie and Max had immediately separated, but Charlie still took a moment to lift both girls in the air—one hand on each—and shake them. So that they "understood" that what they had done was *not* okay.

They hadn't learned that, though. Instead, they'd learned to keep their fights away from the watchful gaze of their big sister.

Like now. In this kitchen with just the two of them, a possibly dead male, and a feral cat. It was the perfect time for them to get a good fight on. But before Stevie could make a solid move, that feral cat charged across the table and launched her seven-pound body at Max's face.

Stevie gasped, horrified, watching the pair hit the floor,

stunned by all the snarling and hissing for several seconds before she realized she should do something.

"No, no, no!" she yelped, attempting to pull the pair apart. But there was so much resentment and hatred between the two, neither was willing to give up.

The feral cat had her front claws dug deep in Max's face. As if she was hoping to rip the skin off completely. Max struggled to her feet with the cat still attached. She gripped the angry beast with both hands and pulled and pulled.

Stevie cringed, watching as her sister's skin was stretched by the deeply imbedded claws.

Terrified about how this would end, she reached in between the pair, ready to separate them with a hard push. But Max abruptly pulled the cat off her face and slammed it down on the table. Angry beyond reason, Max kept the animal pinned to the table with one hand and lifted the other, unleashing her claws.

"Max!" Stevie screamed. "*Noooo!*"

Max, ignoring her as usual, brought her claws down toward the hissing animal she had trapped on the table. But a black paw slammed into her arm, holding it in place.

The black jaguar that had replaced the possibly dead man who had been sitting unconscious at the table glared at Max with bright gold eyes. Then it bared its fangs and let out a roar that had Stevie doing the only thing she could think of . . .

Max gazed into the gold eyes of the big cat glaring at her. He had his back paws in the chair his human form had been sitting in and the front paw not warding off her unleashed claws was on the kitchen table.

Shocked that the dude she'd thought was dead was quite alive and had just shifted into a very big jaguar, Max didn't know what to say or do . . . until she realized that her sister was no longer standing behind her.

Looking over her shoulder . . . and up, Max let out a little growl.

Max pulled her hands away from both cats and turned. "Get

out of the ceiling!" she ordered, using that phrasing because
her sister was hanging by her claws.

"Nope."

"Stevie!"

Stevie crawled into the closest cabinet over the refrigerator,
slamming the door behind her.

Satisfied that at least her sister wouldn't come crashing to the
ground—Charlie got really bitchy when their rental house was
damaged—Max turned back to the table to find only the feral
cat standing there, glaring at her. The jaguar . . .

"Shit!"

Max ran toward the front of the house.

"What's wrong?" Stevie yelled from the cabinet, but Max
didn't have time to answer her. Not when she scented that the
big cat had gone out the front door. Someone had left it open,
probably the triplets since they would most likely head back
this way from their house across the street at any time.

Max ran out on the porch and stood at the top of the stairs,
gaze searching the street.

"Max?" Dutch came around the side of the house, still rubbing his side from where Charlie had hit him with the basketball. "What's wrong?"

"He's out. He's out."

"Who's out?"

They heard screaming from down the street. A kid screaming, "Dad! Dad! *Daaaaaaaad!*"

Running down the steps and through several neighbors'
yards, Max stumbled to a stop, and Dutch crashed into her.

"Oh, shit!" they both gasped at the same time.

The cat had grabbed a grizzly cub lounging in his own yard
and was dragging the poor screeching kid to a nearby tree.

The Ako Pride had ruled the Tanzania cats long before the
Chinese had their first emperor. But it wasn't until the late
1800s that Imani's great grandmother, her great aunts, and
their males had traveled to the American shores. They'd lived

in Harlem in those days, but that's when shifters of other breeds and species had been scattered throughout the country.

If one wanted to find shifter-only towns on the East Coast, one had to go to parts of the South that seemed to be filled with nothing but dogs from the Smith Pack. Not a lot of cats wanted to deal with Smiths in any town or city, but the southern soil seemed to strengthen the Smiths in ways that had made Imani's kin more than a little uncomfortable. When several houses became available on a Queens street a couple of decades back, the Ako Pride had purchased them and moved in. Finding out there were bears a street or two over and wolves in the other direction with their annoying howling every goddamn full moon had almost sent them running back to Harlem. But their cubs had loved having yards, a couple with in-ground pools. Who could willingly leave that? So they stayed and did what all lions did: expanded their territory.

It was Imani's grandmother who'd realized that waiting for more lions to move in would put them at risk of full-humans snapping up newly available homes. So she'd decided to have other breeds of cats move in as houses became available—no matter how annoying those cats might be. Tigers, cheetahs, leopards, jaguars, cougars, lynx—all of them would be welcome as long as they had the down payment and could tolerate the damn howling. It took some time, but eventually the local full-humans found the constant silent staring of unfriendly neighbors more than enough reason to move out to Long Island or out of the state completely. Leaving the Pride with all they'd ever wanted:

Several streets that belonged only to them.

Which meant that when a She-tiger casually showed up with a Smith riding in the car with her, Imani didn't take it well. How could she? It wasn't just any Smith that Cella Malone had brought to her territory. It was Dee-Ann Smith. A She-wolf who was a standout killer in a Pack of standout killers. Only Smith's father was feared more. An oversized wolf strangely named "Eggie."

It was such an annoying move that Imani felt the need to say something in the most diplomatic way possible.

"Who told you it was okay to bring this heifer with you?"

"Mom!" her daughter snapped from behind her while one of Imani's teenage granddaughters snorted out a laugh before quickly turning away.

"That is not friendly," the She-tiger replied with a wide smile. A smile Imani had never trusted and had always wanted to slap off her face. But this particular cat wasn't some lone kitty roaming the world. This was Cella Malone and the Malones were not only Siberian tigers, they were Travelers and, as a group, nearly as dangerous as the Smiths. Just less insane, which was at least something. "Everyone knows that Dee-Ann is a very close associate of mine."

"Who, exactly, is 'everyone'?" Imani looked at her granddaughter over her shoulder. "Ever notice that narcissists always say, 'everyone knows this about me'? Or 'everyone knows who I am'? Is that you, Malone? A narcissist?"

"My daddy says," the Smith cut in, voice low, "that's the way of all cats."

Imani studied the dog a few seconds before asking, "Can your daddy even spell 'cats'?"

"Okay," Malone quickly said, stepping between them, arms out although neither had moved. "Let's keep this civil."

"Why are you here, Malone? What do you want from my Pride?"

The She-tiger's back straightened, her mouth set in a grim line, and she solemnly intoned, "Your firstborn."

When Imani's fangs angrily slid into place, Malone began laughing.

"I'm kidding!" she finally said, wiping away actual tears. "You're all so serious! Loosen up."

"You expect me to loosen up when you bring a dog to my territory?"

"Call me 'dog' one more time . . ."

Imani looked over at the big-shouldered female standing behind Malone. Her short brown hair was covered by a Tennessee

Titans baseball cap; her ancient-looking blue T-shirt had a Pabst Blue Ribbon logo, and her jeans were so old looking, they might have once been worn by an actual old-timey cowboy. The best touch was the brown boots: steel-toed. So when she had to kick someone, Smith could do maximum damage. The worst thing about Dee-Ann Smith, though, was her eyes. Because unlike most of their kind, her eyes didn't change to a different color when she shifted. Imani's brown eyes turned a bright gold when she became lion, but Smith's eyes were an off-putting yellow all the time. It was like having a human pit bull staring at you.

Imani opened her mouth to tell the dog to roll over, but Malone quickly said, "No." She looked back and forth between the two of them. "You know, ladies, we're all on the same side. Working toward the same goal. Protecting our kind."

"I have never been on the same side as the Group," Imani reminded Malone. "My loyalty has always been to Katzenhaus. And if I still worked for Katzenhaus, I can promise you, we would not have an association with a bunch of hybrid freaks."

"Can I shoot her *now*?" Smith pushed.

"*No*," Malone snapped.

Fed up, Imani finally asked again, "Why are you here, Malone?"

"We need your help with something."

It was the way she said it. The way her body suddenly seemed tense. This time, Imani knew the She-tiger was serious because she was trying so hard to hide it.

"With what?"

Malone cleared her throat, glanced away. But the dog, the dog had no such sense. "The de Medici Pride."

Imani felt that tic she sometimes got right under her left eye. It was the only thing she couldn't control with ruthless determination. She hated that tic, but other than using Botox, there was no way to stop it. And no lioness was so insecure as to waste time and money on getting shots in her face. What were they? Full-humans?

"Get off my property, Malone," she ordered both dog and cat. "And I mean now."

★ ★ ★

The cub's father came stomping down his back steps, grizzly hump expanding with each move.

"Stop him!" Max ordered Dutch, pointing at the shifting grizzly.

"Why do I have to go after the bear?" Dutch wanted to know, but Max wasn't really listening.

She ran to the tree that the cat had dragged his prey into.

"Goddammit! Drop that kid! Now!" Stretched out on a high branch, the cat had one paw pressed against the sobbing kid's head and the other across his chest. Glaring down at her, Vargas gave a warning snarl.

"*Let him go!*"

Behind her, Max could hear rage-filled huffing. She turned and came face-to-face with a dozen of her neighbors in their bear forms. There were four grizzlies, two black bears, a polar, three sun bears, and—to Max's great concern—a couple of sloth bears. Usually the most laid-back, easygoing bears there were . . . unless they were aggravated. They could be a little psychotic when aggravated.

And right now, all these bears knew was that there was a cat in their territory attempting to eat their children. Of course, all Zé Vargas knew was what any big jungle cat would know: that some chunky cub lying around in his kiddy pool with no parents around to protect him was easy prey. It didn't help that Vargas was probably pretty hungry, too. Max hadn't thought about feeding him when he'd been conscious. All he'd eaten were those cinnamon buns.

The worst part was knowing she'd never hear the end of this once Charlie found out.

Dutch pushed his way past all those shifted bears and stood in front of them.

"Let's all just calm—" was all he managed to say before he was slapped into a yard three houses over by a livid grizzly bear attempting to protect his child.

Max raised her hands, palms up and out. "Okay. Everyone

be calm. We can discuss this. Remember . . . I'm Max. Charlie and Stevie's sister."

Max grimaced as the roaring response from the grizzlies and black bears reminded her they had not been appreciating her nightly raids on their beehives.

Since trying the calming thing that Charlie was really good at wasn't working for her, Max said, "Zé Vargas . . . if there's a part of you in that tree that still knows you were once a U.S. Marine, you best realize the situation you're currently in and let that goddamn kid go . . ."

The leaves in the big tree behind her rustled and—

"*Ow*," she growled when the big-boned bear cub landed on her back. He was alive but crying. Something she didn't have patience for.

She grabbed the kid's arms and was trying to politely remove him when a shot of black zipped past her peripheral vision— and a bunch of bears tore off in pursuit.

Unable to take her time, she yanked the kid off her back and tossed him to his father.

"Sorry about that, Mr. Kapowski!" she yelled, running after the mob trying to take down her rescue cat.

"What's going on?" Charlie asked Stevie, her eyes narrowing when Stevie jumped at the sound of her voice. Now she *knew* something was going on.

"Uhhhh." Stevie stood in front of the house, twisting her fingers the way she used to before a big recital. Her eyes were unnaturally wide and she was moving around as if she had to pee, but Charlie knew that was simply one of her sister's nervous reactions to an uncomfortable situation.

"You might as well tell me, Stevie. We both know I'll find out anyway."

"Well—" she began just as a black jungle cat shot across the street, turned down Everest Drive, and headed directly into cat territory. Five streets ruled by the Ako lion Pride that even the hyenas didn't fuck with.

"Was that—?" Charlie started, only to stop when a gang of bears raced across the street after the cat. So pissed off it seemed as if they were blindly running right into lion territory. Something none of them did except when they were in their cars, trying to avoid traffic. But to actually walk into that neighborhood . . . in their bear forms?

A few seconds later, after the bears went down the street, Max came into view. She was still human, but only because she ran much faster as human than as honey badger. And right behind her . . . that idiot. Although Charlie did have to stifle a laugh when she saw that Dutch was bleeding profusely from his face, meaning he'd ended up on the wrong side of those bears.

"I've got it!" Max yelled, waving at Charlie and Stevie as she headed down Everest. "I've got it alllllll under control!"

Stevie looked at Charlie, shrugged. "Do I still need to answer your question?"

"Talk to us," Malone pushed. "We need your help."

"If you're going after the de Medicis, you need more than help. You need a mental hospital. For a thousand years, Katzenhaus did not have anything to do with the de Medicis. We didn't help, we didn't hinder. They kept their territories and we kept our own. And all that was for a very good reason."

"Pretending they don't exist is no longer an option for us."

"Then let the full-humans take them down."

"That's not something we should let full-humans handle. We've seen what happens when they get involved in situations we should have managed from the beginning. They *always* make it worse."

Imani shook her head. The She-tiger could say whatever she wanted, but going against the de Medicis was a fool's plan. She knew that from past experience. From nightmares she still had. From the therapist she still saw.

"Forget it, Malone."

"But—"

"Ma!"

One of Imani's daughters strode up to her, with Imani's toddler granddaughter in her arms.

Imani waved her off. "It's all right. I can handle this."

"Cat," was all her daughter said, but she knew her daughter didn't mean Malone. So Imani looked down the street and saw the black cat streaking toward them.

One lone cat was not something Imani would ever worry about, but the zoo-sized crowd of bears behind it . . . that was definitely a bigger issue.

"*Bearsssss!*" one of Imani's neighbors roared. Cubs retreated into homes, some females going with them, while others shifted to their She-cat forms and made a half-circle behind Imani. The Pride's male lions joined Imani on either side.

The cat was running toward them, looking over its shoulder at the bears behind it. But when it saw the cats, it tried to stop, turning into a rolling jumble of paws and claws.

Confused, because she'd never seen a cat as inelegant as this one, Imani kept her eye on him—she now knew it was a "him" from his scent—while her Pride watched the bears.

The bears grotesquely lumbered to a stop. They wanted the interloper but they weren't sure they wanted to fight a bunch of cats to get to him.

The strongest of her males took several steps forward and unleashed his roar. A sound that must have traveled to other nearby neighborhoods because the wolves a few blocks over barked and howled in response.

One of the grizzlies, the oldest of the Kapowski brothers, stepped forward and roared at the lion, but before jaws snapped and claws slashed, a honey badger appeared.

An actual honey badger. In basketball shorts, tank top, and high-top sneakers. Because that was the kind of weird day Imani was having. First Malones and Smiths and now honey badgers.

The honey badger jumped between the two groups, standing close to the interloper cat. She spread her arms out and opened her mouth to speak . . . but all she could do was pant. Hard.

Putting her hands back on her waist, she bent over. How far had she run? From Utah?

"Sorry," she finally got out. "Sorry." She pointed at the jaguar. "He's with me."

They all gazed at the She-badger for a moment, processing that information. Because it was weird information. Why would a badger be hanging around a cat? Ever? In this universe? Before any of them could figure that out, a wolverine showed up. Bloody and bruised, limping as he joined the badger.

"I think we can all calm down," the wolverine suggested when he finally made it close enough for all of them to hear. "This is *not* a big deal."

The bears didn't seem to like that sentiment at all and one of the grizzly males roared at the wolverine.

"Hey, hey, *hey!*" the badger bellowed. "*Don't you yell at my friend!*"

"Max, it's okay. It's okay," the wolverine soothed. "Let's just discuss this like reasonable, civilized—"

With one swipe of his paw, Kapowski sent the wolverine flying down their street. And they all watched him go before refocusing on the She-badger.

"That," the honey badger announced, "was unnecessary."

Kapowski pointed his paw at the cat she was standing in front of.

"No," she immediately replied. "He doesn't know what he is. He's still learning. And he didn't know that chubby kid was your nephew. So I'm telling you to leave him alone."

The bear took two big steps toward her and the badger held her hands up. "Don't make me get nasty, Kapowski."

The bears laughed at the tiny female. Harsh because bear laughter was always particularly mocking in its tone.

But as the bears laughed, the woman slid one hand behind her back and carefully lifted her shirt. She had a knife sheath strapped to her back and with deft fingers pulled the weapon from its holster. Imani had done a lot of work for Katzenhaus. They had trained her from the time she was fifteen with the blessing of her mother and grandmother. And if there was one thing Imani knew, it was a fellow trained combatant. This badger, no matter how small, wasn't going to let her claws and fangs do her talking for her. Not when she could open arteries and remove eyes without working up much of a sweat.

Imani stepped forward, finally ready to intervene, but she heard that sound first. Even from this great distance, she could hear it perfectly. So could everyone else. The cats, dogs, and most of the bears hit the ground or made a mad run for it. Except for Kapowski, who had reared up onto his hind legs to scare off the She-badger. It wasn't until that tranq dart hit his neck that he became aware of anything other than the honey badger and that black cat.

From her spot on the ground, Imani watched the bear blink, stumble back, blink, stumble forward . . . blink . . . and go down like the *Titanic*.

That surprised Imani. She'd been hit by a tranq once, shot by scientists at an animal park in Botswana. It took her ages to finally pass out, only to wake up with one of those damn collars on her neck so that the scientists could monitor her location and vitals. The worst part was the laughter of her mother and aunts before they took the damn thing off, but that was beside the point. A bear shouldn't go down this fast. Especially not a one-thousand-pound bear with a thick neck.

But there he was . . . snoring.

Standing, Imani looked in the direction the shot had come from. There was no one standing in range. Tranq rifles were not long-distance weapons. The shooter had to be pretty close for it to not only hit the target but also get past the target's hide.

The honey badger had slid the blade back into its holster. She crouched beside a snoring Kapowski, her hands on his shoulder. But as soon as she attempted to push him over, his two brothers were there, snarling in warning.

"He should be on his side to sleep this off," the badger explained. "If he's on his back and vomits, he'll choke. If he's on his front, I'm afraid he'll stop breathing. You should get him home. Put him to bed."

One brother leaned forward and roared in her face and Imani

heard it again. That sound of a trigger pull and a projectile racing toward them. She didn't drop down this time; instead she watched.

It wasn't a bear that was hit this time, but the black cat. He'd launched himself at the bears roaring at the badger, claws and fangs out, all four legs spread wide. But that tranq hit the cat right between the eyes, flipping him back and over. When he landed, he was out cold.

"See what you did?" the badger asked the bear. "Causing problems!"

In obvious exasperation, the bear finally shifted. It was the youngest Kapowski, Matt. "*I'm* causing problems? You steal our honey—"

"Prove it!"

"We have video of you!" the third brother yelped, now also human. "Stealing our honey in both your honey badger *and* human forms!"

"Oh."

"—you let your friend try to eat our nephew—" Matt continued.

"If he lost a few pounds, he wouldn't look so tasty!"

"—and you get my brother tranq'd—and *I'm* causing problems?"

The badger stared at him a moment before replying, "Yes."

Then, without another word, she easily hefted the more than two-hundred-pound cat onto the back of her neck like she was putting on a stole, and returned to the streets run by bears.

They all watched her go. In silence. She wasn't running. She wasn't fearful. She was just . . . a honey badger with a live but unconscious cat around her neck.

Glad the drama was over, Imani looked at the bears and ordered, "Mind getting your walking bear rugs off my territory?"

With a few snarls and some snaps, the bears left and the cats shifted back to human and put their clothes on. Everyone's day finally returning to normal.

Shaking her head, Imani turned to go back to her house when she came face-to-face with the She-tiger and the dog.

"What?" she asked.

"Interesting, huh?" Malone asked.

Imani frowned. "What are you talking about?"

Jutting her chin, Malone motioned toward the retreating bears.

"Sorry. I have never found bears remotely interesting."

"Not the bears. The honey badgers."

"I only saw one badger and I didn't find her that interesting."

"The one doing the shootin' was Charlie MacKilligan," the dog explained.

"Even *I* couldn't make that shot," Malone admitted, which was huge. Because Malone was the go-to gal when it came to long-distance kills. It was, in fact, her specialty.

"And the one who combined a long-distance rifle with a tranq gun and created a knockout drug for shifters that wouldn't kill them but could automatically adjust to their body chemistry was their baby sister, Stevie. Although anyone with any sense would just leave her out of this."

"Why is this dog talking to me?" Imani asked Malone.

"Because we need you."

"I'm retired. I'm especially retired if you're thinking of going after the de Medicis. You can just leave me, my Pride, and the entire cat nation out of that shit."

Deciding nothing else needed to be said, Imani started toward her house.

"They're using full-humans," Malone called after her.

"They've always used full-humans. Humans deal for the de Medicis. They spy for them. They kill for them. This is *not* news, Malone."

"The de Medicis are using them as product."

Imani was halfway up the steps to her porch when she froze. Slowly she faced the cat and dog. "What?"

Malone shrugged.

"What kind of product?"

"Well, much to our surprise, given their history, they seem uncomfortable with sex trafficking so they leave that mostly to the full-humans, but anything else the buyer wants . . . From what we can tell that includes hunting, food, and on several recent occasions, ritual human sacrifice."

Imani's mouth briefly dropped open; then she closed her eyes, shook her head, and once again asked, *"What?"*

chapter SIX

Zé woke up and quickly realized that he was, again, naked and on top of the china cabinet. How did he keep winding up here? What was that about?

At least this time he wasn't alone. He had a furry companion cuddled up to his side. Not the dogs, thankfully, but the stray cat that Max seemed to hate. The cat was sweet to him so he didn't understand what her problem was.

"Why are you up there again?"

Zé looked over the side of the cabinet. Max stood below.

"I really don't know. Is this normal for cats?"

"I have no idea. Are you hungry? You must be hungry."

"I could eat."

"Do you need help getting down?"

"No," he said quickly. This time he didn't even have a towel. It was just all him . . . hanging out for the universe to see. "I'll get down on my own."

"Great." She took a step away from the cabinet but then stopped, looked back at him. "By the way . . . did you know it's been forty-eight hours since our last conversation?"

Zé blinked. "Wait . . . what?"

"My sister tranq'd you so you wouldn't be torn apart by bears. She also tranq'd a bear, but he was only out for, like, ten minutes. But he's a thousand pounds, compared to your two-hundred-and-sixty, so that's a substantial difference, right? Anyway . . . thought you'd want to know."

Then she walked off. Just like that. As if what she'd just said was in any way a normal or reasonable conversation!

"Wait . . . *what?*"

Dutch walked into the communications room of the Group's Team Center.

"You wanted to see me?" he asked the She-bear hybrid sitting in front of a bank of monitors.

Hannah was one of Dutch's favorite people aside from Max and Stevie. Just a relaxed female who didn't let the little things bother her. She'd had a very tough life growing up, but you couldn't tell because she handled things so well. Although that mellowness could be because she vented any aggression she might still have in her system on the ice by playing hockey for a minor-league team.

"I thought you should see this." She motioned to the chair next to her and he sat down. "I haven't said anything to anyone else. Yet. You always told me to alert you first if this came up."

"Alert me first?" Dutch didn't remember all the things he'd told Hannah over the years, because he tended to talk a lot sometimes, and couldn't keep track of everything he said. "About what?"

"Just got this from one of our Bulgarian contacts."

Hannah brought up a shot of a hole in a decrepit-looking cell. A big hole. Not neatly dug but . . .

"Oh, God."

"Renny Yang's cell in Bulgaria," she said. "Although once the authorities found out she'd left the country, they haven't exactly been scouring the streets looking for her. Or alerting anyone else to her sudden disappearance."

"They don't want her back," he guessed. "No one would."

Dutch could think of a thousand things he'd rather do than deal with this right now. A thousand things! But he couldn't avoid it. Or her.

He couldn't avoid dealing with Renny Yang. Jewelry thief and bank robber who'd only been caught because she insisted on making very bad choices with men. Oh, Renny was also the mother of his best friend. A mother Max hadn't seen since she was eight. Sure, they'd kept in touch via smuggled cell phones and the occasional letter, but Dutch always got the feeling that Max didn't know her mother as well as she thought she did.

And Renny definitely didn't know her daughter any longer. Because Max wasn't the little girl Renny had left behind. She'd grown up with Carlie Taylor and then Charles Taylor. Charlie Taylor-MacKilligan and Stevie Stasiuk-MacKilligan were her sisters. All these people had taught Max a different way of life. A chance to be something more than a really good thief.

Not only that, but Renny was a true honey badger. She knew how to start shit. She knew how to cause problems. She knew how to blow up a person's life and not feel a bit of remorse about it. And he was afraid that would go for Renny's daughter's life as well.

Sadly, Dutch had always known this time would come. Unless Renny had been put into a specially built prison just for shifters—and there were a few of those around the world—she wouldn't be stuck in Bulgaria for long. He was surprised she'd stayed as long as she had. But Devon, also a bad choice of boyfriend for Renny, had gone too far in the last month. He'd forced Renny's hand by going after Max. And doing that more than once.

Like most honey badgers, Renny wasn't going to let some guy hurt her kid.

"Ric will have to be informed," Hannah reminded him.

Ric—Ulrich Van Holtz to the rest of the world—was in charge of the New York division of the Group while his older cousin was the head of the entire organization. Dutch enjoyed working for Ric. He was calm and rational. A typical wolf, really.

Ric also ran, and was the head chef at, the Fifth Avenue Van Holtz Steakhouse, which meant that every time Dutch went there for dinner or just to chat with his boss, he got food for free. Considering how much Dutch could eat when hungry and that Van Holtz Steakhouses were shifter friendly and offered the kind of meats one could usually only obtain by big game hunting, this was one of the best job perks Dutch could get.

"Can you wait a couple of days before you tell anyone else?" he asked.

"Sure. No one's looking for her, so it's not a problem."

"Thanks, Hannah."

"Need me to do anything else?"

"Find out when she gets to the States."

"You sure she's coming here?"

"Trust me . . . she's coming this way."

Dutch started toward the door, but quickly stopped, facing Hannah again. "Any sign of Freddy?"

"MacKilligan?"

"Yeah."

Hannah spun her chair around. "I thought you said that guy was dumb."

"Dumb as they come."

"I don't see how. He's always one step ahead of me. And I'm good."

"Could he be working with somebody?"

"He must be. Maybe he has a new girlfriend to help him out."

"That sounds about right."

"Also . . . someone else is looking for Freddy. *That* I can tell you."

"Do you know who?"

"No. Want me to find out?"

Dutch shook his head. "Don't bother. We need to just find *him*. Preferably before he gets himself killed."

"It's nice you care," she said with a smile.

"I don't. Not about him, anyway. And Max doesn't care either. I just don't want Stevie to cry. I hate when she cries."

"Softy."

"Again, thanks, Hannah."

She faced her multiple screens. "Anytime."

★ ★ ★

"I tried to eat a child?"

Max nodded. "Sort of. I mean, we assumed you were trying to eat him. You had him by the back of the neck and had dragged him off to a nearby tree. But that tree has a lot of leaves, so we couldn't exactly see what you were doing. For all we know, you were just playing with him. You know . . . testing your claws and things."

Vargas did that thing again. He had done it a lot in the last fifteen minutes. With his elbows on the table, he buried his head in his hands and dug his fingers into his scalp. It was like he wanted to massage his brain but the skull kept getting in his way.

Finally, he looked up again. "Was anyone hurt?"

She waved his obvious concern away. "The kid's fine. His father and uncles are a little pissed but the Kapowskis are always pissed. They're like the pissiest grizzlies on the block."

"I think I'd be pissed, too, if someone tried to eat my kid."

"Allegedly." He frowned and Max explained, "In case there's any legal trouble. We go with 'allegedly.'"

"Legal trouble? As in getting arrested for eating a child? That seems like something one should go to prison for."

"*Allegedly* eating a child . . . actually, allegedly *attempting* to eat a child. And you were having a rough moment. We thought you had completely healed up but it seems the damage to your brain was worse than we thought, so it took a bit longer for your recovery. You feel fine now, though, right?"

"Even if I can't tell whether this is reality or a fantasy world where I'm a cat?"

"Christ, we're not still arguing about that, are we?" Max didn't even bother to keep the annoyance out of her tone. If he couldn't accept this shit after everything that had happened, he'd never be able to move forward, and Max wasn't one to linger on things for long. What was the point? "You now know what you are . . . right?"

Vargas looked down at his hand, watched as claws came out of his fingertips. Watched the skin become covered in fur.

He shook his hand out as if he'd just burned it. But he was

just trying to turn it back to human. Something every kid shifter tried in the beginning.

"Yeah," he finally said. "Yeah, I know what I am. I know."

"It's not a bad thing. It's actually amazing."

"Is it?" he asked.

"Of course it is."

"But I tried to eat a child—"

"Allegedly."

"—then I was hit by a tranquilizer dart—"

"You needed the rest."

"—and I keep ending up naked on your china cabinet."

"Yeah . . . that is weird."

In confusion, his head tilted to the side. "Really? *That's* the weird one?"

"To me. I'm not much of a climber. But I've got a hell of a jump shot. Oh!" She snapped her fingers. "I wanted to ask you if the team you said you were working with knows you're still aliv—"

"Oh, my God!" He started to stand up, but Max put her hand on his shoulder and pulled him back into the seat. "I have to let my team know I'm alive. I have to let Amelia know."

"Who's Amelia?"

"My team leader and friend. We started in the Corps together."

"You can't tell her. At least not yet. Not until you head back home."

"Why not?"

"Because we don't want government types wandering around our bear-only territory. And you need to remember that when you leave. You can't tell anyone about this. They don't know we exist and we need to keep it that way. It's the only way to protect ourselves."

"Yeah, but—"

"Not even your girlfriend."

"She's not my girlfriend. Kamatsu's my friend who happens to be a woman."

"Whatever. Just keep your mouth shut." Max looked at the kitchen doorway, heard her sisters heading their way. "And don't say a word about any of this to my sisters," she whispered.

"You are making my life complicated," he whispered back. "I hate complicated."

"Suck it up, pretty boy!"

Charlie and Stevie walked into the kitchen.

"Hey! You're up!" Charlie smiled wide, surprising Max. Her sister wasn't known for her . . . good cheer. If anything, she was known for her control issues. "How are you feeling, Zé?"

"Better. No headache this time. I'm really sorry about your china cabinet, though."

"It's fine. When I mentioned it to our landlord, Tiny, he didn't even remember he had one."

Stevie sat at the table with several of her notebooks, leaned in, and whispered to Vargas, "Tiny's a hoarder. It's a behavioral disorder and I've come to the realization that he owns lots of real estate, so he has plenty of places to put his shit."

Vargas leaned toward Stevie and whispered, "I don't care."

Stevie laughed in response, which pissed off Max because when she told her sister she didn't care about some armchair diagnosis she'd just made about someone, all she got in return was foaming anger.

Despite her annoyance, however, Max was not going to point out to her sister what a hypocritical douche bag she was, but instead take the opportunity to show both her sisters what a caring human being Max could be. And not the "sociopath with malignant narcissism" that Stevie had once diagnosed during a heated argument.

Max placed her hand on Vargas's forearm, and the cat's green gaze locked on where they touched as she said, "I'm so glad you're feeling better."

The cat's eyes narrowed. "Thank you?"

"And now you understand what you are, yes?"

"Yes. I understand."

"And don't you feel better about that?"

He shrugged. "I guess. I mean, it does explain a few things. Maybe."

"Exactly! You feel better because you now know what you are. A whole new world is ahead of you. Prepare to enjoy the rest of your life."

"I liked my old life."

"Well, you're getting a new one. Be happy!"

"Sure," he said with a low chuckle. "I'll see what I can do."

"Great." Max stood. "I've gotta go." She patted Vargas's forearm, smiled, and said with as much empathy as she could muster, "Well . . . good luck to you. I'm sure you'll do great."

Zé wasn't even listening when Max patted his arm. He couldn't understand why she kept touching him. Or why she kept touching him like *that*. It reminded him of old Mrs. Maducci down the block from his grandfather, who used to pat Zé's head every time she saw him. He'd hated the head pat or anything that felt emotionally like a head pat. And that's how Max was treating him. Like a cute little boy she'd allowed into her yard to get his baseball.

Innocuous. She was treating him as if he was innocuous and Zé didn't like it.

But he had no idea why her sisters reacted as if she'd spit at him.

Charlie spun away from the oven, eyes wide. And Stevie slammed her hands against the table and stood.

"*Max!*" they both screeched at the same time, causing their sister to spin around and take a fighting stance.

"What? What's wrong?" Max demanded, ready to start doing what she'd done to those men who'd kidnapped her.

"You can't just leave him," Stevie told her, hands now resting on hips.

Realizing there was no danger, she relaxed, but her eyes also rolled to the back of her head.

"I can't? Do you want me to get him a limo to take him home?"

"You could call me a cab," he suggested, enjoying her annoyance.

"Shut up."

"Max!" Stevie barked again.

"Can we talk to you outside?" Charlie politely asked.

"No."

Charlie pointed at the back door. *"Get your ass outside!"* she snarled from between clenched teeth.

With another eye roll, Max walked out of the kitchen, her sisters following.

A minute or two later, Stevie's boyfriend came in, took a large stash of bamboo from one of the cabinets, and sat down at the table.

"Hey," he greeted, biting into the bamboo at the same time.

"Hey."

"Where are the girls?"

"Outside. Yelling at Max."

"So a typical morning, then?"

"Based on what I know so far . . . probably."

"You can't just inform him that he's a shifter and then send him off into the world alone."

Max looked back and forth between her sisters before asking, "Why not?"

Charlie threw up her hands but Stevie answered this time. "You've upended the man's world. He doesn't know anything about anything. You have to help him."

"Why?"

"It's the right thing to do."

"I have a lot going on right now. We're in the playoffs."

"He's still your responsibility!" Stevie argued.

"What playoffs?" Charlie asked.

"With my team."

"What team?"

Max and Stevie stared at their sister.

"The *pro* basketball team I'm on?"

"You're in the WNBA?"

"Do I *look* like I'd be in the WNBA?"

Charlie's eyebrow rose. "Because you're not black?"

"Because I'm not ten feet tall. Nor am I fully human sooooo . . . yeah. I'm on a *shifter* pro team, not the WNBA."

"They were interested in you, though," Stevie reminded her.

"Well . . . after they saw my game footage, yeah. But it wouldn't be long before someone started asking questions and I'd end up having to hold back on the court, and you know I can't do that. Besides, the shifter teams offered me more money. Full-human pro teams don't pay women shit."

"Because full-humans don't have to worry about getting trapped in a room with a bunch of grizzly sows angrily demanding fair pay."

Both sisters laughed at that visual until Charlie asked, "When did you join a pro anything, Max?"

"I don't know . . . a *decade* ago?"

Charlie snorted. "Oh, come on." She looked at Stevie but when her sister just gazed back . . . "Wait . . . really?"

Stevie winced a bit before she admitted, "She was voted MVP two years in a row."

"Oh. Okay . . . uh."

"It's all right." Max put her hand on Charlie's shoulder. "You always have so much on your mind. I don't take it personally . . . when you forget I ever existed because all you care about is Stevie."

"Oh, puhleeze!" Stevie crowed. "Don't even attempt to use me as your excuse for being a shitty person!"

Max turned on her baby sister. "*Why can't you ever let me do what I do?*"

"Manipulating Charlie does not change the fact that Zé Vargas is your responsibility!"

"But I don't wanna be helpful." And Max knew she was whining. She couldn't help it. She had more important things to do than help some sad sack who'd just found out what he really was.

Right?

"Didn't he save your life?" Charlie asked. But she revised

that when Max did nothing more than gaze at her silently. "Okay. Didn't he *attempt* to save your life? And doesn't it seem that he would have put his life at risk for you whether you were Max 'Kill It Again' MacKilligan or not?"

"Dammit, Charlie," Max continued to whine. "I fucking hate you."

"I'd hate me, too . . . because I'm always right. I understand how painful that must be for others who aren't always right."

Zé pulled the baking trays out of the oven and stared down at what Charlie had made.

"Croissants," he sighed. "I love croissants."

"I'm not usually a big fan but hers are great." Shen pointed at several on the second tray. "She made those for me. They have bamboo in them."

"You eat a lot of that, don't you?"

He shrugged. "I'm a panda."

"It's a little on the nose, though, isn't it?" Zé asked. "A Chinese guy who's a panda?"

"Says the South American jaguar."

"Touché."

Shen tracked down an obscenely large plate of bacon that had been sitting in the warmer. Zé pulled out the orange juice and milk and plates and glassware.

As they sat down to eat, the back door opened and the three sisters returned.

Charlie pulled Max close as they stood in front of Zé.

"Max is going to assist you," she announced.

"Assist me?"

With one arm over her sister's shoulders, she swept the other in a wide arc. "Teach you the ways of our kind."

"That sounds weirdly sexual. Is this a cult?"

Max rolled her eyes and started to walk off, but her sister yanked her back. When Max tried again, Charlie caught her around the neck and held her.

"This is a whole new world for you, Zé. You need someone to guide you."

"And," Zé said on a startled laugh, "you want it to be *her*?"

Charlie covered her mouth with her free hand to hide her own laugh and Max yanked the other forearm off her throat. "What does *that* mean?"

"I know," Stevie cut in, adorably sitting on Shen's lap, "that my sister may seem like a waste of space—"

"Hey!"

"—but she actually did help me when I started shifting."

"And she knows more than I do," Charlie admitted, grabbing one of the croissants off the plate. "I was so busy trying to keep everyone alive that I didn't really have time to figure out the different scents of bears and cats and . . . whatever. And that sort of thing actually can help. Especially during a firefight."

Zé glanced at Shen. "Lot of firefights among your kind?"

He was only being sarcastic but the "yes" he got from all three sisters was off-putting.

"Okay," Zé agreed, not knowing what else to do. "Where do we start?"

"Our ancient blood rituals!" Max announced.

"No," Charlie said immediately.

"Then let's learn all the different poop smells!"

"*No,*" Stevie said, her lip curled in disgust.

"Answering the ancient question, does rat really taste like chicken?"

"*Max!*" both sisters barked.

The evil woman laughed. "I'm kidding! Everyone knows that the first lesson for any new shifter is how to lick their own ass."

Zé thought for sure one of Max's sisters was about to hit her, and he was going to let it happen. But out of the corner of his eye he saw the largest of the sisters' dogs ease up to the table and take all the bacon in his giant maw.

"Put that bacon back, mister," he softly ordered, without facing the animal.

The dog growled at him, but Zé was really hungry. He wasn't giving up bacon without a fight.

"Put. It. Back."

Another growl. So Zé snarled back.

The dog finally leaned forward and dropped the bacon back onto the plate before stepping away from the table and leaving the kitchen.

Now Zé glared down at the bacon, annoyed. "Ech. It has dog drool on it." He looked at the three sisters. "Can one of you make me more? This time *without* the dog drool?"

Max slammed her hands on the table and brought her face close to Zé's. "How, in all this time, did you *not* know you were a cat? *How?*"

chapter SEVEN

Imani found a comfortable seat against the wall, near the window. That's where she sat and watched. It was her nature. Lions didn't run around, chasing everything that moved. They simply waited and watched until something tasty and weak came along. It was what had made her very good at her job back in the day.

A job she had thought she'd left behind long ago. But she'd realized that she had to get involved this time. The de Medicis were ridiculously dangerous and would blow up the world before they'd let any of their direct bloodline be taken down. Even worse, they were naturally paranoid and inherently mean. The de Medici Pride was ruled by three brothers who seemed to love money more than they loved anything else, but even their love of money didn't explain why they would involve themselves in human trafficking.

No, their motivation was a simple one: They had no respect for full-humans. True, all shifters tended to look down on full-humans, but they also understood that they were all intertwined. That down deep, they were all human beings. Shifters were just better.

But the de Medicis saw full-humans as nothing more than prey. No different from gazelles or wild boars.

Still . . . human trafficking seemed beneath even them.

But when the Alpha male of the Van Holtz Pack and head of the protective organization The Group laid out the evidence that proved the de Medici involvement, that was enough for Imani. The de Medicis were out of control.

Still, the idea of involving herself with the Group—a protection organization that was run by wolves—and the Bear Preservation Council made her almost sick to her stomach. She'd been raised since birth to worry only about other cats, and even among them there was a hierarchy. But here she sat . . . surrounded by wolves and bears and a few cats. Walking into the room, she'd been ready for a fight. Ready to put the drooling dogs and idiot bears in their place so she could take over this situation and manage it.

But it wasn't the rich Niles Van Holtz and his cousin Ulrich who were the problem. Nor was it the perversely sized Bayla Ben-Zeev from the BPC that was making Imani's hairline itch.

It was *him*. Well . . . him and his two friends.

A lion. His grizzly friend. And the weirdly long-legged, maned wolf that turned out not to be a wolf at all.

"This is what comes with intermingling," she'd jokingly whispered to the current New York head of Katzenhaus, Mary-Ellen Kozłowski.

It turned out the three males had been in the military together. In the aptly named Unit—a shifter-only division of the Marines.

The lion male, Benjamin, took the lead and had been talking for at least thirty minutes since Niles Van Holtz had finished. The bear, Oliver, did nothing but pick things up from Van Holtz's desk, investigate each one thoroughly, and then set it back down. Where he set them, though, must have been the wrong place, because Van Holtz moved each thing to another spot seconds later.

And the maned wolf, Bryan, just ate apples that he had in a bag beside his chair.

Benjamin was making the case that he and his two friends should take the lead on this assignment against the de Medicis. He strongly felt that he would be best able to deal with the young de Medici males who protected the older lions that ruled the Pride. "Get rid of them, we can get to the others," he opined.

Imani could tell from the expression on the faces of the Van Holtzes and Ben-Zeev that they were not comfortable with that notion. Not simply because of Benjamin's youth. They'd all been young when they'd started as operatives. The problem was the arrogance. It was, honestly, all too human. Only humans had the kind of arrogance that could get others killed. Most predators had instincts and a need to survive. These boys didn't want to survive; they just assumed they would.

But as a She-lion, Imani believed there was only one way to teach young predators that their arrogance was a dangerous thing. That's what a Pride or Pack was for. Not only protection but to teach those coming up. Either Benjamin hadn't been raised by a Pride or his Pride hadn't done a very good job. An error, but one that could be fixed.

Something Imani was very good at, and the reason these three groups had wanted her involved in the first place: she was a very good fixer.

"I assume," Van Holtz said when Benjamin finished his pitch, "that you'll want Dee-Ann and Cella on this with you."

The kid made that face men make when they want to tell someone nicely "fuck, no."

"The problem with that," Benjamin reasoned, "is the de Medicis know all about Smith and Malone. They're recognizable."

"Yeahhhhh," the cat and dog in question said at the same time.

"But I think we have a great option after what we saw in the Netherlands," the kid went on.

"No, no, no," the Van Holtzes said together, both wolves shaking their very handsome heads. Imani had never seen the two dogs so animated—and adamant—about anything. They'd always been the "reasonable" dogs. Always wanting to give several options and take everyone's concerns and opinions seriously. Blah!

"We are *not* doing that," Ulrich Van Holtz insisted.

"Look, I get it. The oldest sister seems—"

"Psychotic," both dogs said together again.

"That's because of the baby sister," the maned wolf interjected as he tossed a half-eaten apple core toward the trash can but missed it. Much to the annoyance of the elder Van Holtz. "She's really protective of her."

"But we're not interested in her. It's the middle sister . . . and her friends. *Those* are the ones we want."

"Her friends?" Ulrich Van Holtz asked. "Max MacKilligan has friends? Real ones? Or imaginary?"

"Real ones. They're part of her basketball team. They all play pro now."

"You want this situation to be handled by *basketball* players?"

"We've done our research. They've got the skills."

"To play basketball?"

"To kill quickly. Cleanly."

"Cleanly? Like that mess in the Netherlands?"

"That wasn't completely their fault."

"The older sister still won't like it," Ben-Zeev said, her gaze on Van Holtz. "She's made that very clear to all of us."

"Our plan," the lion said with great confidence, "is not to go at them head-on. That's the mistake you guys have been making. We're going to take things a different route, in a safe space, where they know that their options are very limited."

The leaders of the three organizations traded glances.

"Don't get me wrong," Benjamin continued. "We don't, for a second, underestimate these females. That's why we want them for this enterprise. And all of you need to understand that this *is* an enterprise. The de Medicis won't go down without a . . . well, I was going to say fight. But really I mean they won't go down without an apocalypse."

Imani still hadn't said anything but she didn't have to, finding Van Holtz's doggie gaze locked on her. She gave the smallest nod and he said to Benjamin, "All right. But we want Imani as part of your team."

The lion male glanced at her, and she knew that he automatically assumed she was looking down on him. Not only because he was young and male but because he wasn't from a Pride that had been around as long as hers. She was guessing his ancestors were from early 1700s England. Lions, just like her and her kin, but she doubted that one of them had ever set foot on the Serengeti except as part of some paid-for, shifter-only hunting party.

But Imani had no preconceived notions about any cat. She simply watched and learned. As she always had.

So when the male raised a brow at her, she stated, "You guys can do whatever you're planning on doing. I'll simply report back to the heads of all three organizations to keep them in the loop. I'll be the point of contact for everyone. This is your show, guys."

"Sounds good," he lied, even managing to force a smile.

But Imani's smile was real when she promised, "I'm just here to observe and report."

Mairi waited while the men kicked the door open and entered the motel room. She followed a few seconds later, sniffing the air. Freddy MacKilligan had definitely been here, and he hadn't been alone. But he was gone now.

"How does he stay ahead of us?" one of the men wanted to know.

"He's got someone helping him," Mairi guessed. "Someone who's tracking us. Can tell when we're close."

"How do you know that?'

"Because I know how me uncle thinks." She snapped her fingers. "Phones. Get rid of them. I'll get us some burners. No contact with family or girlfriends. No computers or anything else."

"Then how do *we* track him?"

"I'll find someone to help us out. I just need a day or two to—"

"The twins aren't going to like you going off on your own again," he pointed out, making Mairi want to rip his throat out. She didn't . . . but she really wanted to.

"Then keep yer mouth shut and there won't be a problem, now will there?"

"But the twins said—"

Mairi reached up and grabbed him by the jaw, squeezing until she heard a small "crack" sound. She wasn't trying to break it. Not unless she had to.

"I said," she warned again, up on her toes so she didn't have to shout to be heard by the much taller man, "keep yer mouth shut and there won't be a problem. Understand?"

Eyes wide, gawking down at her, he managed a nod.

"Good." She motioned to the room. "Clear this place and head to the hotel. I'll get you new phones and check in with you later."

Mairi walked out of the motel and returned to the rental car. She sat down in the driver's seat and stared straight ahead. She didn't want to deal with Freddy MacKilligan. The idiot. And when she finally tracked him down, she was going to make him suffer for distracting her from what she really wanted, which was Max MacKilligan.

And anything that got in the way of that goal just pissed Mairi off.

Mairi rested her hands on the wheel. Maybe she should just kill the twins. If she got them out of the way sooner rather than later, she could focus on Max.

She liked that idea. Of course, she'd originally wanted to keep the twins around so they could continue to distract all the uncles and aunts. But now they were just getting pushy and annoying. Mairi didn't have patience for that sort of thing.

Thinking on it a bit longer, Mairi realized that she didn't actually have to kill the twins herself. She had another option. One that would free up her time. She just needed to get a few things in order and . . .

"Excellent!" she cheered, pleased with her brilliant decision-making. "Get all that sorted and then I can put a bullet in the back of me cousin's head."

Mairi let out a happy sigh. She did love when things worked out in her favor.

chapter EIGHT

"I just don't see why I'm responsible for him," Max complained.

Nelle came out from her dressing room wearing designer jeans, a designer sleeveless shirt, and six-inch heels that probably cost several thousand dollars. She was putting on gold-set diamond earrings that brought out her dark brown eyes and matched the gold and diamond bracelets she wore on both wrists.

"You feel responsible for him because your sisters say that you're responsible for him. Charlie is your moral compass and there's nothing wrong with that."

Max loved the Manhattan penthouse apartment that Nelle occasionally shared with her family, with its eight bedrooms and two terraces that boasted amazing views of Central Park. Of course, the family could have bought a private island for what they'd paid to get this place but it was in the heart of the city and the Zhaos didn't like to be subtle about their wealth. Not surprising. They were honey badgers. Badgers weren't subtle about anything.

"Really?" Max asked, sitting on Nelle's giant double-king-sized bed. "Because I feel like everything is wrong with it. Because of them, I'm stuck with this guy for however long it takes him to shift on his own and not keep asking that same stupid question about whether he's been drugged or not."

Nelle turned away from the mirror she'd been looking in

and gestured to the other end of her bed. "Should we really be having this conversation with the poor guy just sitting there?"

Max glanced over at a silent Vargas. He was busy watching the BBC World News channel and didn't seem the least bit interested in what they were talking about. She waved away Nelle's concern.

"You know," Nelle went on, "his adjustment doesn't have to be time consuming, especially with all the girls here at the same time because of the playoffs. We round everybody up and we help you help him. It'll be just like old times."

"I guess that's an idea."

"Come on, Max. Lighten up. Just be glad your sisters give a shit about this kind of stuff. I *wish* I had that kind of relationship with my sister. But instead . . ."

When she didn't finish her sentence, Max asked, "But instead what?"

Nelle walked over to a small closet and opened it, revealing Nelle's sister trapped on the floor, hogtied and gagged with duct tape. Most likely by Nelle herself.

"Dude! What the fuck?"

"She deserves it." She glared down at her sister and yelled, "*Because she's a bitch!*" She slammed the door shut, ignoring her sister's muffled threats, and pulled her phone out of her back pocket.

"I'll text the girls," she said with abrupt great cheer.

"You're not just going to leave your sister in there, are you?"

She snorted. "She'll be fine. Gnaw her way out of those restraints in no time."

"Is the only reason you have duct tape in your beautiful apartment so that you can hogtie your sister whenever you want?"

Nelle glanced up from her phone and grinned. "Yes!"

Zé stared across the round table in the coffee shop at the five women gazing back at him. There was Max, her purple hair in two pigtails high on her head, purple bangs hanging into her eyes. Gorgeous Nelle, who had the attention of every man in the establishment. Tock, whose blank expression made him uncomfortable. Streep, who'd been complaining since they'd all stood in line to get their coffee and treats. And Mads, who seemed to do nothing but glare at everyone who came within ten feet of her personal space.

"Maybe we should just get rid of him," Tock finally suggested when no one else had any other ideas.

"We can't," Max said with a sigh. "Charlie really likes him."

"I thought she already had a man."

"She doesn't like him like that. She just likes him. And you know what Stevie will do if *she* finds out—"

Nelle waved her manicured hands in the air. "No, no. Forget getting rid of him."

"For moral reasons?" Zé had to ask.

"Sure . . . if that makes you feel better."

"Is anyone else concerned," Mads asked, speaking for the first time since she'd entered the coffee shop, "that he's taking it so well that we're discussing getting rid of him?"

"No," the others said in unison.

"Okay."

"Besides," Max continued, "I didn't go through all this trouble just to get rid of him."

"Most important," Nelle reasoned, "the hard part's over. He knows what he is, and he accepts it. Now we just have to teach him the basics."

"Good point," Streep agreed.

Then the women went back to staring at him.

Finally, Tock asked, "Sooooo . . . what are the basics we should be teaching him?"

After that question, more confused silence followed. A silence that went on for so long, Zé began to laugh.

"What's so funny?"

He shrugged at Tock's question. "I'm just . . . entertained, which is not something I say very often. Because most people do not entertain me. But you guys . . . ?" He nodded. "Entertainment."

"Awwwwww," Streep said. "You guys, we have to keep him *nowwww*. He's adorable!"

Nelle closed her eyes, shook her head. "He's not a rescued kitten, Streep."

"But still!"

Zé glanced over at Max, one brow raised. Her response? Mouthing, *Oh, my God. Sorry.*

And that only made Zé laugh harder.

Amelia Kamatsu waited outside the office of her boss after he'd given her and her team their next assignment. She was surprised to be called in. She never had been before. What they did was beyond top secret. They weren't spies or anything. That took a subtlety most of her team lacked in many ways. But when the government couldn't take action for political reasons, it called the company that hired her team.

It wasn't an easy job but she did enjoy the freedom it gave her. When she wasn't risking her life in foreign countries for an exorbitant fee, she was relaxing in her secure cabin deep in the Maine woods.

But this was the first time she'd lost one of her men. And she didn't mean "lost" in some euphemistic way. She meant lost. She'd *lost* him. Her team had been attempting to track down Vargas for days and nothing. It was as if he'd disappeared. She hoped, however, that her boss had some news of him. That he was in a hospital somewhere, recovering. Hopefully the damage wasn't too great and he'd be back on his feet soon. Maybe not able to join the fight again, but at least able to live as normal a life as any of them could. That was the least Vargas deserved.

"He's ready to see you now," the receptionist said.

Amelia picked up her briefcase, pulled down the light sleeveless blouse that covered the weapon holstered to the back of her black slacks, and entered the office. She smiled at her boss—until she caught sight of the man sitting at the far side of the room. A man she didn't know.

"David," she greeted her boss.

"Amelia. Hello."

He stood and Amelia reached across his large desk to shake his hand. "Good to see you."

"Please. Sit."

She did, moving her hair off her shoulder so she could get another look at the man watching her. He made her nervous but she didn't know why. Maybe it was those eyes. The way they watched her was . . . off-putting.

"Any word on Vargas?" she asked, eager to get to the heart of things.

"As a matter of fact . . . yes. He's alive."

She let out a relieved breath and relaxed into the leather chair. "Thank God. Where is he? Can I go see him?"

David glanced at the man across the room. "Not right now."

"Why?"

"He's recovering."

"Then I definitely should see him. He's one of my team. I should be making sure he has everything he needs."

"He has everything he needs," the man across the room said.

Amelia smiled. It wasn't a real smile. It was one she'd taught herself a long time ago when she'd joined the U.S. Navy and was surrounded by very sensitive men who couldn't stand a woman who got "mouthy."

"I'm sorry," she said. "And you are?"

"Zezé Vargas is being taken care of and will completely recover."

"Recover from what?"

The man tilted his head, blinked. It was weird.

"From his injuries," the man finally replied.

"His injuries? What kind of injuries?"

"The kind that require healing."

What kind of fucked-up answer was that?

Amelia turned to David, and the man who dined with U.S. senators and vice presidents gave a short headshake. His way of telling her to "stop asking fucking questions, woman!"

"Anyway"—the man stood—"just wanted to give you guys that update. And I'd like that report of yours. Please."

Amelia gripped the handle of her briefcase tighter. She'd

been so busy asking about Vargas, she hadn't put it down. It still sat in her lap.

"My report?"

"Yes." The man walked across the room, his hair brushing his shoulders. God, she would kill for his highlights. It was like a world of browns, grays, whites, and golds in there. How much did that cost? "Your report. Now, please."

Amelia again looked at her boss and he frowned, urging her along with a jerk of his head.

"Fine."

She opened her briefcase and pulled out the report, handing it over to the man.

"Excellent. Thank you both so much."

Then he walked out. Without another word. No explanation. No idea when she'd hear from Vargas again. She couldn't even send him flowers because she didn't know which hospital they'd put him in. Was he still in the Netherlands? Was he back in the States?

What the fuck was happening?

Once the door closed behind the man, David slumped in his chair.

"Wow, does that man make me uncomfortable."

"Who the fuck was that?"

"Don't worry about it."

"What do you mean, don't worry about it? Vargas is one of *my* men."

David folded his hands on his desk and calmly gazed at Amelia.

"What?" she finally asked when he just stared at her in that weird, placid way of his.

"Do you enjoy your life?"

"Excuse me?"

"Do you enjoy living and being happy? Then, if I were you, I'd forget about Vargas. If he contacts you, he contacts you. And if he doesn't, keep your mouth shut and move on with your day."

"David—"

"I'm not joking, Amelia. These are people you do not want to fuck with. Be happy you only had to give up your report."

David turned away from her, focusing on his computer. "The remainder of your money will hit your account in the next hour, including a bonus. Divvy it up among your team as you see fit. And have a good day. I'll let you know when we have a new job for you."

She wanted to argue. She wanted to rip his nuts off. But how would that help her or Vargas?

So she stood and headed back to her hotel room. If nothing else, she had a copy of her report on her laptop and in her cloud account.

At least she thought she did.

By the time she got back to the hotel and went online, it was as if that report—and what had happened—had never existed.

"We need to go back to the beginning!" Streep announced, arms thrown wide, smile gorgeous. "To where this all started!"

"You mean Africa?" Mads asked flatly, and Max was barely able to stop her laugh. Streep hated being laughed at.

"*No*," she snapped back at Mads. "Not Africa. To where Zé began." She rested her hands on the table, leaned in a bit. "You're from Mexico, right?"

Vargas's eyes narrowed and Max wondered how often that was people's first choice when discussing his heritage.

"Yeah," Streep cluelessly persisted. "Like Tijuana . . . oh, and . . . uh . . . Tijuana?"

Max covered her mouth with her hand, and Nelle pressed her face against Max's bare shoulder to stop her own laughter, which did not help the situation.

After a pause, Vargas said, "No. I'm not from Mexico. Are you?"

Streep frowned, confused. "No. My family is from the Philippines. But what does that have to do with anything?"

"Absolutely nothing," Mads growled.

"What is with the tone?"

"Should we do a roundtable of everyone's racial background? Maybe get some DNA tests done? Wouldn't that be fun?"

The Streep-tears started immediately. Right after the trembling bottom lip.

"Why are you so mean to me?" Streep sobbed.

Tock pointed at the watch she had saved for since she was six years old, when she'd decided that her father didn't understand the "concept of time" and what it meant to "manage my life." A ten-thousand-dollar Swiss timepiece that was beyond precise. A watch that was in no way designed for the average person just looking to keep time.

Of course, Tock had informed them at their first team meeting as a junior high basketball team—when she only had a Timex watch with Minnie Mouse's arms telling her the hours and minutes—that she managed her life in thirty-minute increments. If she got something done in ten minutes that meant she had another twenty to do whatever she wanted to do, but whatever she had booked had to be dealt with first. Whether it was homework, team practice, or wild boar hunting. When she booked practice, she expected all of them to honor the time commitment. And that expectation hadn't changed in the last sixteen years.

"We have practice tonight in Manhattan. So what are we doing about Zé?" Tock demanded.

Streep stopped sobbing and glared at Tock. "Does my pain mean nothing to you?"

"I didn't book time for your pain."

"What do you suggest we do?" Nelle asked Tock.

"I'll go to the Katzenhaus Library. The cats keep track of their people, and their library on Fifth digitally links to the library in Germany, which has even more extensive genealogical records." She pulled out a small notebook with a leather cover and a very nice pen. She shoved both toward Zé. "Give me your full name, the names of your mother and father, and your address when you were a kid."

Zé looked down at the notebook and pen and then at Tock.

"*Now*," she pushed. At least this time she didn't tap her watch. To everyone else, she said, "I'll get his background. Maybe he has a local shifter relative who can help him."

Tock stood up, took the pad and pen from Zé's grasp as soon as he'd finished writing out his information, grabbed Mads by her T-shirt, and yanked her out of her chair. "You'll come with me."

"I don't want to come with you."

"I don't care."

"The Katzenhaus Library is only open to cats," Streep reminded her. "They're not going to let *you* in."

"So you'll come with us. You can get us in."

"I'm not a cat either!"

"I'm sure you can charm our way in."

"I'd rather stay—eep!"

With one hand around her neck, Tock lifted Streep up and out of her chair so she stood in front of them.

"We'll meet the rest of you at practice," Tock informed them.

"At the Sports Center?" Max asked, sounding surprisingly eager.

"Are you high?" Tock demanded. "Every playoff team is practicing there. Coach is meeting us at the old center on Staten Island. If you're going to get to practice on time, you'll need to be on the ferry by—"

Now Mads grabbed Tock and pushed her toward the door. Because they all knew that if Tock got too deep into obsessing about travel times, they'd be sitting where they were for another hour. At least.

"Love you guys!" Nelle called after them. "Aren't they the best?" she asked Zé.

"Are they?"

"So what are we going to do?" Max asked, although she was already thinking about getting in some nap time before practice. She loved a good afternoon nap.

"I can get a new phone and call my team to let them know I'm alive."

Max and Nelle just stared at him. They'd already told him once that was not a good idea. At least not at the moment. But they weren't in the mood to say it again. Instead, they got their point across with staring. Then Nelle suggested, "Let's get him some clothes." She leaned in and whispered, "It's strange . . . he smells like Dutch. But he's not Dutch and it's starting to weird me out. Aren't you weirded out?"

"No."

"Well, whatever. Let's get him new clothes." She smiled at Zé. "Won't that be fun?"

Zé shook his head. "I don't have any money."

"Oh. No big. I have *tons* of money." She stood, slinging her thirty-grand bag over her shoulder. "Come on, you two! Let's get this big kitty-cat some clothes . . . and a scratching post!" She held up her phone. "I'll call us a car."

She headed outside and Max leaned back in her chair, smiling at Zé's surly expression.

"It could be worse," she told him. "You could be dead."

"Do you mean dead when we were back in the Netherlands, or when your psychotic friends were debating whether to kill me?"

"Tomato, tomaht—"

"No," Zé quickly cut in, a look of disgust on his face. "Dude . . . just no."

Dez MacDermot, current head of the shifter division of the NYPD, gazed at the young lion male talking to her. The kid had been talking for about twenty minutes but he'd lost her interest ten minutes in.

According to her husband, Mace, fifteen minutes of "miscellaneous conversation" was about all she could handle. "Then you get real bitchy," he'd say, grinning.

What annoyed her about this kid, though, was his condescension. He tried to pretend that he respected her but she knew better. She was used to that, though. Since she'd been part of this particular division of the NYPD she was accustomed to being dismissed by shifters. Because she was full-human. Her husband and child might be lions, but she was just a nice girl from Brooklyn . . . who happened to have a shifter as a mate.

Over time, the cops she worked with, and those who eventually worked for her, grew to respect Dez. Or, at the very least, tolerate her. Her onetime partner and still very close friend, Lou Crushek, explained it to her one day: "You're a crazy human. You terrify them. Because there's nothing more terrifying than a crazy human."

Fair enough. And hell, if it worked, Dez wasn't going to complain.

But listening to this kid ramble was getting on her nerves. She finally decided to cut it short. She had the feeling he would keep going forever if she let him.

When he took a breath, she looked over at the woman who'd accompanied the kid and his two oddly sized friends. Imani Ako.

Before they'd worked together on a few joint NYPD-Katzenhaus cases, Dez had met Imani at some all-lion event a few years back. Imani had introduced herself by explaining that her Pride had wanted Dez's husband as one of their males but the Pride he'd been born into had put a sizable amount on the mating contract. A contract Mace had not been part of or even aware of. He'd been too busy fighting for their country as a Navy SEAL. Even if he had been in town at the time, Mace was not a fan of binding sex contracts with women he didn't know. Especially when that deal was whipped up by his older sister.

"Imani, I—" Dez began, but the kid cut her off.

"Imani is just here to observe," he said, stepping in front of Dez so her view of Imani was also cut off. As if that would miraculously stop her from knowing that Imani was in the room with them.

"Oh . . . Observe. Okay. And you want *me* to . . . ?"

"Observe as well. Oh, and we'd like you to provide a couple of entry teams and three units for what should be simple arrests. Oh, and one of your conference rooms here," he said, gesturing to the rooms that he could see through the glass windows of Dez's office.

Entry teams? Why would they need entry teams? Those were the SWAT teams that crashed in doors during drug raids or dealt with mass shooters. Her department had its own SWAT units, made up of the biggest shifter breeds: grizzlies, Siberian tigers, and lion males. All of them former military. And such teams were necessary for the kind of gangsters they took on. Because nothing in the world was more terrifying than a grizzly drug lord with a meth addiction.

She just didn't think her entry teams were necessary for the kid's project.

Wanting a minute to consider his request but knowing the kid wouldn't stop pushing for an immediate response, Dez used the same technique she employed when she was trying to stop her Rottweilers from attacking neighborhood dogs on a walk: distraction. For her dogs, she just needed treats and a ball. But for these arrogant pricks . . . ?

Dez looked at one of the lion's friends. "So you're a maned wolf, huh? I never heard of those," she lied. "What's the name of your Pack?"

He rolled his eyes and she guessed that he'd had this conversation before. But he still didn't have to sound so bitchy when he said, "I'm not a wolf."

"Then why are you called that?"

"Maned wolf is its own species." It was a statement but he said it like it was a question, with the last word going up a notch. As if he was questioning her intelligence, which just annoyed Dez even more.

"But that doesn't make sense because you have wolf *in* your name. Are you, like, half wolf and half lion because of the mane?"

"No."

"Are you a werewolf?"

There was a moment while all three men gawked at her until the maned wolf arrogantly informed her, "There's no such *thing* as werewolves."

"I'm not sure why the tone? I was told there were no such things as shifters, too—and yet here we are."

Imani cleared her throat behind the lion but Dez kept her gaze right on the maned wolf. Even if the women weren't particularly close, Dez knew that if just one look passed between them, the hysterical laughing would begin.

"Miss MacDermot—"

"Captain," she corrected the lion. "Captain MacDermot."

"Gurl, did you get a promotion?" Imani happily asked, leaning over so they could see each other.

"I did! I am now Captain Desiree MacDermot of the division that no one knows exists."

"Good for you!"

"Ladies!"

Dez looked up at the lion, one eyebrow raised. And she was sure Imani had the same expression.

"Can I continue?" he asked.

Dez tapped her fingers against her desk. That was because what she wanted to do was pull her gun and shoot the kid in the leg. Just to hurt him. But she knew that wouldn't work out well for her. He was representing the Group. Wait. Was he?

Imani, from what Dez remembered, always made it clear she would *never* willingly work for the Group. She had a thing against hybrids and she wasn't a fan of the Van Holtz wolves that ran the organization. And she didn't seem like the kind of woman who would change her mind about anything.

"Who do you work for?" Dez asked and she immediately felt the tension in the room go up ten clicks. But the lion male simply rolled with it.

"We work for a new organization. A sort of offshoot of BPC, Katzenhaus, and the Group. Our work is . . . very specific, though."

"Does your group have a name?"

"I'm sure we do. But you don't need to worry about that. At least not at the moment. I just need you to provide what I've requested. I've been told you're the one woman who can make things happen."

Oh, Christ, this guy.

"I can," Dez replied. "But what about the no-knock warrants you'll need? Those I can't get you. I can, however, call our D.A. She's a coyote. Among the full-humans her nickname is 'Rabid She-Demon.'"

His smile was blatantly insincere. "No need to call the rabid she-demon. We'll take care of any necessary paperwork."

"You'll take care of the *warrants*?"

"Uh-huh. Any other questions?"

"Well—"

"Great! So we're good?"

Dez glanced over at Imani. Was she really okay with this? But, again, she got back that tiny, imperceptible nod from Imani. She clearly wanted this to move forward, which confused Dez even more. Before Imani's retirement, Dez had worked several cases with her and Imani was almost Marine-like in the way she ran her operations. As a former dog handler in the Marine Corps herself, Dez had quickly grown to trust Imani's judgments and decisions. But she didn't trust these . . . males. Not yet anyway.

However . . . Imani *was* here and Dez still trusted her.

So, with a resigned sigh, she said, "Okay. Just give me dates and times and I'll make sure the teams are ready to go."

The lion smiled but this time it wasn't forced. As far as he was concerned, he'd gotten his way.

chapter NINE

"I thought we were here to get *me* clothes," Zé complained when Nelle strutted by in her fifth ball gown.

"I know," Max sighed. "But I forgot how she likes to shop for herself first."

"I'm not going to want anything from here. I'm not really a designer kind of guy."

"And I'm not a designer kind of girl. So I get it."

Nelle spun in front of them. "Thoughts? Concerns? Opinions?"

"No," they both said at the same time.

She rolled her eyes. "I don't know why I bother."

"Neither do we," Max informed her friend. "Can we just get him clothes? Please."

"Fine." Nelle motioned to a sales person. "I'll take this. And we need clothes for this gentleman."

"I'm not wearing clothes from here."

"Why not?"

"One reason: I'm not European. And I feel like you have to be European to shop here."

"He has a point," Max muttered.

"And two . . ." He pointed at the gown Nelle wore. "I'm not shopping any place that charges thirteen thousand dollars for a fucking dress."

Max's head snapped around. "*How much?*"

"Didn't you hear the sales guy? He said thirteen thousand. I heard him. God heard him."

Now she looked at her friend. "Nelle!"

"Oh, for the love of Ming the Merciless. Can we get over the drama about a few dollars?"

Nelle lifted her skirt with one hand and spun away to go change into her street clothes.

"Ming the Merciless?" Zé asked.

"It's from *Flash Gordon*."

"I know where it's from. How does she?"

Max shrugged. "She's a sci-fi fan. Even bad sci-fi."

"There is absolutely nothing wrong with *Flash Gordon*." Slowly she turned her head so that she could gawk at him. "Tell me you're joking."

"Okay," Nelle said, standing in front of them, her street clothes back on. "Let's go. I've already called Ándre and he's waiting for us."

Before Zé could tell her "no" as calmly but as adamantly as possible, Max said, "We are not taking him to any store where a guy named Andre will get him clothes."

"Why not? What's wrong with the name Andre?"

"Let me ask you this first: Is there an accent on the *E* in Andre's name?"

"No." She cleared her throat. "It's over the *A*."

"Is he a DJ?" Max wanted to know. "Because that's the only excuse I'll accept."

Zé laughed at that, ignoring the glare he received from Nelle.

"No. He's not."

"Then no, Nelle. No. We're not going to any store where a guy named Ándre will get him clothes." Max stood. "Come on, cat. Let's go someplace neither of us will feel uncomfortable buying clothes."

Livy Kowalski didn't know how this had become her life: taking pictures of people's weddings to make her living. It was true, art was not always something that paid off during the artist's lifetime. She could think of plenty of artists and writers whose work hadn't made a mark until long after their death.

Yet did any of them actually have to work a Leibowitz wedding? Putting up with a bunch of insane wild dogs that—and she was quoting here—"loved love"?

Even worse? The bride. She was lovely. Just the nicest person Livy had ever met or worked with. Livy preferred her brides difficult, rude, and out of control, so that she could really wallow in the misery of her work. What she didn't need was a shining bride informing her that "Despite your outright bitchiness, you are *awesome!*"

Livy studied the pictures she'd done for the Leibowitz wedding and knew they were so good, she was just going to get *more* work from brides willing to pay anything to have her as their personal photographer.

How had her life become so pathetic?

"Hello, niece."

Livy didn't bother to look away from her work. She'd learned long ago, living with her parents, not to be easily startled. "Auntie. What do you want?"

"You can't even pretend to be respectful?"

"No."

That elicited a chuckle so Livy kept her focus on her work, knowing this was some honey badger shit she didn't want to deal with. Being the "black sheep" of the Yang clan wasn't easy but Livy managed to find a way.

"Have you seen your cousin?" her aunt asked, moving around Livy's office in the Sports Center. For quite a few years now, Livy had been the official photographer of most of the pro shifter sports teams. The job paid her amazingly well and she often used the athletes as models for her artwork, but it still felt like another distraction from her true work. Her art.

Of course, her best friend, Toni, would call her an idiot for all this "whining" and tell Livy to "get over yourself!" And she'd probably be right.

"Which cousin?" Livy asked. "I do have about ten thousand of them."

"That's a bit of an overestimate."

"Considering how many people may be genetically connected to Genghis Khan . . . I doubt it."

"I'm talking about Max."

Livy's hand froze over her keyboard and she finally turned her chair toward her aunt.

"MacKilligan?" she asked for clarification.

"Yes."

"I thought the Yangs didn't consider Max MacKilligan family."

"We don't. But her mother still is."

"How magnanimous of you."

"Cut the sarcasm. You should talk to her."

"Max? We're not exactly friends. She's actively attempted to kill me several times."

"Oh, who hasn't?"

"Thanks," Livy said, returning her focus to her computer screen. "And talk to her about what?"

"Her mother's back."

"Back from where?" Livy's hand froze again. "You don't mean she's back from—"

"Prison? Yes. That's exactly what I mean. And to add to the fun . . . she wasn't exactly allowed to go. If you get my meaning. She just went."

"How the fuck—?"

"It doesn't matter how she got out."

"Doesn't it?"

"What matters is that when she's caught, it's not here."

"I'm not sure how that involves *me*."

"You know she's always been close to our European cousins."

"So?"

"Worked on a lot of jobs with them. And the great aunts would prefer if she returned to Europe."

"Uh-huh."

"Which she may not want to do if her daughter does not go with her."

"Wait a minute." Now her aunt had Livy's *full* attention. "You want me to tell a woman I barely speak to—because we hate each other—that she should leave the family she has here and go off with a mother she hasn't seen in about two decades? Am I understanding this correctly?"

"You are! That's exactly what we want you to do."

"And why should I do this for . . . I don't know . . . *anyone*?"

"Well . . ." Her aunt came closer to her desk and rested her hands on the shiny mahogany. "We'd understand if you don't want to do it. But we'd feel awful that we had to ask you in the first place. So we'd come here . . . every day . . . to see you. You know, to apologize for trying to involve you. That would, of course, include all the aunts, the uncles, the cousins. All of us. Doing our best to make amends. That would, sadly, mean we'd also be spending time around all the sensitive cats and dogs you have around here. Oh! And let's not forget the bears! How we do love the bears. And how they do *love* us. All that sounds like fun, doesn't it?"

Livy gave herself a moment to get control. She had to or she was going to rip her aunt's fucking face off and eat it like the skin off a freshly roasted turkey.

When she knew she had control, she quietly replied, "I'll talk to Max."

Her aunt smiled. "Thank you, niece. You're the best."

"It smells in here," Nelle complained as they sat on the bench next to each other, Nelle's fist under her nose.

"Would you stop? You act like we took you to a pile of clothes we found in the subway. It's an army surplus store."

"I don't understand why we couldn't just stop by—"

"If you mention Ándre—accent over the *A*—one more time, I'm going to beat you to death. And there's ample shit I could take off the walls to do it with."

"Rude."

"Snob."

Max couldn't believe the bitching she was getting from Nelle simply because she'd been forced to spend a few minutes in an army surplus store.

Vargas returned from the dressing room in a pair of blue jeans, a black T-shirt, and thick work boots.

"Seriously?" Nelle asked, lip curling in disappointment . . . possibly disgust.

"What's wrong with it?"

Max had the same question as Vargas. She didn't understand what Nelle was complaining about. It was a basic outfit. Typical of any of the former military guys she'd dealt with over the years, but she couldn't remember any of them looking this . . . tasty.

The Levis cupped his exquisitely formed ass perfectly. The T-shirt had a worn look so that the sleeves were a little tight on his massive biceps and the bottom hung just at his hips. When he put his hands in his front pockets and lifted his shoulders, the T-shirt rose up, giving just a tease of the magnificent abs and narrow hips it was hiding.

"Are you *sure* you don't want to see Ándre?" Nelle practically begged.

"*Shut up about Ándre!*" Max bellowed, startling everyone in the store. Startling even herself.

She cleared her throat. "I mean . . . we don't have time for that." She focused on Vargas. "Let's just get a few more of those *exact* same jeans. And a bunch of those T-shirts in, um, red, dark green, and blue. A nice, deep . . . blue."

Vargas frowned at Max. "Uhhhh . . . okay." He looked at Nelle. "And I promise I'll pay you back once I get a new debit card and have access to my bank account. Or I can write you a check . . . once I get my checkbook."

"Don't worry about it," Max told him, leaning her arm on Nelle's legs so that Vargas was looking at her again with those green eyes. "She's rich. Like, disgustingly, horrifyingly, amazingly rich. You don't ever have to pay her back."

"Oooohhhh . . . kay." He blinked several times before saying, "I'll pay you back, Nelle."

"Sure," Nelle replied. She waited until Vargas had gone back to the denim section before she brutally shoved Max off her lap. "What is wrong with you?" she demanded.

"Well—"

A man who had been lingering near them while they spoke to Vargas suddenly sidled up to Nelle. She turned only her head to nail him with one of her ball-shriveling glares, and said, "Get the hell away from me or I *will* kill you." He smirked and again started to say something, but she added, "You can look in my eyes and tell that I will kill you. You can feel it in your soul. Like a dove when a hawk is nearby. So what you're going to do at this moment is walk away from me. Because if you don't, we both know I'll kill you and that it'll be messy, but that I'll definitely get away with it. Because I'm pretty and I'm rich. And rich people get away with everything."

Frowning, the man looked at Max next and she replied with a fangless but spit-filled hiss that had him quickly scurrying off. When they were again alone, Nelle asked in a whisper, "Are you into him?"

Max knew that Nelle was talking about Vargas but a different full-human male approached, apparently sensing an opening. Nelle dismissed that belief by snapping, "I'm not talking to you, idiot."

With that man gone, Nelle again focused on Max. "Well?"

Max sat back down on the bench. "I wasn't, but then . . . he came out in those jeans and T-shirt . . . god*damn*!"

"You know what it was? He didn't smell like Dutch anymore. I told you he smelled like Dutch!"

"I don't mind Dutch's funk. Unless he's gone to a wolf party. All that tequila does not come through his pores well."

"No. But Dutch might as well be your brother. He's not someone you've ever had a thing for. And Zé was covered in that brotherly funk. But now he's in clothes that only reek of this horrible place, which allows you to drill down to his natural musk." She grinned, crinkling up her nose and nodding her head. "*Musk*."

"Did you have to say that twice?"

"I totally did."

★   ★   ★

They took a ferry over to Staten Island, stopping at a diner that was apparently within walking distance of what both Max and Nelle kept calling "the old sports center." Zé had no idea what that meant but he didn't care enough to bother asking any more questions. Especially when the answers he got were . . . off-putting.

For instance, the diner they stopped at seemed to be manned by very large women with a less-than-friendly attitude toward Nelle and Max, even though they were both being very nice. When Zé asked about it, he was told, "Well . . . they're bears. What did you expect?"

He expected people in a service business to know how to treat their customers! Growing up in New York as a Puerto Rican from the South Bronx, he was used to being treated in a less-than-friendly manner by some. But if service people wanted a good tip or his return business, they hid the bullshit. Not *these* people, though. They let their bigotry hang out there for the world to see. It wasn't color or religion they reacted to, though. It was species and breed.

According to Max, wolves didn't like dogs; dogs and wolves didn't like cats; bears didn't like dogs, wolves, or cats; and absolutely *nobody* liked honey badgers.

"And none of that covers the internal bigotry."

"Internal bigotry?"

"Tigers think very little of lions, lions think very little of jaguars and leopards, grizzlies tend to slap around black bears, jackals find African wild dogs really annoying . . . the list goes on and on." Max took another bite of a burger that was nearly the size of her head before muttering, "It's endless. Just do what we do . . ."

"Which is?"

"Ignore it," the two women said together.

After finishing a meal so large it would kill most people, they made their way down the street to the "old sports center."

"You can wait in there. We've gotta hit the locker room." Max gazed up at him. "Need anything else?"

Wondering why she was looking at him like that, Zé replied, "No. You can go away now."

She chuckled and headed off.

Okay, there was one thing that Zé *did* really like about being around his "own kind," as Max called them. Their reaction to him. Specifically, their reaction to his attitude.

Since childhood, everyone around him had made it very clear they didn't like it. There were comments on his report cards, his grandfather heard about it in parent-teacher conferences, his commanding officers told him often "you have to work on your attitude, Vargas." He'd heard it so much for so long, he'd gotten used to it. But here, among these people . . . ? His attitude didn't seem to faze any of them. He enjoyed that.

Zé made his way into the basketball arena. Women were already practicing on the well-worn court, and none of them were what Zé had been expecting. They represented a broad swath of humanity, including different sizes, different races, different hair colors. So many hair colors, in fact, sometimes on one head alone! And along with the usual array of tattoos came scars. Lots of scars. As if several had been attacked by dogs at some point in their lives.

Hell, maybe they had.

No, this wasn't like the WNBA at all. He knew that when he saw one player who was so tall—well over seven feet—she simply stood under the hoop so that when one of her teammates passed her the ball, she simply tossed it into the basket. Zé sensed that was her only purpose.

Then Max and her friends walked out, all in bright yellow team sweat suits. They were the smallest women there, even though Mads, the tallest of the five, was at least five-eight. In fact, they appeared so tiny next to the rest of their teammates that Zé wondered why they'd be chosen for the team. They were like hobbits in comparison.

Max spotted him sitting in the stands, close to the floor, and waved. She'd been much . . . nicer to him since they'd left the army surplus store. He tried not to be paranoid about her change of attitude but he'd managed to live a relatively long, healthy life so far by being incredibly paranoid.

Turning to speak to another teammate, Max revealed her team's name on the back of her team jacket. The Wisconsin Butchers.

"Well, that's lovely," he muttered.

"What is?" a woman next to him asked.

Zé quickly looked to his left, his hand immediately reaching for the sidearm that wasn't there.

"You're okay," the woman said. "I would never hurt a fellow cat." She scratched a spot under her eye. "Unless he started some shit, of course. You planning on starting some shit?"

"No." He lowered his hand, returned his focus to the team in front of him. Max had taken off her sweatpants and jacket, leaving nothing but her tank top and shorts and revealing the body of a gymnast. Her shoulders and thighs were massive for a woman her size, and her arms were muscular. She cracked her neck and the sound radiated across the arena.

"You don't remember me, do you?" the woman next to him asked.

He looked at her again. She was black. Older. Beautiful. Her dreads were brown, blond, gold, white, and gray. Her eyes dark brown. She wore an African-style necklace made of wood and ivory that looked, at least to his eye, expensive. Her bracelet was white gold and diamonds. But despite the money around her neck and wrist, she wore only casual shorts and a worn Bob Marley T-shirt. The flip-flops on her feet probably only cost her three bucks at an Old Navy summer sale.

"I'm sorry. I don't."

"Well . . . you were in the middle of recovering from brain damage." When he frowned, she added, "You came to our street when you got busted trying to eat a bear cub."

Horrified, Zé closed his eyes and lowered his head. If he could have, he would have disappeared into his seat, never to be seen again by any decent person.

"Don't feel bad," she said with a smile. "If they don't want their cubs eaten, bears shouldn't let them get so juicy looking."

Zé was looking at her again. Gawking might be a better word.

"Oh, don't worry." She patted his knee. "Most of us don't eat humans anymore."

"Most of you?"

"Some hyenas . . . they still have the taste. There are some of them that do cleanup work, if you need it."

"Please stop talking to me."

She laughed and it made her even more beautiful, but holy shit! This conversation was freaking him out.

"The name is Imani Ako." She held out her hand and he took it.

"Zé. Zé Vargas."

"Nice to meet you, Zé." She refocused on the team practice. The players were doing warm-up drills. Not exactly interesting. "Sooo . . . you really didn't know that you were—"

"No."

"Wow. This must be hard for you. I mean, I've known all my life. Was raised to understand both sides of myself. I can't imagine finding out about all this when you're . . . ?"

"Thirty."

"Thirty! Wow."

He really wished she'd stop saying "wow." It was giving him a complex.

She was silent for a bit—thankfully—until she asked, "Do you feel safe?"

Zé frowned. "In life?"

She chuckled. "With the MacKilligans. Those sisters have made quite a name for themselves since they came to our neighborhood."

"The bears don't seem to mind them." Wait . . . did he just say that? Why had he said that? What the fuck did that even mean?

"The bears don't mind for two reasons. One, because the oldest sister can bake her ass off. The quickest way to get any bear on his or her knees? Baked goods. The second reason is because they're all so small, the grizzlies can just slap them right out of the neighborhood if need be. Which I thought they'd do right away when I heard there were honey badgers roaming around. The grizzlies and black bears are extremely protective of their hives. And yet . . . the three sisters are still there. And now you."

"Yes. Me."

"The little one, Max, she was very protective of you when you came to our street. She put those brawny shoulders between a group of confused cats and a gang of really angry bears. That's not something even a honey badger would usually do." She paused for a moment, then added, "I'm lying. Any honey badger would do that, but only for themselves. She did it for you."

"Your point?"

"That protectiveness could fade. Badgers are crazy . . . and mean . . . and hate everybody. Remember that. Because if she changes her mind about you . . . Well, don't let her tiny size confuse you. You might be a large cat but honey badgers are not easy to kill, they're willing to take on anybody, and they won't stop. They'll attack and attack until you either go away or you kill them."

"That is lovely information you just provided. It should be put into verse."

She laughed and Zé had to ask, "Are you here for a reason? Or just to freak me out?"

"Just observing," was her reply but there was something really weird about it. So weird he decided not to engage in any more conversation unless it was about the weather or something else inane.

Thankfully, the silence between them stretched on for quite a bit and Zé had just gotten comfortable again when a male he didn't recognize sat down to his right, leaving only one empty seat between them. Which seemed strangely close considering they had the entire fucking arena to sit in.

Holding a giant soda from the nearby 7-11, the man greeted Zé with a wide smile. "Hey-ya! I'm Dutch. Dutch Alexander. Max's best friend. I was the one who tried to help you when your brain was still healing. You're Zé, right? How are you doing? Holding up? You look really good. Like you're all healed up. Must be a relief, huh? So what's going on? You just hanging out here? Not that I blame ya. Max's friends are cute, right?"

Dutch was chatty. Dutch kept talking. Talking so much that Zé really just wanted him to shut up. But that wasn't happening fast enough for him.

So when the words just kept pouring from the man's mouth, Zé did the only thing he could think of.

Dutch was trying to make Zé feel comfortable and relaxed in this new world he'd been thrust into. He knew how the MacKilligan sisters could be when it came to outsiders. It had to be rough on the poor guy. Right? So he wanted to let the cat know that if he needed someone to talk to after a lifetime of thinking he was one thing, when he was, in fact, another . . . well, Dutch was here for him.

At first, the cat just stared at him. Frowning. He didn't say anything. Just kept staring. Dutch was used to breeds that stared. Cats were big on staring. Lions, tigers, bobcats. All of them tended to stare. Even when Dutch tried to involve the man in the conversation by asking whether he'd always lived in New York . . . Zé continued to stare at him. For at least a good minute. Then, with his gaze still on Dutch, Zé slowly reached over and, with a flick of his wrist, knocked Dutch's soda out of his hand.

The Ako Pride She-lion sitting on the other side of Zé threw her head back and laughed as Zé returned his gaze to Max's team practice.

"You five! Over here!"

Max, Nelle, Mads, Streep, and Tock made their way over to their coach. They'd been practicing for two hours and were exhausted, sweating like pigs. Someone handed each of them a towel to dry off and they slowed down a bit to wipe their faces until Coach yelled, "I said move, move, move!"

There were not a lot of people that Max and her teammates would run for but Coach Diane Fitzgerald had been working with them since they were in high school. She'd actually used the high school team's record to get the job of coach for the Wisconsin Butchers. She didn't need to be a college coach first. Which was fortunate, because she never would have lasted coaching a human college team.

Full-humans could never handle having a She-wolf like their coach as a leader. To put it nicely, Coach Fitzgerald was a vicious animal with few boundaries.

Max adored her.

"Why were you five late?" Coach demanded once they were standing in front of her; her massive shoulders always made her appear as if she was ready to tackle any one of them like a linebacker for the New York Giants.

"Why are you asking?" Max questioned. "You know we'll just lie. We're very good at lying."

"I'm not," Tock admitted. "I believe in painful honesty. The kind that destroys your soul and breaks your mind."

"I was just going to blame my period," Streep interjected. "Talk about my cramping. Then double over, with lots of sobbing."

"While I would quickly move to help Streep and rush her to the bathroom, begging everyone for a tampon as we ran." Nelle looked around and called out, "Anyone have a tampon? Anyone? *Dear God, she needs a tampon!*"

Everyone stared at Mads but all she did was shrug and softly say, "I would have just walked away. I always walk away when I don't want to answer something."

Coach lowered her clipboard, sighed. "Listen, I want to get into the finals. But that means we have to destroy every team in the playoffs. Can't do that if you five start flaking on me."

"When have we ever—"

"Don't even, MacKilligan. Just remember those schedules and get your asses to games and practice on time. Understand?"

"Yes, mistress of power!" they sounded off . . . just to annoy her.

With a frustrated sigh and a hard whack to the back of Max's head, Coach walked away.

"Why do you always hit *me*?" Max demanded.

"Because your head is the hardest!" Coach yelled back.

To the untrained eye, Coach appeared fed up and done with them, but Max knew better. They'd been torturing the She-wolf for years and she adored them for it. Because it was their honey badger attitude that made them such great competitors on the court. Hell, Coach had picked and groomed them *because* they were pain-in-the-ass badgers. She used to say that finding five badgers in the school was a gift from God. At least for her and the girls' basketball team. For everyone else, the five of them were just a nightmare that couldn't graduate fast enough.

"I'm starving," Nelle announced. "Who's up to feed?"

"Let's go back to Manhattan for food," Streep begged. "Some place fancy with excellent service."

Nelle smirked. "I guess I'm paying?"

"That's not necessary . . . unless you just want to."

"There's just no shame, is there?" Mads asked. "You just have no shame."

"Shame is for the weak."

Tock pointed her finger at Streep. "You're getting McDonald's and you're going to fucking like it!"

"No, no," Nelle said, chuckling. "We'll hit the Van Holtz Steakhouse on Fifth. We'll introduce Zé to a shifter's idea of fine dining."

Max nodded. "Oh, wow. Good idea. Cool."

But her teammates knew her too well.

"You forgot he existed, didn't you?" Mads asked.

"Of course not!"

"Don't lie to us."

"He simply slipped my mind," she admitted.

After clucking at her, Streep asked, "Did you even remember that we were going to look up Zé's background at the Katzenhaus Library?" Nope. She hadn't remembered that. At all.

"Of course I did."

Mads shook her head. "You really are a bad liar."

"I'm not. Look at my excellent eye contact. This is skill, bitch."

"So did you find out anything?" Nelle asked Tock.

"Fucking cats wouldn't let us in. And they were really mean about it. Show 'em, Streep."

Streep lifted her tank top to reveal the brutal claw marks that slashed across her belly. A full-human would have needed stitches and possibly a blood transfusion—as well as a decent therapist—but Streep was already healing up. A good thing, too, since Coach would not have cared if Streep's throat had been torn out. *"You don't miss practice!"*

"So we didn't get anything. But," Tock added, "I have a few contacts that may be able to help. I've got calls out. When I hear back, I'll let you know."

"Great."

"But I'll make sure to remind you first since you'll forget all about poor Zé again."

Max flashed a fang. "I will not forget him."

"I bet she won't," Nelle said, grinning. "She was lusting for him earlier."

"Because he no longer smelled of Dutch?" Streep guessed.

"Exactly! Now she just smells—"

"His musk!"

"Yes!"

"What is it with you two and musk?" Max asked. "Because you're starting to gross me out with that word."

"Musk or no musk," Tock suggested, "you better think about making your move before it's too late."

"What are you talking about?"

She pointed and they all turned. In the audience seats, two of their teammates—both cheetahs—were sitting on either side of Vargas. And they were *talking* to him.

Talking!

Max narrowed her gaze on the two bitches and started over there to slap the shit out of them—merely on principle—but Nelle grabbed her shoulder and yanked her back.

"That is not the way to handle it."

"Look at 'em. Talking to him. Whores."

"Wow," Mads snorted. "You went misogynistic fast."

"Christ, you're right." Max put her hands to her head. "What's wrong with me?"

"You like him," Nelle reasoned. "That's all. There's no shame in that."

"Isn't there, though? When, you know, it makes me call my teammates whores?"

"Max, don't overthink this. Enjoy that first flush of liking a guy . . . before you find out what an asshole he really is and dump him by throwing him out a third-story window like you did to Danny Parker in tenth grade."

Max laughed at the memory. "He just screamed," she said, waving her hands the way he had when she'd picked him up and thrown him out that window.

"They're coming over," Streep whispered. "Everybody be cool! Be cool!"

Max watched as her four teammates attempted to "be cool" by striking poses like they were at a 1993 Beverly Hills pool party photo shoot.

She closed her eyes and sighed. "Such idiots."

Zé followed the two players down to the court where Max and her friends were standing. He'd never had women come up to him and open a conversation with "Hey, we saw you sitting here all alone . . . We're cheetahs."

And Zé could think of no other reply than "That is the weirdest introduction I've ever gotten."

They were confused by his response, and that was how his backstory had come out. They were surprisingly nice and he'd laughed when they'd told him he was now "officially part of the spots-r-us club!" Apparently a common joke among jaguars, leopards, and cheetahs.

"We met your new friend here, Maxie," one of them said to Max. "He's cute."

Max took a step toward them but Nelle quickly cut in front of her. "What's going on?" she asked.

"Look, we heard you're trying to help Zé."

"And?"

She put her hand on Zé's shoulder in what he thought was just a friendly gesture. "We can teach him something right now, as a matter of fact. In front of everybody."

"*Whores!*" Streep yelled, pointing a damning finger.

"Okay!" Nelle raised her hands, palms out. "Everyone just calm down. We're all on the same team."

The cheetahs gawked at the badgers—another sentence he'd never in a million years have believed would come from his brain—and one of them asked, "What is going on with you guys?"

"Maybe," Tock interjected, "and I'm just spitballing, why don't you just tell *us* what you're talking about."

"A race. Around the court."

"Why?" Zé asked.

"Are you afraid?" one cheetah asked. "Hate to lose, do ya?"

"Not to be insulting, but I'm taller than you. Way longer legs."

They all laughed, then.

"He really doesn't know what we are, does he?" the other cheetah asked.

"Come on, cutie," the first cheetah prompted. "You don't even have to change clothes. Three times around the court. Whoever gets back here first . . . wins."

Zé sighed, rolled his eyes. But when he looked down at Max, expecting her to agree with him about not wasting his time, she asked, "Scared?"

No. He wasn't scared. But he was competitive.

Leaning down so he could look right into Max's face . . . "Fine. You guys wanna play . . . let's play."

The entire team sat on the sidelines, watching as the two cheetahs and Vargas lined up at one corner. Coach came out of her office to help, her whistle at the ready. She raised her arm. "Get ready! Get set!" She waited another few seconds . . . then blew her whistle. The three took off, charging down the line toward the first turn.

Immediately the cheetahs fell back, Vargas taking the lead.

"Is this just going to humiliate the poor guy?" Max asked, already cringing.

"How does he not know that cheetahs are the fastest land animals?" Tock asked.

"Because he doesn't understand that the women he's racing are *also* one of the fastest land animals in the world. He still hasn't put two and two together."

"That's why he's still floundering," Mads tossed in. "Why he can't shift on his own."

"He's not floundering," Max argued. "He just doesn't see it yet. Hopefully this will help with that and not just humiliate the fuck out of him."

"Believe it or not," Nelle explained, "they're not trying to humiliate him. They're trying to do exactly what you're saying, Max. By pushing that competitive nature he so clearly has."

Max wasn't so sure . . . until they hit the second lap.

Vargas had just shot around the corner when both cheetahs powered by him. So fast that he almost stopped. He definitely stumbled, his eyes blinking wide. He'd most likely never seen humans move that fast. Not in his old neighborhood. Not in a combat zone. Not in the Olympics.

But unlike most full-humans, who would stop, stare, and possibly pee themselves in panic, Vargas didn't stop. He barely slowed down. And after a moment of confusion, he picked up speed. Why? Because he was a competitive cat. He just didn't understand that yet.

The cheetahs slowed down a bit again, giving Vargas a chance to catch up and, honestly, because they had to. Because they could only run at sixty-five miles per hour for short bursts. But as soon as he caught up to them, they took off again. A move that clearly pissed him off.

And they did it again. And again. Slowing down until he caught up and then blasting off, leaving him behind.

The fourth time was when she saw it. Not rage. Not jealousy. Nothing full-human in his reaction. Just determination. Annoyance at himself for being left behind.

It started with his eyes. Those green beauties turning bright gold.

Then his shoulders hunched a bit. And his strides became longer, more fluid.

When the transition hit, it took less than a second. A flash. His human body abruptly covered in black fur, the spots so dark they were almost invisible, only exposed when he passed under certain lights. His shoulders hunched, his arms hanging down. Then his hands were paws, hitting the ground hard, followed by his feet.

In mid-run, he shook himself all over and his clothes flew off. When his front paws landed again, he was full jaguar and, as one, her team did what they always did when they saw a great play: they jumped up and cheered.

It took him a second. He was still running, unaware that he'd shifted on his own. But when he did finally realize it, when he fully understood he was no longer human, he slowed down and then stopped.

Max watched as he lifted one paw after another, his now gold gaze studying each in turn.

The two cheetahs shifted and playfully attacked him, knocking him down, leaping over him. Zé rolled to his back, stretched his legs and studied them. Fascinated by his new form. Fascinated with his new power.

He scrambled back to his feet and faced the cheering players. Then he was charging toward them at full power. Max smiled, but unlike the dogs on her team, she didn't duck. None of the badgers did.

Zé sailed over her with ease, dashing up the seats to the highest row.

That's when Max and her teammates began the chant.

"Zé! Zé! Zé! Zé! Zé!"

And even in his cat form, she could tell he was taking a bow.

chapter TEN

The trunk opened and, for the first time in hours, Devon Martin could see something other than utter darkness.

"Come on, Dev," that familiar voice said, although more than one set of strong hands grabbed him and hauled him out.

He was mercilessly tossed to the ground. Then there was a series of brutal kicks to his gut, legs, chest, and back. Almost everywhere but his head.

When he was sure he couldn't take any more, he heard that voice again.

"All right. That's enough."

The kicking stopped and Dev was able to pull himself up onto his hands and knees. He lifted his head.

"Hi, Dev."

She sat on the trunk of the car with another Asian woman, both of them eating carrots.

Holding up the vegetable, Renny Yang said, "You know, I really thought that when I got out of prison, I would be *dying* for a burger and fries. And that was the first thing I ate. But you know what else they don't have in a Bulgarian prison? Vegetables. And fruit. Something this omnivore has missed greatly."

"I want my shit, woman."

Renny smiled and Dev remembered how he used to love that smile. Now he just wanted to shoot it off.

"You and that idiot double-crossed me," he reminded her. "What did you expect me to do?"

"Not mess with my daughter."

Dev gazed at her. "Your daughter . . . or *our* daughter?"

Renny frowned and eventually looked at the woman next to her. Then they burst into laughter. They were joined by the other Asian females who came out of the darkness and surrounded the car.

"You think I would have had a child with *you*? Some"—her mouth curled in disgust—"*full-human* with absolutely *nothing* to offer my bloodline? Oh, puhleeze!"

"I don't know which is worse," the woman beside Renny said to him. "That you think she'd have a child with . . . *you*. Or that you think Max might be your child and yet you attempted to kill her several times."

"I never tried to kill her. She just . . . just . . ."

"Just, just, just . . . what?" Renny asked. "Didn't stand for being a tool for you to use against me? You know, actually"— she slid off the trunk but didn't come closer to Dev—"it's a real shame that my girl didn't find you first. She's much nicer than I am. Quicker . . . from what I've heard."

"If you're going to kill me, bitch, then kill me!"

"I'm not going to kill you." She held up her hand. "I just got my nails done. Gotta look nice when I see my daughter again. But I want to be able to tell her she has nothing to worry about anymore."

Dev heard them first. A weird, whooping noise that came from the forest surrounding the clearing. He looked around, trying to figure out what was happening. What that sound was. What was coming through the trees toward him.

He forced himself to stand, expecting Renny to immediately knock him back down. But she had her back to him, was adjusting her jeans—on the much-wider ass she'd grown since going to prison—and chatting with the other Asian women. She was ignoring him.

Dev's first thought was to run up and kill her. Just snap her neck. He'd still die but so would she. The bitch who had taken what he'd earned.

But those sounds. That loud, long whooping call. He kept hearing it, coming from all directions. Long whooping, then short. Like barks. Whatever it was . . . it just kept coming. And sometimes . . . sometimes there'd be what sounded like laughing.

Whatever the fuck it was, it was too much for Dev. It terrified him more than the thought of Renny Yang getting away with his money.

Maybe she was just faking him out. Maybe she was just using a sound system to get him to panic. He didn't know. He just knew he didn't want to stick around to find out what that noise was. He couldn't.

Dev turned away from Renny and started running. He glanced back but Renny and the women weren't chasing him. That didn't make him feel better. It made him feel worse. Renny wasn't stupid. She knew that if he got away, he'd be coming for her again. She knew it. So then why was she letting him—

It slammed into him from his right, grabbing hold of his arm between powerful jaws. He turned, trying to get the thing off, but it spun with him. Dev punched at it, but the creature only made that whooping sound again, even with its jaws closed around his arm.

A dog? They were going to use a dog to kill him?

But this "dog" didn't feel right. He used to breed fighting dogs and they didn't feel like this. They didn't make these kinds of sounds.

Headlights came on from behind him and now Dev saw. Now he understood those sounds. Like any kid growing up, he'd loved watching documentaries on predators. Lions, tigers . . . hyenas.

The hyena flipped him over and forced Dev to the ground.

Dev tried to get up but it wasn't one hyena that Renny had sicced on him. There was a whole bunch and they surrounded him, one climbing onto his chest and leaning over him.

He knew, knew this was it and bared his throat, wanting it to be over quick.

The hyenas made that sound again—a whooping combined with that short laugh. And that's when the one on his chest turned its head one way, then the other. Suddenly . . . it was human.

A woman staring down at him.

"Did you really think this was going to be easy?" she asked, her voice husky, almost male. "That you wouldn't suffer? Oh, my friend . . . you will suffer."

Renny heard Dev screaming as the spotted hyena clan devoured him while he was still alive.

Her cousin handed over a wad of cash and Renny handed it to the matriarch of the Clan. Giggling, the hyena walked off, apparently not in the mood to dine this evening.

"You didn't short her, did you?" Renny asked once the hyena was far enough away.

"No, no. Promise."

"Good. I don't need Dev's literal ass suddenly popping up in a river somewhere." Renny held out her hand and accepted the keys dropped in her palm.

"You're going now?"

"I haven't seen my daughter. I need to."

"Maybe you should wait," another cousin suggested and Renny finally noticed that her cousins were looking everywhere but at her. "Max isn't the Yang you left behind."

"She's my girl."

That's when several of the cousins laid into her. One after the other.

"The aunts won't accept her."

"You haven't seen her in years."

"You didn't even raise her yourself. How attached could you be?"

"And she's a MacKilligan now."

"Hardly even that. The MacKilligans don't want her any more than the aunts do. They don't want any of Freddy's girls."

Renny studied the cousins who had spoken. "So you want me to hold that against my own flesh and blood? *Our* flesh and blood?"

"If you think you can bring her into this life—*our* life, you're wrong."

"I have no plans to do anything but see her."

"Renny—"

"I just want to see my daughter. That's all."

Her cousins moved away from the car and Renny got in. She started the vehicle and lowered the window.

Renny leaned out. "I'll let you all know when I'm settled."

"Just . . . be careful."

"With my own daughter?"

The cousins exchanged glances until one finally said, "She's not alone, Renny."

"And she's not normal," said another.

Renny looked through the windshield out onto the field, where she saw a hyena rip off one of Dev's arms and go running into the trees with several of its clan mates following.

She returned her gaze to her cousins. "You're kidding, right?"

They were given a private room in the back of the famed Fifth Avenue Van Holtz Steakhouse. Zé's grandfather had never had much money so Zé had never considered eating at any of the Van Holtz restaurants in this city or any other around the world that he had been to over the years. If there had been a Van Holtz Steakhouse next to a Sizzler in Taiwan, he would have gone to the Sizzler. His appetite—and the appetites of his teammates—made eating at an overpriced tourist trap an unacceptable move in his opinion.

But here he was. At a Van Holtz Steakhouse on flippin' Fifth Avenue, no less. This wasn't the flagship restaurant, though. That was in Seattle. When the server handed him the menu, Zé already knew what he wanted, a T-bone with a side of broccoli. So he put the menu aside.

Max, who sat catty-corner from him, smirked. "You need to look at the menu."

"I already know what I want."

"Trust me," she said, her focus already on the offerings. "Look at the menu."

Rolling his eyes, Zé picked up the menu and opened it. The first page was a list of wines that, even on someone else's dime, he would never order. Wines from the 1800s? Who would willingly pay for that at a chain restaurant? He knew the cost of those wines must be insane because the prices weren't listed.

Already disgusted, Zé flipped the page and immediately saw the listing for his T-bone. Under that listing, however, were *choices* of T-bone. Zé frowned. He'd never heard of there being a choice of T-bone. T-bone was T-bone . . . right? He let his gaze move down the list and he saw bison and ostrich. Not strange, just a little hippy-dippy for his tastes.

But as Zé continued to read, he felt his face get hot and his brain start to hurt. Why?

Because the menu included deer, elk, moose, antelope, buffalo, zebra, rhino, hippo, giraffe. Giraffe!

"What the fuck am I reading?"

"Your dinner options."

"What the fuck is peccary?"

"It's like a pig. A skunk pig, I think. I know people who've tried it, but I'm not risking anything with skunk in the name."

"Capybara?" he asked. "The giant rat?"

"You might like that. They come from jaguar territory."

Zé took a quick look around. He felt like he was being fucked with. Was he being fucked with?

He turned the page and found a listing of seafood, but his eyes widened once he passed the usual salmon, trout, and ahi tuna. Because that's when he hit bearded and ringed seal, walrus, beluga whale, narwhal.

"What the fuck is a narwhal?" he demanded.

"Unicorn of the sea," Nelle replied with a grin.

When Zé got to grilled monkey, he slammed the menu shut, got up, and stormed out. But he only got as far as the stairs that led to the second floor of the restaurant, right by the elevators.

He sat down on the first step, his forearms resting on his knees.

When he'd shifted at the gym, the feeling had overwhelmed

him. But not in a bad way. He'd loved it. Loved the power that surged through his body. The strength.

But, most importantly, it was the feeling of finally being whole. Complete.

After that, he'd—stupidly—thought he'd be okay. That nothing else would shake the foundation on which his world was built. He had shifted into another species. Nothing would shake him because he could change his entire physical being into something completely different.

Then, however . . . he'd seen a listing for grilled monkey in a wine reduction sauce with garlic asparagus and broccoli. When he saw that one could substitute wild rice, he'd snapped.

How could anyone eat monkeys? Looking into the eyes of a monkey was like looking into your own eyes. It was like eating your neighbor. Wasn't it?

"You're still here." Max sat down on the step beneath the one his feet were on, her back against the stairwell wall so she could look up at him. "I thought we'd lost you."

"Grilled monkey? Really?"

She chuckled. "Jaguars eat monkeys, but that doesn't mean *you* need to eat monkeys. You can eat whatever you want."

"I was just going to get a T-bone steak, but you told me to look at the menu."

"You need to get used to it. If you hang around shifters, you're going to see them eat weird shit."

"What do you eat?"

"Depends where I am. When I was in Italy, I found an amazing badger-owned restaurant near Vatican City that made this"—she closed her eyes, took in a breath, as if she were tasting that meal again—"viper Bolognese sauce that *blew* my socks off. It was *utterly* divine. But in Germany, I found this black mamba bratwurst that was just . . . *wow*."

Zé held his hand up. "Wait . . . black mamba as in . . . ?" He shook his head. "When you said 'viper,' you meant—"

"Vipers. Cottonmouth, rattlesnake . . . copperheads. Like that."

"Because honey badgers eat—"

"Whatever we want. Down to the last rattle. And you need to know that and be okay with it." She patted his leg. "You've traveled. I'm sure you've tried the delicacies of other countries."

"Yeah, sure . . . but giraffes? On tonight's specials they had baby elephants!"

"Okay. First off, those are not from out in the wild. Trust me when I say we are not decimating the wild population of any animal. We have farms and ranches all over the world."

"How is that better?"

She snorted. "That steak you're planning to get . . . where do you think it comes from?"

Zé started to argue but quickly realized she was right.

"Everything on that menu is to fulfill the needs of certain breeds. There's no shame in it, and we give back. Most of the tough bastards that are protecting the world's wildlife preserves are shifters. And occasionally, those stories about big game hunters being mauled by lions and such . . . that's usually us. Why? Because we can . . . and because we're dicks. And let's face it . . . those guys are asking for it."

Now it was Zé's turn to snort. He even smiled. Something he didn't really like doing unless he had to. "I never got trophy hunting."

"Who does? Except extreme assholes."

"So what do I have to eat?" he finally asked. "The rat?"

"The capybara is not a rat; it's a rodent."

"What's the difference?"

"I don't know," she admitted. "And the only thing you have to eat is whatever you want. I have to admit, the prime rib here is *really* good."

"Where is she?" Zé heard from down the hall.

He looked over his shoulder and saw a stunning black woman running toward them.

"Max! Have you seen a child of mixed parentage running around?"

Frowning, Zé and Max exchanged glances. Mixed parentage? Really?

"Nope."

"If you see one, let me know."

"How do you lose an entire child?" a male voice snarled and Zé watched in horror as a massive human being stomped toward them. His hair was white with brown layers under it but he wasn't an old guy. Just massive. Maybe four hundred pounds packed onto nearly seven feet of thick bones. But he moved like a much smaller man. Fluid and easy as if all the world had been built for humans of his size.

"Zé, this is Bane and Bo."

"Blayne!" the woman snapped, starting off down the stairs. "My name is Blayne!"

"Whatever."

The male literally stepped over Zé and Max with those insanely large legs so he could also go down the stairs.

"Bo, this is Zé," Max said to the man, which only got Zé a grunt in response.

"If more of them make a break for it," he said, pointing his finger to the very last room at the end of the hall, "grab 'em."

Max nodded. "Sure."

Bo started to turn away but stopped and looked Zé over. "Do you play hockey?"

Zé was so surprised by the question, he began to answer that no, he did not, when Bane . . . sorry . . . Blayne returned and barked, "*Seriously?*" Her voice was so high when she spoke that howls and yips from the other private dining rooms answered her.

"I was just asking. No need to get hysterical. *I'm* not the one who lost *my* child."

Blayne pointed down the stairs. "Check the second floor."

Bo stomped off—was he physically able to just walk or did he only stomp everywhere?—and Blayne went back up the stairs. She, unlike the male, was forced to go around them even though her legs were rather long, too. Just not as long as Bo's.

"Uh, sweetie?" Max called out, catching Blayne's attention. Then she raised her forefinger and pointed up.

Blayne looked up and so did Zé. That's where they discovered a giggling child of, well . . . obvious "mixed parentage" hanging from the ceiling. The disturbing part was that she didn't seem to be hanging from anything in particular. There were no beams or light fixtures. The kid was just hanging there from a flat ceiling. Giggling.

"Holy shit!" Zé exclaimed, forgetting there was a child nearby.

"When did that start?" Blayne wanted to know.

Max only laughed. "When Stevie started doing that, she was about six, I think. She was startled by a squirrel."

"Oh, my God! Oh, my God!" Blayne dramatically pointed down the hall and shout-whispered to her child, "*You get back in there!*"

The child ran—still on the ceiling—to the last room. Blayne looked down at Zé and Max.

"You cannot tell Bo," she whispered to them. "He'll flip out!"

"The man with *tusks* will flip out?" Max asked.

Blayne bent at the waist so that she could put her hands very close to Max's face as she angrily explained, "They are not tusks! They're fangs! Like the mighty saber-toothed cat of yore!"

"Did you know," Zé felt the need to note, "that saber-toothed cats are not really related to modern cats? Like your tigers and lions."

"Stop talking!" Blayne snapped before yelling down the stairs, "Found her!"

She pointed her finger at Zé and Max again and whispered, "Not a word from either of you two! Ever!"

She stormed off and was halfway down the hall when she spun back around, now grinning, and happily told Max, "Oh, and tell Stevie I said 'hi'!"

Max nodded and gave her a thumbs-up. When Blayne was gone, Max muttered, "That bitch is a nut."

A minute or two later, Bo returned. He stopped just below, gazing at them, and asked, "So was the kid on the ceiling?"

Afraid to reveal anything, Zé and Max merely stared back but he seemed to see through their clever silence. He nodded his head, started up the final steps. "Yeahhhh. Blayne thinks I don't know. But I know."

"Let me guess," Max said. "You thought that with both of you being hybrids, your varied genes would just wipe each other out and you'd end up with full-human children. Right?"

"Yep. That's what we thought." He glanced back at them. "Instead . . . we have children that can run on the ceiling. Like lizards."

"They can all do it?' Max asked.

"Yeah. They can all do it. Blayne hasn't figured that out yet, though. She's probably in denial."

"Probably. But you know what? Most of my family lives in denial and they all seem pretty happy there."

The cat went with the prime rib and seemed very happy about his choice. He also ignored the offers to taste the non-poisonous snake dishes that Max's teammates offered him and that was probably for the best. Not everyone was a fan of boa constrictor tartare with mushroom-garlic risotto.

As always, Nelle turned what could have been just a bunch of bitches abusing her friendship into an event. All her wealthy "side-friends," as her teammates called them, stopped by. Cats and dogs from all over the world brought their skinny, influencer asses into the private dining room to drink, eat, and chat while taking lots of pictures of themselves and one another with their phones.

Max enjoyed the scene from a distance, sitting on a wooden cabinet where the restaurant stashed extra napkins and dishes, listening to all the insipid dialogue. She didn't mind insipid dialogue. She simply read news articles on her phone while other people's conversations droned on in the background. Like a movie soundtrack.

"I'm out of here."

Max looked up from her phone and smiled at Mads. "Everything cool?"

"Yeah."

They bumped fists since Mads wasn't much of a hugger. But

when Max realized that Mads wasn't really looking at her, she quickly grabbed her wrist and held her in place.

"Are you sure?"

When she got no answer, Max kept her loose grip on Mads's wrist and slid off the cabinet. She led her teammate out of the room.

"What's going on?" she asked once they were in the hall-way. Again, Mads didn't say anything, so Max guessed.

"Family?"

Mads still didn't answer but she did look more sour than usual, which could only mean one thing . . .

"Are they in town?"

Mads blew out a breath.

"Why? For a heist?"

Mads scratched her neck.

"Shit. For what? Jewelry or bank?"

She rubbed her eye with her fist.

"Oh, God. A bank heist?"

Yeah. They'd been playing ball together for a long time. Words didn't mean as much to them when they were stressed.

Max gave a low whistle and in less than a minute, Nelle, Streep, and Tock were in the hallway with them.

It took even less time and a single look to get across the problem.

"I can't believe your family is going to hit a bank," Streep said, pacing.

"They want you involved, of course," Nelle guessed. Not exactly shocking. As honey badgers they were all really good at stealing, whether it was a basketball from a really bitchy point guard or a terra-cotta soldier from an archeological dig in China . . . badgers were good thieves. Their only real competition being foxes, but the canines always preferred long or short cons to actual break-ins that might require weaponry and heavy equipment.

"I told her no," Mads said, leaning against the door, her arms folded over her chest.

"Her" was the matriarch of Mads's Clan. A very unfriendly

female who felt Mads owed her because the matriarch hadn't killed her when her father had first brought her home.

"But she's continued to move forward on this plan."

"That woman does love a heist," Tock muttered.

Although it wasn't just her. Most hyenas loved a good heist. Anything that required them to strong-arm innocent people: home invasions, car jackings, bank and jewelry heists, and celebrity tabloid reporting.

"Are you at the team hotel?" Nelle asked.

"Yeah."

"You can't stay there. They'll come for you and drag you out of bed."

"She's right," Max said. "You'll stay at my house in Queens."

"*No!*" all her teammates said together.

Max raised her hands, palms out. "Calm down. The bears won't bother her."

"It's not the bears we're worried about."

Max rolled her eyes. "You guys are *still* scared of my sister?"

"*Yes!*" they all said together.

"Oh, come on!"

"You guys can stay at my apartment," Nelle offered. "But only if you're mean to *my* sister."

Her teammates easily agreed to that, but before Max could argue her point about her own sister, the dining room door opened and Zé stepped out.

He looked at Nelle. "I hate your friends."

She nodded. "So do I."

He walked off and Max asked, "Are you going back to my house?"

"Can I tell anyone I'm still alive?" he asked, continuing to move away.

"Uh . . . I'm not actually sure." Because that depended on Zé.

"Then I guess I'm going back to Queens."

"Hold up. I'll go with you." She looked at her teammates. "I'll text you guys tomorrow. Any problems," she said, looking directly into Mads's eyes, "you call me. Understand?"

Nelle put her arm around Mads's shoulders, yanking her back when she attempted to pull away from the show of affection. "Don't worry. We'll be safe at my place." She jutted her chin toward Zé and winked in a way that made Max want to tear her eyes out. "Have fun."

"Ew." Max shook her head at her teammate. "Don't be that girl, Nelle. Just don't."

They got into the back of the car that Max had called up on her phone. The driver, thankfully, was not chatty so they sat in silence most of the way until Zé finally asked, "So exactly *when* can I tell my friends I'm not dead?"

"Never." She looked at him and the passing streetlights reflected in her eyes, making them appear almost white, like something out of a horror movie. "Not unless you want them all to die."

Zé felt a brief moment of panic but it went away so quickly he asked, "Are you fucking with me?"

"Yes." She laughed. "Sorry, couldn't help it."

"Of course you couldn't," he sighed out.

"But it seems like you truly get it."

"It?"

"What you are. What you will always be. What you have always been."

"Ahhh."

"Now that you understand everything, you can tell them whatever you want except the truth. Just remember that each time you do tell a full-human about what you are, you're not just risking yourself, you're risking all of us. Even the cubs you occasionally like to eat," she added with a wink.

"She's right," the driver suddenly added, his gaze watching them in the rearview mirror. "Most of them will never understand."

Zé pointed at the driver's seat and mouthed, *Him?*

"No," Max said aloud. "He's full-human, but he reeks of dog."

"My wife's a jackal," the driver happily offered.

Max gave him a thumbs-up but Zé asked, "Can you go back to being quiet now?"

"Cat?" the driver asked Max.

And Max's response was just to throw her arms up in faux exasperation, her hand nearly hitting his nose.

He pushed her hand away. "Do you mind?"

"Are you mad about something?"

Zé thought a moment, finally admitted, "No. The food, as you promised, was amazing. The drink . . . delicious. Your teammates were not nearly as annoying as Nelle's friends. And Nelle's friends went out of their way to avoid me."

"That's because you don't look like you have money."

"Good. Anyway, all in all, it was a pretty great night."

"Then why are you so cranky?"

"This isn't cranky. At least not my cranky."

"Dear God, what *is* your cranky?"

"Me," he answered, "but more."

"What's terrifying is, I kind of get what you mean."

They fell silent again and Zé wondered if he should apologize for making her think he was mad at her. He wasn't. He hated to admit it, even to himself, but he kind of enjoyed hanging around Max. Or maybe it was simply the way people sometimes feel toward doctors or nurses who save their lives. She had saved his life, literally, and had shown him his true self. So maybe he was simply giving her more leeway than he would normally give any cute girl who kind of irritated him, but was so cute he didn't care.

Eh, he thought, dismissing the idea of apologizing. He wasn't going to suck up to her. So, instead, he relaxed back into the seat and thought about the kind of phone he was going to get tomorrow so he could call his team leader and let her know he was not dead.

As he stared out the window, he felt Max's head rest against his arm.

Assuming she'd fallen asleep, he glanced down at her. But she was wide awake.

"What are you doing?" he asked.

"Resting on your arm."

"Why?"

"Because I want to."

"I don't get a say?"

"Sure. Does my lightweight head on your massively built bicep bother your sensitive cat nerves?"

"Or you could have just asked, 'Can I put my head here?' And I would have just said, 'Yes.'"

"Could have done that," she said, snuggling close, "but, ya know . . . didn't."

chapter ELEVEN

The driver refused to go any closer than three blocks away from Max's street. When she asked why, she was told, "Bears."

It really was the only answer she needed.

Together, Max and Zé walked down the street. They had to stop a few times when one of her neighbors trotted by in bear form or fell out of a tree right in front of them.

"This is so weird," Zé finally admitted. "I feel like I'm in one of those towns in Alaska where they have a polar bear season."

"I know it seems scary but it's not."

"Really?"

"Well, none of these bears have spent months on shrinking ice floes with very little food to eat. They're not starving or willing to get shot just to eat some tasty Alaskan wandering by. Because if there's one thing I know about New York bears . . . they always eat. A lot. Several times a day. But the last thing they want to do is tussle with a cat if they don't have to. So, you know . . . you're safe."

When they were half a block from the house, Zé stopped; it took Max a few seconds to realize it. She looked back at him. "What?"

"How am I going to learn all this stuff? About what bears do and lions and dogs."

She shrugged. "Watch Animal Planet and Nat Geo."

"Pardon?"

"While most full-human toddlers are being left alone to watch cartoons on TV, we were being left alone with Nat Geo. Or PBS. Anything with nature documentaries. My adopted grandfather even had tapes of old programs. That Omaha show."

Zé smiled. "You mean, *Mutual of Omaha's Wild Kingdom?*"

"Yes! That's it!"

"My grandfather used to talk about that show. But he just liked documentaries. Especially anything military related."

She walked back to Zé and stood in front of him. "You'll be okay. This stuff is easy to learn. You've already mastered the hard stuff. Shifting on command . . . ? Stevie learned pretty quick. Charlie can't shift at all. And it took me a while to figure it out. So you're halfway home."

Zé moved closer so that they were only inches apart. "Look, if I haven't, or if I don't . . . I just wanted to thank you."

Max gazed up into those stunning green eyes and decided it was time to make her signature "move." She was known for her "move," and few men could resist it.

So Max made that "move," leaning in until their bodies were touching. Yeahhhh, the "move."

But when Max looked up to continue staring deeply into Zé's eyes, he was gazing at something behind her.

"Yo! What are you looking at? I just made the move."

"Someone's lurking by your house."

"*What?*" Max spun around and tried to see what was there, but as a honey badger, she didn't have the amazing long-distance sight that cats had.

She was worried that Devon or his men had come to get her and that meant her sisters were in danger. So she pulled away from Zé and quickly ran toward the house, keeping her body low. She jumped over the fence that surrounded their rental property and ducked behind the oak that Stevie liked to hide in when she felt the squirrels were threatening her.

Max peeked around the tree trunk and waited. After several

seconds, a hand landed on her shoulder. In the next instant, she had one of her blades out and pressed against the throat of the cat standing beside her.

"Do not sneak up on me!" she whispered, annoyed but impressed that Zé didn't back away from her blade. He knew moving was more dangerous than simply standing still when dealing with a predator.

Without speaking, Zé pointed his finger toward the backyard. Max went around to the other side of the tree and spotted a male lurking near the garage. Finally, she could let out her breath.

"Dammit." She stepped away from the tree and ran toward the male. He was peering into the clear glass doorway of the garage, so he didn't see her coming. She moved silently, without effort, and when she was a few feet away, she launched herself at his back. Once on him, she wrapped her legs around his waist and her arms around his neck, pressing the blade she'd used on Zé to her cousin's throat.

"Hiya, Dougie. Kinda late to visit, isn't it?"

Knowing Max could handle herself, Zé gave himself a moment to . . . uh . . . relax. Although, he had to admit, his current *non*-relaxation was due to Max and that move she'd made just as he'd seen someone trying to break into her house.

Now he was standing here, forcing himself to think about old football plays to help him get rid of the hard-on he currently had.

He'd had past girlfriends who did stripper-like moves to get him turned on, but none had done more with less than Max.

With his erection finally under control, Zé stepped away from the tree and strode across the yard to Max and whatever criminal she was currently dealing with. As he got close, he realized whoever the guy was, he should be happy Zé was around. Because the knife Max had pressed to the man's throat was already drawing blood.

"Want me to call the cops?" he asked.

"Nah," Max replied, resting her chin on the shorter man's big shoulder.

"You can't bury him here," he reminded her, not really in the mood to see her murder anyone. "Besides, won't killing him upset your sisters?"

Max laughed. "I'm not going to kill him because this is my cousin Dougie. Well, one of my many cousins. You may remember him—he and his brothers were at the house with my Uncle Will. They were here when you first arrived."

"You were dribbling a basketball." Zé frowned, trying to remember. "And you were doing that just to annoy your sister . . . ?"

"That's right. And I thought my uncle was staying in Manhattan at that fancy, overpriced hotel."

"We are," Dougie put in. "And I'm not here for you, cousin."

"Then who are you here for?"

"Your father."

It happened so fast, it was almost stunning. Max's always-there smile dropped away and her brown eyes darkened. She released her cousin, stepping away from him and sliding her knife into the back of her jeans.

"What are you talking about?"

Dougie faced her. "The word is he's back in New York and every bastard who hates him is looking for him."

"And you thought he'd be here?"

"Your father has no money. You know that as well as I do. And he's hoping your little sister will give him some. Just like she always does."

"Talk about my sister—while sneering—again and I'll tear your handsome little face off and wear it as a Halloween mask."

It must have been something that either Max had done before or people had no doubt she'd actually do, because her cousin immediately changed his tone.

"Look, *my* father, bastard that he is, is really pushing me to find *your* father . . . bastard that he is. I could use your help."

"If he were here, you know I'd tell you. So would Charlie.

But he hasn't come near us since Charlie threw him in the street and he got run over by a truck. You know, after that funeral."

Zé glanced off, not sure he'd heard that story correctly.

"All right, but if you do see him . . ."

"Wait." Max looked at the house. "I'm gonna check the house. Stay here."

She went to the back door of the house and let herself in. Lights came on in the kitchen and Zé realized that he could actually hear her moving around inside.

"Why are you smiling like that?" Dougie asked.

"I can hear her," Zé replied, fascinated by all the new things he could see and hear and . . . smell.

He focused on Dougie. "What the fuck have you been eating?"

"Copperhead snake in a spicy black mamba sauce." He grinned. "I was out for nearly an hour. Clinically dead for at least fifteen. Totally worth it."

Max returned. She was munching on something from a bag, and he was relieved to see that the bag was a small plastic one. Not big enough for some poisonous viper. But, as she got closer, he saw that she had something hanging from her mouth.

When she was just a few feet away, he realized it was a scorpion. A live scorpion putting up a fight.

"He's not in there," she said, around the thing stinging her while she offered the bag's contents to her cousin. He happily pulled out another live scorpion and immediately bit its head off.

"I appreciate you taking a look, cousin."

"Well, I know MacKilligan luck. I swear all over the place he isn't there, you leave, I go inside, and BAM! There he is."

"Yeah, that is our luck." He swallowed the rest of the crunchy scorpion. "But if you hear from him . . ."

"I'll let you know. Unless Stevie sees him first."

"Oh, come on."

"You know how she is when it comes to our dad. And she

knows what your dad is going to do to him. I can't be the one who rats the fucker out if that happens. But if I see him and she hasn't . . . I'll call."

"Thanks." He motioned to the plastic bag. The one that, to Zé's horror, he now realized was a *wiggling* plastic bag. "Can I have a few more?"

"Oh, here, take it. I have more in the basement."

"Aw, thanks, luv."

He walked off, waving as he went, another scorpion hanging from his mouth.

Max smiled at Zé. "So," she purred, "where were we?"

She expected all sorts of responses to her very obvious offer, but "Nope. No way. Not in this life," had not been one of them . . . or, in this case, three of them.

"What's wrong?" she asked, following him into the house.

"I just watched you share a bag of scorpions with a man." He stopped at the kitchen table and faced her. "*Live* scorpions! In what universe is that a normal thing to do?"

"We had this discussion at the restaurant. Remember? Different breeds and species eat different—"

"I get that. What I didn't expect was to see you *snacking* on live scorpions! Like, 'Hey, want a Twizzler? Maybe some M&Ms? *How about a live scorpion?*' How are you not worried about dying? And before you say"—he dropped his low voice even lower—"'I'm a honey badger,' there has got to be more to it than that!"

"Uh . . . okay. When I was born, still in the cradle and, you know, before my mother went to prison, she used to give me live scorpions to play with. They'd sting me, I'd cry, but eventually I built up a tolerance for their poison. Now I eat them as a tasty snack because scorpion venom doesn't hurt me. I barely feel their stings against my skin. And, to be honest, they are *really* tasty. And crunchy. Like tortilla chips. Tortilla chips that wiggle and attack me."

When Zé didn't say anything for almost a minute, Max guessed, "This isn't helping, is it?"

"No. Not helping."

She thought about storming away. Angry and insulted. But she wasn't really angry or insulted. She simply understood he didn't get it. So she took his hand and pulled him into the living room. She sat him down on the couch and grabbed all the controls for the television, the sound system, and the cable box. She made a few quick purchases on one of the streaming services and began playing the first one.

"What is this?" Zé asked.

Max sat down on the couch beside him. "The story of me. The next one will be the story of you."

The documentary about honey badgers started and, after a few tense minutes during which she felt positive that Zé was simply going to walk out of the house and her life forever, he leaned forward, rested his elbows on his knees, and his chin on his fists. For the next fifty minutes, he stayed glued to what was on the television. When the ending credits rolled, he leaned back again and looked at her.

"You guys are mean."

Zé wasn't sure what he'd expected to see in that documentary. But a small animal that challenged lions, hyenas, African wild dogs, cheetahs, leopards, African killer bees, and humans was not it.

But as he'd watched, he'd realized something very important: Max was definitely a honey badger. She didn't seem as openly hostile as the wild honey badgers in the documentary, but everything else about her was like them.

Now, the question he had to ask himself was what did that mean to him? Was she someone he could live with? A not-nearly-as-hostile-as-a-wild-honey-badger woman with an amazing body, beautiful skin, and a healthy sense of humor. Or was Max MacKilligan going to be too much for him? He honestly didn't know. At least not at this moment.

Seeing the documentary on jaguars might help because he still didn't know exactly what he was about either.

"You want to watch this with me?" he asked, pointing at the new credits rolling on the screen.

"I'm actually hungry again."

She stood and began stripping off her clothes.

"Uh . . . Max. I'm, uh, going through a thing right now and . . ."

"Oh, dude, get over yourself," she laughed.

She finished taking off her clothes. "I'll be back later," she promised before she shifted right in front of him, turning into what could only be called a *giant* version of a honey badger. Especially since most of them weighed, according to the documentary, no more than thirty-five pounds or so. This badger was a healthy one-hundred-and-twenty, just like Max.

Max trotted out of the house and Zé followed, curious to see if she could open the door with those ridiculously sized claws. She didn't try, though. Instead she went to the window and opened it by using her snout. Then she jumped out and disappeared into the night.

"Yep," he said to the air. "My life just keeps getting stranger and stranger . . ."

He continued watching the MacKilligan house from inside his vehicle. The man who'd come out earlier was no one. Definitely not the badger they were looking for.

Not the one he had to find.

He snarled in annoyance and his brother leaned forward, sticking his head through the seats. "Maybe we should just go home. You need to sleep."

"We're not going anywhere. Not yet."

"Well," his other brother said from the passenger seat, "I don't think we should be hanging around here. Because the bears are getting nervous."

"Fuck the bears."

"You know, big brother, you say that; but when they drag us onto the street and start ripping our arms off . . . we won't be able to help anybody. Now will we?"

He hated that his brother was right. Hated it.

"Fine," he growled. "We'll come back in the morning. Ask questions."

"Politely," his brother insisted. "We'll ask questions *politely.*"

Fuck polite. He didn't do polite.

A hand fell on his shoulder and his brother softly insisted, "I'm sure she's fine."

"She better be," he said, starting the engine. "Or I'm going to kill them all."

chapter TWELVE

Zé woke up with Max staring down at him, her body resting against his.

"You were wonderful last night," she purred.

"Don't even try it," he told her, sitting up and pushing her off with his arm. "I know for a fact that I didn't drink enough of that foreign beer you guys had in your fridge to forget anything that might have happened with *you*."

She rolled onto the couch with a laugh. "I'm going to take that as a compliment."

"If it makes you feel better." He yawned, scratched his head, and was a little relieved to see they were both wearing their clothes from the day before. "Where did you go last night?"

"Just around."

Zé frowned, motioned to his cheek. "You have something on your face."

She wiped at it with the back of her hand. "Oh. Yeah. That's honey."

"Are there going to be pissed-off bears this morning?"

"Probably." She tapped his leg. "You still freaked out about me?"

"Less so."

"Good. Then let's get ready and we can go buy you that phone. And breakfast."

"Shit."

"What?"

"I don't know where the clothes we got yesterday are. I think we left them in Staten Island."

"Nah. Nelle had them brought here by . . . somebody. I mean, she just tells people to deliver things and . . . they do." She leaned in and whispered, "There is a world that rich people exist in that I have no idea about."

"How rich is she?"

"It's not her so much as her entire family. It's family money. And there is a lot of both, meaning she has a shit-ton of cousins and a shit-ton of money. Beyond just a few million."

"But she grew up in Wisconsin—"

"That's one of their homes."

"—and plays basketball for the—"

"Wisconsin Butchers!" Then, she balled up her fists and growled out, "*Goooooo, Butchers! Ar! Ar! Ar!*"

Zé leaned back. "What was that?"

"Our team chant."

"That last part sounded like a seal bark."

"Gee. Thanks." She jumped up from the couch and spun around to face him. There was so much energy in Max, she was starting to remind Zé of one of those crazy little dogs that race from room to room because their owners don't walk them enough. "Let's go. Your clothes are probably upstairs."

Zé began to stand as well but spotted someone peeking around the corner of the living room entryway. He was going to point the stranger out to Max when the man spoke first.

"How's my sweetie pie?"

Max's habitual smile disappeared and her brows lowered so much they nearly reached the tip of her nose.

With parts of her face twitching, Max opened her mouth and fangs abruptly replaced her teeth. Not the way he expected either, with two fangs on top and two on the bottom. Instead her entire mouth was filled with fangs. They weren't huge but there were so many that the damage they'd do would be devastating.

Then, without turning around, Max snarled, "*Dad?*"

★ ★ ★

Max faced her father. "Have you lost your fucking mind? Coming here? *Again?* Dougie was already here looking for you!"

"Okay, before you get hysterical—"

"I don't get hysterical," she reminded him. "I just kill things. And you're a thing I'm feeling the need to kill."

"I'm still your father."

"Are you fucking kidding?" She looked at Zé. "Is he fucking kidding?"

Knowing the poor cat wouldn't have an answer, and not caring either way, she again looked at her father. Freddy MacKilligan. Conman. Thief. Idiot.

"You need to go." Thankfully Charlie had spent the night at Berg's house across the street. But she'd be back soon since she liked baking in her own kitchen and she'd promised the Kapowski brothers honey buns for the next week to make up for Zé trying to eat their offspring. So if Charlie found Freddy MacKilligan in their home when she got back . . . there would be blood. And body parts. And a sobbing Stevie who would never recover from seeing her sister kill her father; she seemed to care about that sort of thing!

"Get out now."

"I'd love to." Her father shrugged. "But I need some cash."

Max again snapped. *"Are you fucking kidding me?"* She was trying to keep her voice down since Stevie *was* upstairs with her panda, but her father was testing the strength of her will *not* to kill him. "I'm not giving you any money."

"Fine. I'll ask your baby sister. She's upstairs, right?"

He turned to go bother Stevie but Max grabbed her father by the throat, yanking him back. She knew she was squeezing his neck harder than was necessary, but she couldn't help herself. Plus, he was a honey badger. She'd have to do a lot more than that to kill her father. But at the very least, she could hurt him. She enjoyed hurting him because he so richly deserved to be hurt.

With her hand still on his throat, she forced her father to bend backward until she could look him in the eyes.

"You're going to get out of here and you're not going to come back. Or *I'll* kill you and bury you under the house. We both know I'll do it. Just test me."

To make her point, she shoved him down so he landed hard on the floor. But he was up quickly, unleashing his own fangs and stepping into her. They banged their foreheads together and snarled, drool pooling on the hardwood floor, their claws out, ready to slash.

Max had always been able to anger her father in ways that Charlie never could and Stevie never would. Because Max had no issues that he could toy with. She barely had a conscience. To her, taking out her father would be just one more thing she had to hide from her sisters so feelings wouldn't get hurt. Freddy knew that Max was the biggest threat to his well-being because Max truly did not give a fuck.

She decided in that moment that maybe it was just time to get the loser out but she didn't have a chance.

Zé suddenly grabbed Freddy by the hair and yanked him up and out, dragging him toward the front of the house. Following them, she watched Zé yank open the front door.

"She told you to leave," he said, kicking the security door open. "So you should do that."

He tossed her father out of the house like so much trash, slammed the door, and locked it.

Zé faced her. "What an asshole!"

Max nodded. "Yeah. He is."

"He didn't even do anything. But just the sight of him . . ."

"Irritated you."

"Yes! Just the sight of him irritated me."

"Yeah. That's my dad. He does great with full-humans. But shifters aren't fans . . . except our mothers."

Zé cringed. "Why?"

"Dude . . . if I knew why, I'd tell you." Max went to the door, pushing past Zé. She unlocked it and opened it again. Her father was standing in front of the house now and she could tell just by looking at him that he was about to start screaming. Just to get Stevie's or Charlie's attention.

She stepped out of the house but didn't have to go any farther because her saviors were right there.

"Hey, Kapowskis!" she called out to the four grizzly bears about to drive their kids to shifter summer day camp—including the one almost eaten by Zé. "If you want my sister to have those honey buns ready for you when you get back"—she pointed at her father—"he needs to go."

Those big grizzly heads turned, those cold brown eyes locked on Freddy MacKilligan, and their grizzly humps abruptly grew, giving their already powerful arms and shoulders even more strength.

Freddy glared at his daughter. "You evil little—*aaaaaaaaaah-hhhhhhhhhhhhhhh!*" he screamed, running from the four bears chasing him down the Queens, New York, street.

With a smile, Max went back inside and closed the front door.

"All done."

"What about those kids?" Zé asked, pointing at the cubs through the front windows of the sun room. "Should we leave them outside like that?"

"They'll be fine. Every bear mom in this neighborhood is genetically tuned to the cries of any cub under threat. And one of those kids is the one you tried to eat, so I'm not sure his dad would want him in here . . . with you."

Zé glared. "Thanks for that."

"You're welcome," she said, ignoring the sarcasm in his tone. "And thanks for your help."

Max headed back into the living room and found Stevie standing there in one of Shen's way-too-big Pittsburgh Steelers T-shirts.

"Dad?" she asked.

Max nodded. "Yeah. Dad. Sor—"

"No. Don't apologize. You didn't do anything. What did he want anyway?"

"What else? Money."

She nodded at Zé, who'd followed Max into the room. "Hey, Zé."

"Hey, Stevie. You okay?"

"I'm going to be fine." She held her hand out. "Gimme your phone."

Max let out a sigh. "Dude, don't give him any money."

"I'm not. I'm doing something I should have done a long time ago."

Handing over her phone, Max asked, "What?"

"I'm going to rat him out to Uncle Will. Let his brother deal with him the way he's always wanted to: brutally."

Max couldn't help but be shocked by that response. Well . . . that response from Stevie. No one in the family had ever thought she'd be the one to tell Uncle Will.

"You're going to call Uncle Will? Are you sure you want to do that?"

"I am not letting our sister's therapy go to waste. She has been doing so well."

Max winced a little, glancing at Zé. "Yes, let's tell the world our sister's in therapy."

Stevie stopped searching for Will's number in Max's phone to glare at her. "*I'm* in therapy. Are you embarrassed by that, too?"

"I'm not embarrassed by you or her being in therapy, but perhaps she doesn't want the world to know."

"That sounds like shame."

"That is not shame."

"I've been in therapy a few times," Zé suddenly announced and both sisters looked at him. He shrugged. "PTSD. When I was a Marine. You know . . . being shot at. Things blowing up around me. It takes its toll."

"See?" Stevie said, again searching for Will's number. "He has no shame."

"I'm not asham—"

Max stopped what was about to turn into a tirade. She wasn't going to let her father and sister get under her skin. Not today!

"I'm going upstairs to take a shower and then buy *him*"—she pointed at Zé—"a new phone."

"Did I ask you what you were going to do?" Stevie demanded. *"Because I don't really care what you're going to do!"*

It took all of thirty seconds but the sisters went from general sadness about having such a weirdly irritating father to screaming at each other. So much screaming that Zé couldn't understand a word they were saying.

He thought about stepping in before the two could come to blows but that seemed like a bad idea. Zé had already seen Max's fangs. He didn't need to see them again.

Behind them, though, standing outside the window in the yard, stood Shen. He waved at Zé, urging him to come over.

Zé looked at the sisters, then back at Shen, but Shen motioned again. He walked through the house and out the back door to meet Shen.

"Morning," Shen greeted.

"Hey. You needed me?"

"No."

"Then why did you tell me to come outside?"

"Oh, because you don't want to get in the middle of a MacKilligan sister fight. For a second there, you looked like you might."

Zé glanced back at the house and nodded. "You know, I sensed that wouldn't be a good idea."

"Instincts, man. You've lived this long because of your instincts. Trust them. Besides, it always gets like that when their father comes around. Especially if Charlie's not there for them to focus on instead."

"They're trying to keep it from Charlie."

"Probably a good idea. She *really* hates her father."

"I've only met him once, but I get that."

"Anyway, it's better if you stay out here with me." Shen held up what he had been holding in his hand. "Bamboo?"

Zé shook his head, forcing himself to not look disgusted

about a man offering him what seemed to him to be nothing more than a piece of a cheap chair, and simply replied, "No, thanks."

Shen motioned behind him. "Wanna climb a tree with me?"

At that point, Zé couldn't do anything but look as confused as he felt. "Why the hell, as an actual adult, would I want to climb a tree with another man?"

Shen simply looked at the tree and so did Zé. It was a good-sized tree with a wide trunk. The branches were extremely thick and covered in lush leaves.

"Oh, my God," Zé gasped out. "I want to climb that tree."

"At this time of day, it's best to do it as human. But at night . . . all bets are off."

"Pandas climb trees?"

"I don't really climb," Shen admitted. "I just hang from the lower branch and eat my bamboo."

"And that makes you happy?"

"Stevie makes me happy. Hanging from a tree limb and eating bamboo . . . ? That's just an enhancement to my happy."

chapter THIRTEEN

Max watched her sister disconnect the call with Uncle Will. Their father had ripped off the Scottish side of the MacKilligans for one-hundred-million Sterling. One of the dumbest things that anyone could do. Honey badgers were not exactly known for their forgiving nature, but they were known for their love of money. They liked the security it provided, and if they had to break the law to ensure they had cash, they were willing to do that. Mostly because they were good at it.

They could break into—and out of—almost anything and had no problem working with full-humans. In fact, most badgers lived their entire existence among full-humans, avoiding the shifter world outside their own families.

When Max asked her mother why their kind did that, why they didn't happily join in to all the things the shifter world offered—the restaurants, the sports, the shopping and, most importantly, the protection—she'd only smiled and said, "Because they can smell us coming a mile away."

Max had only been seven when she'd asked that question, so she'd taken her mother literally. Of course other shifters could smell honey badgers coming a mile away! Especially if they unleashed their anal glands! But that wasn't what her mother had meant.

Unlike full-humans, shifters knew better than to trust honey badgers. One never knew when a badger was going to get "fed up with your bullshit" and suddenly just slap the shit out of you or decide "I didn't like the look on your face" and rip it off or one day simply steal everything you own because "you didn't look like you really needed that Ming vase."

Of course, not all honey badgers were like that, but as Max's teammates had shown her, it wasn't always easy to completely remove oneself from a honey badger family.

Even she and her sisters had realized that. No matter how much the MacKilligans on both sides of the Atlantic had made it abundantly clear they wanted nothing to do with Max, Stevie, and Charlie . . . here their relatives still were. Annoying Max and her sisters.

Of course, once Will got his money back from their dad—or he killed their dad—they would no longer have to deal with their cousins and aunts and uncles. That's what Charlie and Stevie seemed to believe, but Max wasn't so sure.

Max watched her baby sister's face and knew that she was torturing herself. She had that look she got when she was worried about all the things that could go wrong. Like when she checked herself into a German hospital because she was giving herself panic attacks over Ebola. She'd made the mistake of reading an article about it. Just a general informational thing, but there'd been enough statistics in it for Stevie to figure out exactly how long it would take for the virus to completely wipe out the entire human population. Most scientists could and probably did figure out the same thing, but those same scientists went on about their day. Maybe made plans for their families if something bad ever happened. But not Stevie. She wanted to save the world and when she realized she couldn't do that without the help of "worthless and uncaring human beings" she had a complete and utter meltdown.

She was in that therapeutic facility for four months before she was ready to check herself out. The psychiatrists were ready to release her after a month, once they got her on meds that helped control her ongoing panic attack, but Stevie kept telling them and Charlie, "I still need time. I'm not ready."

It was what-ifs that made Stevie a brilliant scientist. It was also what made her "sick" sometimes. Max had realized that after knowing Stevie for less than six months, when they still expected her She-tiger mom to come back and get her daughter. Over the years, though, Max had found ways to distract her sister from her anxiety. Some worked most of the time, but only one way worked *all* of the time. Out of necessity, that was the one she used.

Sitting down at the table, leaning back in the chair, Max accused, "You're going to open your big mouth to Charlie, aren't you?"

Stevie lifted her gaze from the table. That deep-in-thought, I'm-about-to-flip-out gaze.

"No, I'm not."

"You are," Max insisted. "She's gonna walk through the door, and as soon as you see her, you're going to start running your fucking mouth." Max did that thing Stevie really hated. She scrunched up her face and began speaking in a high-pitched voice that she always told Stevie was exactly how she sounded. It wasn't, but that didn't matter. Not at the moment. "'Nan-nan-nan-nan-nannnnn. Oh, Charlie, he was here. I don't know what to do. Wah-wah-wah!' As soon as she comes in this fucking house!"

Stevie looked away, took in a breath, let it out . . . then exploded.

Pointing her finger and jumping up from her seat, Stevie screamed, *"You are a fucking bitch and I wish I'd set you on fire when I had the chance!"*

Max jumped up, too, making sure her chair went flying back and hitting the counter behind her. Big, clanging noises always set Stevie off. *"I'm a fucking bitch? You are a worthless, whiny baby!"*

"Hey, hey, *hey!*" Charlie bellowed, rushing into the kitchen from the front of the house and pushing Max and Stevie apart. *"That is enough!"*

"She started it!" They both screamed in unison.

"I don't care! Stop it. Right now!"

They stopped screaming, but they kept glowering at each other. So, to keep the distraction going, Max shoved Stevie and Stevie shoved her back, and then the mutual headlocks began.

By the time Charlie had yanked them apart, Max had a bloody nose and Stevie a split lip.

Charlie shoved them in separate directions and raised her hands, pointing a finger at each of her sisters.

"That's enough. Stevie, don't you have somewhere to be?"

"As a matter of fact . . . I do! Because *I* have a life!" She made that sound Max always equated with the British ladies who starred in movies made from Jane Austen novels, before she stormed back to her room. All she was missing was a full skirt that she could lift when she made her exit.

Instead of laying into Max about giving Stevie "a break," Charlie walked away from her sister and started pulling out what she needed to make her honey buns.

She was putting the supplies on the small counter under the window that looked out over the backyard when she suddenly leaned down and gave a low chuckle.

"You have to see this," she said, motioning to Max.

Max came over to the counter and leaned down next to her sister so that both of them were resting their arms on the wood top. But when she looked outside, all she saw was Shen hanging from the big tree in the yard, which wasn't exactly shocking. He did that most mornings and nights. He hung there with his knees over the lowest limb so his arms could easily reach the bag of bamboo that he placed under it.

"It's Shen," Max said. "So what?"

"Look *into* the leaves."

Max raised her gaze and studied the higher parts of the tree but still didn't see anything. At first. Then she noticed a slight movement. She tilted her head and leaned forward.

"Oh, my God. That's the cat."

Charlie rested her head on her arm and laughed.

"He's climbing trees now?" Max asked. "Seriously?" Then she laughed so hard she had to lean against her sister so she didn't fall to the floor.

"How did you even see him?"

Charlie gave a small shrug. "When I've got my contacts in, it's like I have wolf eyes."

They watched Zé for a few minutes, and Max loved that he was really starting to embrace "the cat within" as Dutch liked to say about cat shifters in general.

But just as Max was about to turn away to pour some orange juice before getting ready to head out, Charlie asked, "So what are you and Stevie hiding from me?"

Max forced herself not to react to her sister's question. She kept moving, even as she asked, "What makes you think we're hiding anything?"

"Instinct. Stevie seemed truly angry, but you . . . you were just trying to distract her. And you only distract her when you want her to keep her mouth shut about something. What's she keeping her mouth shut about, Max?"

Max continued to stare at the tree, where Zé was easily moving around among the leaves. After a moment, she asked her sister, "Do you really want to know the answer to that?"

From the corner of her eye, Max saw her sister open her mouth . . . close it . . . open it again . . .

Finally, Charlie returned her gaze to the tree. "Not really."

They stood there like that for quite a bit until a male head suddenly appeared between them. "What are we staring at?"

Max had scented the kid coming. Felt his light footsteps coming through the floor. Heard the way he rubbed his nose sometimes instead of twitching it like a normal jackal. So when he put himself between her and Charlie, Max wasn't bothered or surprised.

Charlie, however . . .

"Jesus Christ, Kyle!" she practically screamed, her entire body leaping backward so that she slammed into the oven. *"What the fuck, man?"*

Kyle Jean-Louis Parker blinked a few times as he stared at Charlie.

"Sorry you're so unobservant . . . ?"

"Don't be a smart-ass." Charlie brushed her jeans off for no reason Max could see, then did that thing she did when she was startled. Barking at the person who'd scared her just like a dog startled from its sleep. "And where the fuck have you been?

You've been gone for days. For all we knew, you could have been dead!"

"Would you have cared?" Kyle wisely asked.

"That's not the point!"

"I was with my family. Not on purpose, my mother made me."

Kyle was one of the Jean-Louis Parkers. A family of jackals headed by a former child-genius mother who'd given birth to a whole litter of geniuses. For some it was math, science, and language. For others it was art, music, and dance. Only one was born "normal" like her father, but Toni Jean-Louis Parker was the true matriarch of the whole troop while the actual mother played violin for monarchs and prime ministers all around the world.

Kyle was only seventeen at the moment but he tended to irritate his family as much as his family irritated him. Maybe more. So he'd moved into one of the MacKilligans' rooms and paid a very nice rent. It helped that he and Stevie were close friends, each of them understanding the other as only a former child prodigy could.

For most kids his age, being in a house with twenty-something women who barely paid him any attention would be a chance to drink, do drugs, and get laid. But this was Kyle. He'd turned their garage into an art studio and spent hours in there . . . working on his art. No drinking, no drugging, no anything. Except, on occasion, being annoying.

Charlie blinked. "Why are you holding a sledgehammer?" she asked.

"I'm going to destroy my shitty art and start over."

Max gasped. "Awesome! Can I help?"

"Of course!"

"No!" Charlie snapped. "No, no, no, no, no! You're not doing that."

"Why not?" Kyle asked, his voice calm. "I am unhappy with my work—why keep it around? So I can have evidence of my failure?"

"He has a point, Charlie."

Charlie aimed a warning finger at Max. She didn't even have to say the words *Shut the fuck up.* She said it with her glare and that finger. That terrifying forefinger.

"Kyle," Charlie said, keeping her voice calm, "I know what Shen's sister said about your art the other day really upset you, but that doesn't mean you should destroy your work. That doesn't make sense to me. And it definitely won't make sense to your sister Toni."

"Toni has no say when it comes to my work."

"Well, I under—"

"And neither do you. It's my work; I can do what I want with it. And I'm going to destroy it. Now if you'll excuse me."

Max winced. The poor kid. He didn't know what he was dealing with, did he? He was dealing with the same woman who had successfully managed Max and Stevie.

Yeah. Poor kid.

Kyle started toward the back door but Charlie grabbed the head of the sledgehammer that was resting on his shoulder. When she yanked it, she dragged the kid back with it. He tried to keep his grip on it, but Charlie wasn't going for that either. With two good pulls, she took it from his hand.

"Give that back to me," Kyle ordered.

While staring Kyle in the eyes, Charlie held the wooden handle in one hand and the head in the other. Then, with little effort at all, she ripped the head off and dropped it to the floor.

Kyle briefly chewed the inside of his mouth before asking, "Is that supposed to intimidate me?"

Charlie placed the ragged part of the broken wooden handle against Kyle's throat.

"Now listen up, kid. I'm happy to have you here. You pay your rent, you're surprisingly quiet, and you have no friends, so I never have to throw any of them out. But if you think you're going to do something radical to your work, which will force me to deal with that psychotic sister of yours, you've lost your mind. You want to destroy your shit, you take it back to your parents' place first and do it there. While you live here, you pretend everything you have in our garage was made by Michelangelo himself and is *priceless*. Do you understand?"

Kyle cleared his throat. "I've always found Michelangelo overrated."

Charlie pulled the broken handle away from Kyle's neck, her hand gripping it in the center. With her gaze still locked on poor Kyle, she used that single hand to break the wood with what seemed to be very little effort. Because, for Charlie, it *was* little effort. Stevie had always reasoned that all the energy Charlie would have used for shifting instead seemed to go into muscle strength.

"Okay." Max grabbed Kyle by his shoulders and steered him out of the kitchen. "Don't forget the honey buns," she called back to her sister before stopping at the stairs.

"Your sister is terrifying," Kyle admitted in a whisper.

"She is. But no one wants to go toe-to-toe with *your* sister either. So don't do anything that's going to piss them both off. For all our sakes."

"But my work sucks."

"Because Shen's sister says so? Who is she anyway?"

"She is *art*."

"I don't know shit about art, Kyle. I don't care about art. The closest thing I ever had to art was my boy-band poster collection in junior high."

"Not sure that's something I'd brag about."

"I thought it was awesome."

"You do know there are amazing singers and bands and artists that are"—he waved his hand in her direction—"you know . . . Asian . . . right? Music based on the culture of your people that you can really be proud of as opposed to"—he cleared his throat again—"boy bands."

"What's wrong with boy bands?"

Kyle gave a quick shake of his head. "Forget it."

"Look, I can't help you with this problem you have. Mostly because I don't care. But I also can't afford for my big sister to be annoyed by you right now. And I also don't want to *deal* with you. It's nothing personal."

"No. I get it."

"So I'm going to pass this shit off." She turned her head and yelled up the stairs, "Stevie! Kyle wants to destroy all the fancy art he has in the garage!"

"*Oh, for fuck's sake!*" Stevie yelled back.

Max nodded. "There you go," she said to Kyle, patting his shoulder. "Now you can deal with her. Honestly, you'll be better off in the long run. Because if you keep talking to me, I'll just bury you alive. Literally. I will *literally* bury you alive."

"I have to say, Max, I enjoy your directness."

Max snorted. "Yeahhhhh . . . I'm pretty sure you're the only one. See how unique you are, Kyle? Like Mozart or John Carpenter."

"John Carpenter? The movie director?"

"The *brilliant* horror movie director."

"Wow." His eyes blinked wide. "Mozart and Carpenter in the same sentence . . . okay."

It was as if they were debating on the works of Truman Capote and Gore Vidal. But they weren't. They were debating about phones.

Phones!

For the last hour Max had discussed every phone in the goddamn store with some teen kid who seemed way too young to be legally able to sell anything. This intense, deep, ridiculous conversation on phones.

Zé didn't understand it. He just wanted to get a phone. Any phone that could make calls and receive calls.

He just wanted a phone!

"Now tell me about this one," Max said, pointing at another phone that looked just like all the other phones they'd looked at. Sizes might be different but that was it! *That was it!*

Zé grabbed a phone that he thought wasn't too expensive but also wasn't ridiculously large. He dropped it on the counter.

"This one."

"Wait. We still haven't looked at—"

Zé slammed his hand on the counter, making all the people in the store jump. All except Max, who only smirked at him.

"This. One."

"Yeah, let's go with that one," she said to the teen.

As the kid went through all the steps necessary to get the phone set up for him, Zé glanced down at Max standing next to him. She was just standing there, not speaking. She didn't seem upset or hurt or annoyed or anything. She was smiling but he'd already learned that smile told him absolutely nothing. So he asked.

"Have you just been fucking with me for the last hour?"

When she burst into a round of snorted giggles, bending over at the waist, Zé rolled his eyes and tried to say, "Not cool." But what came out was . . . a growl. A low, rumbling one that came from deep in his gut and worked its way up and out of his throat.

It startled him and the poor kid but just made Max laugh harder, which he did not appreciate.

"Would you like a cover for the back of your phone?" the kid asked.

Annoyed the kid was still bothering him with bullshit, Zé snapped, "Just pick one."

The kid went around the counter, grabbed the first thing he found, and rang up the sale. He took the new phone out of the box and put the case on it. He told Zé what his new number was and gave him the phone while pushing the box with the charger toward Max.

They went out of the store and onto the street. Zé stopped and stared at his phone.

"What's wrong?"

"I don't remember Kamatsu's number." He shrugged. "It was in my phone."

Zé rested the top of his phone against his chin, trying to remember which of the phone numbers in his brain belonged to his team leader.

When Max started laughing again, he glared at her. "What now?"

"Unicorn," she gasped out.

"What?"

She took the phone from his hand and turned it around. The color of the case the kid had picked out for him was bright pink glitter, which Zé had noticed but not cared about. But the white unicorn with rainbow-colored wings that decorated the back was too much for him. Just too much.

"Goddammit," he snarled, snatching the phone from Max and returning to the store to scare the kid into changing it for a simple black protective case. He didn't have to try too hard to scare the kid. Apparently just staring at him did the trick. The whole exchange took only about three minutes but when Zé got back outside, Max had been slammed over the hood of a cop car and her wrists zip-tied.

"What the hell's going on?" he demanded, not really thinking about the fact he was mouthing off to cops.

A big, blond, uniformed male pulled Max off the car.

"Out of the way, house cat," the blond ordered as he pushed past Zé.

"Whatever you do," Max told him before she was unceremoniously shoved into the back of a police van, "do *not* tell Charlie. Understand?"

Of course he understood . . . but he wasn't going to listen.

There was just one problem: he didn't have anyone's phone number or any money. He'd been planning to get all that together back at the house when he had access to Max's computer.

Zé looked up at the corner street sign, and that's when he remembered where they'd planned to go *after* they left the phone store.

Nelle was in the middle of a wonderful massage while her teammates got mani-pedis when the front door was battered open and cops came charging in with weapons out.

The full-human women giving them the in-home spa day

screamed and dropped to the ground, most of them sobbing in fear.

But Nelle and her girls . . . well, they were honey badgers. They weren't hard to startle but they were hard to scare.

Big NYPD lions and bears grabbed each of them and as they zip-tied their wrists in front, one of them warned, "We're being nice here, badger. Don't make us regret it." Female cops got Nelle clothing from her room and let her put it on since she'd been naked under the sheet while getting her massage.

"What are the charges?" she asked, ignoring the laughter of her bitch sister from the other room.

The grizzly holding her didn't answer, just pulled her out of the apartment. But Nelle could still hear her sister from inside, cheering, "*This is the best day ever!*"

The bitch.

Mads was glad she'd only agreed to the manicure. Her teammates didn't have on shoes, and the thought of walking around without shoes in fucking New York City made her skin crawl. Honey badgers might be hard to kill but diseases were different from a knife or a gun. Diseases were worse than any serial murderer when it came to killing shifters.

As they were removed from the building, none of her teammates seemed to show any concern. But Mads was concerned. Because she was worried this was her fault. She hadn't gone to her family's heist despite the multiple calls and texts that had hit her phone the night before. But maybe the cops thought they could get to her family through Mads and her friends.

The thought made her sick to her stomach.

Her teammates had always been tolerant of the hyena side of Mads's family. Tolerating the rudeness, the mocking laughter, and the inappropriate "man moves" of her male cousins. But if they were all being dragged to a police station because of her family, Mads wasn't going to do what she usually did when her family got out of hand: walk away and ignore it. Nope. Not this time.

The cops opened up the van doors and began to put each of her teammates inside. But just when it was her turn, she saw Zé run around the corner. He had not yet noticed her. Glancing back and forth between the Siberian tiger male on one side and the black bear on the other, she decided to risk it, and let out one of the whooping calls that came from the hyena side of her family. A communication skill only her teammates knew about because it would weird out other shifters, who already hated hybrids on principle.

The full-humans walking down the street looked around— and up . . . which was just weird—in confusion at the sounds they heard, but Vargas immediately stopped running and those bright green eyes locked on her and the NYPD van.

He ran toward them but the tiger lifted her up and threw her into the van. They slammed the doors closed and locked them, but they hadn't bothered to secure Mads or the others to their seats since there were two grizzlies and three lions in the van with them, confident that so many trained apex predators could eventually dismantle four honey badgers.

But, as a team, Mads and her friends had been playing against bears and cats for years, often communicating with nothing more than a look or a hiss. Using that look, Mads sent her teammates into immediate action.

Streep stood up, her eyes rolling into the back of her head, and dead-dropped right there on the van floor. For added drama, she began convulsing.

Nelle and Tock dropped to the ground beside her.

"Help!" Nelle called out. "Help her! Dear God! Someone please help her!"

One of the grizzles glanced down at Streep. "She'll live," he muttered.

Streep immediately sat up. "I'll *live*?"

"Look at you. You're already better."

Insulted—Streep had really been putting her all into that seizure—she snarled, "Shoes."

Nelle raised a brow. "Shoes?" They hadn't used that code

word since the last high school party they'd attended with the football team.

"Shoes!"

"Okay, okay. Shoes."

Streep and Nelle looked at Tock and, after a second, she sighed and agreed, "All right. Shoes."

Nelle, Tock, and Streep immediately launched themselves on the cops.

They weren't trying to kill anyone, sticking with general punching and hair pulling. Shifters or no, these were cops after all. Instead, their goal was distraction, allowing Mads to return to the back doors, unleash her claws, and tear a healthy rip into the metal. Using her hands to bend the metal back, she opened up a hole big enough to stick her head through so she could yell at Zé, "Chicken legs!"

"What?" he yelled back, running after the van now that it had pulled out into traffic.

"Chicken legs! One word! Three *Z*s and three fours. Two exclamation points! And an asterisk!"

Strong hands grabbed Mads by the shoulders and yanked her back into the van.

At that point, they were all secured to the benches and one of their NYPD captors snarled, "I told you not to make us regret being nice."

Nelle gave her sweetest smile and a shrug. "Oops."

When the cops stopped glaring at them, Nelle softly asked Mads, "What were you yelling?"

"The password. For my phone."

"What the fuck for?"

"So he could get into my phone. It's still in your apartment."

"Who are you expecting him to call?"

"Max."

"He was with Max. She texted me and said they'd be coming over after he got his phone so we could all have lunch together. Did you see her with him?"

Mads shook her head. "No. He was alone." Which meant only one thing: Max had been picked up, too.

"Well, he can still call someone who can help us," Mads insisted. "At the very least get us some bail money."

"The only people he knows aside from us are MacKilligans. You know what that means."

"I only have Stevie's number in my phone."

"But Stevie panics, and when she panics . . ."

All four of them blew out breaths while Mads desperately hoped that Zé never found her phone.

Stevie rushed into the kitchen, where the lingering scent of honey buns still filled the air. She had to get into the city for a meeting with the ballet company and Kyle's sister, Oriana. A ballerina prodigy, Oriana was about to get her chance at a lead role in a ballet with music written by Stevie. Something that Stevie had offered just to help Oriana out; it had never occurred to her that it was as big a deal as it was turning into. She'd already gotten calls from major media outlets asking about her "return to music."

They were all acting as if Stevie was giving up her scientific work but she hadn't. In fact, she was taking over the lab of her ex-boyfriend's brother, who had kidnapped her and tried to remove her ability to shift. He'd "disapproved" of hybrids and, in his mind, Stevie represented the potential horror of what a hybrid could be. As if it was her fault that when she shifted into her animal form she became a tiger-striped honey badger that weighed more than two tons. "More than two tons" since she'd recently discovered she'd put on weight, which wouldn't normally bother her except that she'd also noticed her shifted form had gotten bigger, too . . .

That was starting to freak her out. But instead of focusing on something she definitely had no control over, she decided to focus on her new lab and the ballet. Two very positive things! Her life was currently full of positive things! She was in love with the sweetest panda ever—and, oh, my God! He loved her back—her music was flowing out of her the way it used to when she worked on it daily as a kid, and going through the files she'd found in the lab had been fascinating. As well as terrifying. Her predecessor had been brilliant but he'd also been a sick motherfucker. That's why she didn't feel guilty for biting him in half.

Her phone rang and she pulled it out of the back of her jeans pocket. She looked down at the screen and frowned at seeing Mads's name.

"That's weird," she muttered, about to answer the call. But then . . .

"Stevie? Is that you?"

Stevie turned and saw a honey badger female standing near her back door. A honey badger she didn't know. With a panicked scream, she flipped herself up and caught hold of the ceiling with her claws.

The honey badger gazed up at her. "Huh. Max never told me you could do that."

Stevie blinked, retracted her fangs. She might not recognize the face but the voice . . . she'd heard that voice a few times through Max's cell phone.

"Renny?"

"Hi, sweetheart."

Stevie now retracted her claws and easily landed on the ground. "Renny? Is that you?"

"I know. A little older. My ass is a little bigger. But it's me."

Stevie threw her arms around Renny and hugged her.

"I'm so happy to see you! Have you seen Max yet?"

"No. Not yet. I was hoping she'd be here."

"She went out, but she'll be back later." Stevie stepped away from Max's mother. "They let you out early? That's wonderful! I thought you had a few more years to go."

One side of Renny's mouth curled up and Stevie saw her sister in that smirk. Then she knew. She knew!

"Oh, Renny . . . you escaped, didn't you?"

Renny shrugged. "I had to get rid of Devon. He was a threat to my baby."

"I understand that but . . . I mean . . . wait . . . you've already killed someone? How long have you been out?"

"A few days."

Stevie pressed her fingers to her temples and tried, very hard, to remain calm.

"Renny, you can't stay here."

"I'm not leaving until I see my baby."

"Your *baby* is a grown woman who could go to prison for harboring a fugitive. Which you are. You're a fugitive and I'm not letting my sister go to prison for you."

"Sweetie, I get it. I'm not trying to cause a problem for any of you guys, but—"

"And if Charlie finds you here . . ."

"Charlie loves me."

"Wow . . . you *have* been gone for a very long time."

Stevie heard the front door open and her sister and Shen coming into the house. Shen had gone with Charlie to help deliver all those damn honey buns.

Her sister was heading down the hallway toward the kitchen so Stevie did the only thing she could think of: she shoved Max's mother down the stairs that led to the back door.

A few seconds later, Charlie walked in with empty foil containers.

"Hey," she said, tossing the containers into the sink. "Everything okay?"

"Ummm . . ."

Charlie faced her. "Okay, what's wrong?"

"Nothing," Stevie lied, wondering how she was going to tell her overprotective sister that there was a fugitive in their house. But before she had time to say anything, her phone rang. It was Mads again.

"Stevie—"

"Sorry. I have to get this." She answered the phone but was shocked to hear Zé's voice on the other end.

"Wait. Slow down, Zé. What's happened?"

Shen entered the kitchen, and what she was hearing from Zé must have shown on her face because her boyfriend stopped in the doorway and asked, "What's wrong?"

She held up a finger so she could hear the rest of what Zé had to say.

"Okay," she finally replied. "Give me your new phone number and I'll set up an account under it. I'll send you some cash so you can get a car and meet us there."

She frowned and repeated, "Max doesn't want you to tell Charlie?"

Stevie lifted her gaze. Her sister stood right in front of her, only a few inches away.

"Oh. Uhhhh . . ."

Charlie took the phone. "What's going on?" When Charlie apparently didn't hear anything, she said, "Zé, don't make me angry."

Stevie moved her position a bit, hoping that Charlie hadn't spotted Max's mother. Of course, there was always the risk that Renny might just come out of that little staircase to say "hey." The She-badger didn't seem to understand boundaries.

Charlie reached into one of the cabinet drawers and pulled out a notepad and pen. She jotted down the number Zé gave her and handed it to Stevie.

"Okay. Yes. We know where that is. I don't care that she didn't want you to tell me, Zé. I'll handle this."

Charlie disconnected the call and handed the phone back to Stevie. "Send him money and a car, but bring him back here." From the table, she picked up her small backpack, which held her wallet, phone, and a .45 Glock. Stevie grabbed the bag and wouldn't let go until Charlie gave her the gun. Of course, Charlie probably had a gun holstered to both her legs but at least they wouldn't be easy to get to.

"I'll go with you," Stevie said.

"No. You and Shen stay here."

"But, Charlie—"

"I will handle this."

Nope. Stevie didn't like the sound of that at all.

"Charlie, promise me you won't kill anyone." When her sister's response was to give a cold laugh, Stevie stepped closer and insisted, "I mean it. Do not kill anyone. Not over this. You have to promise."

"I warned them—"

"I know. But now they've involved cops. You can get away with a lot, but you can't get away with killing cops. And besides, it wouldn't be right. So promise me." Charlie's jaw clenched because she didn't want to promise that, but Stevie wasn't backing down. "Promise me or I start screaming."

Still Charlie didn't answer so Stevie stomped her foot and roared, shaking the windows throughout the entire house.

"Okay, okay!" Charlie barked. "I won't kill anyone. Today."

Hell, that was more than Stevie had actually hoped for, but she didn't hug her sister, simply said, "Cool."

Charlie stormed out and Stevie waited until the front door slammed shut before letting out the breath she'd been holding in.

"Why do I smell strange honey badger?" Shen asked, plopping a bag of bamboo onto the table.

Dusting herself off, Max's mother returned from her spot near the back door. Stevie swept her hand toward her and said, "Shen . . . this is Renny, Max's mom. Renny, this is my boyfriend, Shen."

"Wow!" he said happily. "Max's mom! It's so nice to . . . wait . . ." His happiness quickly faded. "Aren't you in prison? For, like, another five or ten years?"

When Stevie silently folded her arms over her chest and Renny just smiled that smile that told everyone she was Max's mom, Shen simply faced forward, grabbed a bamboo stalk, and began eating.

Considering the current situation, it was the safest thing he could do.

chapter FOURTEEN

Max looked around the conference room of the NYPD shifter division. She was surrounded by crystal-clear reinforced glass, so she could see everything going on. At one point, she looked into the office next door. Inside were a woman and two males she didn't recognize, and Dee-Ann Smith. Her absolute favorite wolf to torture!

As soon as their eyes locked, Max put on her biggest grin and happily waved at Dee-Ann with her zip-tied hands.

The men and woman laughed as Dee-Ann snarled and looked away from her.

Yup. Her favorite person to torture!

Before she could lower her bound hands, one of the cops grabbed them.

"These were behind your back."

"Were they?" she asked.

He released her and snarled, "Fucking badgers." Then he stormed away, leaving her alone.

About thirty minutes later, Max was shocked to see her teammates dragged in. Why were they here? They hadn't done anything.

Each of them was led to a chair and pushed into it by a much bigger uniformed shifter. Then the cops left and a new team came in. They were all dressed casually in jeans and T-shirts, each with a single holstered firearm, but none of them had badges, so they weren't detectives Max would expect. She was always interrogated by detectives—at least in major American cities. In other countries, it varied.

After the five of them were seated and the very large, unidentified shifters were comfortably situated around the room . . . nothing. For at least forty-five minutes. Max wasn't exactly shocked, though. It was an interrogation move. Keep the perp waiting in the hopes that he or she would get worked up and reveal all when the cops entered the room. Although the police outside the room, the ones Max could see through the glass, didn't seem the least bit interested in them. When a few did notice, they just appeared confused by what was going on. Probably because the NYPD had other rooms that were used specifically for interrogation. So why were she and her team here? In this big glass room? And who were their guards? Max didn't recognize any of them.

Eventually, while Max was wondering if she could jump out the window and fly—she wasn't planning on doing that, but she did enjoy wondering what it was like to fly—three males entered the room along with a black woman who looked familiar to her.

"Hello, ladies," the lion male said. "I'm Benjamin."

"Benji!"

The lion smirked before correcting Streep. "Benjamin." He gestured to a grizzly. "This is Oliver." Then pointed at the shifter beside him, whose animal scent Max didn't recognize. "And this is Bryan."

"Benji, Ollie, and Bri!" Streep cheered.

The three men glared at her but the lion quickly continued. "Anyway, I know you're wondering why you all have been brought here and—"

Tock pointed at the black woman, who was now quietly sitting in a corner, drinking from a large travel cup. "Who's that?"

"That's Imani. She's here to observe."

"Why didn't you introduce her? Are you dismissing her very presence because she's a woman?"

Uh-oh. Tock was putting on what the entire team called her "Feminist Warrior Wear—trademark pending."

Unfortunately, Tock always seemed to aim her anger-spears at the wrong targets.

"Can I go on?" Benji asked.

Poor kid. He'd only spent three minutes around them and already he was annoyed. Imani, however, seemed to be thoroughly enjoying herself.

Max remembered her now. She lived a few streets over, in lion territory. She'd been there when Max was trying to protect Zé.

"Please," Nelle said, flashing her award-winning smile and ingrained old-money politeness. "Go on."

"As I was saying," Benji began, "I know you're all wondering what you're doing here and—"

"Ohhhh, shit," Mads breathed out, cutting the cat off, and Max saw the color drain from her teammate's face.

As one, they all looked at the front of the room through the glass and Max immediately realized that things had just gone to shit.

Dez watched Smitty pull back a bit.

"Do y'all see that?" Smitty said in his Tennessean drawl. "Don't think I've ever seen a honey badger show fear."

"Who is that?" Mace asked, enjoying the bag of popcorn he'd brought with him. Dez had invited him and his best friend, Smitty, because she sensed there would be drama and her hubby, lion male that he was, did love drama that he was not involved in. Smitty had also brought along his cousin Dee-Ann, but unlike the boys, she saw the woman standing outside the conference room and instantly shook her head, pulling out her phone.

"Who are you calling?" Smitty asked.

"Everybody," she muttered.

An answer that Dez found particularly disturbing.

★   ★   ★

Apparently Zé hadn't understood her command *not* to call her sister. Because here Charlie was, gazing at them with a completely blank expression on her face from outside the room.

Benji stupidly motioned her in with a twitch of his hand and Charlie slowly entered. She didn't speak, just looked at everything. Sizing it up, figuring it out, judging and preparing.

"You must be the big sister, huh?" Benji asked. "I've heard a lot about you. I'm Benjamin and—"

"Oh, my God!" Tock suddenly snapped. "Just get on with it! You are taking way too much time with this."

"Fine." Benji motioned for Charlie to take a seat but she just stood there. Still not speaking, that blank expression on her face.

Honestly, Max found that blank expression much more terrifying than Charlie's obvious-anger face. But that could be because she really hadn't seen that expression before. It was new and Max wasn't crazy about new when it came to her family.

Benji took a moment to let the silence settle before he said, "We want you five to work for us."

"We're not rats," Mads announced. "I won't tell you anything about my family."

Nelle cringed and Max informed her teammate, "That's not what he's talking about."

"It's not?"

"No. So shut the fuck up."

"Your teammate's right, of course. You see, we know how talented you all are and we want to put those talents to work for us."

Nelle smirked. "So you're starting a basketball team?"

"Of course not." He stretched his arm out, hand open, and the grizzly turned over a batch of red folders. "We'd like to utilize your other talents."

"Our other talents?"

"We're not fucking anyone for some spy job."

Max turned in her chair so she could look at her teammate.

"Again, Mads, I don't think that's what he means so maybe *shut up*."

"Again, she's right," Benji said with a smile. "I'm talking about your other skills."

He tossed one of the folders across the table so it landed in front of Tock. "Three months ago, uranium stolen from a Russian lab, the entire event somehow managing to take thirty minutes—precisely."

Another folder landed in front of Nelle. "A year ago, a truck-load of gold bars taken from outside the Vatican."

A folder in front of Streep. "Six months ago, a billionaire—who escaped justice even though he liked his conquests . . . rather young—found with a bullet to the back of his head and his two-hundred-million-dollar impressionist art collection gone."

He stopped and stared at Mads. "Shockingly, I have nothing on you. Either you're really good or . . . very boring."

"That's just rude," Tock muttered.

"But your family," he said. "Now that is some fascinating shit. But we didn't have space for the number of folders we'd have to use."

Benji moved around the table until he stood behind Max. Now he slowly leaned around her and placed a thick red folder on the table in front of her.

"Then there's you, Miss MacKilligan." He stood straight and patted her shoulder. "And then there's you."

He began to pace around the room. "I mean, where do I start? The diamond heist in Uruguay? The missing Gutenberg Bible from Paris? Or the tapestries stolen from the Vatican Gallery of Tapestries? That's a good one, too. Happened in the middle of the day with a full crowd of tourists mulling around, waiting for the pope to arrive for a visit. Now that, ladies, is skill."

Max focused her gaze on the unopened folder. She couldn't look at her sister because she knew Charlie wouldn't be happy. In fact, she might hate her. Charlie had tried so hard to keep both Max and Stevie out of trouble and away from a "typical MacKilligan career."

She knew Charlie wouldn't just be disappointed in her, but ashamed, and that was something Max couldn't deal with. Because the only other person Charlie was ashamed of was their father and Max never wanted either of her sisters to see her that way.

"What is the point of this?" Mads asked, the only one among them who seemed to have found legal ways to occupy her time between basketball games.

"You work with us, none of this ever gets out."

Mads sat up a little straighter. "And if we don't work with you? Then what?"

"Sweetie . . . what do you think? We have enough evidence to put you all away for a very long time. Well"—he glanced at Mads—"maybe not you, but all your family. And not just here in the States, but in places where you don't want to go to prison." He leaned down so his head was right by Max's. "Just ask your mom about that."

Wow. He'd gone there. Had gone there hard. And her friends were none too happy about it either. The four of them jumped up from the table—despite their bound hands—and started yelling at Benji. The guards he had with him immediately rested their hands on their holstered weapons. And the cops outside the glass had finally found something interesting to watch in this conference room.

Only Max stayed in her seat because . . . because . . . did it matter? Any of it? Now that her sister knew the truth. Now that she knew everything, would Charlie ever forgive her? Or just push Max out of their lives as she'd done to their father?

Max couldn't even think about it. It was too horrible for her to even . . .

It was instinctual, the way Max shoved herself and the chair she was sitting in back and out of the way. Because she didn't hear anything. See anything. She simply sensed a change in the air around them as Charlie launched herself across the table and directly into Benji. She didn't take him to the ground, though. Instead, she forced him into the wall that was a solid fifty feet behind him.

Benji laughed and grabbed her upper arms, pushing her back. "I heard you'd be the problem here. The Group, Katzenhaus, BPC . . . they may all be scared of you. But I'm not, freak. Now get her out of my sight," he ordered his team.

A male grizzly grabbed Charlie's left arm and a She-grizzly grabbed her right; together they led her back toward the door.

"Now," Benji continued on, "where were we?"

Charlie stopped halfway across the room, pulled her arms free, and spun around to face Benji again.

"What?" Benji asked. "What are you going to say, Miss MacKilligan, that I could possibly give a fuck about?"

It seemed that Charlie was trying to say something. She kept opening her mouth to speak but nothing was coming out. Max had never seen her like this. Charlie almost *always* had something to say. Usually something precise, brutal, and definitely threatening. Yet this time . . . she kept trying but there was nothing. Not a word.

Fed up, Benji simply flicked his hand toward Charlie, and the bears again grabbed her arms. This time, instead of leading, they began to drag her from the room. They got a few feet but abruptly stopped again. It took a second, but Max realized that the reason the bears had stopped was because Charlie had stopped.

With her head down and her entire body shaking, she refused to move.

Each bear took an even stronger grip on her arms with both hands and again tried to drag her from the room. It should have been easy. They were grizzlies. Max, herself, was once sent flying about a mile through trees when she'd startled a grizzly female camping in the Alps with her family. But no matter how hard those two pulled, Charlie wasn't moving.

"What the fuck are you two doing?" Benji demanded. "Get her out of here."

"We're *trying*," one of the grizzlies snarled.

When Charlie finally lifted her head, her eyes hadn't shifted

to wolf gold, the way they sometimes did during a firefight or
fistfight. Instead, they were . . . bloodred. Like all the capillar-
ies had broken at the same time.

The muscles in her neck bulged, her shoulders seemed to
extend so that they were even bigger, and her combination
of badger fangs and wolf fangs extended but the canines also
seemed to grow thicker and longer than usual.

Max thought for sure her sister was finally going to shift.
Maybe not into a badger or a wolf, but into something else.
Something amazing.

But no. She didn't shift. God knows, she didn't need to.

Charlie turned her hands so that she could grip the forearms
of the bears holding her and then, with a roar that shook all
that surrounding glass, Charlie lifted her arms—and the bears.
She lifted the motherfucking bears!—and crossed her arms,
sending the grizzlies hurtling in opposite directions.

"Down!" Max screamed to her teammates as a grizzly flew
over them and crashed into the glass walls, nearly shattering
them. The people in the office next door jumped to their feet
in shock.

Weapons were drawn but Benji quickly threw up his hands.
"No! Don't shoot her!"

Because he knew that if he killed Max's sister, the only thing
he'd be doing would be running for the rest of his life. Max
wouldn't stop until she killed him. And if he killed her, her
teammates wouldn't stop until they'd killed him.

Benji and his crew would need to manage Charlie without
killing her and, Max had to admit . . . she couldn't wait for
them to try.

Mace and Smitty both jumped up, ready to move. Both
males were former Navy SEALs and were used to taking action
as soon as there was trouble. That was just the way they were.

"Stop!" Dez yelled before they could go out the door.

Mace gawked at her. "You're not going to do anything?"

Dez went to the door herself, opened it, and ordered her people: "Stand down! Now! You do nothing. Absolutely nothing."

"Dez!"

She faced her husband. "I was told to observe. Nothing more. The kid said he can handle it."

"That kid can't handle shit!"

"Don't get in the middle," Dee-Ann told them.

"You, too?" Smitty asked his cousin.

"I've been up against that one," Dee-Ann said, gesturing toward the older badger sister. "And if you like your body parts still attached *to* your body, don't get your dumbasses in the middle."

Once she'd tossed the bears holding her away, Charlie flexed. And it was terrifying.

Still, Max knew that at least *she* was safe. She always knew she was safe with her sister, no matter how mad she might be at Max. Unfortunately, her teammates didn't have that same sense of security; hands grabbed Max and yanked her down. She managed to bang her head on hard wood and was rubbing it when she found her "afraid of nothing!" badger friends cowering under the conference room table.

"We have to get out of here," Streep desperately whispered. "She'll kill us all!"

"We could burrow out," Nelle said, getting out of her zip ties easily. Actually, they all could have gotten out of their zip ties but that would have just pissed off the cops.

"We might burrow into an actual jail," Tock explained, reminding them that they didn't know the layout of this building.

"Let's go for that office next door," Max suggested, deciding it was best to get her friends out of here. "On my mark, three . . . two . . . one!"

They bolted from under the table as something—something generally human—crashed onto the floor a few feet away from them. Still, they kept moving, with Max shoving them from behind. They scrambled out of the conference room and into the office next door. When Max turned around to slam the door behind her, Imani slipped past her into the office as well.

"Don't mind me," she said as she moved across the room to stand by the only full-human. A Latina woman with a short haircut, a badge around her neck, and a handful of popcorn caught between her fingers.

Max moved to a part of the glass that hadn't been damaged by the grizzly toss and watched her sister.

Charlie was attempting to make her way across the room to get to Benji but all his guards were getting in her way. One swung at her from the front, but she caught his arm and twisted. Max cringed, hearing the splintering of bone. While Charlie was busy with that male, another came up behind her with a gun and hit her in the back of the head. Should have taken her right out. Should have. Didn't.

Still twisting the arm in front of her, Charlie reached back with her free hand and grabbed the hand holding the gun. She tightened that hand into a fist until Max could hear more bones breaking. Charlie snatched the gun from all those broken fingers and swung her arm back, hitting her assailant across the face.

Max got ready to move, terrified Charlie would do what she always did when she got her hands on a gun during a nasty fight. Go for the headshots. But with one hand, Charlie dropped the clip and cleared the chamber. Then she tossed the gun away and started toward Benji again.

The breath Max let out was shaky, but relief flooded every cell. If Charlie started killing people in the middle of a police station—shifter or no—this would end so badly, and Max didn't even want to think about it. So she didn't; instead, she assumed Stevie had asked Charlie not to kill anyone. It wouldn't be the first time she'd asked and probably not the last. So she kept the request for important times like this.

The final group of six guards attacked Charlie at once, throwing her to the ground and surrounding her. She disappeared from sight as the guards swarmed her. Mads immediately put her hand on Max's shoulder. She was afraid Max would run to her sister's rescue.

But that was not her plan. For many reasons.

The guards continued to kick and punch for several long seconds but, eventually, they slowed to a stop and then separated, revealing a hole where Charlie should be. The curious canines practically stuck their heads in that hole while the cats and bears just dipped their fists in to see if it was a true hole.

While they were distracted, a clawed fist came up through the flooring near the door. Seconds later, Charlie crawled out, covered in concrete and wood.

"I feel like we should warn them," Nelle softly suggested, but none of them moved. None of them tapped on the glass or gestured wildly to the angry female sneaking up behind the guards. They didn't do any of that and Charlie went from sneaking to galloping down the length of the conference table. Literally, she *galloped*. On all fours. Still human but, you know, galloping.

By the time one of the She-tigers turned to see what was happening, Charlie had launched herself over the group, directly at a stunned Benji.

The guards scrambled to un-attach her from Benji's head, but now that she had her hands on him, Charlie seemed in no mood to let him go.

She wrapped her left arm around his neck tightly, probably choking him, and fought off the guards with the other. She was mostly just pushing them back until she grabbed one of the chairs that had been abandoned by Max and her teammates.

Lifting it up, Charlie swung it, hitting the guards in their heads or chests. After knocking most out or, at least, to the floor, Charlie pulled Benji to the table, tossed him on it, flat on his back. She wrapped her hand around his throat and proceeded to drag him across the tabletop until she reached the end. He was punching her, but nothing seemed to stop her. She yanked him off the table, put him on his feet, took a step back, and then she kicked him. Right in the chest, sending him exploding through the glass conference room door.

By the time Charlie followed him into the bullpen of cop desks, the lion had crawled across the floor. He was shaking his head, trying to stop himself from passing out, most likely.

Charlie started after him but a roar stopped her.

It was the two who'd come in with Benji earlier. The grizzly was huffing, ready to charge, and the other one . . . the . . . the . . . ? What the fuck was that thing? Was he a wolf? Or a fox? She'd never seen a wolf or fox with such long legs—ridiculously long legs.

Both males had shifted and the grizzly shook his head, his anger setting off the cops in the room. None of them wanted to watch a grizzly mauling.

Charlie faced the males and, without hesitation, began to walk toward them. Another bear, a polar cop with a long white ponytail and a gray-and-black beard that made him look like a criminal biker, tried to grab her. Not to hurt her, though. To stop her from getting hurt. But Charlie just pushed his hand off her arm and, when the grizzly went up on his hind legs and roared, Charlie kicked him right in the nuts. When he bent over from the pain, she grabbed his giant grizzly head with both hands and proceeded to slam it into the polar bear's desk. Again and again and again. When the wolf-fox thing came at her, she finally spoke, growling out a dismissive, "Oh, please!" before she backhanded the wolf-fox into the conference room so she could continue bringing down that grizzly's head on the polar's desk.

Then it came. The sound every human rhapsodized about. You know, all that *Lion King* shit.

Benji's lion roar reverberated across the room and probably outside, confusing people on the street.

Charlie dropped the unconscious bear and faced him.

Benji launched himself toward her, front and back legs stretched out, maw open, fangs flashing—

And Charlie swung her fist—once. It collided with Benji's face and sent the four-hundred-pound cat spiraling across several desks and through a bathroom door.

Charlie stood there a moment, waiting for another attack. But everyone who'd come for her was out cold or still recovering.

Finally, she let out a long breath and turned her head toward the office they were all hiding in. Well . . . "hiding" might not be the right word since the whole fucking room was made of glass.

Charlie strode over to the office and shoved the door open. That's when Max realized that her teammates were hiding behind her. Seriously! Hiding! Honey badgers!

But Charlie didn't notice any of them. Instead, her gaze locked with Dee-Ann Smith of all people.

She pointed a finger. "Your husband and his uncle—"

"Had nothin' to do with this," Dee-Ann quickly said. Usually the woman spoke as slow as molasses but not this time. "None of these people work for the Group, BPC, or Katzenhaus. And they ain't cops. The Van Holtzes kept their promise to you."

"That better be true, Smith. Because I warned them. I warned them all."

"I know. It wasn't us. This was all them."

"Them who?"

Smith shrugged. "Got me. Ain't heard a name yet."

"Fine." Charlie's eyes—which had thankfully returned to their boring brown—lasered over to Max and her hiding teammates. "You five—out. Now."

Max's teammates ran out of the room and Charlie turned, following them. She assumed Max would be right behind them and she was right. She would . . . in one second.

Max walked across the room and immediately Dee-Ann backed up, throwing up her hands. "Woman, do not kiss me again!"

"Awwww, Dee-Ann. What about our love?"

"Get your sister out of here before these cops get real cranky."

Laughing, Max walked out and caught up with her friends and sister at the elevator. Her teammates were huddled together against the wall but Charlie was just standing there, quietly, seething. She was quietly seething.

Max decided to take over. "You guys find a cab when we get downstairs and we'll—"

"No," Charlie said, watching the numbers on the wall that

told her which floor the elevator was currently on. "They're coming with us."

"Why?" Nelle asked, her voice ridiculously shaky.

Slowly, Charlie looked at the four of them over her shoulder and growled out between clenched teeth, "Because I said so."

Max didn't really think much about her sister's statement until she realized that her teammates were silently crying. From fear.

Good Lord! The drama with these idiots.

chapter FIFTEEN

Rina knew she wasn't alone. She was reaching for the light switch when she realized that she could see fine in the dark. Always could. She had to keep reminding herself that she wasn't all that human.

So, instead of waiting for her eyes to "adjust," she simply looked around her cabin and saw them. All of them. Most sitting on chairs or the chaise lounge or the desk, watching her. One of them, however, was holding her sister from behind, a knife to Tina's throat.

"Hello, niece," one of the older ones said. "I'm your aunt. By marriage, but still . . . You can call me auntie. Isn't that nice?"

Rina sat up, but when she started to get out of bed, the one holding her sister pushed the knife into her neck. Not all the way, but just enough to bring blood and a bit of panic.

"Now, now. Let's not forget we're all ladies. Yeah?" her "auntie" said. "We're just here to talk. You up for listening? I was told you two speak English . . . yeah? 'Cause I don't know any Italian and I ain't about to learn now."

"Where are my men?" Rina asked, proving she spoke English.

"Those full-humans?" Her auntie laughed and the women with her joined in. "Yeah . . . they're all dead," she explained, her laugh abruptly ending. "You didn't really think they'd stop us from gettin' on your fine boat here, did ya?"

The woman pulled one leg up, resting her foot on her knee.

She wore thick work boots like a man would. "We'll make this fast, yeah? You see, little girl, this could have been a little skirmish between gods. But then you released the Kraken . . . didn't ya? And now the Kraken's running free."

"What?"

"It's Greek mythology. Thought you two would know that."

"Italian," she reminded them, punching her chest.

"It doesn't matter. You released the Kraken, and now she's going around, terrorizing the villagers."

"I still do not understand—"

"Mairi," another one said. "You let out Mairi."

"Mairi hates us," her auntie explained, "because we didn't dig her out of prison. That's what she wanted. And if it had been almost any of our other kin, we would have done it."

"But Mairi's a right bitch, ain't she, Ma?"

"That she is, my darling girl. Our Mairi's a right bitch. And you two let her out." She studied Rina for a moment. "Do you know why we're here, luv? Do you know how we found out where you are? Because Mairi told us. She wants us to kill you. And we could have, as you see. Poor Mairi, though, she keeps forgetting something about her aunties: Her uncles may be blood . . . but we're just family. Married into this shit, didn't we? We *know* we're dealing with a right bitch and we don't want her back. Because once she's done with you two and those three illegitimate Yanks, she'll be coming for us. She only told us where you two are because she wants"—she waved her hand, gesturing around the cabin—"all this tacky shit. And if she were any one of me other nieces, she could have it. But she's the Kraken and we need her dead."

The auntie stood and walked across the cabin. "So when I heard from her, I stopped and thought: Which is worse? Dealing with you two crazy cows, who blew up me husband and sons, or that psychotic cunt? That's when I knew: I had three choices. One, I could just come here with me girls and kill ya both. Which, I have to admit, crossed me mind. Two, I could do nothing, and let Mairi kill ya when she's done with the Yanks. Or three . . . I could let you know that the Kraken wants you dead. I went with three. And all I gotta say is, you two better get rid of her before she comes back here and gets rid of you."

"We could hide," Rina pointed out. "She will never find us."

"Oh, you think so?" The auntie laughed and shook her head. "All this money you made and not a brain in either of your heads. She's a badger. Finding shit is what we do. The farther underground you go, the easier it is for us to find ya."

"You did not find us."

"We weren't lookin', were we, girls?"

"Nah," all the other women said.

"Do you know why, my Italian princess?"

Rina sighed. "Because we had the Kraken?"

"Exactly. And if we had liked the Kraken, even a little bit, you'd both be dead. Be grateful we don't like her. That being said, she's still family. Her uncles and cousins won't want to kill her. Being loyal to each other is all we got when we have to go up against lions and hyenas and shit. You, however, don't seem to have a problem with all that. So we'll leave it to you."

The auntie nodded at the one holding onto Tina, and Rina's sister was immediately shoved to the ground.

"We've done what we can for ya," the auntie said. "You take care of Mairi and you stay away from ours, and we leave you be. But if you try to come for us again—especially me sons—it'll be the last time anyone outside the family ever sees you. But I can promise you one thing, niece: it won't be over quick for you or your sister. Remember that when you think about fucking with the MacKilligans again."

She raised her hand, made a circular motion with her forefinger. Instantly the other women slipped out into the darkness, disappearing. Not making a sound. Just going. The yacht wasn't even docked. They anchored in open waters. And yet . . . Rina never heard them actually leave.

Tina sat down on the bed next to Rina.

"This," her sister pointed out, again speaking in their language, "has not been working out for us."

Slowly Rina turned her head toward her sister and told her plainly, "Shut the fuck up."

"I am in love with whoever this guy is."

Irene Conridge looked up from the book she was reading. Her former protégé was grinning at the computer screen, entertained by what she was seeing. Of course, Miki Kendrick was entertained by many things. Unlike Irene, who found most things annoying and a distraction to her work.

"So you have the hacker locked down?" Irene asked.

"Nope."

"Then why are you boring me with this conversation?"

Miki glared at her from under all that curly hair. Of course Irene also had curly hair but anytime she brought that up to Miki, she would just grumble, "It's not the same, dude," and they were meant to leave it at that. Of course, Miki was African American, so that could have something to do with it, but Irene didn't let things like race or religion or any of the usual reasons human beings disliked each other affect her life. Instead, she saw people in one of two ways: annoying . . . not annoying. It used to be "stupid . . . smart" but she'd found that there were so many stupid people in the world, she began to run out of people she could allow into her life. Even smart people tended to be stupid and the frustration was more than she could handle. So she'd settled on "annoying . . . not annoying." It worked for her.

"I said one fucking thing," Miki complained, "and it wasn't necessarily to you."

"So you often speak to yourself?"

"Sometimes. I find myself quite interesting."

"That's called delusion, dear."

Irene hid her smile when she saw that middle finger raised in her direction.

"You've been working on this for quite a while," Irene reminded her. "I don't mind your staying in my New York home, but is there any chance you can find the culprit before my daughter gets her second doctorate?"

Miki turned in her chair, resting her arm on the back. "While your middle son has gotten his . . . what was it again? That 'degree' "—she said with air quotes—"at Jiffy Lube?"

"He's taking a gap year, thank you very much. This is just a temporary delay before he—"

"Makes it to a BMW dealership as head mechanic?"

"Engines are hard."

"Are they, though?"

Irene lowered her book, raised an eyebrow. "And how are your two friends doing? The one who dresses like she's expecting Coco Chanel to come visit? And the tall one who knows all about how a bicycle works!"

"It's called a hog," Miki shot back. "And motorcycles like that are part of the American—"

"Criminal underworld?"

"I was going to say landscape."

"Ah."

They glared at each other but they weren't remotely angry. This was just something they liked to do. Ever since Miki had bravely walked into her office at the university and asked if Irene would be her doctoral advisor. Only the bravest students ever did that because most of the students found her "terrifying." And Irene rarely said yes, but there was something about the tiny young woman in cutoff shorts and steel-toed Doc Martens that she'd found interesting. At the time, neither Irene nor Miki knew that one of her best friends was a wolf. Then again, Miki hadn't known that Irene's husband was a wolf as well, although the two wolves were from vastly different Packs.

Now, however, Miki not only had a canine best friend, but a wolf mate of her own, a wolf pup that was turning out to be smarter than Miki and Irene combined—which was a terrifying thought for either of them—and both of them were forced to help shifters survive in an increasingly horrifying world.

These insult-breaks were something they did to keep long periods of work entertaining. No one else understood them, but no one else mattered.

Irene had just returned to her book when her husband, Niles

Van Holtz, stormed into the room. He looked around, walked out again, but returned a minute later with a suitcase.

"Get packed up," he ordered, opening the suitcase. "Both of you. We have to get out of here."

Irene watched her husband begin shoving random things into the suitcase. There was no rhyme or reason to what he was grabbing, but he was canine. She was surprised he didn't just grab a bone and make a run for it.

"Is there a reason we're escaping?" she finally asked when he slammed closed her laptop and shoved it into the suitcase.

"The MacKilligans. The oldest. I'm pretty sure she's coming to kill us all."

"Holtz, perhaps you should calm down and tell me—"

"Why aren't you moving?" he demanded. "Do you want to live without skin?"

At that point, Miki had turned around in her chair again. "Live without skin? What now?"

"Yes! She promised to skin us!"

"You know it's not really that easy to skin a person, right?"

"What?"

"I'm a hunter," Miki explained. "Me and my girls—"

"My girls and I," Irene corrected.

"Stop it. We go hunting all the time. And it's not easy to skin a deer, and they have that thick hide you can pretty much grab and pull. But humans . . ." She lifted her left hand and with her right began to simulate removing human skin. "Our skin is so thin, you've gotta be real careful about removing it. It's not like skinning an orange."

Holtz turned to Irene. "Why are all our full-human friends weird?"

"I didn't major in psychology," Miki said before Irene could reply, "but I'd say you draw weird to you."

"No one asked you, tiny female."

There was a knock at the door and it opened to reveal her cousin-in-law's giant mate filling the doorway. The woman boasted shoulders Irene imagined Neanderthals once had. They were enormous!

"Hey there, cousin!" Dee-Ann greeted Holtz, her Tennessee Titans baseball cap low on her head. Irene often wondered if the She-wolf could see or if she was so canine, she simply sniffed her way around. "Whatcha doin'?"

"We're leaving. Ric told me what happened with those idiots and that psychotic badger. We warned them and they didn't listen. Now I have to evacuate my family from the state."

"*Or* you can calm down," Dee-Ann suggested, "and not worry. Charlie MacKilligan knows it wasn't y'all."

"You do understand 'y'all' is not a word?" Irene once again reminded her.

"I'm supposed to believe," Holtz said, "that the woman who threatened to skin me and my wife in the dark of night if we went near her sisters is rational enough to know we didn't have anything to do with this?"

"Yep."

Holtz looked at Irene and she repeated, "Yep."

"Besides, she made her point," Dee-Ann continued. "Beat those boys and their friends within an inch of their lives, sending a very clear message."

Holtz shook his head. "They're lucky she didn't kill any of them."

"That was not luck, cousin."

"Stop calling me cousin. I am *not* your cousin."

"What she did was very precise. She knew exactly how much strength to use to do the most damage without killing her prey. That's the mark of a real killer."

"And you know that because . . . ?"

"How do you think?" Dee-Ann smiled. "My daddy taught me well."

Miki snorted as she tapped away at her keyboard. "Anyone else hear banjos playing anytime this woman speaks?"

Dee-Ann's wolflike gaze immediately locked on Irene's protégé. "Well, ain't you the cutest, tiniest, little full-human I ever did see? I could eat you *right* up."

"I guess we're done here," Holtz said quickly, trying to escort Dee-Ann out the door.

But Miki Kendrick had been around wolf packs all her life and, just in general, was a difficult woman to terrorize.

So she laughed and shot back, "Bitch, I'm a black woman from the wilds of Texas. Trust me when I say I can have your wolf ass hunted, stuffed, mounted, and displayed in my living room before the day's over."

"This has been fun!" Holtz interjected into the following silence before he shoved Dee-Ann out into the hallway and left Irene and Miki to their work.

chapter SIXTEEN

The drive back to Queens in a limo ordered by Nelle was so silent that Max was sure her teammates were going to burrow out of the vehicle at one of the red-light stops. Because every time Charlie crossed her legs, every time she let out a loud breath, practically every time she blinked, the others jumped.

It was like they were expecting her to beat them to death right there in the car. But Max knew she wasn't mad at them. Charlie was mad at *her*. Because she knew exactly how Max had made her money over the years. The things she'd done. The people she'd ripped off. Yeah, she liked to pretend she was sort of being Robin Hood. At least in the sense that she only ripped off people or organizations that she knew had the insurance and money to handle the loss.

But did it matter? She was still a thief. Just like the MacKilligans and the Yangs.

Max hadn't known about her teammates, though. Not once had any of them discussed what illegal jobs they had done or were doing, aside from Mads occasionally asking for their help when she needed to get out from under her hyena family's claws.

The limo pulled to a stop in front of their house and Charlie got out.

"Everyone in the house. Now."

Max waited for the others to start moving but they just sat there, staring at one another. Terrified.

"Oh, my God. Would you guys just go!"

With sighs and grumbles, they got out of the limo and tromped into the gated yard.

Charlie was about to go up the stoop stairs when she heard Berg call to her from his house across the street. "Get inside," she ordered the women. "I'll be back in a second."

She headed across the street to her boyfriend and Max jogged up the stairs to the front door. But it opened first and Stevie motioned her in with a quick wave of her hand.

"What?"

"Just come on!" she whisper-screamed at her.

Max glanced back at her teammates and, after making sure that Charlie was still talking to Berg, they all hustled into the living room.

"We have a problem," Stevie said. She was no longer whispering, but still kept her voice low.

"What problem?"

She motioned at Max's teammates. "Can they keep their mouths shut?"

"You're kidding, right?" Because seriously.

"Fine." She clasped her hands together and straightened her back. "Your mother was here."

Max stared at her sister. "Whose mother?"

"*Your* mother, dumbass. I told her she had to go, but she wants to see you."

Confused, Max scratched her jaw. "She was *here*? They let her out?"

"No. They didn't let her out."

Later, Max would be ashamed at how long it took her to understand what her sister was telling her. What she was explaining. Especially because it was so obvious.

"Oh, my God. Does Charlie—"

"No, but I don't know what she'll do when she finds out."

"Kill us all," Streep whispered desperately.

Max briefly closed her eyes. "Ignore her," she told her sister.

"You better call her." Stevie handed Max a small notepad with a number on it. "Before she shows up again and Charlie sees her."

"Or," Nelle suddenly suggested, "you could just tell Charlie what's going on."

"Oh, you mean, tell her that every time my mother comes here, we're aiding and abetting a fugitive and might go to prison?"

"I'm sure it's just jail time."

"Thank you, Tock," Stevie replied. "That's very helpful."

"Are you being sarcastic?"

"Very."

The security door opened and Charlie came into the house. She stalked into the living room, stopped, and her gaze moved over all of them.

Max steeled herself for the explosion of rage and disappointment. Ready to shield her friends while accepting all the blame for what had happened. Because it was her fault. All of it. She'd made them all vulnerable.

After a few moments of utter—and painful—silence, Charlie announced, "I'm going to bake cupcakes."

She stalked from the room, leaving them standing there . . . stunned.

"Is that . . . code or something?" Mads asked. "For, like, murdering us?"

"*No*," Max barked. "It means she's going to make cupcakes. My sister doesn't lie or use code when it comes to baking."

"So what do we do?" Streep asked. "Do we make a run for it?"

"My sister has a high prey drive. Making sudden moves will just catch her attention. I suggest we all get comfortable and—"

"Wait for death?" Tock asked.

"I was going to say watch TV, but whatever works for you, sweetie."

"Before you do anything," Stevie said to Max, "you may want to check on the cat."

"Fuck! Did that thing piss in my bed again?"

Stevie crossed her arms over her chest. "Not the cat. *The* cat."

"What weird phonetic shit is that?"

"I'm talking about Zé!"

"Oh! *That* cat!"

"Yes!"

"Don't get that tone! I've got a lot on my mind at the moment."

"He's been really worried about *you*! And he was the only one. The rest of us were just worried about what Charlie was going to do to the cops who arrested you."

"Which was *epicly* terrifying!" Nelle admitted.

Stevie's shoulders sagged. "She promised me she wouldn't kill anyone."

"She didn't kill anyone," Max reassured her.

"That we know of," Tock muttered.

"And she didn't touch one cop." She motioned to her teammates. "Bring Stevie up to speed. I'll be back."

"Where are you going?"

"To find the cat."

"He's in the backyard," Stevie told her.

Max nodded and headed through the living room. But when she reached the dining room, she heard Charlie in the kitchen—slamming bowls.

"Nope," she said to no one in particular. Then she spun on her heel and went out through the front door.

Zé sat on the ground, his back against the trunk of the tree he'd climbed earlier that day. He'd completely forgotten about calling Kamatsu because he'd been sitting in a tree worried about Max and her teammates. He'd wanted to meet Charlie at the station but the car that Stevie had sent for him brought him back to Queens. When he complained, Stevie had said, "I do what Charlie tells me, because she's not going to yell at me."

He assumed she'd meant Charlie would yell at him. Unfortunately, he had no idea which precinct had a "shifter-only division." And since he wasn't about to wander around New York state looking for it—or to ask cops if they had any shifters working in their office—he just stayed at the house and hoped for the best.

"Are you listening to me? Because my next question is very important."

Zé looked up at the kid he'd met about an hour ago. He apparently lived here with Max and her sisters. His name was Kyle. He was a great artist. Brilliant, in fact. A prodigy, like Stevie. And he enjoyed living with the MacKilligan sisters because they didn't bother him. Not like his own family did, because his family didn't understand boundaries.

And Zé knew this because the kid had told him all that and much, much more while he'd been standing there, blathering along as if Zé had done anything to warrant such an attack of annoying-ness.

"So," the kid continued on, "have you ever done any nude modeling?"

"Okay, that's it." Zé got to his feet. "I'm out of here."

He could track Max down later. Because this whole conversation was just weird.

"Are you ashamed of your body? You shouldn't be. It's quite nice."

"You need to stop talking to me."

"Why?"

"Because you're freaking me out. And I don't freak out easy."

"How am I freaking you out?"

"Because you're a teenage boy asking a grown man if he wants to pose nude for him. If I didn't know better, I'd swear you were just a cop attempting to frame me." The kid wanted to debate this but Zé held his hand up to silence him and walked away.

As he moved out from under the tree, he saw Max coming toward him from the front of the house.

He couldn't believe how relieved he was to see her. He wanted to rush up to her but he waited where he was until she reached him.

"You're back."

"I am. You told my sister."

"I did. I called Stevie but she put me on the phone with

Charlie and I don't like lying to her. Of the three of you, she does seem the most rational."

"Most of the time."

"Hi, Max," the kid said, now standing near them.

"Heya, Kyle."

"Zé won't pose nude for me. I think he's worried it will put his sexuality into question. Would you please convince him that he is a very virile heterosexual male and that as a woman, you would love to have sex with him, so he can feel confident in his straightness and see this as the artistic request that it is?"

"Sure!" Max said, nodding and smiling and walking. Walking right over to the back door of the house, opening the screen, and yelling into the house in a singsongy voice, "Charlieeee! Kyle keeps asking Zé to pose nude for him and making the poor guy uncomfortable!"

Charlie's voice, however, was *not* singsongy when she barked, "*Goddammit, Kyle! Stop doing that! Or no cupcakes for you!*"

Kyle blinked and was extremely calm when he asked Max, "Your sister is making cupcakes?"

"Yes, she is."

"Fine. In honor of your sister's cupcakes, I'll let it go. But," he added, "I consider what you just did a hate crime against art."

"Of course you do."

Kyle nodded at Zé. "Zé," he said.

"Child," Zé said back.

Zé watched Kyle walk to the garage and disappear inside, closing the door behind him.

"Why did he go into the garage? I'm worried what that implies."

"Don't. He turned it into an art studio."

"So he really is an artist?"

"Yes. And a very good one. He's also a little nuts."

"Honestly, your entire house is kind of a freak show."

"I know. Isn't it great?" She pointed at Zé. "Did you ever get in touch with your girlfriend?"

"I don't have a girlfriend."

"The Japanese chick. At least I'm assuming she's Japanese."

"You mean Kamatsu? She's not my girlfriend . . . and I completely forgot to track down her number. I need a laptop so I can get to my online storage."

"I'll get you a laptop. You wait here." She looked at the back door but started to go around the house.

"Where are you going?"

"Charlie is anger-baking," she said, stopping by one of the windows that looked out over the side yard. "And the last thing you want to do is walk into the middle of that."

"Why?"

"Because she starts ranting. And when she starts, she doesn't stop . . . for a long time. She has a lot of rage-stamina."

"Do you and Stevie make up a lot of terms that involve your sister doing mundane things and anger?"

"Yes!" she replied. She pushed the window open and snuck her way into her own rental home so that she could avoid her sister . . . baking.

Zé let out a breath. "Utter freak show."

"Hey! Cat!" a voice called out from behind Zé. He looked over his shoulder and saw an obscenely large man across the big yard on the other side of the chain-link fence. He motioned Zé over with several waves of his hand. With nothing else to do and a little curious about what the large man could want, Zé walked across the yard and around an in-ground pool he hadn't noticed before.

"Yes?" he asked when he stood before the large man who had to be at *least* seven feet tall. Freak show!

The man lowered himself and whispered, "Is Charlie baking?"

"Why are you whispering?"

"Shhhhhh! Fucking cat! Just answer the question!"

"Yes. She's baking. Should I alert the media?"

"What's she making?"

Zé remembered what Charlie had threatened Kyle with. "Cupcakes, I believe."

"Cupcakes . . ." And the man said that word as if he was

talking about something sacred. Like the Lost Arc of the Covenant or the Shroud of Turin.

"Thanks, cat," the man said before he jogged away, again moving with an ease that Zé would expect of a shorter, leaner man.

As he stood there, wondering, Max came to stand beside him with a thin laptop in hand.

"What are you doing over here?"

"Talking to what I believe was some freakishly sized bear."

"That's pretty much the entire street, dude. What did he want?"

"To know if your sister was baking."

"What did you tell him?"

"I said she was."

Max's eyes grew wide. "You didn't tell him *what* she's baking, did you?"

"Cupcakes, right?"

"Oh, God. They know about the cupcakes." Her gaze scanned the street. "They know about the cupcakes . . ."

Charlie placed another two trays of cupcakes on the dining table to cool and returned to the kitchen. She reached into the cabinet above the fridge and took out several jars of honey. She placed them on the kitchen table with all the other items she needed to make the cupcakes and the icing.

Wiping her hands on a towel, she walked back into the dining room and stopped, staring at the grizzly who'd opened her window and was stretching his long arm inside, his fingers attempting to reach the cupcake trays.

Placing her hands on her hips, Charlie asked, "Whatcha doin', Lloyd?"

The bear stopped, his gaze locked on the floor, refusing to look up at her.

"Uhhhh . . . nothin'?"

"Is that a statement or a question, Lloyd? Because it sounds like a question. Like you're not sure. Are you not sure what you're doing, Lloyd?"

"He's sorry," his wife said, pulling him away from the window. "He's sorry. We're just going to sit out here and wait until you're done."

"Sit out there?" Charlie walked to the window and leaned out. They were everywhere. Sitting around her yard, in the summer sun, chatting and waiting—for her cupcakes.

Well, now she knew what had happened to the dogs. They usually stayed in the kitchen with her while she baked in the hopes that she'd drop something on the floor. But now she knew they were under her bed.

She reared back from the window. "Stevie!"

Charlie returned to the kitchen and again opened the cabinet above the fridge. The place where Stevie usually hid when bears invaded their house or yard. She was definitely not there, nor had she burrowed a hole into the ceiling of the cabinet so she could escape through the house.

Hearing a laugh, Charlie went to the butcher block by the small window that looked out in the backyard. There was Stevie, chatting with the bears while she sat on Shen's lap. With the panda so close, Stevie wasn't freaked out by the grizzlies and polars—the "man-eaters," as she liked to call them.

Seeing her sister so comfortable and casual around people who used to make Stevie hide in trees made Charlie so damn happy, she didn't think she could stand—

"Hey, Charlie."

Startled by the voice, Charlie drew the .45 she always holstered to the back of her jeans before she'd even turned around . . . to find it pressed against her sister's head.

"*Dammit, Max!*" Charlie quickly removed her finger from the trigger and lowered her weapon. "Don't sneak up on me!"

"You didn't smell me right behind you? Did you not take your allergy meds?"

Charlie returned her gun to her holster and walked to the cabinet where they kept the meds. Charlie's were for allergies and general anxiety. For Stevie, extreme anxiety, occasional depression, and period cramps. There was nothing in there for Max. Charlie wouldn't say her middle sister didn't have any issues that could benefit from a little medication, but they weren't issues Max would admit to.

"What's going on?" Charlie asked after taking a couple pills and then spritzing her prescription nasal spray up her nose.

"So Zé opened his mouth about the cupcakes—"

"Yeah, I saw the invasion in our yard."

"It's quickly turning into a teddy bear picnic. I thought I'd go out and pick up some liquor."

"We're throwing a party?"

"We will be. Berg said he could get everyone else to chip in food and their barbeques so you can just focus on the cupcakes."

"I guess I need to make more cupcakes," Charlie reasoned when she thought about how many bears were in her yard and how many cupcakes they could put away. Of course, if they could offset that with some steaks, hotdogs, and burgers, the cupcake demands would ease a bit. "Could you pick me up some other stuff while you're out?"

"Yeah. Sure."

Charlie opened a drawer, searching it for the little notepad she kept there. "Have you seen my notepad?"

"Oh. Here." Max pulled it out of the back pocket of her cutoff shorts. "Sorry. I forgot I had it."

Charlie took the notepad, grabbed a pen, sat at the kitchen table, and worked up a list of things she wanted her sister to pick up for her. As she worked, she could *feel* Max's gaze on her.

"What, Max?"

"I'm sorry."

" 'Don't mention cupcakes around bears' is not something that's on the list of must-knows for the freshly shifted. Zé will figure it out."

"No. I don't mean that. I mean, everything else. I'm sorry about all that."

"It's not your fault. You have skills any black ops team would kill to harness. It's their own fault they got their asses kicked."

"That's not what I mean either."

Confused, Charlie pulled her attention away from her list. "What are you talking about?"

"About . . . everything I've done. What they were going to use to blackmail me. You know . . ." She looked away, scratched her forehead, shrugged. "That stuff they talked about."

"Oh. That stuff." Charlie went back to her list.

"Yeah. I'm . . . I'm sorry if I disappointed you."

"Disappointed me?"

"Yeah. I have no excuse and I won't try to make any. I just hope I can—"

Charlie leaned back in the chair and gazed up at her sister again. "I'm sorry . . . what are we talking about?"

Max let out a frustrated breath. "You know, the stuff I . . . stole?"

"Yeah. What about it?"

"I guess I'm confused."

"About what?"

"I thought you'd be mad."

"About what?"

"The stuff I stole!"

"Oh." Charlie tore off the sheet with the list and stood. "I knew."

"You knew what?"

"I knew about the stuff you stole."

Max took a step back. "You knew?"

"Of course I knew."

"But you never said anything."

"What was there to say?"

"That you were disappointed in me. That you were disgusted. That you were—"

"Whoa! Whoa! Whoa!" Charlie came around the table. "I would never say any of that to you because I never felt that way. All three of us have done whatever we needed to do to keep us going. The money you brought in kept us solvent, allowed us to watch out for Stevie when she was in countries where we could never afford to go to without funds. Each of those jobs you took and, by the way, knocked out of the fucking park, kept us alive. How could I hate you for that?"

"So you were aware of every job I did?"

"I think so. Unless you snuck some in."

Max moved closer. "And what about you?"

"What about me?"

"What were you doing?"

"When?"

Now Max was inches away, her finger pointing in Charlie's face. "I did all my jobs in the six months I was *not* looking out for Stevie. So when *you* were not looking out for Stevie, what did you do? You know, to keep us *solvent*?"

Charlie handed Max the sheet of paper before going back to her cupcakes. "And make sure you don't forget the flour."

Zé waited by the black SUV Max had pointed out to him before she went into the house to talk to her sister. When she came out the front door, she seemed . . . upset.

"Are you okay?" he asked as she stomped by.

"Get in the car."

"Okay."

She electronically unlocked the doors and he got into the passenger side.

"Is it me or is this vehicle excessively large?"

"It was built for bears," she said, moving the seat up until her chest was practically one with the steering wheel.

"Um . . . maybe I should drive. You know, since my feet can actually *reach* the pedals."

He waited for Max to tell him to go to hell or to just laugh at him, but she didn't do either. Instead, she texted someone on her phone. She got an immediate reply and started the SUV.

"What's going on?"

"I need to make a stop before the stores."

"Okay." She kept gripping the steering wheel, so he asked, "Max, you seem a bit . . . tense. Is everything all right?"

She turned the SUV off and took out the keys. "You're right. You need to drive." She handed him the keys.

Zé held them up. "You could have just kept them in the ignition."

"It's a symbolic gesture!"

chapter SEVENTEEN

The Bugatti pulled to a stop in front of the SUV and Max leaned forward to get a closer look. She couldn't believe that her mother would steal a goddamn Bugatti! Why not steal a yacht? Or a private jet? If someone is going to lose their mind about their car being stolen, it's the guy willing to drop a few million on it!

"Who the hell is that?" Zé asked, but Max was already getting out of the SUV. She was too excited to wait.

As she closed the door, her mother was already throwing herself into Max's arms. They hugged, holding on tight, neither speaking. What was there to say?

Over the years, once Max had been able to travel without her sisters, she'd attempted to see her mother. Many times. But Bulgaria had a tough penal system and her mother was considered a highly dangerous prisoner. So they'd kept in touch with letters and smuggled-in phones.

So this, this very moment, was the first time they'd held each other in years, and it meant everything to Max.

"My beautiful girl," her mother said in that growly voice of hers. According to Yang family lore, her mother hadn't been born with that voice but had gotten it after she and one of her brothers got into a nasty fight and he slammed Renny against a table. He'd been trying to knock her out, but he'd misjudged the distance and her throat took the hit. Which turned out to be very bad for her brother once Renny caught up with him. His arm was successfully reattached once she'd finished hitting him with it, but it never quite worked the same.

Renny stepped back, still holding Max's hands. "Look at you. You look just like me when I was your age." She pointed at Max's chest. "You have better tits, though. Those real?"

"Yes, Ma," Max said, laughing. "They're real."

"Lucky girl. I didn't even bother getting bras, they were so small. Just put some Band-Aids over my nipples, a tank top over that, and out the door I went."

"Ma."

"Sorry, sorry. Just a little jealous." Without moving her gaze from Max, Renny jerked her head in Zé's direction and asked, "Who's the cat?"

"That's Zé Vargas."

"He's cute. You fucking him?"

"Not yet."

"I'm feeling objectified."

"Shhh, pretty kitty," her mother said, ignoring the follow-up hiss. "No one's talking to you."

The music started outside, and Charlie couldn't believe how fast the bears could get a party started. Maybe it was because they didn't need much. A couple of whole cows already butchered, a farm's worth of potatoes and corn to boil and roast, and a few industrial-sized barbeques carried from their nearby homes like they were carrying a six-pack of beers. Get that together and you had yourself a bear party. Apparently her cupcakes would just be a "lovely dessert" as one of the She-bears noted when she passed through the dining room.

The security door at the front of the house opened and closed and Charlie called out, "Did you get the flour? Or did you forget again?"

"If you need flour," said a voice that did not belong to Max, "I can get you flour."

Putting down the bowl she'd had in her hands, Charlie faced the doorway.

"Do I know you?" she asked the woman standing in her kitchen.

"You know, I would say we've met, but we really haven't. We just sort of keep passing each other in the most interesting of ways."

"Oh, yeah?"

"Yeah. You tranq'd someone on my street from, I believe, the roof of this house, and I witnessed you kicking the ass out of some very strong male apex predators."

Okay. Charlie remembered her. She'd been in the conference room, but she hadn't involved herself in any way. She hadn't spoken, hadn't helped the ones attempting to recruit Max and her teammates and, when things really got nasty, she'd gone into the office next door and stayed there.

"Now before you pull that gun you've got behind your back . . ." When Charlie frowned, the female tapped her nose. "I can smell the gun oil. Anyway, before you start doing what you do so well, I have an offer."

"You want my sister to work for you."

"Yes."

"And her teammates."

"Yes."

"By blackmailing them?"

"No. I never would have gone that route, but you know what they say: boys will be boys."

"That's why you didn't do anything. You were letting them fail."

She shrugged. "A She-lion teaches the younger generation by letting them get their asses kicked. Usually the ass-kicking comes from a clan of hyenas but you did a very good job."

Charlie rested her hands on her hips. "So what is this? You're hoping I'll force my sister to work for you? You've got something on me you think you can use to get me to help you?"

"Look, kid, I know you can't be blackmailed. I know you can't be forced. And I fully understand the extent of your dangerous nature." She smirked. "That's why I want to hire you."

"Hire me to do what?"

"To do what you do for your sisters, but this time for others."

"You can hire the Dunn triplets if you want a protection unit. I have other things to—"

"No, no. I don't want you to protect and serve. That's what we have cops for. I want you to do what you do for your sisters: protect and destroy."

They did look alike. The pair of them. The same height. The same face. Even many of the same mannerisms. But there was a difference. The thing that drew Zé to Max was the same thing that made him keep a healthy distance from her mother. He just didn't know what that thing was or why his reaction was so vastly different from one woman to the other.

"I can't believe you stole a Bugatti. Why not just wear a sign that says, 'Hey! I'm a fugitive'?"

"Oh, you're such a little worrier."

"That's the thing, Ma. I'm not."

Max's mother leaned against the Bugatti's door, putting that expensive paint job at risk.

"So why couldn't I come see you at that house you guys are living in?" Renny asked.

"Not sure Charlie would be okay with a fugitive coming to call."

"Must you keep bringing that up?"

"Ma," Max said, grabbing her mother's hands. "I am so glad to see you. You have no idea how glad I am. But I don't want you back in prison. I want you free to live your life. I want you to be happy."

"Happy? Sweetie, we're honey badgers. We're rarely happy. We're bitter and angry. And that's okay. That's what gives us our edge."

"I'm happy."

"You are?"

"I'm almost always happy. I'm happy you're here. I'm happy my sisters have met men that can tolerate them. I'm happy Charlie's making cupcakes tonight. So yeah . . . I'm happy.

Aren't you happy? Now that you're out of prison? Because you should be happy. I want you to be happy."

"Well, I'm not depressed. Among the Yangs that's considered . . . happy-ish. But stop worrying about me. I want you to start thinking about the future."

"The future of what?"

Her mother let out a long, pained sigh. "The future of your life, dumbass. I'm back now. So start thinking. What do you wanna do? Where do you wanna go?" Her brown eyes suddenly lit up. "What do you wanna steal? The whole world is ours for the taking. So let me know where you wanna go from here."

Before Max could say anything—if she was going to say anything—her mother kissed her cheek and hugged her again.

"I'll text you in the next day or two. Okay? You think about what you want and you and me, baby . . . we're on our way."

Her mother gave her one more hug, waved at Zé, got into her Bugatti, and then pulled out in such a way that Zé knew he'd never willingly get in the car with that woman if she were driving.

"Your mother seems nice."

Slowly Max turned to face him, her eyes wide.

"Okay. I'm lying. She doesn't. But she clearly loves you. That must be nice."

"It's great." She nodded. "It's great."

She walked toward the SUV. "Come on. We still have to get stuff for Charlie. And liquor. We need to get lots of liquor."

Zé got into the driver's side and started the engine. "Do you want to talk?"

"I'm not one of those girls," she said, staring out the passenger-side window, "who sits around, endlessly analyzing her feelings. If you want any of that shit, talk to Stevie."

"Okay. Fair enough. So what do you need now?"

She looked at him, stared at him intently. "You know what I need right now?" she said in a husky whisper.

Zé cleared his throat. "What?"

"Ice cream."

"Huh?"

"I need ice cream. Two scoops. Chocolate and honey almond. On a sugar cone." She pointed. "There's a place not far from the house. Just go up this street and take a left."

"If it's ice cream you want . . . then it'll be ice cream you shall have."

Because the bears kept coming in and out of the kitchen, they moved their conversation to the front of the house.

By the time they'd finished and Imani had handed Charlie her business card and told her to "think about it and call me," Max and Zé were double-parking in front of the house.

"Hi!" Max greeted Imani with a big smile as she stepped out of the vehicle. "I remember you. You tried to blackmail me, and my sister kicked the asses of your friends. And despite this, you're here. With me. That seems like a bad idea."

"Max," Charlie said, "it's okay. Let her go."

"You should thank my sister, because she's the one person who can stop me from tearing out your throat."

"Wow." Zé took Max's arm, pulled her away. "Talk about not subtle."

Imani returned to the cat side of town and Charlie returned to the house. But she didn't want to go inside, so she sat on the stoop stairs.

Zé had a few bags of groceries but he stopped before going past the fence and said, "Why are we doing this?" He put the bags down and walked to the far side of the fence.

"Hey! Bears!" he yelled into her yard. "Get over here and take this stuff if you want liquor."

A small herd of bears tromped out of her yard, went to the back of the SUV, and grabbed all the groceries. Zé led them inside by heading around the house. That way Charlie wouldn't have to move from her spot on the stoop. She also noticed that Zé's arms were now empty.

"Typical cat," Charlie joked when Max sat down beside her on the stairs.

"He *is* turning out that way." She motioned in the direction that Imani had taken. "Want me to deal with her?"

"No."

"I don't mind."

Charlie laughed. "That I know." She slipped Imani's business card into her pocket. "So what took you so long getting back?"

"Do you really want to know?"

"Probably not."

Max cut through the house and went out into the backyard. She found her teammates lounging by the pool and the big bears relaxing in the water. She motioned to the girls with a wave of her hand and led them into the garage. Kyle was there, working on sketches, but he had his noise-canceling headphones on and didn't seem to be aware of anything but what was on his giant sketchpad.

"What's going on?" Nelle asked.

"That bitch was here. From earlier today."

"Which bitch?" Tock asked. "There were a lot of bitches in that room. Bitches and bastards. Unless you're specifically talking about the canines. Then the room was also filled with sows and boars and—"

"Please stop," Max begged her teammate. "The older black chick. Who didn't do anything except watch us."

"Ohhhhh," they all said.

"Wait," Nelle said. "She was here? Why was she here?"

"That's what I'm trying to find out. More importantly, who does she work for?" When her teammates all shrugged, Max said, "Nelle—"

"I'll find out."

"Good. Find out and then I'll know if I need to kill her. I won't let her push my sister into something she doesn't want to do just to protect us."

"I'm on it."

"Did you see your mother?" Mads asked.

Max nodded. "Yeah."

"How did it go?"

"Amazing."

"And?"

"She's already talking about us working together."

Mads frowned. "Seriously? 'Hey, honey. Boy, have I missed you these past two decades. Let's go rob some people'?"

"I'm sure she didn't mean it like that," Nelle argued, shoving Mads aside with a very nice hip bump. "She was just probably really excited to see you and wasn't thinking."

"I'm sure that's true," Max agreed. "Anyway, I'll see her again later. I'm not going to worry about it right now."

"So," Streep interjected, "we're *not* going to talk about the fact that on our off-time we're all thieves? Except for Mads, I mean."

"I steal magazines from doctors' offices all the time," Mads admitted.

"Why are you in doctors' offices?" Tock asked.

"To steal magazines."

"Okay." Max went over to the metal shelf where she kept still-boxed basketballs and took one out. "Let's go practice a little before we eat."

"Why?"

"So when Coach is busting our proverbial balls about not being at practice today, we can tell her—without lying—that we still practiced."

"Niiiiice," her teammates quietly cheered before heading outside.

Max started to follow but Kyle's voice stopped her. "You MacKilligan sisters do live fascinating lives."

Walking to the table where he was working, Max wrapped her arm around him and rested her chin on his shoulder.

"I thought those were noise-canceling headphones."

"They are. But I'm a jackal." He rested his smudge-covered hands on her arm. "I can hear someone washing dishes, like, six blocks away. These just cut down on the noise. Nothing truly cancels it out for me."

"I'm sorry. Did we scare you?"

"Not at all. I like you guys. I especially like Nelle."

"Everybody likes Nelle. But you are too young for her and too poor."

"But I *will be* rich and will need a beautiful woman on my arm to impress people I do not care about."

Max laughed and kissed the kid's cheek. "You are too cute."

"Forget it, MacKilligan," he teased. "You're much too short for me."

It was the dark chocolate cupcake that made it clear to Zé why the bears had come into the MacKilligans' yard and then patiently waited. He'd never tasted anything so amazing before and he was a connoisseur of dark chocolate. Whether it was truffles or cake or ice cream. A very picky connoisseur, in fact, but Charlie had made a believer out of him.

She even used a proper dark chocolate ganache on those cupcakes.

When he went to grab four more and some polar bear attempted to get between him and what he wanted, Zé bared his fangs and hissed. When the polar paused to wipe the spit from his eyes, Zé grabbed his treats and walked away. He sat down in a lounge chair and watched Max and her teammates playing ball against a few of the locals. To say they were wiping the floor with those guys would be an understatement.

"Hey!"

Zé let out a very long, very loud sigh.

"Damn," Dutch complained. "I haven't even said anything. Yet."

"Just your presence annoys me."

"People love me."

"I doubt that."

"And after I did you a favor."

"Really?" Zé asked, licking chocolate ganache off his fingers. "And what favor was that?"

"I took care of everything with your company so that they and your girlfriend know you're alive but don't know you're a shifter."

"Shit," Zé snarled at himself, lowering the half-eaten cup-cake. "I forgot to call Kamatsu again. And she is not my girl-friend. She's my team leader." He looked at his watch, winced at the time. "I'll call her in the morning."

"Why are you going to call her?"

"Because she's my friend. Do you have friends? Do you know what that's like?"

"I have friends. And you can't call her. What are you going to tell her?'

"What do you mean?"

Dutch moved his chair closer. "What are you going to tell her about where you've been? What you've been doing? How you healed so fast? Your blood was all over the place."

"I'm sure I can come up with something."

"Come up with something—or admit the truth? Because you look like someone who thinks he can get away with telling the truth. Except you can't. Not now. Truth is off the table."

"But isn't it easier to—"

"What? Explain to her how you can shift into a big cat? That Max is a honey badger? Max's best friend is a wolverine? That Max plays on a pro basketball team filled with shifters? Do you really think you can tell her all that and not have her think you've gone insane or, even worse, believe you, and *tell the world*?"

"She wouldn't do that."

"I know you believe that, because she's your friend. But what if you're wrong? Then what do you tell these people"—he looked out over the bears filling the MacKilligans' yard—"when your friend's government comes for them and their kids?"

Zé wanted to tell the man he was wrong. That he didn't know Kamatsu. That his battle buddy would never betray him. But Zé also knew the risk was too great.

"So you're saying I have to give up my entire life?"

"No," Dutch said with a dismissive wave. "Don't be stupid."

"But you said—"

"Just don't tell her the truth. Have your story ready before you see the woman. Then lie your ass off."

"And my old job? Can I go back to that?"

"If you want, but now that you know what you can do, why would you want to?"

"What does that mean?"

"Full-humans will just hold you back. Because you can't reveal what you can do. You can't unleash your claws. You can't unleash your fangs. You can't roar."

"You roar?"

"No, I'm a wolverine. Still, I can bite through thick human bone, which is helpful during a nasty fight. But I can't do that if I'm standing around with a bunch of full-humans watching me, because we all know they'll ask questions. They're all so nosy."

It took a few seconds for Zé to understand what was happening, but when he did, he asked, "Wait . . . are you pitching me something?"

"My organization is always looking for good people, and we love former military. We pay top dollar and everyone knows exactly what you are and what you can do. It's something to think about when you're ready."

"Would I have to work for you directly?"

"No. Asshole. But just so we're clear, I'm always around. Max is my best friend."

"So?"

"What? Are you actually going to sit there and tell me you're *not* interested in—owwwwwwwwwwwwwwwww!"

Shocked by his scream of pain, Zé looked up to see that Charlie had Dutch's ear and was twisting it to the point that Zé was worried she'd tear the damn thing off.

"You will not bother Zé," she told Max's friend. "You will not talk to Zé. You will not annoy Zé. You will not interact with Zé at all. Do you understand me?"

Dutch pulled away, stumbling into a grizzly that roared a little and pushed Dutch back.

But Zé was impressed. Dutch didn't hit the floor and start crying, which would be what Zé would expect after having a six-and-a-half-foot man attempt to shove you to the ground.

"I can talk to whoever I want to!" Dutch told Charlie while holding his ear.

Charlie moved in on Dutch. "Not if you're missing your tongue."

"I'm telling Max."

Zé smirked when Dutch took off through the crowd and that smirk turned to a large grin when Charlie put a plate of dark chocolate cupcakes in front of him.

"If Dutch bothers you again, you just let me know. He lives and breathes because I allow him to. I'd happily enjoy reminding him of that."

He pointed at the cupcakes. "These are the best, by the way."

"Thank you. I'm glad you're enjoying them." She sat down in the chair next to him. "Can I ask you a question?"

"Sure."

"Did Max go see her mother today?"

Zé choked on the cupcake he'd just bitten into, sending a spray of chocolate across the ground.

"Okay. Thanks."

"No, no." He grabbed Charlie's hand before she could stand up and walk away. "I did not say 'yes' to that question."

"You kind of did."

"I don't want to get in the middle of this."

"There's nothing to get into the middle of, Zé. Don't worry. I'm not going to flip out or anything. It's her mother. I would never get between them. I just wanted to make sure."

"How did you find out?"

"Imani Ako, the She-lion from a few blocks over. She was here. She told me. I thought she was going to use it to black-mail us, but no. She just wanted to tell me. Trying to gain my trust, I guess."

"I really think Max is going to tell you."

"It doesn't matter," Charlie admitted. "If my mother came

back as a zombie, I'd be, like, 'Mom! You're home!' " she jokingly cheered, pumping her fists a little. "So, you don't have to
tell her anything. I just . . . needed to know. For myself."

Zé watched Charlie MacKilligan for a moment before he
guessed, "You're worried she's going to leave."

It seemed that Charlie was about to answer but then she
patted him on the shoulder and said, "I'll wrap up some more
of these cupcakes for you and hide them in one of the high
cabinets. After I accidentally shot Mr. Longchester from down
the street—when he sniffed out some cake in our cabinets one
morning—we haven't had a problem with any more break-ins."

Once Charlie was gone, Stevie jumped into her empty seat.
"What did Charlie want?" She leaned in. "Does she know
about Max's mom? Did she ask about that?"

Zé stared at Max's sister. "I can't express to you how much
I'm *not* getting in the middle of this."

The party eventually wound down. Barbeques were hefted
up and taken home. There was no leftover food—there never
was when bears were involved—but paper plates and disposable
utensils were cleaned up. Trash-bagged and taken to the large,
bear-proof Dumpsters outside the fence. Max and her sisters
didn't have to lift a finger. She liked the way the bears knew
how to show their appreciation.

Her teammates were going to go back into the city and get
hotel rooms, but Charlie stopped them at the door.

"You're staying here . . . aren't you?"

As usual, the four idiots were too terrified to say "no" to
Charlie so they all headed down to the finished basement,
planning to sleep together on sleeping bags and air mattresses
like they used to when they were in high school and at away
games.

After making sure all the bears were gone, and then shoo-
ing Kyle away from the garage so he could get some actual
sleep—he was still a growing jackal!—she made her way back
to the house. But before she went through the door, she sniffed

the air and followed the scent to the big tree. That's where she found Zé. He was hanging out on a limb and texting on his new phone.

"You going to spend the night up there?" she asked.

"I wasn't planning on it. But Kamatsu managed to get my new number and she's been texting me like crazy. She wants proof it's really me. She's been asking me a ton of questions that only *I* can answer. It's very annoying."

"She's worried about you."

"Yes, which I really appreciate. But I'm also bored now." He began typing, staring at his screen while saying what he was writing. "I'm done. I'm going to bed. Do not bother me again until sometime tomorrow."

Max grimaced. "That's a little abrupt, isn't it?"

The phone vibrated with an incoming text.

" 'Okay,' " he read from the screen, " 'now I know it's you. Talk to you tomorrow.' "

Happy with that reply, Zé started down the tree, slipped, flipped, and landed on his feet right in front of her.

"I bet you *wanted* to do that," she prompted.

"Yes. I did. Beautifully handled, don't you think?"

Max jammed her hands into the back pockets of her shorts. "Look, Zé, I hope tonight wasn't too much for you. I mean, my mom, watching bears feed, fighting for the cupcakes . . . Dutch. I know this kind of existence isn't for everyone."

"I actually had a relatively pleasant time. Except for Dutch. But your sister handled that."

"You and Charlie. I don't get it. I love Dutch. He's fun, he can eat frozen meat because he's got that wolverine jaw, and he's not afraid to eat a rattler if there's one slithering around. What?" she asked when Zé just stared at her, not saying anything.

"Are you two . . . together?"

Max laughed. Hard. She couldn't help it. "When it comes to Dutch . . . I've seen too much." She stopped, glanced up. "That rhymed. Huh. Anyway, one time he got drunk at homecoming and somehow managed to set himself on fire. If Tock hadn't been there to put him out, the rest of us would have let him burn. But he's my boy. He always has my back."

"But I don't have to worry about him, right?"

"Worry about him?"

"Yeah. Worry about him getting in my way."

"I'm not a building you're trying to climb. And no. You don't have to worry about Dutch."

"Good," he said, a small smile on his lips. "See you in the morning."

But Max wasn't going to let him get away with that. When it came to sex, cats might play games but honey badgers didn't and he might as well learn that now.

Zé was about to go into the house when Max cut in front of him and blocked his way.

"Something wrong?"

She went up on her toes and slid her hand behind the back of his neck. He watched as her lips came close, already parted and lush. She didn't wait for him to come to her; she simply made her wants known. And he liked it.

When her lips touched his, he grabbed her waist and pulled her close. Both her arms went around his neck and her tongue slipped into his mouth.

They should have been testing and easing into this. Finding out what each other liked through exploration. But there didn't seem to be a question to answer. It was as if they both just knew.

She sank her hands into his hair, digging her fingers into his scalp. He began growling at the sensation and pushed her against the wall next to the back screen door. The kiss quickly grew out of control. He pushed his hand between her thighs, brushing his fingers against her covered pussy. In return, she wrapped her hand around his denim-encased dick and began stroking.

Their intensity grew, both of them pushing each other. Any second, he knew, they'd start ripping off each other's clothes. Right out here, in the backyard.

Max pulled her hands away, only to place them on his shoulders. She pushed him around so that he had his back to the screen door; then aggressively stepped into him. Sadly, the screen was not as strong as the wall and their combined weight took the whole thing down.

With mouths open in shock, they gawked at each other. Then, from somewhere deep in the house, Charlie yelled out, "I am *not* fucking paying for that, you two horny idiots!"

Mairi lowered the long rifle. She'd been using the scope to watch her cousins. She had no intention of shooting Max. That would be too easy, now wouldn't it? She wanted a proper fight with her. It had crossed her mind to start shooting people at that party. But this was the States, wasn't it? And something like that would make big news. Random "extremely large innocents" shot at a summer party. "News at eleven!" She'd be in an American prison faster than she could spit, so it was best not to get off track.

She carefully took her weapon apart and put it back in its case. She locked the case and made her way off the small, full-human–owned house to the waiting vehicles down the block. She secured her case in the back and got into the passenger side. They headed back to the city and the hotel they'd been staying at.

Although she hadn't really forgotten about Freddy MacKilligan, she wasn't actively looking for him. She could deal with him later. She'd let her female kin deal with her twin aunts first, and then she'd find that idiot and twist him until he coughed up the location of the money he'd stashed. She refused to believe he was smart enough to steal it back from the twins alone. He must have had some help, but he was protecting whoever that could be. Mairi knew it must be a woman. Some young thing too stupid to know what she was getting herself into, but smart enough to steal a hundred million and hide it from nearly *everyone*.

She had no idea how Uncle Freddy was smart enough to

pick such competent women to help him—and get them pregnant—but so stupid he always managed to get his money stolen by someone else. That man . . . a walking disaster if she'd ever seen one.

But she'd worry about him later. She had other things on her mind right now. Like why they were pulling into this parking lot behind a closed shopping mall.

"What are we doing here?" she asked the full-human behind the wheel.

"Got orders to come here, ma'am. Not sure why."

The first shot took the driver's head clean off. The next few took out the men in the vehicle with her.

Mairi dropped down, hands over the back of her neck to protect herself.

More shots took out the ones in the second vehicle as well. Then silence.

She waited, not remotely surprised when the door to her vehicle was wrenched open and big hands grabbed her and dragged her out.

"Come on, lads—" she began to say but they simply shot, using handguns this time. The shots kept coming and coming. She thought they'd never stop. A few even hit her in the head. A couple quite near the heart.

Those hurt. A lot. She could feel them burning into her, searing past flesh and bone directly into organs.

These men didn't speak. They were professionals. And she knew her twin aunts had sent them. Because her Scottish aunts would have made sure of one thing if they had arranged this operation: that she was shot in the back of the head where the neck bones meet the skull. These men didn't do that. Well, they thought they had. One of them turned her over and shot her right in the back of the head. But not where it would kill her. Not *there*.

They burned the vehicles—with her men inside—but took her and dumped her into the plastic-covered boot of one of the Cadillacs. They drove off, and an hour or so later came to a stop. She heard the men standing around, chatting, laughing. Having a very nice time until they were ready. They opened the trunk and reached for her.

Mairi attacked then. Their weapons were holstered and they hadn't expected much of a fight from a corpse so she had free rein.

She wrapped herself around the first, tearing his throat out with her fangs and spitting the blood and bits of artery into the eyes of the man next to him. That one had a big butcher's knife in his hand to cut her up. She grabbed it and cut his throat before burying it in the head of another. She fell with the body of the man she was wrapped around and rolled forward away from him.

By now the rest of her assailants had retrieved their weapons. They started shooting, but those earlier shots—the ones that didn't go straight through her—they'd already been expelled from her body or were stuck in her thick skin. These new ones didn't do any more damage than the first. They hurt, but as long as they didn't get her in that one spot, they couldn't kill her.

She killed three of the last four quick and took a moment to watch the terrified young man who took off running. She got into the car, the keys still in it, and went after him. When she reached him, she slammed him with the front of the vehicle. Not enough to kill him, though. Not yet.

She stopped the car and got out; paused a moment to finally pull out a few of the bullets that were burning nasty holes in her thick badger skin.

Giving an all-over shake, she walked over to the man. Despite his battered legs and destroyed hip, he was desperately trying to drag himself away. It amazed her, the way full-humans fought for their lives. Even when they knew they were done for. It was the one thing their kind had in common with the weak bastards. The will to live.

"Now where you going, my lad?" she asked before grabbing his left foot. His right was barely hanging on by its tendon so she didn't bother with that one. "No use trying to get away when we still have to get better acquainted."

"No!" he begged. "Please! No!"

"Don't start with all that yellin'," she told him as she dragged him back toward the car. She could hear his fingers digging into the asphalt, trying to stop her from taking him. "Not that I mind yellin', ya see. I just think you should wait."

She pulled him alongside the car and dropped his leg, put her foot on his back, and gazed down at him. "You know, at least until you really have something to scream about."

chapter *EIGHTEEN*

Max woke up on top of Zé with the morning sun blasting through the living room windows.

They'd fallen asleep like that a few hours before after binge-ing late-night reality TV repeats involving people in love with criminals just getting out of prison. Considering her mother's unannounced return, it seemed apropos.

After going through the back screen door—which woke everyone in the house up—sex had seemed awkward at best. Not that Max wasn't still down for it. Oh, she was. But having her teammates *and* her sisters so close that even full-humans with no enhanced senses could have heard them was some-thing even *she* couldn't do. Not for their first time. And after that kiss Max was definitely sure there would be a first time and quite a few more. She didn't believe in never-ending love between males and females—they just weren't built for that unless they were canines—but she did believe things could last for a while if the two people clicked.

And she felt that she clicked with Zé. She really enjoyed the way he just sort of hung out. Watching, learning, but not div-ing in. Not getting into her business. Trying to "fix" things, as many men enjoyed doing. Maybe it was the cat in him that she liked so much, which was shocking since, ya know, she had ac-tively attempted to kill that cat roaming around their property.

Max rubbed her eyes and quickly realized that she hadn't woken up simply because she was ready to greet the new day. Nope! It was because she'd known she wasn't alone with her cat.

Three females stood on the other side of the coffee table.

Stevie waved at her and mouthed, *Sorry.*

Next to her was Charlie; her lips pursed, her eyes mid-roll.

And next to both her sisters was their Aunt Bernice. The unofficial leader of the American MacKilligans, mostly because no one else wanted the job except Freddy, but that would be a goddamn disaster.

"Mind untangling yourself from the house cat and getting your ass outside so we can talk?" her aunt ordered, as was her way.

True, Max could launch herself across that table and tear out her aunt's throat with little to no effort, but it entertained her more to grin widely and cheer, "Auntie Bernice! I'm so glad to—"

"Shut up! And move your ass!"

See? *Much* more entertaining.

Zé knew as soon as Max was awake. He felt her lashes blink against the skin of his neck. Felt her breath quicken when she realized they weren't alone.

He'd never been so attuned to anyone before. The closest was his teammates when they were on a job, but that was about life and death. About surviving when the firefight started.

This, though . . .

He hadn't wanted her to go but he'd scented someone new in the room and that's when he discovered that he not only knew what Max's sisters smelled like, but if one stood behind him, he knew exactly which one it was.

Smirking a little, he sat up and dropped his legs to the floor. He studied his hands and, with just a thought, he changed his hands to claws.

Texts began pouring into his phone at that moment. All from Kamatsu. She wanted to meet him at a Starbucks in Manhattan at noon. He knew he had to go, even though he had no idea what he was going to tell her. But the more he thought about it, the more he realized that if he tried to put her off . . . she'd keep digging. It was in her nature. She never backed off anything.

Yeah, it was better if they met and talked. Otherwise, she wouldn't stop.

Deciding he needed a shower and to change his clothes first, Zé quickly texted Kamatsu back, agreeing to her demand. Just as he hit Send, he heard screeching tires and car doors being slammed. He didn't think much about it, assuming it was some local teens acting like idiots. But then someone banged on the front door.

Zé stood and moved through the living room until he reached the doorway into the day room. He was about to walk to the front door, where someone was *still* banging, when the door was torn off its hinges and the thick wood came slamming into the room.

And all Zé could think was, *Charlie is* definitely *not going to want to pay for that.*

They went out the back door into the yard. Kyle was already up and setting off on a jog, with Dutch along to keep the kid out of trouble. Although Shen had been officially hired to protect Kyle, they all kind of kept an eye on him. None of them really minded. The kid was obnoxiously cute, with ego enough to fill Penn Station, but there was still something about him that stopped at least Max and Charlie from killing him.

"So," Bernice began as soon as they were alone, "which one of you geniuses told your Uncle Will your father was back in town?"

Stevie raised her hand and Charlie blinked, eyes wide. "You did?"

When Stevie nodded, Charlie and Max began to politely applaud.

"Stop that!" their aunt barked at them. "Your idiot father—"

"Or your idiot brother," Max muttered.

"—actually requested a sit-down with your Uncle Will to 'discuss' all this."

Max and her sisters stared at their aunt, their minds attempting to grasp what she'd just told them. When they finally understood, Stevie merely shook her head and sadly sighed out, "Oh, Dad." But Max and Charlie just started laughing and didn't stop.

Their father had to be the dumbest motherfucker! Will would do nothing but kill him.

Charlie was the first to get herself under control. "What exactly does he think that 'discussion'"—she asked, using air quotes, like her aunt—"is going to accomplish?"

"He says he's got the money," Bernice replied.

"I thought the twins had the money," Max said.

"They did, but then he took it back. Now he has it."

"How is that possible?" Charlie wanted to know. "The man can barely tie his shoes, much less use a computer to transfer money anywhere."

"Obviously he's working with someone else; we just don't know who."

"I've been trying to find that out." Max pointed to Charlie. "Irene Conridge set me up with some full-human hacker she knows. They've been working on it for a bit now."

Stevie suddenly snarled. "Conridge? Why that bitch?"

Max raised a finger to her sister. "You need to get over whatever issue you have with Conridge."

"Contact Conridge," Charlie told Max. "Find out if the hacker knows anything yet."

"Why are *we* getting in the middle of this?"

And, again, Charlie and Max looked at their sister in surprise. Usually she wanted to help everyone. She felt for *everyone*. Maybe now, though, with the help of her new medications, she understood that not everyone deserved her help.

"Because part of that is *our* money," Bernice reminded them. "And Will is so pissed, he'll just kill your father without waiting to find out where it is. It could be anywhere in the world, and the family wants it back."

"Except the family doesn't consider us part of it," Max reminded her.

"Well, if ya wanna be, get our money back."

"Yeahhhhh, we don't."

Bernice's eyes narrowed and she took a step toward Max, but Charlie quickly stepped between them.

"Let's play nice, ladies," Charlie said, before telling their aunt, "Although my sister has a point. Why should we get involved? This is Dad's fuckup and your fuckup for letting him get away with it in the first place. I don't think that falls on us."

"You ungrateful little—"

"*We're* being ungrateful?" Stevie suddenly yelped, moving around a stunned Charlie so she was right in their aunt's face. "All of you went out of your way to make sure we felt as excluded as possible; you let Charlie's poor grandfather take the full financial responsibility of raising three girls even though only one was his actual blood relation, when any of you could have taken us in or just sent us a little money to get by. And you have the nerve to stand there and call *us* ungrateful?"

"What's happening?" Max asked Charlie. Like her older sister, she was stunned and impressed by Stevie's outrage and ability to explain it without breaking down into sobs or shifting into a two-ton animal that could destroy the neighborhood.

Bernice pointed an angry, damning finger at Stevie, and Max waited for the vitriol that would follow. But, after a few seconds, she lowered her hand and softly admitted, "You're right. We were cunts."

"Seriously, Charlie," Max said, turning to her sister, "what's *happening?*"

There were three of them. Big. Tall. With black hair and gold eyes.

The one in front, the biggest of the three, barged in, those gold eyes sweeping the room.

"Where is she?" he growled out.

Since Zé didn't know what or whom he was talking about, he didn't respond.

The man stormed closer. "I said"—now he stood over Zé—
"*where is she?*"

The roar of words blew Zé's hair off his face and he went
from a human wondering what was going on to a cat that
sensed danger.

He backed up, moving into the living room, his fangs easing
out of his gums, claws bursting from his fingers. He shifted,
shook off his clothes, and let out his own roar.

The raging man took a moment to look at the two men with
him. Then he shifted and turned into what kind of looked like
a tiger, but not one Zé had ever seen before. Because despite a
few orange stripes he could barely make out, most of the tiger's
fur was black. As black as Zé's.

Then, still towering over Zé, the tiger roared. It wasn't like
a lion's, but it made Zé's sound like a squeak. Yeah, it was loud
and powerful and shook the windows of the house.

At that point, Zé was pretty sure he was dead, but that had
never stopped him before. He charged the much bigger cat, but
ended up flying across the room and out the window with one
paw-slap to the head.

Max ran into the room just in time to see poor Zé slapped
out of a closed window, the glass exploding across the yard.

Pissed, Max hissed and launched herself at the tiger, shifting
in midair.

"Badger!" one of the other tigers warned. "Badger! Badger!
Badger!"

She landed on the shifted cat's back and dug her fangs into
his fur-covered neck, hoping to reach an artery.

The tiger shook himself, sending Max flying. She hit the
wall, dropped to the floor, and scrambled back to her feet. She
hissed again and charged. The cat tried to slap at her again, but
she ducked under his legs, ran under his chest, and latched onto
his balls. As she sank her fangs into the skin, he went up on his
hind legs and roared, trying to slap her off with his front paws.

"Jesus Christ!" one of the other tigers yelled. "Get her off!
Get her off!"

Human hands grabbed her around the waist, but a separate fist began punching her.

"Let him go!" one of the other men yelled at Max.

A flash of black dashed past Max and Zé returned, tackling the one punching her. That man shifted to tiger and their roars and growling rumbled across the floor as they knocked over furniture and got dangerously close to the TV Max loved. Small price to pay, though, for this much fun.

"*Fuck!*" the last human male exploded. "More badgers!"

Her teammates leaped onto the Siberian tiger and did their best to work their way either up to or down to major arteries. Behind them, Zé and the other tiger rolled by. Considering how much smaller he was than the other cat, Zé was doing pretty well for himself.

They all heard it then, and everyone froze. Because they all knew the sound of a Mossberg 500 tactical pump-action shotgun. Okay, maybe no one but Max actually knew that's what it was, but still . . .

Charlie stood under the archway, her grip on the weapon steady and in control.

Christ, Max adored her big sister.

"Now," Charlie began, their aunt Bernice standing behind her, "we can all relax and retract fangs and claws from important body parts, put our clothes back on, and have a calm, rational conversation. Or," she added with a big grin, "I can start murdering everyone that's not related to me by blood!"

That's when Max's teammates made a run for it, disappearing up the stairs. Disgusted, Max released her grip on the tiger's balls, dropped to the ground, shifted, and yelled after them, "Are you fucking kidding me? *She didn't mean you!*"

Charlie shrugged. "I kind of meant them. Wouldn't do to have witnesses."

Zé had claw marks on his sides and back, and fang bites on his neck. There was blood pouring from his wounds and his head hurt, but despite all that . . . he'd never felt so fucking amazing before in his life.

He pulled on jeans, and a now dressed Max came over to clean up his wounds.

"Don't sweat it," she said to him. "The bleeding will stop in a few minutes, these will be completely healed in less than twenty-four hours, and you'll probably only have one or two scars where that tiger went a little too deep."

"Thanks."

"You're welcome." Max kept her face down, focused on his wounds.

"Keep looking at me like that," Max warned, "and I'm going to fuck you right here."

"Promise?"

"Hey!" that growly voice barked at them. "I want my sister! Where the fuck is she?"

Max handed Zé the alcohol wipes and started to walk across the room to the tigers, but Charlie said, "No, Max."

Max stopped immediately. When they'd started training with their neighbor, Charlie had made Max agree to one thing: "When I tell you to stop, you stop." Even then, at fourteen, she'd had that calm delivery. Not soft-spoken so much as rational. Very rational.

At the time, Max had easily agreed, not thinking it would be that hard to comply. It turned out that it was surprisingly hard to stop in the middle of a fistfight or firefight. Especially if someone had managed to piss her off. In the end, though, it was the rule she'd been most glad her sister had made her commit to. Charlie had saved her life with that one short sentence—"No, Max"—more than a dozen times.

Charlie still held her weapon but had the barrel pointing at the ground. She motioned Max to step back with a jerk of her head.

"Stevie," she said when Max had moved back to Zé's side. "Come down."

"Nope."

The only order that Charlie had ever forced Stevie to follow was "run." So if they asked her to do anything else and she wasn't in the mood or too freaked out, she just didn't do it.

The tigers looked up to find Stevie hanging from the ceiling above them.

"Stevie," Charlie tried again. "Get down here."

"Forget it. There's three of them. Three man-eaters! Why not just serve us up with some Tabasco sauce?"

Charlie closed her eyes, took a breath, and ranted, "*Stevie MacKilligan, get your ass down here!*"

"Okay, okay." She could have just dropped to the floor but she scuttled across the ceiling and down the wall until she could stand directly behind Charlie.

"Are you hiding behind your sister?" Bernice asked.

"Don't harass me."

Charlie ignored the bickering behind her and informed the invaders, "I don't know who your sister is."

"You're lying."

"Call my sister a liar again," Max warned.

"Okay." The one who hadn't bothered to shift at all quickly stepped into the middle of the room, a forced smile on his face. "How about we take this down a notch and I start off with introductions. We're the Malone brothers. I'm Shay." He pointed at the smaller brother—small being relative at six-four. "That's Finn. And this big lug here"—he dropped his hand on the biggest brother's massive shoulder and was immediately tossed off—"is our older brother, Keane."

"And your sister is Cella Malone?" Max asked. But the look she got from all three tigers told her, in no uncertain terms, that they were *not* the brothers of Cella Malone and how dare she even suggest such a thing!

"Sorry. Just a question."

"Our sister is Natalie Malone and—"

Keane yanked his brother out of the way and finished his sentence. "—she's seventeen, deaf, and was last seen in the company of Freddy MacKilligan. That was a week ago."

Max locked gazes with Stevie. A lifetime of conversation passed in those two seconds before Stevie pointed at her unadorned wrist and said, "Look at the time! I, uh, need to go get ready. I'm supposed to be doing something with ballet and my music in the city so . . . yeah . . . I need to go. Away."

Like Max's teammates, Stevie disappeared up the stairs and Max whispered to Zé, "If I tell you to run, you run."

Then she turned and faced her eldest sister. She raised her hands to her chest, palms out, and slowly and carefully moved toward Charlie.

"Now, Charlie, I know that's not what you wanted to hear. That's not what anyone wanted to hear. And I'm sure that—" Stevie silently ran back down the stairs with her backpack slung over her shoulder, Max's teammates following behind. She paused long enough to grab their aunt and, as a group, they all quickly rushed toward the kitchen to escape what was about to happen. "I'm sure that we can all discuss this without anyone getting—"

Before Max could get out "upset," her sister's roar of rage exploded all around them.

The males of Imani's Pride had just pushed the cubs out of the kitchen chairs so they could eat the children's eggs and toast. Imani was about to yell at them—again—and order them not to do that anymore, when the entire house shook.

The males bolted from the table, one of them roaring, "Earthquake! *Run for your lives!*" before they all ran outside into the streets.

One of her young granddaughters turned to Imani and asked, "Why do the males get to eat first again?"

Imani crouched in front of her and answered to the best of her ability: "Because the gods have a terrible sense of humor."

Keane Malone knew he was angry. He was proud of his anger. He kept it close to him; tended to it like a lover. But even he had to admit, his anger was nothing compared to Charlie MacKilligan's rage.

For the last ten minutes—while he'd pressed an ice pack to his abused balls—they'd all stood there while she ranted and screamed and threatened death to the man she still called "Dad." At first, he'd thought it was a performance. Something to get him off her old man's back, but as it continued and her face got redder and her muscles pulsed and he was sure her increasing blood pressure was going to make her heart explode, he realized, nope. This was not a performance.

This was hatred. He knew hatred and this was definitely hatred.

Keane's hatred and anger were directed at those who had killed his father all those years ago, when he and his brothers were still young. But Charlie MacKilligan's hatred and anger were directed right at her father. And, if Keane were Freddy MacKilligan, he'd be hiding right now.

But he couldn't let himself be distracted. He wanted his sister back and he wasn't going to stop until he got her.

"Look—" he began but the younger badger shook her head at him and her eyes were really big and she looked about ready to panic, which was strange. Honey badgers weren't prone to panic.

Once Keane stopped talking, the little badger crouched in front of her now seated sister.

"Hey," she said softly, "why don't you go bake something, sweetie? It'll help you think."

Bake? She wanted her sister to bake? His baby sister was out there somewhere with an idiot and these heifers wanted to bake?

Again, Keane opened his mouth to speak and *again* the badger gave him that crazy look.

"Yeah," Charlie MacKilligan said. "Yeah. I'll bake. Baking's good. Bears love when I bake."

And like that, she got up and walked out of the room.

Pressing her hand against her upper chest, the small badger let out a very shaky breath and stood. She was cute but she reminded Keane of a Muppet. Maybe it was the size and the purple hair.

"Okay, now that I've got that managed—"

"My sister," Keane pushed.

"Yeah, yeah. Sorry. Look, I don't know what to tell ya. We always knew our father was an asshole but we didn't know he was *this* much of an asshole. But the one thing I can tell you is that he would *never* tell us about your sister. Not in this world or the next."

Charlie walked back into the room. She was already mixing batter, a stainless steel bowl tucked into the crook of her arm; the other hand stirred its contents with a wooden spoon.

"You know," she ranted, "it's like he goes out of his way to fuck with our lives. Like it's his goal to make me crazy. Why does he want to make me crazy, Max? Because he's making me crazy!"

Abruptly, she spun around and stalked back to her kitchen.

The Muppet went back to their conversation as if her sister hadn't interrupted. "However, our father is being hunted by most of our family. Chances are very high he may be caught soon and quickly killed."

"What about our sister? That just puts her in more danger."

"If one of our family catches up with Freddy, you won't have to worry. They're not going to kill a pup."

"Cub."

"Whatever. They'll probably just leave her there. With the body."

"What the hell does—"

"And you know what else?" Charlie MacKilligan demanded as she stalked back into the room with a muffin pan, each cup filled with batter. He'd never seen anyone make batter that fast before. His mother baked muffins but she took way longer.

"I should have killed him when I had the chance," she continued. "When I was, like, nine, I had the chance to take him out. Thought about it, too. But my mother took the knife out of my hand and told me I shouldn't kill my own father. She said it was wrong. Morally. But you know what? I think *she* was wrong. I think I absolutely should have killed my own father. I should have! I really should have!"

And off again she went, back to her kitchen.

"I'll put the word out with the family, though," the Muppet

said, still not freaked out by any of that muffin-baking rage. "Let them know about your sister and that she is to be brought in alive and unsoiled."

"Wait . . . *what?*"

"Don't panic. My male cousins aren't that bad and my female cousins wouldn't let them get away with it, anyway."

Charlie MacKilligan returned again. This time she had a tray of freshly baked muffins.

"Blueberry?" she asked.

Completely freaked out, Keane stepped away from her. "How did you make those so fast?"

She shrugged. "These just came out of the oven. I've been baking all morning." She jerked her thumb toward the windows. "I've got bears to feed."

"Oh, shit!" Shay barked as Finn hissed in warning at the bears standing outside the windows gazing in.

"And just so you know," Charlie MacKilligan said, her voice now calm again, rational, "if you'd hurt me or my sisters, those bears would have torn all of you apart. Just FYI, if you decide to come back here without an invitation. But you know what?" She handed Keane a giant blueberry muffin. "You and I understand each other perfectly. You hate Freddy MacKilligan. I hate Freddy MacKilligan. You won't let him harm your sister. I won't let him harm *my* sisters. My God, it's like we're twins."

She motioned to the muffin. "Go ahead. Try it."

Keane glanced at the Muppet, but all she did was shrug noncommittally.

He went ahead and bit into the top. After a few seconds of chewing, Keane couldn't help but grunt a little in appreciation.

"I know, right?" MacKilligan agreed as if he'd set off fireworks and written a five-star review. "They *are* great! I don't have a lot of skills, but the few I do, I've made sure to master."

Max walked the Malones out to their car. She wanted to see them get into their vehicle and drive away.

"Next time, boys, if you want to come by, you should call or something. We're not a family you want to sneak up on."

"Our sister—"

"If we hear *anything*, we'll let you know. I promise."

The cat nodded and opened the passenger door. He was about to get in when Max asked, "Quick question: so you're *not* related to Cella Malone? Because I know her already and she could probably help with this."

"We don't deal with that side of the family," one of the brothers said. And the bitterness in his voice . . . damn.

"Got it."

Without another word said, the brothers got into their giant SUV and drove away.

Once they were gone, Max dropped her head back and let the sun warm her face for a bit. It felt like things were spiraling out of control but she refused to panic.

"Hey," she said, when she sensed Zé standing behind her.

"Hey. I need to go out."

"Just grab a set of car keys from the table by the door and go for it."

"Want to come with me?"

Max faced him. "Where you going?"

"The city to meet with Kamatsu. I've got to come up with something to tell her, thought you could keep me from putting my foot in my mouth about all this. Unless you need to stay here."

"So I can listen to my big sister rant for the next four hours about how shitty our father is because he's now kidnapping underage deaf girls? Which, by the way, I don't want to discuss again."

"Where's that big bear of hers? Can't he listen to her complain?"

"He's on a job with his triplets. But he'll be back later. Can you wait for me to shower?"

"Sure. I need a shower, too."

He reached out and Max's first instinct was to rear back because when people usually reached out for her, it was to punch her in the face. But she stopped herself in time and Zé placed his hand against her cheek. Big fingers slid along her jaw. His touch was gentle but she knew from last night that it didn't have to be.

"Sorry you had such a shitty start to your day," he murmured, still stroking her face.

"Sorry you had to experience the Freddy Effect. People come into our orbit and they are tragically swept into the gravitational pull of his idiocy."

"Don't sweat it. We've all got family members that make us want to go back in time to destroy that particular bloodline."

Max laughed and stepped around Zé, but she stopped and added, "By the way . . . smaller cats don't usually fuck with bigger ones. It's a tiny matter of survival."

"You fucked with 'em."

"Of course I did. I'm not a cat. I'm a fuckin' honey badger and by this claw"—she held her hand up—"I fuckin' rule."

chapter NINETEEN

Zé walked into Starbucks and saw Kamatsu sitting at a table, no doubt nursing one of her herbal teas.

"You want anything?" Max asked, motioning to the counter.

"Regular coffee," he said.

"Okay." She caught his arm before he could move off. "And don't forget that whatever lie you tell is for the safety of others."

"Right. I can do this."

"You can do this."

By the time he was heading directly to her table, Kamatsu had already spotted him. Neither of them liked to sit with their backs to the door. Wisely, she'd grabbed a round table that allowed them to sit on either side and monitor the activity around them.

Kamatsu grinned when she saw him, standing up and giving him a hug. "I'm so glad to see you."

"I'm glad to see you, too."

They sat down opposite each other and Kamatsu's smile instantly faded.

"What the fuck's going on?" she practically snarled at him, keeping her voice low so she couldn't be heard by others over the piped-in music. "I thought you were dead. Where have you been all this time? What happened to your phone? And who was that guy who came to David's office and took the report?"

"Well—"

"Whoever he was," she continued, "he or somebody hacked

into my computer *and* online storage and took all copies of the report. I have no backups. I have nothing. Did you tell them to do that?"

"Of course not."

"Then what is happening? You better tell me *right* now."

"Hi!" Max said, bouncing over to the table with two venti coffee cups and a large plate of honey buns.

"Can we help you?" Kamatsu asked.

Max's smile never wavered. "Nope!"

She put a coffee in front of Zé, pulled a chair over, and sat close to him. She pushed the plate sort of in the middle of the table and offered, "Honey bun?"

Confused and pissed, Kamatsu sat back in her chair. "No."

"Zé?" He shook his head. "Cool. All for me."

She dragged the plate close again and dove into those things as if she hadn't had two of her sister's giant blueberry muffins in the car. "So what are we talking about?" she asked around a mouthful of bun.

Ruth Barton walked down the street with her friends. She-bears she'd known for years, since she'd moved into the neighborhood with her husband and four cubs. Of course that was twenty years ago and times had changed. Nothing she couldn't handle, though. Her kind were survivors, after all.

Thinking about changing times, she stopped in front of what everyone in their little neighborhood now called "The Honey Badger House." She wasn't a fan of badgers. Mostly because they ate her honey. She and her husband had hives and since these badgers had moved in, those hives had been raided more than once. It was annoying.

But any time she complained, her husband insisted, "But have you tried that oldest one's honey buns?"

She had and he was right. So, for now, she kept her mouth shut. But still . . . stay out of her hives!

After letting out a grunt that had her friends chuckling, she unlocked the gate in the picket fence and stepped into the front yard. The oldest badger was sitting on the porch steps, so Ruth didn't have to knock on the door or go into the house. She could simply drop off the tray that her husband had taken when he'd brought home a dozen honey velvet cupcakes from the party the night before. It had turned into his breakfast.

"I wanted to return this to you," she said.

"Thanks, Mrs. Barton," the badger said, taking the tray and setting it down next to her. Then nothing.

Which was strange, because usually when Ruth dropped off trays from her hubby, Charlie had something to complain about. Not *to* Ruth or even about Ruth, but just complaining about everything in her life. Something about her allergies. Something about her father being a worthless piece of crap. Or just about the weather. One time she simply blurted out, "The sky looks weird, right?"

But now, sitting on her front porch, she wasn't saying anything. Just sitting.

Ruth began to walk away, but it just didn't feel right.

So, grudgingly, she asked, "Is something wrong?"

"I'm fine." But Ruth had raised four cubs into four strong sub-adults and she knew when those sub-adults were upset. That's what she saw right now.

"Are you sure? Because it seems like something is definitely wrong. Do you want to talk about it?"

"No, I'm . . . I'm . . ." Charlie took in a ragged breath. "I'm *not* fine!" she exploded before bursting into hysterical, savage tears.

Kamatsu crossed her arms over her chest, crossed one leg over the other, pursed her lips, and stared at Zé. He knew that look. It was not a good look.

He took a moment to recall the lie that he'd worked out with Max during the drive over here. He didn't want to get any of it wrong or leave any holes. If he left holes, Kamatsu would tear the entire thing down.

But his pause must have been too long because Kamatsu moved her gaze to Max and said, "He was telling me where he's been all this time. And what's been going on."

Zé cleared his throat. "You see—"

"It's all my fault," Max said, surprising Zé. Fault? They hadn't said anything about fault.

"It is?" Kamatsu asked.

"It is?" Zé asked.

"Yeah." She dropped the bit of bun she had left, wiped her hands on a paper napkin, and began, "You see, this guy was trying to kidnap me because of my mother. Long story, won't go into it. Anyway, when they took the hood off my head and I looked around, I saw Zé. And I said to myself, hold up. This guy shouldn't be here. He's not one of them. My mistake was, I was entirely too friendly and they believed that Zé was trying to help me, which, okay, he was, but they weren't supposed to know. Unfortunately, at that point, they did. And all hell broke loose. It was a total clusterfuck of my own making, which is why my big sister does not like it when I do these sorts of things on my own. But I knew if I told her about it beforehand, she would just flip out because, honestly, this is all because of my dad when you get right down to it. And now that we know he's kidnapped that seventeen-year-old deaf girl . . ." She shook her head. "I gotta tell ya, though—and I *know* my sister wouldn't want to hear this so I didn't say it at the time—I don't think he's having sex with this girl. He's definitely using her for something but I don't think it's sex . . . Oh, my God!" She slapped her hands against the table. "The hacker! She's probably the hacker!" She pressed her fist to her forehead. "That's how he got that hundred million. It was her. Of course. Now it makes sense. We all knew he was too stupid to do it himself so it must have been this girl. And, really, the best thing I can say about my dad is that the one thing he's *not* going to go to prison for is being a disgusting weirdo. Sadly, not because he has a moral high ground, but because he doesn't want to get his ass kicked in general pop."

Max rested her arm on the back of the chair and nodded. "Yeah. I'm right about this. Can't tell my big sister, though. Not yet. She hates him so much, she won't want to hear it. She'll just think I'm making excuses for him. But I don't make excuses for my dad. That's my baby sister. She makes excuses for him. Oh!" She sat up straight again and Zé noticed that her hands were moving with each sentence. Almost every other word, which was fucking incredible because she was talking so fast. The whole thing was intense. "But I was soooo proud of her today. Since she's been on this new medication, she has been rational and calm and not one tear shed! And I was so proud when we were talking to our Aunt Bernice and she was doing that thing she does where she tries to push the blame for our father onto us when she could have killed him, very easily, when she was growing up with him. A pillow over that pinhead and none of us would be having this conversation. Anyway, she did that thing and my baby sis totally took her down. She stood up for herself. She didn't back down. And when she did get angry, she didn't shed one tear or shift into a two-ton striped honey badger that could destroy the neighborhood. It was awesome!" She pointed a finger at Zé. "But don't tell her I said that."

She fell blessedly silent but that didn't last. "What were we talking about? Oh, yeah! So, anyway, I realized that Zé didn't know what he was. And although I could have left him there and let your team rescue him, I felt it was my duty to tell him what he is. I mean, he did try to help me so now I had to help him. Of course, there was a delay because he got really hurt during the firefight. Well . . . it was more knife-fight-slash-animal-mauling than it was a firefight, but anyway, he was really hurt but I knew he'd be fine in a couple of days. Even with that traumatic brain injury, I knew he'd be right as rain in no more than three days. And then once he was back on his feet, I would be able to tell him, 'Dude, you're a big black cat!' But, of course, he didn't believe me. So I had to prove it to him and that took some time and then he had that setback and tried to eat that bear cub and the bears all wanted him dead. But my sister fixed that by making honey buns for them for the next week or so and that usually works great. At least with the grizzlies and black bears. The polar bears, it helps if she uses more whale blubber, but she hates working with whale blubber. She does, however, enjoy working with bamboo for the pandas."

Max looked back and forth between Zé and Kamatsu and finally ended with, "And here we are. Anything else you need to know?"

Kamatsu pushed her chair back and stood. "Can I talk to you outside, please?" she asked Zé.

"Yeah. Sure."

She stalked out of the Starbucks and Zé gawked at Max.

"What?" Max asked with a shrug.

He didn't even answer her. Just went outside, wondering who in Starbucks would be the first to call the cops.

Once Zé and his team leader were gone, Max looked at the people staring at her, including the baristas behind the counter. As they stared, she spread her arms wide and, as one, the entire room burst into a standing ovation.

"Thank you. Thank you," she said to her fellow shifters, the only customers in the establishment. "I love you all!"

"I don't know what the fuck that was," Kamatsu laid into him as soon as he reached her. "And I don't care. But if you wanted to leave the job, all you had to do was tell me."

"I never said I—"

She stalked off and Zé had to jog a little to catch up to her.

"I don't know what that embarrassing performance was about, but if she is a tenth of the crazy she seems to be, then the last thing you should be doing is fucking her!"

"I'm not—"

"I don't care! She's mentally ill! Get her help!" She stopped. "What is she? The boss's daughter or something? Did he ask you to protect her? Because what she needs is a mental hospital, not a bodyguard."

"You don't understand, she's—"

Kamatsu threw up her hands. "I can't listen to this anymore. I can't!" She turned and stalked off again. "Just . . . I can't. I'll call you some other time. Just let me know if you want in on any jobs, but . . . if not . . . I just can't . . ."

Then she was gone.

Zé turned to head back but Max was already standing behind him.

"See?" she said. "They can't accept the truth."

"What the fuck was that?"

"What was what?"

Zé took a moment to get control. Because he wanted to yell. He wanted to yell so badly. But the thing he was starting to learn about Max was that although it might *look* as if she was doing random shit, she never really was. Even if the plan was made up between one breath and the next, she still always had a plan.

When he knew he had control, he said, "I thought we were going to lie to her. I was repeatedly told by you and everyone else I've met in the last few days that the truth could only hurt everyone and I needed to lie and lie and lie again."

Max nodded. "Yeah. You need to lie."

"But you didn't lie. You didn't lie at all."

"I know. That was okay, though."

"How was that okay?"

She looked at her phone and he felt the urge to grab it from her and toss it into the middle of the street. But then she took his hand and began walking in the opposite direction, tucking her phone into the back of her jeans.

"See," Max explained, "the plan was to lie and that was a very good plan. It was a safe plan. And right now you need safe plans. At least until you get your feet under you and you can figure all this shit out without too much worry."

"Okay."

"But I've been doing this sort of thing my entire life and sometimes the truth is perfect . . . because no one fucking believes the truth. You saw her face, right? She didn't believe anything I said. She thinks I'm insane. It's perfect."

"But everyone in Starbucks—"

"Is one of us."

"What?"

"Yeah. I didn't know that the Starbucks we were going to is the one that's so close to the new Sports Center until we got here. Everyone that works there and everyone that happened to be in there at the time . . . one of us. It was perfect."

She stopped and pointed at the giant building that took up the entire city block.

"This is the Sports Center," she said before dragging him through the big doors. As they walked through, he saw a lot of people doing a lot of sporty things. There was a massive gym. A sports medicine facility on the upper floors. An entire stadium in the back. A skating rink. And a Starbucks.

He pointed. "There's a—"

"No. Not that one. It's filled with full-humans. And they never have enough honey buns."

Max continued walking, pulling Zé along.

"Now, I had never been to this place when we first got here a few weeks ago. All the other finals and playoffs I was in took place either at the old Staten Island Sports Center or the Sports Centers around the country . . . or world. Depending on who the finals were against. This place was just built in the last few years. Our first playoff game will be here and I'm so excited. I mean, this place is nice, right?"

She took him to a stairwell that was off the main area. Two large security guards stood in front of it and one of them looked at Max and smirked.

"You start a fight . . ." the security guard warned.

"I won't. Promise."

Max opened the door and they went down a flight to the next level. She opened another door and walked in. Zé followed and froze in the doorway. It was just like what he'd seen upstairs except that he knew almost all these people were shifters. The insane variation in sizes. The way they looked at each other—either sizing them up or threatening them. Even the way they walked. The bears lumbering. The canines trotting along. The cats appearing and disappearing among the crowd until they vanished completely.

"Stop staring," Max said, pulling him along. "You look like you want a fight."

Not only was the place packed with shifters, it was geared specifically toward shifters. The stores had giant mannequins; the restaurants offered "whale blubber steaks" and "foot-long antelope hotdogs," and the massive gym had treadmills right in the window. On one of those treadmills was a woman running at least fifty miles per hour.

He pointed. "What's going on—"

"Tiger. Like the cheetah, they can go fast but only in short bursts. But the wolf on the treadmill next to her . . . ? She can trot like that for several hours. Oh! You should see this." Still holding his hand—which he really didn't mind at this point— she dragged him into the gym, past behemoths casually lifting weights that only Norwegian guys trying to get into the *Guinness Book of World Records* could lift.

"This," she said. "You should try this out at some point."

He didn't know what she was talking about until he saw a very wide, very tall tree with lots of limbs and branches that leopards and jaguars were climbing while holding something in their mouths.

"Are those zebras?"

"Not real zebras. And you have an array of fake zebras and antelope to choose from."

"An array?"

"You know—adult or . . . baby."

"Nope," Zé said, turning back toward the exit. "Can't handle this."

"You should try it! It'll be fun."

She caught up to him just as he stepped out of the gym.

"Okay, okay. I see this was too much."

"And weird. Don't forget weird."

Max took his hand again. "Let's get something to eat."

"I'm not eating whale blubber."

"Of course not! You need meat. Polar bears need whale blubber."

"I just feel like I failed them, you know?" Charlie admitted to the She-bears currently taking care of her. Someone made her lemonade, another got her cheese and crackers, and they were all sitting òn her porch, listening to her whine. "I should have taken better care of them."

"They're still alive, aren't they?" Ruth asked. "Because let's face it, that was a long shot."

"I didn't even know Max still played basketball."

"And she got MVP one year . . . or was it two?" Cathy Jakes said. When Ruth glared at her, she added, "I just know because I used to play a little college ball back in the day and I'm a big fan of the Butchers."

"The who?"

"Her team, dear."

"Oh, God." Charlie rubbed her forehead. "I don't even know the name of her team. What kind of sister am I?"

"I doubt she cares," Ruth insisted. "Your sister is not like . . . anyone, actually."

"Very true," Mrs. Jakes agreed. "And Stevie is flourishing. Isn't she, girls?"

"She saw me the other day," Mrs. Demming said, "and she didn't scream and hide in the tree . . . like the last seventeen times she saw me. This time, she just softly begged for death as I walked by. That's a *huge* improvement."

Charlie sat up a little straighter. "You know what? I'm sorry, ladies. All this whining. Dear God, I'm annoying myself!"

Ruth patted her knee. "Charlie MacKilligan, you need to have faith in yourself. You're an excellent sister who loves two females most people would find very hard to like, much less love. You protect them with your life and you care about others. That's more than most these days."

"Thank you." Charlie smiled at the She-bears. "I really appreciate this and . . . Oh, my God!"

The She-bears looked around, ready for any danger.

"What is it?" Ruth demanded. "What's wrong?"

"Sorry, sorry. I didn't mean to . . ." Charlie pointed and the She-bears turned to look at the street.

"Gurllll," Mrs. Jakes growled. "Look at the fuckin' Bugatti." When her friends stared at her: "What? I like cars. In fact, I'd kill my husband for that car."

"Don't bother," Ruth muttered. "You couldn't get your big bear ass in there."

"Who is that?" Mrs. Demmings asked, sniffing the air. "Badger. Another aunt?"

"Not quite." Charlie blew out a breath. "It's Max's mom."

"Oh. That's nice." Ruth blinked, looked off. "Wait . . . isn't she in prison?"

"She was."

"But she was paroled? Or pardoned? Anything?"

Charlie shook her head.

"Awww, kid, you are having a day," Ruth sighed out.

"You're telling me."

An older version of Max walked through the open gate and stood at the bottom of the porch stairs.

"Hiya, Charlie."

"Hi, Renny. It's great to see you."

"You, too, sweetie. It's been so long. You have grown into a beautiful woman. Your mom would be so proud."

"Thanks. That means a lot."

Renny glanced at the She-bears and asked Charlie, "Uh, think we can go somewhere private and talk for a few minutes?"

"No!" all the She-bears barked before Charlie could say a word.

Those determined looks on all those bear faces told Charlie there was no point in arguing. "I guess, no."

"Not a problem. We can talk here . . . with these bears."

"Sure. What's up?"

"Now that I'm back—"

"Illegally," Ruth muttered.

"How's that going, fugitive?" Mrs. Demmings tossed in.

But Renny, like Max, just ignored them. "—I've got some things going. Some plans I'm making. For my future."

"Okay." Charlie nodded. "That's great."

"And I would love to have my daughter by my side. You know, making up for lost time. Real mother-daughter bonding."

Charlie fought her need to frown. She didn't know why Renny was telling her this.

"Okay," Charlie said again. "I'm sure Max would love spending some time with you. You should just ask her."

"I did float the general idea by her. But I think if you let her know it would be okay for her to go, she'd be more ready to venture away from you and Stevie."

"Max has always ventured anywhere she wants to."

"Well . . . not exactly. I mean, she told me that she was expected to stay with Stevie for up to six months at a time."

"I took six months and she took six months. It's what we had to do to keep our sister safe from the idiot our mothers had insisted on fucking." Charlie knew she was getting pissed, so she forced herself to calm down. "What I mean is . . . we came to an agreement. I didn't force her."

"No, no. Of course not. Sure. But I think she felt she, you know, *owed* you."

Anger. "Why? Because my mother and then my grandfather took her in when the Yangs wanted nothing to do with her, and you were too busy being locked up in prison because you listened to fucking Freddy MacKilligan? You mean like that?"

It looked like Max's smile, but it was nothing like Max's smile. Because it was cold. It was a cold smile that Renny had. But she was still Max's mother and Charlie wasn't going to get between them. Not now. Not ever.

"Yeah," Renny said, "something like that."

"I'll tell you what I always tell her: She owes us nothing, because she's our sister and we love her. And she can go and do whatever she wants and we'll always be here for her. End of story."

"Sweetie, that's perfect! Now if you could just tell her that directly—"

"Wait a minute," Ruth cut in. "Do you want Charlie to *pressure* Max to go with you?"

"Of course not!"

"Then what *are* you asking for?"

"Maybe you should mind your own business."

"Maybe you should fuck off before I maul that leathery badger skin right off that ass."

"Okay," Charlie said, quickly jumping in. "I'll make this clear for everybody: I am not going to pressure my sister to do anything. Whether it's to stay or to go, she has free will. She can make up her own mind. Okay? Everybody happy? Great."

"That's fine," Renny said, taking a step back. "That absolutely works for me. I just wanted to make sure we understood each other and it seems we do. I just wanted to ensure you wouldn't put any undue influence on her. That's all."

Charlie jerked up so fast that she made the She-bears jump. She needed to get herself back under control, even though she was getting to the point where she might not be able to maintain it.

She raised both her forefingers and turned her head so she didn't have to look at Renny while she forced herself to calm the fuck down.

It took a few seconds, but once she knew she had proper control, she faced her sister's mother and precisely and succinctly explained, "Never, in the history of the universe, have I or will I get in the way of you and Max. Not now. Not ever. Do I make myself clear?"

"Yes. Perfectly clear."

"Good. I need you to go away now. Please." Because she couldn't keep from punching her much longer.

"Sure. No problem. It was great seeing you again, Charlie."

Charlie sat back down on the stoop and, after Renny had driven away, Ruth took her hand.

"Oh, Charlie-girl."

"Before we go any further, I just need you guys to be honest with me. Did I mis—"

"No!" Ruth said before Charlie could even finish. "Charlie, you did not mis-read, mis-hear, mis-interpret. You heard what we all heard and understood it correctly."

"Thank you. I wanted to make sure."

chapter TWENTY

Will was going over paperwork and he was in a bad mood. One was not linked to the other. He was in a bad mood because a lot of questions were being asked about his plane being blown up. Coppers from this country and his own were asking too many questions and he didn't like it. You'd think the bastards would just be glad they didn't have to scrape MacKilligan guts off their tarmac, but no. Bastards had all sorts of questions.

Will didn't like answering questions. Never had. And he wasn't about to start now.

They kept saying they wanted to prove—or disprove— that the explosion had been a terrorist thing. But the bastards knew better. They all knew the MacKilligan name and what it meant. They were just trying to trip him and his boys up. Wasn't going to happen, now was it?

Will's nose twitched, that familiar scent hitting his senses like a bloody rock to the head.

Jumping up, he spun around and she stood there in the shadows of the hotel suite, watching him.

"Hello, Mairi. Come to kill yer old Uncle Will, did ya?" he asked.

His niece smiled. A mean smile. She'd always had a mean smile. Even when she was a wee thing, playing with her cousins at Will's house. "Actually, Uncle, I've come to make a deal."

He put his papers aside. "A deal? What kind of deal?"

She stepped out of the shadows and Will saw the damage to her face, neck, and arms. She'd been shot and beaten.

"I get you dear Uncle Freddy—and your money—and we forget all this . . . trouble."

"Trouble? You mean helping those Italian bitches in their attempt to destroy us? Destroy our family?"

"To be fair, those Italian bitches are family, too. So I didn't really go *against* the family, now did I?"

Talk about splitting hairs.

"I thought you'd been trying to find Freddy . . . and couldn't. What's changed?"

"Let me worry about that. I just need to know we have a deal."

"All right," Will said. "You bring me Freddy—alive—and we forget *all* this."

"Great!"

He watched her leave. She didn't say another word. He didn't need her to.

"You really trusting her, Da?" his son said from the doorway that connected their suites.

"I trust she's found a way to bring in Freddy," he replied, picking up his paperwork and dropping back into his chair.

"And if she brings him in?"

"We'll deal with her after that."

After their meals of burgers and fries in the food court—thankfully made of cow and not rhino as the server had suggested—the plan was to explore the Sports Center a little more. But a text came from Nelle asking Max and Zé to meet Max's teammates uptown. They grabbed a cab outside the Sports Center and went to the address Nelle texted them. By the time they reached the location, Nelle and the others were waiting for them in front of a large, five-story building.

As soon as Max reached her teammates, Zé heard her ask, "What? What's going on?"

"We need to get in there," Nelle replied, gesturing to the building. "But they won't let us in."

"Who won't let you in?"

"The fucking cats." She glanced at Zé. "No offense."

Max moved around her friends to stand right in front of the large double glass doors, and Zé waited beside her. She politely knocked, then raised her hand and waved. She included that winning smile and Zé did actually expect the man to allow them entry. But the security guard behind the doors gave her the finger and Zé had to grab her arm before she could pull the knife holstered under her T-shirt.

"Why don't we just break in?" Tock asked. "We're all apparently really good at it."

"I say we just blow through those doors and start beating the shit out of people." Max grinned. "You guys up for that?"

When they all instantly agreed, Zé quickly stepped in front of them.

"Wait, wait. How about we *not* storm the gates like barbarians?"

"But we're descended from barbarians," Max replied.

"Yes. I'm sure you are. But what's in there that you need to get? Is it something I can buy for you online so we don't have to beat the shit out of anyone?"

Streep took his hand in her own and dramatically gestured to the building with the other. "Zé, the truth about who you are is in that building. Hidden away from you by these cruel, *cruel* asshole cats. No offense."

Zé attempted to pull his hand away but Streep held tight. He tried again and still she wouldn't let go. So he yanked it away and kind of hissed at her. Didn't mean to do that last part but it came out.

"Give me a moment," he said to Max and her teammates before walking up to the glass double doors. He politely knocked and the security guard snarled, "What?"

"Are you closed right now? Because here on your door, the sign with your hours says you're open." He leaned back a bit and looked up at the signage over the door. "And this *is* a fucking library."

"Do you have an entry card? This library is open during these hours only if you have an entry card."

"I don't. Can I get one?"

"It's expensive."

And the guy said that as if he *knew* Zé couldn't afford it, which did nothing but piss Zé off. This motherfucker didn't know what he could or could not afford.

"I'm more than willing to pay for an entry card."

"Do you have an appointment?" the guard asked. "Because if you don't have an entry card, you need to have an appointment to come in. But I'm guessing you people don't have that either."

Zé's neck got tight. "You people?"

"He's talking about badgers," Max said from behind him. "It's not a race thing."

"Are you sure?" Because the man was a big, blond, Aryan-looking motherfucker. And it definitely sounded like a race thing.

Max came to stand beside Zé. Pointed through the glass at the guard. "See that hair? That's a mane. A lion mane. He's a cat."

"Uh-huh."

She now pointed at Zé for the "lion's" benefit. "He's a cat, too."

The guard looked Zé over. Then looked over Max and her teammates. "You need to choose a better class of friends, house cat."

Zé grabbed the big metal handles on the glass doors and told Max, "I'm going to tear these fucking doors off."

"Calm down," the guard said. "Calm down." He unlocked the doors and pushed them open. "No need to get bitchy."

Zé stepped back so that Max and the others could walk through first and not be locked out again. Especially since he wasn't exactly sure what they were looking for. He needed their help in this foreign world.

Once the ladies were inside, he followed, matching the guard glare for glare until he turned the corner to enter the main room.

"You're responsible for your friends!" the guard yelled after them. "They steal anything, bucko, it's on."

"Bucko?" Zé snarled, turning around, but Max grabbed his arm and pulled him away. "What an asshole."

"Lion males vary. Some are great. I know a few I just love to hang with. Others . . . you want to throw them from a very high building, headfirst. "

"If you really want to get them, though," Nelle said softly, "go for the hair. They've got such a fucking thing about their hair."

Walking onto the main floor, Zé felt like he was definitely in a snobby library with a lot of very snobby people working in it. These were not the helpful librarians he remembered from his grade school days, like Mrs. Juanita and Miss Frannie. Those two ladies didn't have much to work with at his old public school but they did their best and they did it with a smile—when the kids weren't going out of their way to make their lives hell.

But the librarians here . . . geez.

They went to the counter, where two males and one female ignored them. And continued to ignore them until Tock banged her fists on the wood and yelled, "*Two minutes is too long to be standing here waiting!*"

"Quiet, rodent!" a male cheetah snapped. "The cats here are attempting to expand their knowledge. Something that *you* should try."

Tock was on the counter and almost over it when Mads grabbed her around the waist and yanked her off.

"We need your assistance," Nelle said kindly.

"Do you have an appointment? We only assist those who have an appointment."

Zé put his hands on the counter and leaned forward so that he was eye to eye with his fellow male cat. "*You people* are starting to really piss me off," he growled. "Now, my friends are saying they need assistance—*give it to them.*"

The cheetah hissed. Zé snarled back.

"Good Lord!" the female said, pushing the cheetah out of

the way and taking over. "I swear. You house cats and your drama."

"Bengal tiger," Max said to him so he understood the insult.

"I can't express to you how much I *do not* care what she is."

"Knowing what they are makes it easier to know whether to run or not."

"How can I help you?" the tiger asked, wide gold eyes blinking at them.

Tock, calm once more—she never let her rage linger the way most honey badgers did—said with a hand wave toward Zé, "We'd like familial information on this jaguar."

The tiger nodded. "Of course. How far back would you like to go?"

"The beginning of time?" Mads asked flatly and Max had to ball her fingers into a fist and dig her nails into her palm so as not to laugh in the tiger's face. She was the only one being helpful, after all. It would be silly to piss her off.

"How about a shorter time span?" the tiger sweetly suggested. Maybe it was easier to be pleasant when you knew you were an apex predator. "For instance, three or four generations?"

"Actually," Nelle said, "just one."

"Just one? Ohhhh." She leaned in and whispered to Zé, "Were you adopted?"

Zé leaned in and whispered back, "No."

The tiger pushed a pad and pencil in front of him. "First name. Last name. Current address. Address where you grew up, if that's different."

Zé quickly printed out the information in architectural-type block letters and pushed the pad back across the smooth surface of the desk.

"I'm not sure how long this will take," the tiger explained. "We may need to look in our written archives since some families don't want their offspring tracked by anyone, especially a database."

"Are you talking about doomsday preppers?" Max asked.

"Full-human or not . . . they are *everywhere*."

She walked off with Zé's information and Max turned to Tock. "Did you hear something?"

Tock looked around, leaned in, and whispered, "You mean about that delivery of diamonds coming in from South Asia?"

Max scratched her forehead. "*No*. I mean about Zé."

"Oh. Oh!" Tock stood up straight. "Wait . . . what?"

"When you couldn't get in here before, you said you were waiting to hear back from contacts you had. Did you hear something from them?"

"Um . . ." Her teammates exchanged glances with Tock and she said, "Why don't we wait until—"

"Got it!" the tiger said, coming back to the counter with a smile and a couple of pages printed out. "Here's what we have." She held the pages out but Zé didn't take them. He just glared at them as if expecting them to strike. Like a coiled copperhead.

After an awkward few seconds while the She-tiger held those pages out and Zé stared, Max took them.

"Thanks."

Since she wasn't going to stand there holding the pages out for Zé, she simply looked at them herself, but didn't see anything shocking . . . until she did.

"Huh."

"Huh?" Zé repeated, a note of panic in his voice. This from a man who'd been through the weirdest life change ever and had shown few-to-no signs of panic when not in a full-blown fever . . . until now. "Why are you *huh*-ing? What is there to *huh* about?"

"Well . . . you are in the Katzenhaus system, which would allow what is called the 'Cat Nation' to keep track of you. That way if something happens to your immediate family, they can track any relatives you may have in other states or worldwide who might be willing to take you in. To raise you. If there's no one, you could be taken in by an adoption agency or foster system that handles fellow cats or shifters as a whole."

"Yeah . . . and?"

"See, I was under the assumption that only one of your parents was a shifter, and since you never mentioned your dad, I just guessed that he didn't tell your mother what he was, went out for a pack of cigarettes one day, and simply didn't come back. Sadly, it's somewhat common for the bigger cats. Although it usually happens more frequently with the hybrids. And my dad."

"Waiting for you to get to the point."

Max cleared her throat. "But according to this, both your parents were cats. Your mother was jaguar on her mother's side."

"My grandfather raised me on his own after my mother and grandmother died."

"Yes," she said, wishing she could avoid going on.

"How did they die?" Nelle gently asked Zé.

"Car accident."

Max cringed. "Or a fight with a hyena Clan."

"Sorry?"

Fuck it, she thought. She might as well tell him everything and handed over the document. "It specifies what happened to your mother and grandmother. In the full-human world, the death certificate probably says car accident. But in ours . . . the truth is that your mother and grandmother were in the wrong neighborhood at the wrong time during the wrong Pride-Clan fight. The deaths were accidental—the hyenas just saw cats and overreacted—but it's very clear that your mother and grandmother were part of the shifter world."

Zé stared at the papers in his hand but he didn't say anything. Just stood there . . . staring.

Then, abruptly, he walked out.

"Well," Mads muttered, "he's off to kill every hyena he sees."

But that actually wasn't Max's worry. She saw a bigger issue and, raising her gaze to Nelle, she saw that her teammate saw it, too.

"Go, Max," Nelle urged. "*Go.*"

Max ran out of the main library, past the snobby male lion,

and through the double glass doors. When she hit the street, Zé was already stepping into a cab at the end of the block. She charged toward him, but the door closed, and the cab was already moving when Max reached it. She picked up speed, dashed around a few full-humans walking down the street, and when she passed the cab, she abruptly turned into the street and threw herself in front of it.

The cab wasn't going terribly fast. But fast enough to ram into Max's small body and send her flipping into the back of one of those refrigerated trucks. She bounced off it, hit the ground, rolled toward the cab from the power of that bounce, and went right under the wheels of the vehicle . . .

"Fuck!" the driver screamed when that insane woman rolled under the cab's wheels. He hadn't been able to stop in time and the front tires definitely went over her body.

The poor cabbie hit the brakes and gripped the steering wheel, unable to do anything but pant and pray to St. Francis Cabrini in Spanish.

After a few seconds, shaking and beginning to sob in despair, the cabbie opened his door to step out. But Zé leaned forward, reached his arm through the opening in the protective glass, and caught the man by his shoulder.

"Hold on one second," he suggested.

"But—"

"I'm fine!" Max said, appearing by the poor driver's passenger-side window and waving with that happy smile on her face.

Not surprisingly, the cabbie screamed in terror at the sight of her. A few days ago, Zé would have done the same.

"I'm sorry," she said, moving to the back passenger door and getting into the cab with Zé. "I didn't mean to scare you. I, uh . . . tripped. But I'm fine."

Although she stated this with an actual tire track imprinted across her face like some cosmic joke.

"Really," she insisted when both men just stared at her. "I

promise. I'm a-okay." She gave the thumbs-up with both hands as if that gesture alone would fix everything. It didn't. So Zé told the cabbie, "It's fine. Just go."

The cabbie got back into the vehicle, wiped his eyes and blew his nose with some tissue, then drove on.

Zé rested back in the seat and gazed out the window, not in the mood to talk to anyone. He had too much on his mind. Thankfully, Max seemed to sense that and she didn't try to engage him in conversation, nor go on and on about some other weird shifter factoid. She didn't do any of that. She just sat on her side of the cab and gazed out her own window.

But halfway through their trip, Zé felt her hand cover his. A simple, quiet gesture he appreciated more than he could say. He turned his hand over and interlaced his fingers with hers.

And that's how they stayed for the rest of the journey.

Daley "Dale" Malone closed the video chat, slipped his tablet back into his desk drawer, and pulled out his chemistry books. But as he sat there, trying to focus on his work so that when he started college in a few weeks, he'd be ahead of everyone else . . . he knew he wasn't alone.

Even worse, he knew they'd been standing there for a while.

He turned his office chair around and faced two of his brothers.

"Do we have to tell Keane?" he asked.

Because Keane was the one he was worried about. Keane was the eldest. The toughest. The angriest. Not that he didn't have a reason to be angry. He did. None of that, however, made him pleasant to be around. Especially for Dale, who was the youngest of the Malones.

Actually, Dale was simply the youngest male. His sister, Natalie, was a year younger than he but, of course, she got treated like a princess by everyone else. Not because she was deaf either. To the immediate family, her being deaf simply meant she couldn't hear. Like some people were born with blue eyes and others with brown, some people were born deaf and some were born hearing. And if you really wanted to get into a fight with the Black Malones—as the other Malones insisted on calling them—all you had to do was suggest that their baby sister's deafness was some kind of defect or disability. It wasn't. Not for her. Or for them.

Their older brothers, however, continued to protect her like a weak doe in the woods because they insisted on believing that she was as sweet and innocent as the day she'd been born. To quote his brother Shay, "a victim waiting to happen."

And in the Malone brothers' collective mind—and Dale wasn't considered a "Malone Brother" because he was "too young, too naive, and too fucking stupid," according to Keane—their sister was currently a victim. A poor, sad, kidnap victim taken by some disgusting older man. Dale knew better, though. He knew because there were no secrets between him and Natalie. They were so close in age, they were like twins. There were, however, secrets between Dale and Natalie and *everyone else!*

It was a commitment they'd made to each other when they were toddlers and they kept it to this day. But when it came to their younger siblings, the Malone brothers didn't care about commitments.

Dale was yanked out of his chair and dragged through the family home like a feral cat they'd found under the bed.

They reached the kitchen on the first floor and shoved Dale inside with no mercy. No kindness! Why was he always so mistreated?

"Tell him," Finn ordered when Dale came to a stumbling stop in front of a feeding Keane. His eldest brother was hunkered over a big bowl of Irish stew their mother had made them, big arms resting on the wood table, black hair nearly hiding those disturbing gold eyes that never seemed to miss a goddamn thing.

"Tell him," Finn said again.

"I don't think there's really anything to—"

Shay bumped him in the back, shoving him forward. "*Tell him.*"

Dale cleared his throat. "The thing is," he began, "I promised her—"

Before he could finish, Keane turned his head and locked that cold, merciless gold gaze on Dale, his mouth moving as he very slowly chewed his food. It shouldn't freak out Dale as much as it did; it wasn't as if he hadn't been in this situation many times before. But there was just something about the way his brother did that . . . while staring at him . . . that made Dale want to make a run for it.

And even though he really couldn't see his brother's eyes, it didn't matter. He could *feel* them.

Dale swallowed and said, "Okay, before everyone gets hysterical . . . she's fine. She realizes she made a mistake and she's going to come home soon. She just . . . wants to fix a few things before she does. I tried to talk her out of it, but you know how she is once she makes up her mind. She's just like you, Keane. But she is okay. I just talked to her."

Keane stopped chewing. He swallowed. He kept staring.

"What?" Dale finally asked when the staring kept going and going.

"How long have you known where she is?" Finn asked.

"I actually *don't* know where she is. She's been on the move. Constantly."

"But you've been in touch with her. All this time. And didn't say a word to anyone? Even Mom?"

"She really wanted to do this on her own without you guys."

"Your seventeen-year-old baby sister wanted to do this on her own and you think that's not a problem?"

"I don't know why you're all mad at *me*. I didn't do anything! She did it. And you guys were the ones who went after the MacKilligan sisters, which is probably why she thinks she has something to fix. Again, not something I was remotely involved in. So I don't see why everyone is all—ow. Ow. Ow! Ow!"

Shay, gripping Dale's shoulder and squeezing, nearly crushing it with his goddamn tiger-grip, leaned down and reminded him, "Until you have your growth spurt, short stuff, and your fangs fully come in, you may want to just tell Keane what he wants to know."

"I'm telling you what *I* know. I don't know what she's up to. I didn't know she'd be going. And I'm not exactly sure when she'll be back. She just told me she would be coming home soon and that she was completely fine. That's all I know."

Keane continued to stare at Dale for another full two minutes—really! It was two minutes! He counted!—and Dale forced himself not to look away. Not to avert his eyes. He forced himself not to do anything because he knew his brother would see that as a sign that Dale was lying. And if he thought Dale was lying, this thing could go on for the next twenty-four hours. So Dale kept his gaze steady and waited.

Finally, after what felt like a lifetime, Keane returned his gaze to what was directly in front of him, spooned more Irish stew into his mouth, and chewed. Slowly. Methodically.

Finn put his arm over Dale's shoulder and walked with him back to the stairs. "Next time you hear from her, tell us right away. So that we don't have to worry about lying to our mother when we tell her that you're *not* buried in the backyard. Understand?"

"That you're threatening your own brother with death because our sister is always more important than *I* will ever be? Is that what I'm supposed to understand?"

"Yes!" Finn nodded and smiled at Shay. "Is it me or do you think the kid finally gets it?"

chapter TWENTY-ONE

Xavier Vargas opened his front door and found his grandson standing there, filling up that doorframe as he always had since the time he was fourteen. He wasn't alone today, though. For the first time since high school, he'd brought a girl home.

Some Chinese girl with purple hair and sneakers that matched. She didn't even reach Zé's shoulder she was so short.

"What are you doing here?" he asked.

"We need to talk," Zé said, pushing his way past Xavier and entering the apartment they'd called home the kid's entire life.

"About what?" he asked, closing the door.

He started to follow Zé, but a knock at the door had him opening it again. The purple-haired girl stood there.

She gestured toward Zé. "I'm kinda with him."

"Then get in here," he told her and waited until "her majesty" made her grand entrance.

He pointed to the room he used as his living room and office. Yeah, the apartment was small but it was better than what he used to have growing up.

Xavier went to his kitchen, took three bottles of beer out of the refrigerator and grabbed an opener from the drawer, then took the extremely short jaunt to the living room, which was about two inches away from the kitchen. Although a wall did separate them, which was nice and a feature not everyone in the building had.

He handed out the beers and took the top off his grandson's, then his own, then was about to do the same for the girl but she had already used her teeth to remove the cap.

Deciding not to focus on that bit of tacky for longer than was necessary, Xavier faced his grandson.

Zé began to speak but Xavier stopped him. "You know what we have to do first," he reminded his grandson.

With that damn eye roll, Zé touched the top of his beer bottle to Xavier's, then to the girl's. Xavier followed suit.

She seemed to enjoy that bit of politeness Xavier insisted upon, grinning like a happy idiot before downing some of her beer.

"It's American beer," he told her when she grimaced a little after swallowing. "None of that fancy foreign shit in my house." He looked at his grandson. "So what do you want?"

"Wow," the girl said. "You two are *not* friendly to each other? Is this the typical dynamic between you? Because I *love* my Pop-Pop. He's like the greatest guy! So sweet and funny and—"

"Stop talking," Zé ordered.

"Okay."

She wandered away, going to the bookcase that took up the entire wall that separated the living room from what Xavier still considered to be Zé's bedroom. She studied the titles of the many books there. Books he'd been collecting—when he could afford to—since he was a child.

"How could you not tell me?" Zé asked.

"Tell you what?" Xavier asked.

"Don't try that bullshit with me, old man. You know *exactly* what the fuck I'm talking about."

Xavier stepped into his grandson. "Listen to me, you little shit. You might be ten feet taller than me and wider than this apartment, but talk to me like that again and *I will put you down*."

"You know what would be nice right now?" the girl suddenly said, quickly stepping between Xavier and his grandson. "Chili. Chili would be soooo nice right about now. You see, my sister's mother—we're half-sisters so I'm not being weird by calling her 'my sister's mother'—she used to say that so many problems could be easily rectified if people just sat down over a big meal and *talked* to each other. She used to say that World War Two would have never happened if"—she took a moment to swallow at this bit—"Hitler, Stalin, Roosevelt, and all the rest actually sat around a big table and talked over a delightful meal of beer and chili. I'm not sure I agree with her," she added. "Hitler seemed pretty determined, but, ya know . . . the general spirit of what she was saying is true. Especially when dealing with family. So why don't I see what you have in your refrigerator and maybe I can whip up something we can eat while calmly and rationally discussing all this, like the loving family you are. How does that sound?"

Xavier looked up at his towering grandson and his grandson glowered down at him.

Yeah, Xavier didn't think that would really work.

Max wasn't exactly surprised when the two men exploded into a Spanish-language argument that left her in the dark. She had taken Spanish when she was in high school but to be honest, even if she'd lived in Spain for the last twenty years, she wasn't sure she'd understand a word these two were saying. Not with the yelling and the speed at which they were yelling those words.

She'd known this might happen. After seeing that information they'd gotten from the cat database. After one look at that thing, she *knew* that Zé's grandfather had known long before Zé was out of his mother's womb that the kid would be a shifter. How did she know? Because one of the pages was a document that entrusted Zé's care to the Katzenhaus Trust if anything was to happen to his mother, grandmother, or his grandmother's mate, Xavier.

Not only that, but Xavier had signed it. His signature was there on the copy of the document that had been printed out. Right after the signatures of his wife and daughter.

So, of course, he'd known. The question now, of course,

was why he'd kept it all secret from his grandson. Why hadn't Xavier helped him as he'd developed into an adult? Especially during puberty when Zé was probably confused and scared, wondering what the fuck was going on with his body. Instead, he'd forced his grandson to bury that part of himself, to completely ignore his shifter side. Why?

Those were the questions that probably needed to be answered the most, but screaming at each other wouldn't get them there.

Still, her plaintive, "Hey, come on. Can't we discuss this rationally?" was just not doing the trick. So she did what she had to do and it wasn't pretty.

Max unleashed a nasty, vicious hiss, opening her mouth to reveal all those horrifying fangs as a copious amount of spit flew from the back of her throat and sprayed both men.

Then, with those fangs still hanging out for the world to see, she said, "Both of you stop or I *will* unleash my anal glands. And I can promise you that the funk alone will kill both of you. The only species *not* bothered by that smell are the canines. Neither of you are canines. *So let's stop the fucking bullshit!*" she roared before immediately calming down and softly adding, "Okay?"

Wiping spit off the side of his face, his grandfather accused, "You're dating *honey badgers* now?"

That's when all the fight left Zé. It just left.

Not only did his grandfather know what Zé was—and had known for Zé's entire life—but he *knew* that world. If he knew honey badgers, the man *knew* the shifter world. Shen had told him when they were hanging out in that tree at the MacKilligan house that the honey badgers didn't usually associate with other shifters. They stuck with full-humans, blending in so they could manipulate and use them for their own profit and entertainment. Like Rasputin. Like the Borgias. But one fang-filled outburst from Max and his grandfather had known what she was and that he didn't want his only grandchild hanging around her. Meaning Xavier Vargas could have easily raised his grandson in the shifter world without any assistance from anyone.

But he hadn't. Instead, he'd lied by omission. When Zé had come to him confused and a little scared because he could run faster than anyone in his class, or could fall from trees and the second floor of buildings and not get a scratch much less a broken arm or leg like his friends, or when he'd hissed at his high school football coach because he'd grabbed Zé's shoulder, pissed about a missed play, Xavier Vargas could have sat Zé down and explained it all to him so that he didn't feel like a weirdo freak among his full-human friends.

But, again, he hadn't done that. Any of that. He'd just let his grandson go around feeling like an outsider, when the world he truly belonged to was right next door. A world that Xavier understood and seemed to be more a part of than any full-human who had fallen hopelessly in love with a cat or dog or bear.

Knowing that, understanding that, was too much for Zé. Just too much after everything else he'd experienced the last few days.

He carefully placed the untouched beer onto one of the end tables by the couch and walked out the door of the apartment he'd been trying to get his grandfather to leave for the last decade.

Zé walked out, and into what he hoped would be his new life.

Max put her beer on the coffee table and started after Zé. But she stopped just as she reached the end of the couch.

It was true, she didn't have much family. With her mom in prison, her father an asshole, and both sides of her family wanting nothing to do with her. But Carlie, Charlie's mom, had told her from the day she'd arrived at their little Connecticut home, "Max Yang-MacKilligan, you will *always* have a place with us. Do you know why? Because you're family, baby. And family is family. Now please stop choking Mrs. Merchant's cat and put it back out on the fire escape. I know it scratched you, but it's just a cat, Max."

"Family is family."

That's what Carlie had taught Max.

But it was *Charlie* who'd taught Max that family only mattered "if they are in it with you. To the end. Do or die."

Carlie had been Max's family because she'd been in it until the end and she *had* died trying to protect three little girls, only one of whom was actually her responsibility. She could have grabbed Charlie and run, leaving Max and Stevie behind, but she hadn't. She'd fought to protect them all.

Could that have been the wrong choice? Maybe for others, but not for Carlie. Because she had lived to do what was best for her girls. It had always been about "her girls."

Max looked over her shoulder at Zé's grandfather, and she didn't see a man with an irrational hatred of shifters or a selfish bastard who didn't want a freak for a grandson. She saw devastation on that face because of the past choices Xavier had made. But until grandfather and grandson talked this out, Zé would never know if those choices had been made with his best interests in mind or not.

Max looked around the living room but didn't see any writing paper. Making a tough choice, she grabbed one of the books off the shelves, grabbed a pencil that was lying on the coffee table, and jotted down the address of her Queens home. A move that would have Charlie gasping in horror. She didn't have much time for reading but she treated books like gold.

"When you're ready," Max told Xavier as she placed the book on the table and rushed out the door.

She didn't bother with the elevator but instead ran down the stairs, hoping to catch Zé before he left the building. But she was too late. She rushed through the front door, past the people hanging out in front of the building because it was too hot in their apartments with only shitty fans to fight the summer heat.

A few men whistled at her or made comments but when she looked directly at them, they all quickly turned away. If she were in a different mood, she might amuse herself by torturing them, but she didn't have the time or energy. Instead, she walked toward the street a few hundred yards away, again hoping to find Zé before he took off.

"Max."

She stopped and turned. Zé sat on a bench. As if he'd just given up halfway into his "stalk off."

Relieved, she walked over and stood in front of him. He didn't look at her or say anything. Just sat there with his head bowed.

Max kind of wished Nelle was here. She was really good with the emotional stuff and could tell Max what to do. This was definitely not Max's thing. She was all about the action, about rectifying problems rather than discussing them. And, more than once, Stevie had pointed out how horrible Max was with "anything that has to do with human emotion."

Still . . . she was all Zé had at the moment.

Reaching out, she placed her hand on Zé's head and, when he didn't jerk away, dug her fingers into his hair.

He wrapped his arms around her legs and pulled her close, pressing his cheek against her stomach.

They stayed like that a while, neither one speaking or noticing the world around them.

chapter TWENTY-TWO

Berg walked up to Charlie's house, and the first thing he no-ticed was that the door was new. He didn't want to think too much about what had happened to the old door because he was sure it was something bad.

He entered the house and saw damage to the wall from where—he was guessing—the old door had hit it, justifying his earlier concern.

From there he entered the living room. The first thing he noticed was that one of the windows had been boarded up. Yep. Something bad.

Letting his gaze sweep the room, he saw Zé stretched out on the couch.

"You okay, man?" Berg asked, assuming that at some point the new shifter had gone through that window. He'd been around the MacKilligan sisters long enough to know it was extremely possible.

"Yeah, I'm fine," the cat replied on a very long sigh, which was not the reaction Berg had expected. Especially if Zé had been in some kind of fight. Most shifters found fights exhila-rating, not sad. Yet the way Zé was gazing up at the ceiling . . . he appeared sad.

"Where's Max?" Berg asked.

"She went to get Chinese food."

"Okay."

Zé didn't say anything else so Berg continued on through the dining room and into the kitchen. That's where he found

Charlie. If she'd had another crazy day with her family, he'd find her baking, because that was how Charlie dealt with her stress. But that was not what he found.

Instead, the woman he loved was sitting at the kitchen table with her head resting on her stretched-out arms, and the three dogs he didn't really want at her feet. He knew this was bad because even the *dogs* seemed depressed.

"Charlie?"

She sighed, sounding a little like Zé. "Yeah?"

"What's wrong?"

"Nothing," she obviously lied.

"Are you sure? Because you seem a little bummed."

"No, not at all."

"Okay."

"Just wondering where I went wrong with everything."

Not just went wrong with some specific thing, but with *everything.* Oy.

"Where you went wrong with what?" he asked, wanting her to be specific.

But nope. "Everything. Where I went wrong with *everything.*"

Berg tried to find a space for his foot on the floor between Charlie and the dogs. When he didn't hear a yelp from any of the three on the floor, he crouched next to Charlie and brushed her curly hair off her face. "What's going on? Talk to me."

She sat up straight but didn't look at him.

"I think I'm a horrible sister," she suddenly announced. "I'm ruining their lives. At least I hope it's *ruining* their lives and that I haven't already *ruined* their lives. I want them to still have a chance."

"Charlie, that's crazy. You haven't—"

"I think I should move out and let them enjoy the wonders of life."

The wonders of life? Seriously? He hadn't been gone that long. What the fuck could have happened since he'd left on a last-minute protection job with his sister and brother the night before to bring out "the wonders of life"?

Berg hadn't known Charlie *that* long, it was true. She'd exploded into his life and he'd been figuring her out ever since. But even though Charlie and her sisters were different from other shifters he'd ever known, the three of them were also the *fiercest* beings he'd ever known. It was as if Charlie had been created out of steel, Max titanium, and Stevie gold.

But in less than twenty-four hours, the strongest woman he'd ever known had been reduced to a crumpled mess talking about "the wonders of life." What the hell had happened?

"Okay," Berg said, standing up. He reached down, put his hands on Charlie's hips, and lifted her out of the chair.

"What are you doing?" she asked, but she didn't seem to really care whether she got an answer or not.

Berg carried her into the living room and over to the couch.

"Move your legs," he ordered Zé, settling her down when the cat finally moved a bit so there was some space.

He turned on the TV and put one of Charlie's favorite horror movies on: *The Exorcist III*. Because . . . why not?

Berg left the two depressed shifters and stepped out of the house just as Max was pulling into a spot right in front.

"Hey," she said when she stood at the back of the SUV, opening the door so she could get the food. "What's up?"

"What happened with your sister?"

She stopped, looked at him. "Nothing. Why?"

"She seems to think she's ruined your lives . . . ? Does that sound familiar?"

"God," Max said with an eye roll, and reached into the back of the SUV to start carrying the food into the kitchen. "She didn't blow up anything, did she? Did the Feds come by? Should I smuggle her out of the country again?"

"I'm not talking about Stevie. I'm talking about Charlie."

Again Max stopped, turned to look at him with one of the bags of Chinese food in her hands. "What are you talking about?"

"Did you guys get into an argument or something?"

"Me and Stevie?"

"No. Charlie."

"I don't argue with Charlie. I argue with Stevie."

"Well, something's wrong. She's depressed and—"

"Stevie?"

Now he was getting frustrated. "*Charlie.*"

"Charlie doesn't get depressed. It's her anxiety that really gets her."

"I know that, but at this moment she's thoroughly depressed. I've never seen her like this."

Max thought a moment but finally shrugged. "As long as she's baking—"

"She's not baking."

"She's not baking?"

"Nope. She was just sitting in the kitchen with her head on the table. No baking."

"Get the rest of the food," she said, shoving the bag she held into his arms before running into the house.

Max found a miserable Charlie sitting on the couch with a miserable Zé, both of them watching *The Exorcist III.*

"What's going on?" she asked her sister while turning off the TV.

"Nothing. Why do you ask?" But Charlie spoke with no strength to her voice. No animation. She wasn't even annoyed that Max had turned off *The Exorcist III*!

"Okay, what the fuck happened?" Max pushed. "Is it Dad? Did he do something? Do I need to kill him before Stevie gets home?"

"No, no," Charlie replied, suddenly appearing alert. Concerned. She sat up, clasped her hands in front of her.

"Max," she said with great intensity, "it's not your job to manage Dad. You shouldn't feel that pressure."

What the fuck . . . ?

Berg hustled by with several bags of Chinese food, heading to the kitchen.

"I don't feel pressure," Max said. "And it's no one's job to manage Dad, but we do it anyway because Dad's a fuckup."

"I never should have asked you to get involved. It was cruel and unfair to you." She shook her head. "I've been holding you back from life, Max, haven't I?"

"Actually, you've been holding me back from prison. That's a good thing."

"I should have done better by you. I should have been there for you. When you needed me. I didn't even know you played basketball. I never thought of you as a team player."

"I'm a team player with other *badgers*," she said as Berg strode back outside to get more of the food she'd purchased. She'd assumed she'd be feeding the triplets as well. "Our general hatred of others makes us perfect together. But I don't understand why you'd need to know any of that. It's not like I came in every day and said, 'Hey! I play basketball.' We had other things to worry about. More important things."

"How could such an important part of your life not be important?"

Wait . . . what?

"It's like I turned you into some sort of cult member who blindly followed me around as I ordered you to drink the Kool-Aid."

"Sweetie, we discussed this. It was Flavor-Aid that they drank and I would have drunk it, too, if I were a full-human with guns aimed at me. It wasn't like they had a lot of choices. I, however, have many choices."

"Do you, though?" Charlie asked in a tone Max hadn't heard in more than a decade. Not since high school when Charlie's English teacher had introduced her to philosophy. For weeks she read the works of Nietzsche, Sartre, Plato, even Karl Marx. Then she'd analyze everything in her life and the lives of Max and Stevie. It got so bad, even her grandfather stopped listening to her, taking to hunting down wild boars on the Pack property rather than sitting through another painful dinner with "Immanuel Kant-You-Shut-The-Fuck-Up?" as he liked to call her . . . to her face.

"Do you have choices," Charlie asked, "or am I just making your life hell?"

"At this moment? Hell comes to mind. But I don't think that's what you mean."

"You play pro basketball," she said, "and I've never been to a game. I've never cheered you on. I've never pointed to you and said to some stranger sitting next to me, 'That's my sister.'"

"So?"

"That's what sisters do, Max. They are there for each other, listening to each other's boring stories, and forcing themselves to sit through a sport they detest just to support the ones they love. It's called being family."

Berg returned with more bags. "How much food did you buy?" he demanded, marching by.

"If we were remotely normal," Max told her sister, "that's what we'd do. But we're not, Charlie. We're not a normal family. So we do what we have to and that's okay. It never bothered me."

"It should have. It should have bothered you."

Max's gaze slipped over to Zé, who was no longer stretched out on the couch, despondently gazing up at the ceiling. He was now sitting right next to Charlie, staring at her with his mouth slightly open. He'd known Charlie less than a minute, in the grand scheme of things, and yet he knew this discussion was completely insane.

"I'm destroying you by holding you back. And I can't let that go on."

Now *truly* scared for her sister, Max asked Charlie something she'd never asked her before. "You're not thinking of . . . hurting yourself . . . are you?"

"What?" she asked, the old Charlie quickly coming back. "No! Of course not."

"Are you sure? Because you kind of sound like you are."

"Max, we both know I'd never give Dad or the rest of the MacKilligans the satisfaction."

Giving the perfect response to Max's question meant Charlie wasn't too far gone, but Max still didn't understand what was bothering her big sister.

That was until Zé softly asked, "Charlie, did you happen to see Max's mother today?"

At first, Max couldn't believe Zé had brought Renny up after she'd specifically told him not to. She wondered why he would do such a thing and when this was all over, she planned to yell at him for, like, five seconds over it. But before she could really be mad at him, Charlie snapped back, "What does that have to do with anything?"

Max shifted her gaze back to her sister. *What does that have to do with anything?* Max repeated to herself. If Charlie didn't know Renny was back in the States, then her response should have been, "You better tell me that your mom has been granted an early release." But she didn't say that, because she already knew. She knew Renny was back because Renny had been here.

"You saw my mother?"

Charlie let out a little breath. "She stopped by,"

"She stopped by and now you're morbidly depressed and *whining* about what a horrible sister you are?"

"I wasn't whining. I don't whine."

"You've been whining!"

"It was a little whiny," Zé agreed.

"You let my mother get into your head," Max accused.

"Don't be ridiculous. This has nothing to do with—"

"You *absolutely* let my mother get in there and allowed her to fuck things up. That's why you're acting like this. She did this to you!"

"That's crazy. And not true."

"Okay. Then what did she say to you?"

"Nothing really. Just that . . . you know . . . she'd like to spend more time with you. Maybe travel together. It's been a long time. She probably just wants to get to know her only daughter better."

"Uh-huh. Was that how you felt immediately after the conversation? Or did you feel annoyed and pissed when she first left, but then you started thinking and wondering and worrying that maybe she was right?"

"I wouldn't say—"

"*Charlie.*"

"Okay, maybe a little. I was mad, but I realized that she probably had a point."

"Dear God, woman! That's what she does! Like a brain-eating disease, my mother worms her way in and destroys from the inside. And you let her do it!"

"That's not what happened."

"It is! And do you know how I know that? Because she taught me how to do it. While I was in my crib, playing with live scorpions—"

"That still freaks me out," Zé muttered.

"—that badger was teaching me how to fuck with people without raising a claw. It's what she's *really* good at. Better than stealing. Better than destroying her enemies. My mother knows how to get into someone's head and before you know it, you're covered in guilt and shame. That's not even a honey badger thing!" Max admitted. "Most badgers just come at you like the infected in *28 Days Later*. But not my mother."

"Oh, my God." Charlie leaned forward, dropped her head into her hands. She sat like that for about a minute until she finally admitted, "You're right. That's exactly what she did."

"I know. I do it to Stevie *all* the time."

"Yes, but you do it so she doesn't wallow in her misery and then accidentally destroy the world. Not just to get what you want out of her."

Berg, his brother, and their sister, Britta, came by with more bags of Chinese food. "So much food!" he complained. She knew the triplets were going to eat the majority of it with or without anyone's help, but she'd let him live in denial.

"Your mother, however," Charlie continued, "did it just because she wants you to be her jewelry-heist buddy and she wanted *me* to get you to do it."

"Yeah," Max told her. "That's my mom. In fact, your mom *told* you that's my mom. She told you to be prepared for that."

"I can't believe I fell for it."

"It's not surprising, really," Zé reasoned. "You just don't

want your sisters to resent you for what you've had to do over the years to keep them and yourself alive. You made choices. Tough choices. But everybody does. Especially when you're caring for others. The question is, were you doing it for a good reason? Because you cared and you wanted to keep them safe? Then you have nothing to feel bad about."

After hearing that, Max couldn't help but stare at him, wondering if he would see how that statement applied not only to Charlie but to his own grandfa—

"What?" Zé asked Max. "Why are you looking at me like that?"

Nope. He didn't see it at all. Typical.

chapter TWENTY-THREE

The dinner turned out to be a surprisingly relaxed event, which Zé hadn't been expecting but was exactly what he needed.

Because he still didn't understand why his grandfather had done it. Why he'd told him nothing. Why he'd allowed Zé to feel alone in the world when he could have been part of something much bigger. All those years of never fitting in, from grade school through high school through the Marines, Zé had always felt out of place. Off.

Yet sitting here, among all these strangers in a Queens house, he felt completely at home. He didn't know why. He couldn't say he had anything in common with anyone. Even Max. But that didn't seem to matter to anyone. In fact, for the first half hour, once they'd all gotten their food and returned to the living room so they could have the TV on in the background as they ate, no one spoke. Not because anyone was angry or Charlie was still upset—if she was, she didn't show it—but because they were eating. And wow, could all of them eat.

There was no talk of diet or workout regimes or anything else as they downed the Chinese food Max had brought back to the house; the majority smothered in honey—honey chicken and broccoli, honey garlic beef, honey General Tso's chicken, honey shrimp and green beans. Max and the triplets seemed to enjoy all that while Zé and Charlie focused on the non-honey foods.

It never occurred to Zé that he would eat nearly as much

as everyone else, but he did. Easily. And if he hadn't stopped himself, he sensed he could have kept going.

Watching the triplets eat, though . . . That was interesting. There was some snarling and snapping when arms reached over or around to grab at cartons of food from the living room coffee table and it felt almost like the three siblings were preparing for hibernation. He wanted to ask if they actually were, but he didn't want to be rude. Not when everyone was having a nice time.

When they'd mostly finished, except for the occasional nibble of the leftovers, Zé thought about asking Max if she wanted to go to a movie. Or maybe out for coffee. Someplace it could be just the two of them. But then Kyle came in through the front door and, without even a "hey," went right through the house and out the back.

It wasn't long after that Shen came in as well.

"You guys seen Kyle?" he asked, and then he spotted the food. "Ooooh. Is that from Honey Panda?"

"Yep. I got you bamboo chicken, bamboo beef, steamed bamboo, and bamboo fried rice. I put it in the fridge for when you got home."

"You're the best, Max. Thanks."

"What do you need Kyle for?" Charlie asked.

"I've got to take him into the city."

"Family dinner?" Max asked, snuggling close to Zé's side before she explained, "Kyle hates family dinners."

"Worse," Shen replied, using his fingers to dig out whatever leftover chicken he could find in the General Tso's container. "Surprise birthday party. Oriana and Stevie are waiting for him."

Charlie snorted. "No one should be forced to go to any party, but especially a *surprise* birthday party." She briefly made gagging sounds. "Can't think of anything worse."

"Even if it's your birthday?" Shen asked.

"It's not my birthday."

"No. But it's Kyle's. It's Kyle's birthday. Actually, yesterday was Kyle's birthday but the party is today."

"It's his birthday? Did you know this, Max?"

"No. But I can tell you in all honesty, I wouldn't have cared even if I did know."

"Ech," Charlie said, dismissing her sister with a wave of her hand and getting to her feet.

"Where are you going?" Berg asked.

"I'm going to find the kid. Eighteen is huge. He has to celebrate."

"Really?" Max questioned her sister. "He *has* to celebrate? Isn't that something you can do or not do?"

"*No*," Charlie told her in a tone that brooked no dissent.

Max shuddered. "Now I'm having birthday flashbacks."

"I don't want to hear it." Charlie stepped over bodies to get around the table. "Your parties were always major events and I made sure everyone had a good time. Even you, Max."

"I enjoyed myself grudgingly. Grudgingly!"

Britta pointed at the window that Zé *hadn't* gone through during the brawl with tigers. "He's making a run for it."

Charlie took off toward the front of the house and Zé had to admit he was impressed she could move so swiftly considering she was probably still digesting all that food she'd just eaten.

She returned a few minutes later, her arms wrapped around the waist of a struggling and much taller Kyle.

"Got him!" she said with obvious pride. "Here, Shen."

Charlie handed Kyle off and gestured to the others. "Let's go. All of you."

"Go?" Berg asked. "Go where?"

"To Kyle's surprise party." She blinked, looked at Shen. "How can it be a surprise if he knows?"

"I can't answer that."

"Why are we going to Kyle's party?" Dag wanted to know. "Even he doesn't want to go."

"A kid's eighteenth? This is important!"

"Do you know who I am?" Kyle demanded. "I'm Kyle Jean-Louis Parker! Artist, prodigy, and bon vivant. And the only party I plan to attend is the one for my gallery opening!"

Charlie studied the kid. "Do you have a gallery opening?"

"Not at the moment," he finally admitted.

"*Then shut up!*" She jerked her thumb over her shoulder. "Shen, get him in some clean clothes. You guys, let's get ready. We meet at the SUV in ten!"

Max rested her head on Zé's shoulder. "Zé and I are going to stay here. Ya know . . . some alone time." She gave her sister an exaggerated wink to, uh, get her point across, Zé guessed.

"Fuck the cat on your own time. Let's go! Let's go! Let's go!"

Charlie waited by the SUV for everyone else. She could still hear Kyle bitching about not wanting to go but she had no patience for it. The kid would one day regret not having celebrated such a big milestone. No, it wasn't like turning twenty-one, when a boy could legally drink, but Kyle didn't drink anyway. So this was more about celebrating life! Managing to get to eighteen was an achievement. Especially for Kyle, who had the unique ability of pissing off almost everyone he came into contact with.

She heard doors closing from inside her house and at the triplets' across the street. She knew everyone was coming. With a sigh, she looked at the text on her phone from much earlier in the day. It was from Imani. Charlie didn't want the She-lion at the house when either of her sisters could come wandering in and wonder what the fuck was going on. But meeting at a party? Well . . . this was Kyle's party. For all Charlie knew, three people could show up, including Stevie and Oriana because it wasn't as if Kyle surrounded himself with friends. Or family. Or anyone, now that she thought about it. Still, she could make the meeting work since it was at a club.

Charlie texted the club info to Imani and stuffed the phone into her back pocket seconds before the front door opened and Shen walked out, carrying Kyle with one arm the way he might a sack of potatoes. Behind them were Max and Zé, and Charlie ordered her sister to text her teammates the details for the party.

Max stopped walking. "Why the hell would I do that?"

"Just do it."

"Oh, is it so the kid will have people at his party?"

"It's like you want me to start screaming."

"Calm down," she said, pulling out her phone. "I'm sure they'll come."

The triplets came from across the street and, together, the group piled into the SUV.

As soon as the doors shut, the complaints started. From everyone.

"Shut up!" Charlie yelled. "We are going to this party. We're going to have a good time. And I don't want to hear anything else *about it*!" She waited a beat for her yell to fade. Then she added, "Understand?"

"Yes," they all groaned except Kyle.

"What I don't think you understand," the kid spouted, "is that I consider this a form of kidnapping and I plan to—"

"Shut up, Kyle," the entire group told him.

"Rude," he muttered, but at least he did shut up.

"Whatever happens," Max told Zé while he stared out over the packed dance floor, "just don't start swinging."

Frowning, he asked, "Why would I just start swinging?"

"*Maaaaaaaax!*" a voice screeched seconds before Bane— sorry . . . Blayne—the woman he'd met at the steakhouse, attacked Max from behind, wrapping her arms and legs around the much smaller woman.

Slowly Max turned her head to look at him. "Now do you see?"

"Cocaine?" he asked, assuming that would explain the woman's risky behavior.

"Nope. Sprite. Maybe Pepsi."

"Actually," Blayne said, dropping to the ground and gliding to a stop in front of Max, "none of those things. Shirley Temples. Six of them." She pumped her fist into the air and screamed out, "Woooooo-hoooo!" Then she grabbed Max's hand and dragged her out onto the dance floor. That's when Zé realized the woman had on roller skates.

Why was she wearing roller skates? At a club?

"Want a shot?" Berg asked him, motioning to the bar.

"God, yes."

The bartender poured four shots of tequila for Zé and the triplets. They each picked one up and were about to knock them back when Nelle and Mads abruptly ran up to them and began slapping the tequila from their hands.

"What the hell, man?" Dag demanded.

"You don't want that tequila," Nelle said, grabbing the bottle off the bar and expertly passing it off to Tock, who hustled it away while Streep put her hand to her forehead and seemed to pass out in front of Charlie, clearly attempting to distract her from what had just happened.

"Okay, then!" Nelle said before walking away.

"What the fuck was that?" Zé asked Berg.

"I'm guessing poison."

"It's tequila. How bad can it be?"

He shook his head. "No, I mean literal poison."

"Sorry about that," the bartender said, pouring the four of them fresh shots from a tequila bottle Zé recognized. "I didn't know they'd put that shit behind the bar."

"This is going to be an interesting night, isn't it?' Zé asked the triplets and the three just laughed.

Max watched Blayne perform what she seemed to think constituted dancing. It wasn't. It was just a horrifying show of "Blayne moves." Even worse, those moves were done to "Funkytown." A song she only knew because her Pop-Pop had listened to that sort of seventies crap when he was driving Max, Stevie, and Charlie around before Charlie got her driver's license.

"Come on!" Blayne urged. "Dance with me!"

"To this seventies shit? Don't they have anything from this century?"

"It's a seventies-eighties dance party!"

"That explains the white people in Afros."

"Those are African wild dogs!"

"That means nothing to me."

The music switched to Donna Summer—another singer she knew because of her Pop-Pop—and Max was done. She turned to look for the closest bar and then Zé, but instead found her baby sister. When they spotted each other, Stevie stopped and stared at her.

What are you doing here? she mouthed to Max.

Charlie, was all Max had to say in return.

With a laugh and nod, Stevie started off but abruptly stopped again and motioned to Max to come to her.

"What?" Max asked when she stood next to her sister.

"Livy asked about you."

"Livy who?"

"Your cousin."

Max frowned, confused.

"The one you've threatened with death many times?"

"Still unclear."

Kyle sat at the bar nursing his virgin Bloody Mary and wondering when this night would be over.

"You're here!" Oriana greeted, putting her hand on his shoulder. "We didn't get to say 'surprise' to you."

"Seriously?"

"I promised Mom I'd make sure you got a party."

"I'd rather be home. Doing *anything* else."

"I know, but Mom feels bad she couldn't be here." When Kyle simply stared, Oriana added, "I know. She's rarely here for our birthdays."

"It's hard to turn down the King of Spain."

"At least *try* to have a good time."

"How?"

"There are kids your own age."

"Are they all African wild dogs?" When she shrugged, he said, "Yeah, I'd rather be home."

"At least stay until we cut the cake. Stevie ordered it just for you."

"Meaning?"

"I think it's made to look like one of your pieces. The one that got some award."

"*Many* of my pieces have gotten awards."

"Oh, my God! I can't with you anymore. Just stay until we cut the fucking cake," she snarled before storming off.

Max found her cousin hanging over the balcony railing, her camera aimed at the crowd below.

Briefly, Max entertained the thought of shoving Livy over the railing but she knew that would only piss off Stevie and she'd never hear the end of it. Not in the mood for the yelling that would follow such a move, she simply called out, "Livy! You wanted to see me?"

"Gimme a sec."

That "sec" turned into five long minutes and by the time her cousin had removed herself from danger, Max was cracking her knuckles, entertaining the idea of punching Livy in the face for keeping her waiting. Damn artist types.

"Sorry about that."

"Took you long enough."

"I said sorry, bitch."

Max stepped into her cousin's space but Livy quickly pushed her back. "Before you get out of control . . . I wanted to let you know that the aunts came to me."

"All of them? Because we have a lot."

"They sent one representative but she spoke for all."

"I guess it's about my mother?" Christ, her mother had only been back a couple of days and despite her being gone for two decades, Max had to admit . . . she was already sick of her!

"The aunts are hoping she goes back to Europe."

"So they should tell her that. Why are they bothering me? Or *you* for that matter?"

"They're bothering me because they don't want to even suggest they're opening a line of communication with you since they consider you more MacKilligan than Yang."

"Bitches."

"And they aren't telling her anything because they don't want to look like they're forcing her out. Even though they're hoping to force her out through you."

"Through me?"

"They probably figure she's not going anywhere unless you go with her."

Exasperated, Max finally asked what she'd been thinking for days now. "When did *I* become the center of this chick's life?"

"She's your mother!" Livy yelled back with a laugh.

"Yeah . . . I guess. I mean, don't get me wrong. It's been great actually seeing her. But I don't necessarily want to become traveling buddies with my mother. I work alone. Plus, I've got the playoffs coming up and we *are* getting into the finals."

"Oh, that's right. You play basketball. Right? I forgot how much I *don't care*."

"Don't bitch at me because you don't have any trophies."

"Look, I'm just telling you what those old biddies wanted me to. What you do is up to you."

Max sighed. "I guess it couldn't hurt to spend some time with her. She did just get out of prison."

"I think that's actually called a prison *break*."

Max ignored that and continued, "And I have missed her. So maybe I could give it a year or so."

"If you really want to."

"Why wouldn't I want to? I'm her daughter. Daughters should *want* to spend time with their mothers." She frowned a bit. "Right?"

"Maybe asking me isn't such a good idea. My mother and I don't exactly get along. You know, since she keeps calling me 'The Mistake.'" Livy briefly eyed her. "But, in all honesty, it doesn't really seem like you want to go."

"I guess I don't. I've got a lot going on here and I just met a guy. He's extremely hot."

"Did you try to throw this one out a window, too?"

"I never try, I succeed. And I haven't had to do that with him. Plus, he's a cat, so he'd land on all fours anyway." She blew out a breath. "It's my mother. I can at least give her a year. At least until she can get back on her feet financially. It has been a while since she's done any real work. Safes and alarm systems have changed drastically in the last twenty years."

"What are you talking about?" Livy asked.

"You can't tell me the aunts have been giving my mother money since she's been locked away."

"Of course not. You know the family rules. But she has that guy's money. Devon, right? I heard she took him out, by the way. Let the hyenas eat him." Livy shuddered. "That is so gross."

"Wait." Max couldn't give a shit about Devon. "What do you mean she has Devon's money? She's never had Devon's money."

"Yeah, she did. Before she got banged up in Romania, she handed it off to one of the Beijing Yangs. How do you think she got that Bugatti?"

"She *stole* it?"

"That would be less than subtle for a fugitive on the run. She bought that shit. With money. That she has. Because she has Devon's money. The Beijing Yangs laundered it and put it in an account for her, taking only a thirty-five-percent cut."

Max shook her head. "If that were true, don't you think she would have . . . I don't know . . . told me? You know, since Devon *was* trying to kidnap me to use me as leverage to get the money back."

"Yeah, I don't really know anything about that. But this all seems awkward now. I feel awkward." She weakly gestured to some random spot. "I'm gonna . . . walk away now."

Livy scurried around Max but before she could get away, Max called out, "Wait."

"God, are you going to make this more awkward?"

"No. I just have a question."

"What?"

"Would your mother do the same thing to you?"

Livy thought a moment before replying, "Probably." Then she shrugged. "But that's the way of the Yangs. Let me re-phrase. That's the way of the Yang women."

"Would you do that?"

"No. But I'm an artist and according to our aunts, my life choices just make me an idiot they're all ashamed of."

Max shrugged. "But I wouldn't do it either."

"In all honesty, Max, you were raised by different people."

"You were raised by Yangs."

"But I'm also half Kowalski. No. Wait. Forget that. The Kowalskis aren't any better. In terms of who really raised me, though . . . that would be the Jean-Louis Parkers. Kyle's family. When I met Toni, my life changed. *I* changed. That's why my mother hates them with the fire of a thousand suns." Livy smiled, laughed a little. "She blames them for my being a—and I'm quoting here—'loser that takes pictures.' Aaaah. A mother's love," she joked. "But don't worry about it. Your mother isn't doing anything ultra-weird. She's just being a honey badger."

"Yeah. Sure."

Her cousin disappeared back down to the club and Max soon followed her.

As she went down the stairs, she saw Stevie again.

"Everything okay?" she asked. "Did you find Livy?" Stevie stopped a server going by with a tray of fancy-looking hors d'oeuvres. She took two off with a napkin and held them out for Max.

"What do I want with those?"

"They're honey puff pastries."

"Oooooh. Thanks, dude." Max shoved both into her mouth at the same time and nodded. They were good.

When Max had swallowed her food, she asked her sister, "Can I borrow five bucks?"

"Hey!" Stevie called out to one of the people working the party. "Tell the DJ to forget this slow stuff. Remember, dance, dance, dance!" While she said this, she hopped on one leg, took off one of the bright orange Converse she'd taken from Max's room, and removed a small stack of tens and twenties. She handed the whole thing to her sister.

"I'll pay you back," Max said.

"Whatever. I've got to make sure that cake arrived. I'm so proud of it!" She tugged Max's sneaker back on and walked away.

Max tracked down Charlie. She was sitting at a small table, chatting with Kyle's oldest sister, Toni.

When she sat down, Toni moved off and Charlie told Max, "I don't hate her as much as I thought I did."

Max waited for Charlie to add more about Toni. It seemed that she would add more. But other than "That's all I have to say," she didn't.

The pair sat for a while until Charlie stated, "This music reminds me of riding in Pop's car."

"I know, right?"

Charlie glanced down at the small stack of cash that Max had laid on the table. "What's that?"

"I owe you money."

"Since when?"

"Not sure. But I owe you money."

Charlie pushed it back toward Max. "Keep it."

"It's yours."

"I don't want it."

"I owe it to you."

"What is wrong with you?" Charlie snapped. "If I need money, I'll ask for it."

"Yeah, but—"

Charlie swiped up the cash and proceeded to shove Max forward so she could stuff it into her back pocket.

When Max began to argue, Charlie closed the fingers on her right hand, like she was clamping someone's mouth shut, and snarled, "Zip it!"

The pair sat in silence for a bit until Charlie smiled and said, "Totally feel like we're back in Pop's car."

Kyle had almost reached the exit when his eldest sister's best friend, Livy, grabbed his arm and dragged him back into the club.

"I want to go home."

"I know." She pushed him against the bar. "And you can as soon as the rest of your siblings get here and you ooh and aah over the fucking cake. Think you can handle that?"

He blew out a breath.

"Oh, I'm so sorry people love you enough to throw you a party, Kyle."

"You don't have to sound so mean."

Livy snorted. "Obviously I do. Just stop being ungrateful."

"I'm not ungrateful. I just don't want to be here. But, since you insist—"

Kyle jumped when he heard a symphony of thuds, and he quickly turned toward the round table a few feet away. Four women were facedown, each gripping a shot glass.

"Are they dead?"

Livy glanced over. "For the moment."

"*What?*"

"Don't get hysterical."

"I'm *not* hysterical. Maybe we should call an ambulance or something."

"See? That's hysterical. And those are Max's teammates. She plays ball with them."

"Which means what . . . exactly?"

She shrugged. "Badgers."

The four women began to move, each of them slowly sitting up. When they all seemed alert, they slammed their shot glasses down on the table.

"Woo!" one of them cheered. "That was awesome!"

Kyle pointed. "So they're drinking . . . ?"

"Tequila laced with rattlesnake venom."

"Of course they are. Because that's completely normal behavior at an eighteen-year-old's birthday party."

Dag stared at Zé for an uncomfortable amount of time, then said, "You know you're kind of small to be going after Siberian tigers, right?"

"Amur," his sister said.

"What?"

"They're actually called Amur tigers."

After gazing at his sister for an uncomfortable amount of time, Dag refocused on Zé. "I mean, black bears don't fuck with us. Because they're smaller."

"Thank you, Dag," Zé said. "That's fascinating information."

"Okay," Britta said, looking around the table. "Are we really not going to discuss this Freddy MacKilligan thing? I mean, is this some weird online thing? Is he going to end up on one of those news shows where they bust perverts? I just don't understand why none of us are discussing it!"

"We're not discussing it," Berg reminded her, "because it sets Charlie off and no one wants to sit through another one of those Freddy-related rants."

"They do go on," Dag complained.

"Do you really think he's actually having a thing with this girl?" Britta asked, her face twisted into an expression of utter disgust.

"Max thinks he's just using her for her hacking skills," Zé pointed out.

"That does make sense. Sadly. He's not a man who understands basic boundaries."

"I've only met the man once," Zé admitted, "but I don't like him."

"No one does," Berg said. "But do you think these Malones are related to Cella?"

Britta nodded. "Probably. I mean, how many Irish Siberian tigers could be running around Queens?"

Nelle sidled up to the table and took Zé's hand. "Come with me," she ordered.

Zé allowed Nelle to pull him away from the table, but he noticed how Britta's gaze locked on poor Nelle.

"I think Britta believes you're pulling me away for nefarious reasons."

"Who?"

"The grizzly female?"

"Whatever." She led him into one of the hallways and handed him a hotel room keycard.

"Whoa, Nelle. You're really sweet but—"

"Please don't make me give you the speech."

"The speech? What speech?"

"You don't want to know. Now, you take that, you go get my girl, and my driver will take you to the Kingston Arms hotel. I got you guys a suite with a hot tub. Feel free to get room service or drinks out of the minibar. It's all on me."

"You know I have my own money, right? I don't actually need charity."

"Of course I know that. But you don't have access to it at this minute and watching you two constantly be thwarted by family and friends is getting painful."

Zé smiled and kissed Nelle on the cheek. "Thanks, Nelle. I appreciate it. And—"

"I know. You'll pay me back. Now go. My driver, Gavin, is outside, and you better head out before the karaoke starts."

"Karaoke?"

"I really can't think of a bigger boner killer than African wild dogs singing."

Honestly? Neither could he.

Max wasn't planning on dancing until Dutch showed up at the party. He grabbed her hand and spun her out into the middle of the dance floor. From there, they busted into the Hustle, with Streep and Tock on either side of them. The wild dogs loved it.

Her big sister, however, just looked horrified. She dropped her head and covered her face until Max noticed the female who sat down at the booth with her.

She grabbed Dutch's hand and he spun her into his arms.

"Hey," she said as they moved together, "isn't that the She-lion from the street near our house?"

"Yeah."

"She was at the thing."

"What thing?" he asked, as they moved from the Hustle into the Bump.

"At the NYPD office. She was with the guys who were trying to blackmail me and my team."

"From what I hear, those guys are still in the hospital. So she's here on her own."

"Spin me to Tock."

He did.

"Did you or Nelle ever find out what team those guys belonged to? The ones at the NYPD office?"

"Nope. There's nothing on them. And if Nelle can't find out—"

"Got it."

She Hustled her way back over to Dutch. "Dance me to Charlie."

Her friend took her hands, pulled her in, and lifted her. Then he carried her over to the table.

"What are you two doing?" Charlie asked.

"I am impressing the masses," Dutch said with a shoulder shimmy, then he shimmied his ass back to the others.

"I *begged* you to get better friends," Charlie only half-joked.

Max pulled a chair from another table and put it right beside the woman harassing her sister. "You shouldn't be here."

Charlie scratched her forehead. "Max—"

"If you think you're going to blackmail my sister like you tried to do to me, I'll make sure the only thing you know for the rest of your miserable life is *pain*."

"Imani, could you excuse us?" Charlie said.

"Yeah. I'll text you tomorrow."

Max waited until the She-cat had walked away before turning to her sister. "Are you letting that bitch blackmail you?"

"I need you to calm down."

"I need you to grow a set. Don't let her push you into anything!"

"I'm not!"

"Then what are you doing?"

Charlie shrugged. "I'm taking a job."

"A job?"

"Yeah."

"Doing what?"

"Hopefully . . . helping people. She'll give me the resources I need and the intel, and I do what I do."

"You don't even know her."

"No, I don't. But I don't get a bad vibe from her either. And she's not stupid." She rested her elbow on the table and her chin on her fist. "I don't know. But I want to give it a try."

"Why?"

"I need a job, Max. I need to do something with my life. Something that provides regular money that I don't have to worry about laundering."

"Is this about my mother again?"

"No. It's about me."

"You're putting yourself at risk. Putting *us* at risk."

"We're *always* at risk. We're MacKilligans. Which is also the reason this is the closest I will ever get to a government job. So I'm going to try it out."

Max knew her sister was probably right, but she wanted to talk to Imani. She left the table as Charlie yelled, "I'm not running after you! I'm not!"

"Good!"

Zé walked through the club with the keycard that Nelle had given him burning a hole in his back pocket.

He was trying to find Max but everyone kept getting in his way. He'd never been so popular. He wasn't sure he *wanted* to be that popular. But the wild dogs kept introducing themselves. He didn't know why. And the cats and wolves kept sort of challenging him with looks and the occasional body slam. He also didn't know why.

Honestly, he just wanted to find Max and get out of here.

When Dutch landed on the ground in front of him, Zé stepped over him and kept going.

"Aren't you going to help me up?"

"Nope."

Zé did stop at the bar, though, when he saw Charlie standing there . . . seething. And the woman seethed well. Arms crossed over her chest, brown eyes flashing. And every predator in the room avoiding her.

"Hey, Charlie. Are you okay?"

"She's making me crazy!"

That was direct.

"She makes me crazy, too," he admitted.

"I'm just trying to do what's right for me and our family. So I don't need her shit."

"I understand."

"Why does everything I do always have to be about my sisters?"

"It doesn't."

"Are you just agreeing with me?"

"No. But I can tell you and Max are close. She just wants you to be happy and you just want her to be happy. The pair of you are running around, trying to make each other happy. It's sickeningly sweet. Or would be if she wasn't always covered in military knives under her clothes and even now *you* have a .45 holstered to the back of your jeans."

Charlie looked over her shoulder. "Oh, can you see it?"

"No. The T-shirt covers it."

"Great." She gave a small smile. "You really care about Max, don't you?"

"She's insane and dangerous and has managed to convince my old team leader that I am taking advantage of a mentally unstable woman. How could I *not* care about her?"

Charlie's snort turned into a laugh, her wide smile lighting up her face.

"Come on." She grabbed his hand. "Let's go find her. I'll slap her around a little bit, then you can take her home."

"That's big of you, Charlie."

She wrapped her arm around his back. "Isn't it?"

Max lost Imani in one of the hallways. She sniffed the air but there were tons of cats and dogs in the club, making it hard to focus on just one scent.

Thinking she caught the female's scent going down a flight of stairs, Max followed. But when she opened the first-floor door it was another hallway with exit doors at each end.

"Fuck."

She sniffed the air again but she couldn't catch anything specific.

Making a guess, she took a right and went through the exit.

Imani had already made it to the end of the alleyway by the time Max stepped outside. She followed, but abruptly stopped.

"*Seriously?*" she demanded, turning to again face the cousin who wouldn't let it go. Whatever "it" might be. "Woman, what is wrong with you?"

"Just wanted to tell ya," Mairi said, "I'm going to find your da and bring him to Uncle Will. Let him deal with his bastard half-brother." She suddenly grinned. "He's gonna rip 'im apart."

Max waited for more but when she didn't get any, she shrugged and said, "Okay."

Her cousin continued to grin for a little longer but it eventually faded and she asked, "What do you mean, 'okay'?"

"Is there another meaning for 'okay'? Some Scottish slang meaning I'm unaware of?"

She took a few steps closer to Max. "You know what Uncle Will's gonna do to him . . . yeah?"

"I'm aware. So's Charlie. You might make Stevie cry . . . for about five minutes. If that's the reaction you're hoping for. Other than that, I don't know what you want from me. Or why you're even bothering to tell me."

This time, Max stepped closer until she was inches from her cousin. "What do you really want from me, cousin?"

"I guess just a challenge. Something fun to do."

"You think this is fun? Tracking me down at a party you weren't invited to, hiding in an alleyway that you *hope* I'll come through at some point in the evening, and talking to me when neither of us likes each other? You think that's fun?"

"Terrorizing you is fun."

"So you don't have friends."

"What?"

"If you had friends, sweetie, you'd be hanging out with them. Not 'terrorizing' me. And yet here you are. Have you thought about joining a club? You're . . . foreign. Don't your people love soccer?"

"Football."

"Oh, come on. That's not *really* football. Until you people have a Mean Joe Green on your team, you don't know what football is."

"Who?"

"One of my grandfather's favorite football players. He was amazing. You can catch some of his plays on You—"

"Stop talking!"

"There's no need to yell. I understand your unhappiness."

"I am not unhappy."

"Really? Because you don't really appear happy."

"*You know what I really want from you, cousin?*" Mairi exploded.

"Again with the yelling."

"I want to see you suffer!" Mairi suddenly hissed, true badger rage filling her up, turning Mairi's pale skin a bright, angry red. "I want to see you in torment before I finally *end* you."

"God, sweetie," Max told her with intense honesty. "That is the saddest thing I've ever heard."

Mairi's entire body twitched a bit. "*What?*"

"Don't you think that's a sad way for you to live? You don't even know me, but you spend your days hating me. Plotting what you're going to do next. And I know you want me to hate you back so we can have this big . . . badger war? I guess. But I could not give a flying fuck about you." She shrugged. "Sorry."

That badger rage exploded and her cousin grabbed Max by the throat, slamming her against the wall.

That's when Max began laughing. She couldn't help it. Because even when the crazed bitch was punching her in the face, even when she was choking her with her bare hands, even when she was reaching for one of the knives Max had on under her T-shirt . . . Max couldn't get past the fact that the terrifying and horrible Mairi MacKilligan was letting Max get to her simply by doing what her mother had sort of done to Charlie earlier that day.

With one hand still gripping Max's throat, Mairi used her free hand to raise the blade she now held high above her head. Based on her aim, Max knew that she wasn't going for the heart, which was the second-best way to kill a honey badger. She wanted to stab her in the face. She wanted to scar her.

It was like she had something to prove, but Max didn't know what it was. That she was a better fighter than Max? That she was stronger? Meaner? Deadlier? Did any of that matter? Even with Max dead, Mairi's life would still suck. Max's death wouldn't fix that for her.

The knife came down, and Max raised her forearm at the last second. The blade tore through skin, flesh, and bone.

And still Max laughed. Despite the pain.

Then Charlie was there. Coming in behind Mairi and yanking the blade away from them both. She yanked their cousin to her feet and began stabbing at her. Hitting her in the neck, the chest, even the face; gripping Mairi's hair so she couldn't get away without losing a good chunk.

Something that she actually did when she couldn't stand being hit with the blade anymore.

Max cringed when she heard that horrible sound. Charlie left standing there with a blood-covered knife and part of Mairi's scalp dangling from her fist.

Charlie screamed as their cousin sprinted away from her. A scream of rage and warning.

Until she winced from pain, Max hadn't realized that Zé held her arm.

"Charlie!" Zé ordered, getting her sister's attention. "Hold Max's arm. I'll be right back." He waited for Charlie to replace him and then he ran back into the club.

They didn't speak to each other but they were no longer mad either.

Zé returned quickly with a club T-shirt. He crouched beside her and began to wrap the wound. "We should take her to the hospital."

"Why?" Max and Charlie asked together.

"The knife went through the arm. There might be nerve or tendon dam—" He shook his head. "Okay. Forget it."

"Just take her home," Charlie said.

"You coming with us?" Max asked.

"And ruin Stevie's night?"

"I thought it was Kyle's night."

"Stevie planned this shit. It's now her night. Besides, I can't go home."

"I swear to God, Charlie. If you go after that crazy bitch—"

"I'm not going after Mairi. At least not until we figure out how we're going to deal with her. I just can't go home right now because I promised Stevie I'd do 'Ode to Billy Joe.'"

"You promised that on purpose?"

"I love that song."

"It's ten thousand years old."

"And it has aged like a fine wine." She pulled out her cell phone. "I'll get you guys a car."

"We have one already," Zé said. "Nelle got us a limo and a hotel room."

That made Charlie laugh out loud but Max was mortified. "Seriously? She seriously did that?"

"She's trying to help a man out."

"We'll take her limo, but we're going home." The last thing Max wanted right now was to be in strange surroundings. "Okay?"

"Fine with me." Zé helped her to her feet, which was nice.

Charlie started to walk away but Max grabbed her arm. "Do *not* tell Stevie or my team about Mairi. Not a word. I'll tell them myself when I feel like it."

"Fine."

"And I've decided."

"Decided what?"

"You need backup."

"In general?"

"No. Mary Mother, some days . . ." She took a breath. Began again. "I'm saying, you need backup on this job for Imani."

"Because I didn't kill Mairi right off? I wanted the bitch to suffer!"

"I don't mean that either. I mean you need backup on this job and that's what I'm going to do for you. I'll be your backup."

"So you can steal my job before I even get it?"

Max gritted her fangs. Because her teeth were fangs now. "Charlie, I swear to God!"

"Do you two do this all the time?" Zé asked.

"Yes," they said together.

"I'll have backup, Max," Charlie told her. "Imani's letting me pick my own team."

"From the cretins who couldn't defend themselves against you?"

"Why do you keep arguing with me?"

"Because we're doing this. You go on that job, I'm with you."

"Forget it. We're not—"

"*I'm dying!* Why are you being mean to me when I'm dying?"

"You're not dying!"

"I could be. And wouldn't you feel bad not giving me what I want?"

"Dude, I don't even know what that means."

"I know and that's all that matters." She motioned for Zé to leave through the alley rather than going back into the club. "Oh, and by the way . . . thanks for saving my life."

"Yeah, sure. Although we both know you could have taken that bitch out at any time." The club door opened and then Max heard her sister ask, "Why *haven't* you taken her out yet?"

"Don't you find her sad?" Max asked. "I find her so sad."

"Why?"

Max stopped and looked at her sister while Zé still held onto her wounded arm. "Unlike me . . . she doesn't have a Charlie or a Stevie. She's all alone. That's gotta suck."

"What does she expect, though?" Charlie asked, finally heading back into the club. "With that fucking personality."

chapter TWENTY-FOUR

Zé worried that he'd made a mistake by not taking Max to the hospital. Once they were in the limo Nelle had lent them, heading back to Queens, Max slept cuddled up against him. She held her arm with her other hand; the blue T-shirt appeared even darker than when he'd first put it on. But the blood on it had dried. So had the blood on her head and face, though it didn't hide the multiple bruises where her cousin had repeatedly punched her. She winced a few times in her sleep but that was the only sign she was in any pain.

When they reached the house and Zé was about to carry Max inside, she suddenly sat up, eyes blinking the sleep away.

"Are we home?" she asked.

"Yeah."

The driver opened the door and Max immediately got out without needing Zé's help. As she stood in front of the house, waiting for him, she tilted her head one way, then the other. Each time a sound like a shot went off and Zé gazed at her, half-in and half-out of the limo.

"Was that you?" he asked.

She looked over her shoulder and smiled at him, the dried blood crinkling.

Max started toward the house and Zé followed her inside, where she walked straight to the kitchen. By the time Zé joined her, she stood in front of the sink with the water running.

He waited off to the side, ready to help when she needed it, and watched her remove the T-shirt on her arm. She handed it to him and slipped her arm under the faucet, letting the water beat down on the skin. Zé cringed, imagining the pain she was feeling. Until the blood washed away and he saw there was no more than a raised scar on each side of her arm.

"It's still healing," she explained when she saw him staring. "On the inside. The scar will fade some over the next few days, though."

With the blood on her arm gone, she stuck her head under the running water. When she'd washed the blood off, she wrung her wet hair out and finger-combed it off her face.

"How do I look?" she asked when she was finally done. Somehow, she was grinning. He didn't understand how she could be grinning.

"Not as horrifying as I would expect."

He motioned to the kitchen table. "Sit up here. I'll put something on the other wounds."

There was a first-aid kit under the kitchen counter. He pulled it out, opened it, but ended up doing nothing but gawking into it for a few seconds.

"What's wrong?" she finally asked.

"Did you know your sister put several knives in here?"

"That was me. In case we're ever held hostage. I figure if they need to keep us alive, they'll probably let one of us use the first-aid kit."

Zé was about to ask why she would plan for such an event. Why she would even think like that.

Then he remembered how he'd met her . . .

Zé dug under the tactical knives—there were three—and pulled out some bandages, alcohol swabs, and a cold pack for the swelling. He placed them on the kitchen table next to Max's leg and moved so he stood right in front of her. Using his forefinger, he lifted her chin so he could examine the wounds on her face. But she was staring at him in that way again.

"You've gotta stop," he said, attempting to avoid her gaze.

"Stop what?"

"Looking at me that way. I'm trying to take care of you here."

She placed her hands on his hips and pulled him closer, spreading her knees so he could press up against the table. And her.

"Now you're torturing me?" he asked.

"Don't mean to."

"Liar."

Her hands slid under his T-shirt, dragging her fingers against the skin.

"You want me to stop?"

"I want you to get better."

She frowned in confusion. "Huh?"

"You were beaten by your own cousin tonight. Remember?"

"That was, like, an hour ago."

The sentence was so ridiculous Zé could do nothing but laugh. But then Max pulled him closer and lifted her face to his.

He knew they should wait another day or two. More time for her to recover.

Max wasn't waiting, though.

Max appreciated that Zé was trying to give her some time. And, if she were anyone else, she'd probably need it.

It wasn't what she wanted, though. She was tired of waiting. She was tired of being interrupted. So she did the only thing she could think of.

She grabbed his dick.

It was through his jeans but she knew that wouldn't matter. And she was right. He was already hard. So her hand on his dick made him groan; his eyes closed, head dropping forward.

"This isn't fair," he growled.

"I never promised I'd be fair," she replied, tightening her grip. "I don't want fair, Zé. I want you. Now. Fuck me."

His hands cupped her neck and his lips were on hers. He slipped his tongue into her mouth and it moved in such a way that she could only think about him going down on her.

She unzipped his jeans and was about to push them off his hips when he suddenly pulled back. "Wait, wait—"

"You have *got* to be kidding me!"

"It's just . . ."

He seemed to be struggling for words and she was in no mood to help him. But he slid his hand under her ass and lifted her off the table. "Not in the kitchen," he mumbled. "Your sister will kill us both."

He had a point. Charlie could be a little OCD about her kitchen, and she did her baking on that table.

Zé didn't try to take Max upstairs, though. He just dropped her ass on the dining room table and went to work pulling down her jeans. She had pushed his jeans down by his knees but held him back a few more seconds while she reached down to get a condom out of her back pocket. When Zé saw it, one brow went up.

"What?" she asked, tearing it open. "I have knives in my first-aid kid and guns taped under the kitchen table. Are you really surprised I have condoms at the ready?"

He agreed with a nod and she slipped the condom over his cock.

Zé slid his hands under her ass and pulled her forward, letting her legs rest on his forearms. With one thrust he was buried inside her and Max let out a surprised bark.

"Too much?" he growled, his green eyes now gold.

"Are you kidding?" She gripped his shoulders. "Just loving the fit."

She spread her legs wider to give herself more room and let him take over, doing nothing but holding onto his shoulders or arms, and letting him fuck her.

It felt so good and he was so deep, her toes began to curl in her sneakers.

Then she saw that he was watching her. Those gold eyes locked on her like she was some prey he'd seen running through the jungle. She leered back, wanting to challenge him.

"You've gotta stop doing that," he told her. "If you keep looking at me like that, I'm going to shoot my load right this second."

"Do it," she ordered. "I've got more condoms upstairs and we've got all night." To make her point, she tightened her muscles around him and he swore under his breath. "Come on," she urged. "Come on. I can take it. I can take anything."

That dragged him over the edge and he was coming hard, his hands still gripping her ass. She could feel the tips of his claws resting just beneath his skin, ready to be unleashed.

He thrust again and again, until he finally stopped. He placed his hands on the table and leaned down a bit, sweat dripping off him.

"Too much for you?" she asked, leering at him.

He didn't say anything, just yanked her off the table and carried her up the stairs. He was still buried inside her when he took her into the room she pointed out. Her room at the end of the hall. He dropped her on the bed then and turned away to remove the used condom and take off his clothes.

"More condoms over there," she said, pointing to the drawer next to her bed. But he didn't go for them yet, choosing instead to take off her sneakers and jeans while she slipped off the holstered knives around her chest. But as he tossed her jeans away, he stopped and studied the holsters she also had tied around both calves. They held four of her knives. He took those off, too, and then crouched in front of her, yanking her close. Before she could say anything—like suggesting that maybe he get her a wet washcloth to wipe up a bit—he had his head buried against her pussy and his lips around her clit. He tugged and licked at it, burying two of his fingers inside her.

Max fell back against the bed. Although she hadn't come when he had, her clit was still extremely sensitive and just the feel of his mouth on her had her legs trembling. Her groan turned into a hiss and her back arched as she came against his mouth.

When she came down, she realized he was still going. Not only that but he'd bent her legs at the knees, and pinned them to the bed with both arms.

She growled and grabbed his hair, not sure whether to push him away or pull him closer.

He kept going, though, using his tongue and mouth on her clit. Moving between sucking and flicking.

Max thrashed against him, desperate to come again.

She loved how forceful he was being. Challenging her like she challenged him.

"I . . . I can't . . . I . . ."

She exploded again. Her cries filled the room and she tried to close her legs.

But he still didn't let her go.

"No," she begged this time. "No. I can't. Not again."

This time, he just sucked her clit. Sucking and sucking, pinning her tight to the bed, not giving her any chance to get away. To fight. When she came that third time, she called him every name in the book and tore the sheets beneath her with her claws.

When he made her come that third time, Zé released her so he could grab a condom from the dresser. He put it on and grabbed her ankles as she lay limply on the bed. He flipped her over and, instead of making her get to her knees, he put a pillow under her hips and entered her from behind.

"God," he groaned into her hair. "You're so wet."

He took his time this go-round. Moving his hips this way, then that. Seeing which move seemed to work for her. Which one she seemed to enjoy more. Then something happened.

Zé thought he'd have all the time in the world this time. Thought she'd be out of it for a good twenty minutes or so. But her energy came back hard and she pulled her knees up so that she was curled tight with her ass up high.

Max tightened her muscles around his cock, making him crazy. It was like she'd trained for this shit. He'd never felt anything so intense and so amazing at the same time.

"Faster," she urged. "Harder. As hard as you want."

She was driving him nuts again and already he was ready to blow. Way quicker than what he'd wanted because she was putting up a fight. He loved it.

He slid his hands under her T-shirt and bra, which she still had on even after removing her holstered weapons. He gripped her breasts, teased her nipples. On a whim, he nibbled at her ear and the back of her neck.

She responded to that last move immediately; her hands grabbed his, her hips slamming back against him. He bit the back of her neck harder and she cried out. Her muscles clamped down on his cock again as she came and this time he came with her. Both of them groaning and sweating into her shredded sheets.

When they were done, Zé rolled away from her and she dropped facedown onto the bed. They stayed like that for a while, the sound of their panting the only thing they heard . . . until they realized they weren't the only ones panting.

Zé sat up and Max looked over her shoulder.

"Out!" she ordered the three dogs standing in the open doorway, and they took off running.

She laughed. "Perverts."

Max grabbed some of the leftover Chinese food and a couple of beers, bringing them back to her room. They ate in silence but watched each other the entire time. When they finished, Zé picked up all the trash and took it downstairs. Max went to the bathroom, grabbed a clean washcloth, and ran it under the water.

When Zé walked in, Max crouched in front of him, using the cloth to carefully wipe his dick. Then she tossed it away and replaced it with her mouth, sucking him in deep until he hit the back of her throat.

His fingers slid into her hair and he massaged her scalp as she did the same to his cock. She didn't rush it, taking her time to lean back until only the head remained in her mouth, and then going deep again. She hummed a few times, too.

Zé dug his fingers in deep, curling her hair into his fist. She thought he was about to come, but he pulled her off him and brought her up. His kiss was rough and demanding, slamming her into the bathroom wall. His hands explored the rest of her, tugging her nipples, slipping into her pussy, playing with her ass.

Eventually, he turned her around and forced her over the sink. He opened the medicine chest above her head and found the condoms. Then he was inside her again. Fucking her again.

She was beginning to worry she'd never get enough of his cock. It felt so good.

He used two fingers to grab her clit, tugging and twisting until she came again. But he wasn't done, so neither was she. He continued to play while he continued to fuck and Max could do nothing but come, too.

The sun was just coming up when he found her on top of him, taking her time to slowly fuck him. She had his hands pressed against her breasts, her head thrown back as she enjoyed herself.

He loved the way she moved. Her hips writhing, pressing down on him. All the while she squeezed him with her pussy, making him insane.

"You feel so good inside me," she said, smiling down at him.

Gripping her waist, he leaned up, catching one nipple in his mouth. He tugged it, got it wet, blew on it, sucked it. Anything to make her squirm. Then did the same to the other one.

When they finally came, it was mostly with hoarse groaning. It was all they could manage at this point.

As Max lay on top of him, nearly falling asleep again, Charlie's voice boomed from below, "*You two better not have been fucking in my kitchen!*"

Zé chuckled. "Told you it was a good idea to move out of her kitchen."

"Yes, yes. The cat's always right. Now close the bedroom door before the dogs come back."

chapter TWENTY-FIVE

"I want you bastards to stay out of my room!"

Keane looked up from his breakfast to see his baby brother stomping around the kitchen with his backpack over his shoulder.

"I don't like when you guys are in my stuff!"

"What are you talking about?" Shay asked.

"You know what I'm talking about. You *all* know what I'm talking about!" He pointed an accusing finger at them. "It's not my fault what's going on with Natalie. And I told you she'd be back! So stop blaming me! I've got enough happening in my life right now!"

Then their baby brother stormed out of the house, heading to one of his science or math summer classes in preparation for college, Keane guessed.

"What the fuck was that about?" Finn asked.

"I'm not sure going to college right now is in his best interest," Shay said, devouring his oatmeal. "Maybe he should take one of those gap-year things."

"Fuck that," Keane snarled. "He's going to college. And if either one of you mentions 'gap year' to him, I'll break your legs."

"Can I just say"—Finn rapped his knuckles against the table—"it's always a delight being around you, big brother."

Charlie handed over a plate of muffins to Zé and smirked when he thanked her and went out the back door humming. She hadn't seen him that relaxed since he'd arrived.

Her sister was still upstairs asleep, which was also a change. Usually Max was coming in the back door, covered in honey and bee stings. For her not to spend the night raiding local hives was definitely something new.

Stevie had opted to spend the night in the city at the Jean-Louis Parker home so that she and Oriana could get up early and get right to work on their ballet. Shen stayed with her, of course. Kyle, however, had returned at daybreak and gone right into the garage to work, which was where he was at that very moment. If he'd had fun at his party, he didn't really show it. The kid seemed a little young to be *this* stressed out, but Stevie hadn't been much better when she was eighteen.

Of course, it was because of Stevie that Charlie felt the need to keep an eye on Kyle. She knew how hard child prodigies were on themselves. These were driven, determined children, who wanted nothing more than to do their work and be brilliant at it all the time. Bumps in the road weren't easy for them. A small bump could sideline them for days, months, even years. A large bump could put them out of commission forever. Unlike Max, who had been rolling with all sorts of drama hitting her life, Stevie didn't simply roll with her problems. Sometimes she made what Charlie called a "panic-run," meaning she charged through some problems without even bothering to look up because she was so determined to put them behind her. But sometimes, and these were the times that really worried Charlie, Stevie would get depressed. So depressed that Charlie was nothing but relieved when her baby sister checked herself into a mental health recovery center.

Not wanting Kyle to suffer that kind of depression—few people were as aware of their mental health as Stevie, including Charlie herself—Charlie made sure the kid ate regularly, got exercise, took some time off from his work, and found some friends his own age. Well, she hadn't managed that last one. Kyle was a lot to take. Regular kids didn't want anything to do with him. Charlie was sure that her seventeen-year-old self would have stuck his head in one of the school toilets and flushed. Still, there had to be kids he could hang with. Kids who got him, even if they weren't necessarily geniuses themselves. She just had to find them.

Until then, though, she could continue to watch out for the ego-driven little bastard she'd come to like so much.

"Morning," Max said as she entered the kitchen. She'd showered and put on clothes but she was still half-asleep from what Charlie could tell. She poured herself a large mug of coffee and sat down at the kitchen table.

"Want a muffin?"

Max gestured to the dough Charlie was working. "What are you making?"

"Quick-rise cinnamon buns."

"I'll wait for one of those."

"Cool. How's your arm?"

"Fine. My knife wounds always heal faster than my gunshot wounds. Do you find that?"

"I try not to get shot too often."

"Bitch."

"Did you have a good time last night?"

Max's head dropped. "Okay, I told this to Nelle and apparently, I'm going to have to tell you: we're not doing this."

"Not doing what?"

"Talking about me and Zé."

"Awww. You're shy about your love."

"Oh, get a grip."

Charlie began to sing, "Max has got a boyfriend. Max has got a boyfriend. He's in a tree-ee, eatin' mu-u-u-fins."

"Seriously?"

Max didn't appreciate her sister's laughter when the coffee hadn't kicked in yet.

"Are you done?" she demanded when the laughter-snorting began.

"Yes. I'm done. Sorry about that. I had a moment."

Max ran her thumb along the rim of her coffee mug and asked something she'd just been thinking about. "What should I do about Mairi?"

"I thought you didn't want to do anything."

"I started thinking—"

"Uh-oh."

"—she'll probably try to get to me by hurting you and Stevie. Especially after what we talked about last night. I really
fucked with her head."

"Like mother, like daughter?"

"Something like that."

"We can try to lure her to us."

"Think that'll work?"

"Maybe."

"She did tell me she was going after Dad. That she had Uncle Will's blessing to do it."

Charlie was silent for a few moments.

"What?" Max asked.

"I'm trying to think about how I can use that to our advantage."

Max sat up in her chair. "But what about Dad?"

The sisters stared at each other until they both exploded into
laughter.

"You are too funny," Charlie said when they finally stopped
laughing.

"I know." Max drank more coffee before asking, "So this
new job of yours . . ."

"I haven't officially signed up yet. It's just a test job."

"When is it?"

"I don't want you coming."

"I don't give a fuck."

"Max."

"I. Don't. Give. A. Fuck. I'm going. I will have your back.
It'll be like old times."

"Old times. You mean a couple of weeks ago when we
charged into that lab to get Stevie?"

"That, too. Anyway, I'm doing this. With you. Whether
you like it or not."

"Max—"

"If you say 'no' again, I'm unleashing my anal glands. Right here. While you're making your cinnamon buns."

"Come on, Max! You know that leaves a residue I can't get off the furniture! Remember when we were living with the Pack? Pops never forgave—"

"Hey, hey, hey! That was because of that sneeze. When Stevie blew pepper in my face. I didn't do that one on purpose."

Charlie finished rolling her dough and cut the log into equally sized circles. She was putting them on a metal baking sheet when their front door slammed open. Max wondered if the Malones had returned but it was her teammates who busted into their kitchen.

They were all talking at once, trying to tell Max something. But she couldn't understand a word. It was Charlie who silenced them with a barked "Shut up!"

They did, moving behind Max. That's when she noticed that Mads wasn't with them.

"What's going on?" Charlie asked.

"It's Mads," Nelle said. "We all just got here to pick up Max for shootaround—"

"For what?"

"Informal practice before tonight's playoff game. Anyway, we were just walking through your gate when Mads's family showed up."

Max put her coffee down. "All of them?"

"No. But a few of the stronger males."

"We tried to intervene but things were about to get nasty and—"

"Yeah." Max pushed away from the table. "I'll deal with it."

It was an old trick Mads's Clan had learned when Max and her team were in junior high together. They didn't try to fight Max and the others. They knew how dangerous that was because honey badgers didn't back down. Even young ones. And each of them had a family or, at the very least, a Pack that wouldn't let the hyenas get away with killing them outright. So they used a different, crueler tactic: They made Mads suffer for what her friends did. So, if the team tried to pull Mads away from her cousins to get her out of a bad situation, it was Mads who got the wounds. Who got the scars.

It was shitty but very hyena.

Of course, they were no longer in high school and Mads didn't have to go anywhere with anyone if she didn't want to.

When Max and her teammates made it outside, one of Mads's male cousins was already pushing her into the back of a truck. It wasn't that Mads couldn't fight them, it was that she *wouldn't*. To this day, she still felt like she owed these assholes.

Max, however, was about to show Mads that she didn't owe them anything.

The teammates had almost reached the truck but the hyenas decided to meet them, their claws already unleashed as they came face-to-face . . . well . . . it was more like face-to-chest since most of them were several inches taller than the badgers. But that was okay. Her team knew how to take on bigger players.

Max reached under her shirt to get one of her blades but before it even cleared the holster, one of the hyenas went down. Then another. Both screaming from the pain in their legs. More of Mads's hyena cousins jumped off the back of the truck but as they advanced, they went down one by one. Looking over her shoulder, Max saw her sister standing on the porch. She had a .9mm with a suppressor attached so the neighbors wouldn't complain about the noise.

Charlie jumped over the railing with her hands wrapped around the gun, finger still on the trigger. As she moved closer, two more hyenas attacked . . . two more leg shots. Actually . . . knee shots. She shot them in the knees, ensuring they went down and stayed down at least for a couple of days. Knee damage wasn't as easy to get over as a regular leg break.

Max's teammates scrambled back, away from Charlie as she strode across the yard, then jumped over the fence to land next to the truck. She aimed her weapon at the skull of the last hyena standing. She walked him back until he couldn't go any farther because of his vehicle, and pressed the weapon against his head.

"I know you," Charlie said after staring at him for a few seconds. "We went to high school together. You used to call me 'fat thighs' behind my back."

Max and her teammates cringed. That was not something a man wanted to be remembered for saying to a woman when that woman now had a gun pressed to his forehead.

"Listen," Charlie went on, "I'm going to explain something to you: You don't come to my territory and fuck with my sister's friends. Because if they're my sister's friends, they're under my protection."

One of the hyenas on the ground attempted to stand up, so Charlie shot him once in the shoulder blade.

Max knew her sister's precision with a gun was not in question. Charlie would make sure she didn't hit any major arteries or organs. But what she did do, what Max was *sure* her sister did do . . . was cause as much pain as she possibly could.

The hyena's intensified screams proved that.

"So, if I were you, I'd leave now. Mads, out of the truck, please."

Mads slipped out of the vehicle and went to stand behind Max with their teammates.

"All right," Charlie said, stepping back and motioning with the gun. "All hyenas in the truck. Time to go. Come along, fellas, let's hop-hop-hop along. Thank you!"

Not once did Charlie raise her voice. Not once did she lose her temper. Because she didn't have to do any of that.

The hyenas fled and, after lowering the weapon, Charlie faced them.

"You all right, Mads?"

"I'm . . ." Mads cleared her throat. "I'm fine. Thank you."

"Any more problems with them . . . you let me or Max know. Okay?"

"Sure."

Charlie headed back to the house, then stopped, looked at them. "I've got muffins if you guys want some."

Everyone nodded but continued to stand behind Max. Clearly they were still terrified of Charlie and this probably hadn't helped.

But once she reached the front door, Charlie stopped and barked, "The muffins are *not* getting any fresher."

Max watched her friends power-run to the house, terrified to piss off the most dangerous woman they knew, but also the only woman willing to protect them when they needed it.

chapter TWENTY-SIX

The first half hour of their meeting involved listening to their coach yell at them because they had not been at the team meeting with everyone else. They were video chatting through Max's laptop so that they could witness the full extent of Coach's rage and not just hear it over the phone. Not that her anger wasn't valid. They did have a playoff game *that* night and "You five idiots have the nerve not to be here?"

"It's not my fault," Max argued. "I was busy having sex!"

The entire team of Wisconsin Butchers cheered until Coach Fitzgerald snarled and barked, her wolf fangs fully extended.

"And she was attacked!" Nelle threw in, attempting to help.

"By her own cousin!" Tock added.

"If she were my *cousin, I'd beat the shit out of her, too!"*

Streep burst into tears. *"Why are you being so mean to us?"*

"Oh, stop it!"

The tears ceased immediately and Streep flatly replied, "Fine."

After that, the rest of the meeting involved going over plays and plans and warnings about the kind of death they'd be subjected to if they were even a minute late to the pregame bus that would pick up the team at the Kingston Arms.

"Can't we just meet you at the arena?" Tock asked, looking at her watch.

"What did I just say?"

"No need to yell!"

When they finally logged off with Coach and the rest of the

team, Mads leaned back in her chair and remarked, "You had sex on this table."

The rest of the team reared back, lifting their arms and hands off the hard wood, but Max quickly pointed out, "I cleaned it. Before we sat down."

"You didn't clean it that well."

"Shut up."

That's when Nelle adorably crinkled her nose at her.

"What the fuck was that?" Max asked.

"You and Zé." She crinkled her nose again.

"We're not doing this."

"We're not doing what?"

"Doing this girlfriend thing."

"Aren't we girlfriends, though?" Streep asked. "Aren't we best friends? Friends forever. B-F-Fs!"

"*No!*" the other four said.

"So no cute shit," Max informed them. "No girly shit. Or I start throwing people out the window."

"We're on the first floor, so no one cares, Max."

"Thank you, Mads."

"I saw Imani talking to your sister," Tock suddenly announced. "In the club last night. What was that about?"

"Shhhhh!" Max stood and did a quick check of the kitchen, living room, and the backyard. When she saw Charlie outside with Zé, Shen, and Berg, playing with the basketballs she and her teammates had left lying around the yard, she returned to the dining room.

"Okay. This is the deal: Charlie agreed to work for Imani. On a test job."

"What?" Nelle asked. "Why the hell would she do that?"

"Is Imani blackmailing her?" Mads wanted to know. "Because if she is, I'm going to chew that She-cat's legs off."

"That seems excessive." But a very hyena thing to say. "And unnecessary. Imani's not blackmailing her. Charlie wants to do this. She wants a job."

"Can't she just bake professionally?" Tock asked. "Once I hit that diamond shipment, I can definitely buy her a store."

"And then you'll use her to launder the money."

Tock nodded. "Probably."

"I think she's trying to get away from that."

"Is she going alone?" Streep asked. "Is she a Dee-Ann Smith now?"

Every shifter involved in work outside the norms of society—or at least *shifter* society—knew the Smith name. They were the ones you went to when you needed untraceable weapons or a car stripped and made to disappear or a whole hog for a luau—that was because quite a few of them had wild hog farms. But Dee-Ann Smith and her daddy, Eggie Ray Smith, were known for being killers. Nothing more, nothing less. They didn't do rescue missions. They didn't do heists. They didn't involve themselves with anything except taking out people who had done something that had made them a liability. Luckily for the world, they'd both ended up working for the Group, which meant they used their kills for good. Or what Tock, the team's philosopher, called "relative good." Mads, however, had played *Dungeons & Dragons* since she was eleven and she liked to call it "chaotic good."

Whatever one called it, that's what Dee-Ann Smith and her tiger girlfriend, Cella Malone, did for a living and they were very good at it. The question for Max was what was her sister about to get into? Could she be like Dee-Ann Smith and just kill on order? Charlie had done a lot of things over the years, but there had always been a reason. Maybe not a valid one, depending on whom one spoke to, but at least *Charlie* felt it was valid. That's what Max needed to make sure of. She needed to know that her sister was going to do something that, at the end of the day, she could be proud of. Or at the very least, something she could live with. A MacKilligan with PTSD was like a Godzilla with rabies: a situation that was not going to end well for anyone.

"You're going, aren't you?" Mads guessed.

"I have to. She's my sister, I don't know who her team will be; I need to make sure this thing is legit. Not a setup. Not a way to use her for something else down the line. And I want to have her back."

"Then we'll go, too," Nelle said, looking around at the others for agreement. "We'll all go . . ." Everyone's gaze settled on Tock.

"Can you fit that into your schedule?" Mads asked Tock.

With her gaze locked on them, Tock stretched out her hand, picked up her phone. She put in her twenty-digit passcode and opened up her schedule program without even looking at her phone. Just at them. "What day?" she asked Max.

"Tonight. After the game. But I can't ask you guys to—"

"It's in my schedule," Tock said after typing into her phone again.

"How many thirty-minute blocks did you give us?" Mads asked with great sarcasm.

"Hopefully enough for your lazy ass."

"Okay!" Nelle cut in before it became nasty. "That's it. We're all in this. We're going to do this to support a woman that at least four of us are absolutely terrified of. But we're going to do it because she had Mads's back when she didn't have to. So we do this together," she said, swinging her forefinger in a circle, "because we are . . ." She prompted again as they all gazed at her continuing to make that big circle with her fingers. "Because we are . . ."

"What?" Max finally asked.

"Girlfriends!"

Streep clapped happily in agreement. Tock looked again at her watch. Max and Mads just made sounds of disgust until Mads suddenly said, "Uh-oh."

"What?"

"We're not alone."

They all sniffed the air and then looked up.

"Why are you up there?" Max asked her baby sister, who hung from the ceiling.

"I wasn't going to stay, because it looked private, but then it got interesting. So I stayed."

"I thought you were doing that ballet thing."

"I did. But Oriana was a little hungover and she vomited

on the current prima ballerina of the company and . . . at that point, I figured I'd just go home."

"And listen in on my business."

"I don't know why you're getting so bitchy. It's not like any of you have inside voices."

"Not a word to Charlie. Understand? And get down from there!"

"Be caref—" Nelle winced when Stevie hit the table.

Mads shook her head. "You're half cat, but you didn't even *try* to land on your feet."

Zé walked into Max's bedroom. She was stretched out on the mattress, gazing up at the ceiling, her hands behind her head. He stretched out beside her.

"What are we doing?" he asked.

"Thinking."

"About what? Life? Death? Existence?"

"Underwear."

"Underwear?"

"Yeah."

"Lucky underwear?"

"No. Just underwear that matches my uniform." She sat up. "You are coming tonight, aren't you?"

"Of course. Your sister already invited me."

She got up and went to a pile of dirty clothes on the floor. He would need to get her a proper laundry basket. Just having dirty clothes lying around one's room was tacky. "Stevie must like you if she invited you."

"Stevie didn't invite me. It was Charlie. I'll be attending with her and the triplets."

Max faced him, three pairs of bright yellow panties in her hand. "Wait . . . Charlie's coming? To the playoff game?"

"Yes. Then she said you, your teammates, and Charlie would be going off to kill a bunch of people after the game."

Max's eyes widened and she might have stopped breathing. "Charlie told you that?"

"No, that was Stevie."

Those wide eyes slammed shut and she now gripped her dirty underwear. "She can't keep her mouth shut!"

"It's not her fault. I just happened to overhear her talking to Shen, who swore up and down he wouldn't say a word, but I was on top of the china cabinet again."

"What is it with you and that china cabinet?"

"I don't know, but I am so comfortable up there." He watched her for a moment, then asked, "Want me to back you up?"

"No. I want you to protect Stevie."

"She's got a giant panda to protect her."

"And he loves her. He'll make stupid mistakes because of that. You won't."

"You worried about your crazy cousin?"

"Yes. We want to lure her out or track her down or something—"

"Bring the fight to her."

"Something like that, but we don't know how yet. Until we get her, though, anyone close to me is in danger because that bitch is nuts."

"Am I close to you?"

"Yeah, but you can take care of yourself. Also . . . you can take out my cousin without taking out the entire neighborhood. I can't count on that with Stevie."

"Because she's a genius and might blow up the place?"

Max gazed at him for several long seconds before replying, "Sure. Let's go with that."

"You know, based on your tone, I feel like there's something about your baby sister you're not telling me. Is there?"

"No." She started toward the door.

"Are you lying to me?"

"Probably."

"You going to wash those in the sink?"

"Ewwww. No. I'm putting them in the washing machine."

"Don't most women hand-wash their underwear?"

"I'm not one of those. I don't buy underwear that can't handle the delicate cycle on a washing machine. Who has time for that shit?"

"Many women. Some of whom I've known."

"Good for them. They can have their delicate lacy things. I like my shit cotton and sturdy."

"There's something you should know," he called after her just as she'd stepped out the door.

"*God*," she whined. She walked back into the room. "What else did Stevie say?"

"A lot of things but nothing you have to worry about."

"Then what?"

"After last night, you and me . . . I got it bad for you."

"Bad for me? What does that mean?"

"That I could possibly, kind of, with the right incentive . . . fall in love with you. Maybe. Possibly. It feels a little soon but for some unknown reason that feels right. I'm just not sure, but I thought I'd warn you. I also may change my mind. So you should stay on your toes."

Max sat down next to him on the bed before asking, "Could you *be* more cat?"

"I think, with very little effort, the answer to that is yes. Besides," he added, "I need to hear that you love me first before I can even begin to commit to the effort it would take on my part."

She gave a sound of disgust and walked out again.

"I'll take that to mean that you're madly in love with me!" he called after her.

"Don't."

The feral cat that lurked around Max's house came out from under the bed and climbed her way up Zé's leg. When she'd curled into his lap and, eventually, rolled onto her back so he could rub her stomach, he told her, "She's definitely madly in love with me."

Max came down the stairs and went out of her way *not* to think about what Zé had said to her. She didn't have time.

She had to wash her underwear, get her team bag together, take a nice long nap, and then get into the city so she didn't miss the pregame bus. The rest of her team had already left. It was one thing if they were all late, but it was something else entirely if Max fucked up on her own. It would be easier for Coach to suspend her from the game and she didn't want that.

She walked into the kitchen and stopped at the entryway. It seemed Stevie had lent Charlie a fan shirt, but Max's big sister did not seem comfortable.

"Do you have anything in a size other than extra small?" Charlie asked.

"Your tits look like they're having a fight under there."

"They *are* having a fight. And I fear a tragic outcome." Charlie looked at Max. "Do you have a bigger shirt? I want to support you at this thing."

"Forget the T-shirt!" she suddenly exploded. "We have a problem."

"God, what now?" Charlie began to roll her neck, already stressed. "Is this about the Malones' sister? That poor girl."

"Fuck the deaf girl!"

"Whoa!" Stevie raised and lowered her hands. "Let's just calm down . . . in fact . . . this"—she continued to raise and lower her hands—"is the American Sign Language sign for calm down."

"Why is there no door here?" Max asked, motioning to the kitchen entrance. "We need a door here."

"Dag walked through it one day before he had his morning coffee. He took it right off its hinges."

"What's going on?" Charlie asked. "Why are you freaking out?"

"I'm not freaking out."

"You *are* freaking out. Which is weird, because you never freak out," Stevie noted. "That's why I was always positive you were a sociopath. And I haven't seen any evidence to the contrary."

"Zé said he's falling for me. What does that even mean?"

"It's obvious," Charlie mockingly replied. "It means he's leaving you for a *different* hot Asian girl."

"Exactly! He's leaving me for another hot Asian girl!"

"No!" Stevie jumped up from her chair and grabbed Max's forearms. "That is *not* what that means." She smiled. Her expression was sweet and kind and all Max wanted to do was rip that smile off her sister's face and wear it around the neighborhood like a Halloween mask. "He's falling in love with you. And you love him back! I can see it. This is so wonderful!"

"Why?"

"It means you're not a sociopath because you can love others! Aren't you glad to know you're not a sociopath? I know that Charlie and I are glad. And relieved!"

Charlie counted backward. "Three. Two."

And it was on "one" that Max dropped her underwear, grabbed their baby sister by the hair, and took her to the floor. "Take it back!" she screamed. "*Take it back!*"

Reaching down, Charlie untangled Max from Stevie's hair and pulled the pair apart.

"Stop it! Both of you!"

"He loves you!" Stevie yelled . . . from the safety of the ceiling she was now—wisely—hanging from. "You might as well suck it up!"

"I will kill you," Max threatened.

"Everyone just calm down." Charlie placed her hand on Max's shoulder. "There are worse things in the world than extremely hot guys falling in love with you."

"Like what?"

"I hear nuclear war is bad."

"You're just going to have to get used to this," Stevie informed her. "Once cats make up their mind . . . they're done. You could marry someone else and have twenty kids and Zé will still be living under your porch. Because he's a cat! So you are stuck with him. For *life*."

Jumping straight up in the air, Max slapped Stevie off the ceiling and into the dining room.

"*You bitch!*" Stevie yelled.

"Nice lateral jump," Charlie noted.

"Can't play shifter ball if you don't have a lateral jump. Especially when you're going up against cheetahs and tigers. Those striped bastards can jump, like, fifty feet!"

chapter TWENTY-SEVEN

Everything had changed in minutes. Maybe even seconds. Max was about to settle down for her nap when a text came in to Charlie's phone. She'd frowned, responded, and left the kitchen. Leaving her fresh-from-the-oven cinnamon buns alone, with bears already lurking in the yard, ready to pounce.

That was when Max knew something was up. She'd followed her sister to her room and when she saw Charlie taking out her Glock and holstering it to her jeans . . .

"The time changed, didn't it?"

"Yes. I need to go now."

"I'm going with you."

"You've got your game."

"The way we work? We'll make the game."

"Max—"

"And the team's coming with me."

A confused, flustered Charlie faced her. "The *entire* Wisconsin Butchers team is coming?"

"No, dumbass, just my girls. *My* team."

"Absolutely not!"

"They insisted."

"I've never worked with them."

"I have."

"I don't know what their skills are."

"I do."

Unable to come up with a satisfactory argument, Charlie just snarled. "Fine. Get ready. We leave in five minutes."

"What you guys want me to do?" Stevie asked from the ceiling.

"You really need to stop doing that," Max warned her.

Charlie drove and they met Nelle, Streep, Mads, and Tock at an address downtown. Imani met them there as well.

"I'm sorry about this last-minute change. But we need to move now rather than tonight."

"Then let's go," Charlie pushed. "My sister has a playoff game tonight and none of us are missing it."

Imani nodded and ushered them into the empty building.

"This will be our office. Eventually," she told them as they followed behind her. "It'll be nice once I get it up and running."

"Is there a name for this organization of yours?" Streep asked.

"Still working on that, too." She stopped at an elevator and pushed the Down button. As they waited, she looked the small group over before stating, "I didn't expect all of you."

"You tried to blackmail all of us," Tock reminded her.

"No. That wasn't me. And all that information has been destroyed."

"Charlie tell you to do that?" Max asked.

"No. The whole thing bothered me. So I made it go away."

The elevator arrived and they went to a secure subbasement. There were black vans equipped with elaborate communication and media centers so that whoever worked the van could keep in contact with the rest of the team.

"Here are your lockers. You can find body armor in the room over there. There are a lot of sizes; you should find what you need." She pointed to another room. "Weapons in there. Everything you could possibly—" Max smirked as her teammates charged into that room, practically knocking Imani down. "Ooooo-kay." She gestured to Max and Charlie. "You two don't feel the need to run into the room to see what's available?"

"I doubt it's better than what we have." Imani laughed until Max said, "No. Seriously. We have a lot of connections."

"Oh."

Making the decision not to discuss this any further, Imani handed a folder to Charlie. "Here's the information you need."

Charlie looked everything over and immediately frowned. "The de Medici Pride? I never heard of them."

"I have." Max looked at her sister. "A lot of our weapons are from their people."

"That's awkward."

"I doubt you'll find any de Medicis there today," Imani said. "And don't worry about that for now. First, we take on their businesses, then we take them on. Any questions? Need anything from me?"

Charlie shook her head. "Nope."

"Then good luck."

Charlie waited until Imani had gone back upstairs before asking Max, "You sure you want to do this? You sure you want to drag your friends into this?"

Streep walked out of the weapons room carrying a military-grade Gatling gun. The kind used by a door gunner in a military copter trying to get soldiers out of 'Nam.

But the smile on Streep's face . . . it was like she'd just stumbled into a room filled with diamonds.

"Dragging?" Max asked her sister. "Is that what you *really* think I'm doing?"

Miki walked to the door and opened it. She was about to walk out when Irene asked, "Where are you going?"

"Taking a break."

"Right now?"

"Yes. Right now. Why?"

"It seemed you were on the brink of discovering something. So I'm surprised you're leaving."

"My eyes are killing me. Besides, a little coffee is just what I need. Want me to bring you some back?"

Irene didn't respond, simply walked away. She used to do that anytime Miki went over something in her dissertation that Irene didn't agree with.

Of course, that never stopped Miki from sticking with her decision if she knew what she was doing was right. And this was right.

She walked out of the Van Holtz town house and went down the street. There she caught a cab and traveled to a diner off the Jersey Turnpike.

Miki sat down in the booth and smiled.

The girl looked up from the computer she was working on.

"Hi," Miki said. "I thought we should talk."

Pointing at her ears, the girl shook her head.

"You're deaf?" Miki asked and was rewarded with a head tilt and a confused frown.

"No problem," she replied in American Sign Language. "I used to be hot for this guy in junior high. He was deaf so I learned ASL. Now . . . are we going to keep this bullshit up?"

Slamming her laptop shut, the girl replied verbally, "What do you want?"

She was definitely deaf, but had probably lost her hearing when she was a child.

Still using ASL and speaking softly at the same time so the kid could use both, Miki went with blunt. "You need to put the money back."

"Are you going to turn me in?"

"I could. But I was you. Once. Almost did hard time. Hard *federal* time. Kid, you don't want that."

"What do I want, O' Magic Wizard?"

"A challenge. I've seen your work. You're good, but you get bored easy. Right? Is that why you got yourself into this? I have to tell you, my real concern is that you won't live much longer. Because you're dealing with people who will kill you and it will mean nothing to them."

"They have to find me first."

"Don't get cocky. I found you. So, give the money back and go home to your family."

"Not yet." She shoved her laptop into a tote bag and pulled the straps onto her shoulder. "I have things to do first."

Miki reached across the table and grabbed her hand. "You are fucking with actual gangsters."

She leaned down and said, "And I come from an entire *family* of gangsters. The MacKilligans don't scare me."

Watching her leave the diner, Miki took out her phone. She'd hoped to avoid this, but . . .

"I found them," she said when she got an answer. "But I'm thinking that you better move fast."

Charlie had slipped into the role of team leader quite naturally. Of course, Max's teammates made that easy. They started off joking and not taking things as seriously as they should, which had always been their way. But when Charlie snarled, they reacted so quickly and intensely, the question of who was in charge never came up.

Body armor was put on while Max and Charlie made decisions about what weapons to bring. They packed up a black van and, with Tock driving, headed off.

They were nearing the docks when Charlie got a text on her phone. She looked down and said, "They're already on the move."

She typed into the keyboard and called out, "New address on the GPS, Tock."

"Got it."

"You ready for this, Streep?" she asked, since Streep was the only one not in body armor.

"Yep." Then she dug into her purse and pulled out lip gloss.

"Seriously?" Mads asked.

"Shut up."

chapter TWENTY-EIGHT

H e heard the knock at the door of the house they were "borrowing" and opened it.

She was tiny but cute, staring up at him with bright eyes and glossy lips.

"Hi!" she said. "My car broke down and I was wondering—"

He closed the door in her face.

"That was rude!" she yelled.

"Go away, badger. I'm not in the mood to play with you."

One of the bosses helping to take inventory came out of the office. "What the hell was that?"

"Some badger. Probably came to rob the place."

"Kill her," he said, turning back toward the office.

"Really?" That seemed a little harsh. Even for grizzlies doing illegal shit.

"Just do it. No witnesses."

He shrugged. "Okay."

Opening the door, he stepped outside. The badger was walking toward the long driveway. "Hey!" he called out. "You can use the phone."

"Great! Thanks!"

She ran back and, with a big smile, stepped past him into the house. He waited until he closed the door, then grabbed her around the throat and crushed her scrawny little neck. When she stopped moving, he tossed her by the stairs and walked to the office.

"All done," he told the bosses.

"Good. Deal with the body when we move out tonight."

He nodded and turned back toward the door he was guarding. But he stopped and looked at the staircase. The *empty* staircase.

"Uh . . . gentlemen?"

"What?"

"I think we have a—"

She plunged the blade into his inside thigh. When he grabbed it to stop the bleeding, dropping to his knee, she rammed the same blade into his throat.

He dropped to the ground and she gazed down at him for the brief moment he had left. And he watched her crack her neck one way, then the other. Bones knitting themselves back together in a way that didn't seem possible. But it didn't matter anymore, did it? Not anymore.

Who invites a girl in just to crush her neck? Rude! Good thing she was a honey badger or she'd be dead! How tacky would that be?

"What the hell's going on out here?"

Streep raised the Desert Eagle .44 she'd taken from the weapons room—a gun that she'd *always* wanted but never wanted to blow the money on—and took quick shots. A weapon of this power was an absolute necessity in a room with six big bears in it. She caught three with one shot each to the neck, chest, and gut respectively. Not sure she'd be able to hit her targets with the rest of the bears coming at her so fast, she ran to the front door, pulling it open. She dropped to a crouch and waited.

The first bear ran out of the office but Charlie was now in the doorway and she pulled the trigger of her own weapon. Clean headshot. The second bear came out and she got him, too. Also a clean headshot. Streep had always heard from Max what a good shot her sister was, but . . . wow.

The third bear avoided the office doorway altogether and came through the wall next to it, tackling Charlie to the ground. But Max was on top of him and she hammered one of her tactical knives into his throat. There was so much blood, so quickly, Streep knew her friend had hit the aorta.

No matter where on the body she struck, Max always hit an artery if she wanted to.

Mads grabbed Streep's arm and pulled her to her feet. "Stay behind us."

"Got it."

Charlie wiggled her way out from under the bear's body and got to her feet.

"You all right?" she asked Streep, who was so shocked by the question she didn't answer right away. Then she remembered what the first bear had done to her neck and pressed her hand to her throat. The bones were nearly done putting themselves back together, so she smiled at Charlie.

"I'm fine."

"Then let's move."

Max followed her sister into the hidden depths of the New Jersey mansion. She could hear men talking in the long hallways. Could smell that they were shifters. And she could smell something else. Something that shocked her.

Easing around a corner, Charlie looked inside one of the rooms. After a few seconds, she pulled back and pointed at Streep, Tock, and Nelle. Then she pointed at the room she'd looked in. She started forward and motioned for Max and Mads to follow her.

As Max passed the room, she glanced in.

That's what she had scented along with shifters. Full-humans. Bound and waiting to be sold. Not all of them were women. They didn't have to be. They were just full-humans, none of them truly prepared to face off against shifters with no moral center.

Pissed, Max put away her gun and took out another tactical knife.

She moved her shoulders to loosen them up and waited for her sister. Her team leader.

Charlie found the room where the most voices were coming from. She started to move to the door but stopped, looked up . . . and grinned.

Max raised her gaze and saw the air vent. She loved air vents.

Zé looked away from all the ballerinas twirling on the stage and glanced at his watch again.

"We've got tons of time. Stop worrying."

He nodded at Shen's words, glad there was at least a five-second break from the goddamn chewing. Because the panda never seemed to stop chewing. How did Stevie put up with it? She said she found it soothing, but . . . how? How did anyone find that noise soothing?

Zé dug his fingers into his hair and scratched before he looked at Shen and said, "Can I ask you a favor?"

Shen grinned around the bamboo stalk in his mouth. "Sure!"

"Go away." Zé pointed at the audience seats across the aisle. "Over there."

To his surprise, Shen's grin didn't waver. "It's the chewing, right?"

"I like you so much, dude, but the *chewing*."

The panda stood, chuckling. Though he was a couple of inches shorter than Zé, those muscular and massive shoulders, chest, and arms made him much wider. There was no denying the damage the man could do if he was pushed too far. But at the same time, there was something about him that still suggested "adorably rolly-polly," like any panda in the zoo.

"Look," Shen said before moving away, "I'll check in with Stevie, give her a little reminder that we've got somewhere to be. Okay?"

"Thank you."

"No problem. Just relax. No one likes an anxious cat. I'm worried I'm going to find you hanging from those chandeliers up there."

Zé nodded but then quickly asked, "Wait. Is that something I can actually do?"

Shen shrugged. "Probably. But I wouldn't do that here. I'm pretty sure those chandeliers would cost a fortune to replace."

Deciding not to focus too much on whether he could hang from the ceiling or not, Zé realized the panda was right. Zé was anxious about getting to the Sports Center on time, which really surprised him. Max was playing in a basketball game, not making a speech at the United Nations.

Still . . . he wanted to be there early so he could get his seat, a hot dog, and beer, and watch his girlfriend—

Hold up. Girlfriend? He was thinking of Max MacKilligan as his *girlfriend?* The crazy female who'd decimated an entire team of well-trained mercenaries with her badger teammates? Or who didn't seem too concerned that he'd almost eaten a child? *That* woman he was thinking of as his *girlfriend?*

It was true, Zé really didn't have a type, but if he did, it sure as fuck wouldn't be a Max MacKilligan!

"Hi!"

Zé jumped a little, surprised by the female voice beside him.

"I'm Mandy." She held out her hand. "And you're Zezé Vargas."

He looked at her but didn't say anything.

"I see." She lowered her hand. "A little paranoid, are we? Understandable, I guess, considering your line of work."

"Do I know you?"

"No. That's why I introduced myself. Remember? I'm Mandy."

"Why are you talking to me?"

She smiled. "I have an offer for you."

"You have an offer for a man you don't know? So you're a prostitute?"

That smile disappeared and those eyes went from brown to a bright and dangerous blue.

"Do I look like a prostitute to you?"

"Well—" Zé blew out a long sigh. "I don't know how to answer that without getting punched in the face, soooo . . ."

Charlie waited until Max and Mads had disappeared into the air vents. Then she waited another forty-five seconds before she kicked the door in.

Her weapon was already raised and she nearly took her shot, but the bears were ready for her. And smart. They were using some of the full-humans as their shields. One bear had two in his arms, raising them so high, they protected his head.

"Hello there, pretty girl," he said behind the two sobbing women he was holding hostage. "Smelled you badgers coming a mile away."

Pressing the left side of her body against the doorframe, her weapon raised so that she was locked on target, Charlie said, "Hello, Paddington. How are we going to play this?"

"First, before we can do anything . . ."

Charlie heard him grunt and one of the bears behind him punched his fist into the ceiling. A few seconds later he yanked Mads out of the air vent, slamming her to the ground with such force, Charlie was worried he'd sent her through the floor. The same bear reached back up and snagged a snarling, hissing Max out of the vent, too. Her sister put up much more of a fight, trying to wiggle out of the grip that held her.

But neither badger could get away, and their guns and a few knives were tossed aside before they were pinned to the floor by several bears.

"Now that we've got that cleared up," the lead bear went on, "let's discuss whether you're going to sacrifice all these full-humans just to get to us?"

"Katzenhaus?" Zé repeated, staring at the business card Mandy had given him. "You guys run that snobby library, right?"

"*That library*—" Mandy stopped, took a moment to stare off at the stage filled with dancers. When she seemed calmer, she cleared her throat and said, "Katzenhaus is a protection agency. We protect the cat nation all over the world."

"Uh-huh."

"I'm a recruiter."

He held up her card. "Yeah. I read that."

"And you seem to have what we may be looking for."

"You do know I just found out I'm a cat."

"Yes. I'm aware. And we're the ones who can teach you what you need to know."

"Could you teach me to hang from the ceiling?"

She frowned. "Why would you want to hang from the ceiling?"

"Why *wouldn't* you want to hang from the ceiling?"

"Okay." Mandy stood and Zé had to admit that the woman definitely moved like a cat. Of course, she also moved like a hooker. "When you want to be serious, call the number on the card, and we can talk about your future. Sound good?"

"Yeah."

"Excellent."

She turned away from him and strutted off without making a sound, despite those six-inch heels.

Zé leaned back in his seat and studied the card in his hand.

"Hey, darlin'," a new female voice said from his right.

Zé jumped again, this time hissing a little.

"Sorry 'bout that," the woman wearing a Tennessee Titans baseball cap mocked. "I always forget how nervous y'all are."

"You're not a cat," he told the woman sitting next to him.

"Definitely not."

"Pitbull then?"

Her yellow eyes narrowed. "Gray wolf. And a Smith."

"I don't know what that means."

"Dee-Ann Smith's the name."

"And howling is your game?"

Those eyes narrowed even more. "You really didn't know all this time that you were a cat? Because you sure as hell sound like one."

Charlie lowered her weapon.

"You're right," she admitted. "I wouldn't hurt full-humans just to get to you."

"That's excellent," the lead bear said, although he didn't lower his shields. "Now we can have a nice discussion about how we should move forward from here. Because you need to understand something. The people we work for, they won't tolerate some worthless badgers fucking with their money stream. Do you understand what I'm telling you?"

"I understand."

"So, maybe it's best that you and your friends walk away before we crush you like the beer cans we drain on a Saturday night."

"That's a good plan." Charlie threw her gun on the ground and the bears slowly lowered their human shields.

The lead bear released one of the women so he could point a gun at Charlie's face.

He smirked, putting his finger on the trigger. "Now I'm debating what *I* should do."

"Really?" Charlie asked. "Because I'm not." She took in a breath, then bellowed, "*Badger fight!*"

Darren didn't know how he'd gotten here, why he was here, or if he'd leave here alive. He just knew he was chained and about to be moved to another location. The bizarrely large men who seemed to love anything with honey on it had been getting ready to give them all injections. Those injections were filled with something that knocked all the captives out. Every time Darren got one of those shots, he'd wake up in a new place. At this point, he no longer knew which country he was in. He assumed he was in America, though he'd started in Canada.

But as the large men had been getting those shots ready, they'd suddenly stopped what they were doing and lifted their heads, sniffing the air. And, as they'd sniffed, they'd begun to growl at each other. Like some kind of weird warning. A few minutes later, they'd grabbed several of the prisoners to use as shields seconds before that woman had busted through the door.

At first, Darren had thought she was a policewoman, coming to rescue them. But she'd been alone and other than the body armor and her weapons, she'd had no badge or any markings on her equipment that suggested she was law enforcement. Then her friends had been dragged out of the ceiling and he'd given up all hope, ready to be taken wherever the large men were planning to take them.

Until the woman had screamed something. Darren couldn't quite make it out. Whatever her words had been, her friends seemed to understand. Despite the grip the men had on the backs of their necks, the women were able to turn and face their captors; their skin stretching in a way that was terrifying to say the least. Then Darren saw claws and fangs and those two women attacked with such viciousness, he backed up even farther against the wall he was near and began to pray.

The attacking women climbed the large men holding them and dug their claws into their necks and faces. They used their fangs to tear off bits of them. The nose of one. The lips of the other.

The other large men jumped in to help, grabbing the women from behind. They ripped off one and threw her across the room. She hit the wall and landed on the ground. Not even a second later, she rolled over and got on all fours. With a snarl, she charged, climbing the back of another large man and slamming her claws into his skull.

By now, the woman who'd kicked in the door had picked up her weapon and she began firing. Carefully, though. Not spraying the room. No, she shot with precision. Head shots when she could get them. Neck or chest shots when she couldn't. It took at least two head shots to take down each large man. At least six shots to the throat or chest to kill them that way.

Before Darren knew it, the large men were bleeding out on the floor and the women were unlocking his chains.

"You all right?" one of them asked.

"Yes," he said, unable to look at her. Her face and neck were completely saturated in blood and bloody drool still poured from her mouth.

But still, she was letting him go. He would always be thankful for that at least.

★ ★ ★

Nelle opened the locks and removed the chains.

"Come on!" she ordered the full-humans. She didn't yell, but she made sure to command them. That always worked better in situations like this. Then she said it again in a few other languages just in case.

Streep and Tock helped move the people out of the house. Just as they got them into the yard, a semitruck came toward them on the driveway. The transportation for the "product" they were selling, which was how the shifters had referred to the full-humans.

"Go!" Nelle yelled at Streep and Tock. "Get them down to the buses!"

While her teammates took off, she charged back into the house. As she went for the stairs that led to the lower floors, Charlie and the others were coming up, with even more freed full-humans. Her friends were covered in a good amount of blood, so Nelle wasn't too concerned about anyone not friendly coming up from the basement.

"Truck coming," she warned.

"You and Mads take these people out," Charlie ordered. "Get them to the buses. Max and I will meet you back at the van."

"How do you want to do this?" Max asked her sister. "Straight on or roundabout?"

Charlie motioned to the office window and the lawn outside it. "How about underground?"

Nelle and Mads handed the full-humans in their care over to Streep and Tock. "Meet us at the van!" she yelled, running back to Max and her sister.

She didn't feel right about leaving them on their own—

Mads caught her and they stopped, watching as the MacKilligan sisters came up through the ground and jumped onto the truck from opposite sides.

They climbed up the doors and leaned into the open windows.

Max had one of her blades in her mouth. When she reached the window, she grabbed it and began stabbing the driver.

Charlie, a clean killer, just fired her weapon twice into the cab.

Max leaned farther in, her little legs just sort of hanging out the open window, making Nelle and Mads laugh, but she still managed to stop the truck before it ran directly into the mansion.

Done, the sisters jumped down and motioned toward the van.

Charlie reached the van and got in. The rest of her team followed seconds later.

The buses had already driven off and were going in another direction, into another state. There the full-humans would be cared for until they could figure out what was next for them. These weren't necessarily undocumented workers or women about to be sold into sex slavery. They could have been picked up for no other reason than some freak shifter was in the mood to hunt and eat a blonde.

Whatever the original plans had been for them, Charlie had made it clear to Imani: no matter what these full-humans might have seen . . . no one was allowed to kill them to keep them quiet. They could threaten. They could blackmail. They could give them money to shut them up. But Charlie wouldn't be part of any operation that involved killing people who had just been unlucky enough to be kidnapped by shifters.

Tock headed the van back to the city. They weren't returning to the office they'd started at. They didn't have time.

"To the Kingston Arms," she told Tock.

"Don't we have to get this back to the office where Imani met us?" Max asked.

"Tock!" Charlie barked.

"We've got two hours to get back to the city, get showered, and meet the pregame bus!"

Max rubbed her nose to hide her smile.

"Are you coming to the game, Charlie?" Nelle asked.

"Yes. I want to see my sister play." Charlie paused for a few seconds, then added, "So you bitches better win—or I'm going to be upset."

Slowly, Charlie turned her chair around to focus on the computer screen while Max's teammates shrank down in terror.

Charlie glanced at Max over her shoulder, but the sisters had to look away from each other before they started to laugh hysterically.

Because that would be wrong. Wouldn't it?

chapter TWENTY-NINE

At the arena, they had floor seats. Zé might not have been impressed by that if the entire arena had not been filled to capacity. The crowd was already cheering and antsy, desperate for the game to begin. It was like watching an NBA game with half the audience sporting green and white and the other half yellow and blue.

An entire world underneath the full-human one and Zé had never felt more at home.

Zé sat with Charlie and the triplets on his left and Stevie, Shen, and Dutch on his right. Dutch had originally sat down next to him, grinning like an idiot. But when Zé slapped the man's popcorn, soda, and giant pretzel with cheese onto the floor, Stevie insisted he move.

"Not long now," Stevie said, clapping her hands together.

"You are so excited."

"I love watching Max play. She's not just a good athlete. She also has winning showmanship."

"I hear you did, too. When you were six."

"I still do. Someday you'll have to hear me play with my band. They're all former child prodigies, too. And I do a mean Jimi Hendrix."

"On guitar?"

"That, too."

Zé was going to ask what she meant but she said to him first, "Hear you are my babysitter tonight."

"I doubt you'll need it. You have a giant panda."

Shen held out a bamboo stalk. "Want a bite?"

"No."

"You guys don't know what you're missing," he said before beginning his nonstop chewing.

"That doesn't irritate you?" he asked Stevie.

"I fall asleep to it. It's the most soothing thing to me. And I'm the one who finds Enya's music a little loud and abrasive."

They waited in the hallway, the two teams side by side; Max already bouncing on her toes. Ready to go. Ready to destroy the other team. But in a totally nonlethal way, of course.

Nelle was on her phone, taking selfies. Streep was doing yoga stretches to stay limber. Mads was staring down tigers on the opposite team. Tock was looking at her watch. It was the same thing every time, but Max never got bored by it. Only this time, both her sisters were in the crowd. Charlie hadn't been to a game since Max was in high school. And once she'd found out Nelle had a limo driver to take the five of them to and from the games, she'd stopped coming altogether. It didn't bother Max as much as it would have probably bothered others. Actually, it hadn't bothered Max at all. Not when she knew her sister had a lot more important things to focus on. Like keeping them alive.

It was just nice that finally, after all these years, they could do this and enjoy it.

Mads tapped Max on the shoulder and pointed. Renny stood at the end of the hall, away from the entrance.

"Shit."

"Tell her you'll talk to her after the game."

But Max didn't want her mind distracted by anything. Not during a playoff game.

She ran down the hall to her mother.

"I just wanted to wish you luck," Renny said when Max reached her. "Some of your aunties are here, too."

"They are?"

"Yes. I also think they have money on the game, though."

"Of course they do."

"Anyway, given any more thought to my suggestion? About you and me . . . traveling together for a while?"

"Yeah."

"Great. And?"

"No."

Her mother blinked. "What do you mean, 'no'?"

"I mean no. There's no other meaning for 'no.' But let me know when you're back in town. We'll go to lunch."

Max turned to walk away but her mother caught her arm and pulled her back around. "You have to give me some kind of explanation."

"No, I don't."

"Give me one anyway."

"You want an explanation? You had Devon's money the whole time."

"Is that really a big deal? I knew you could handle him."

"Of course I could handle him. That's not the point. You also put my sisters in danger. That's definitely not okay. You also could have sent us some of the money."

"For what?"

"Oh, I don't know. To give our grandfather's Pack some cash since they were the ones taking care of your kid. Or we could have given some to Charlie so she could have gone to college. At the very least you could have told me you had it. But you didn't."

"So you're saying you want a cut now? Is that it?"

Max pointed at her mother. "And that's why I'm not going. Appreciate the invite, though."

"Max, you can't just leave it at that."

"I'm not leaving it at anything. I'm just not going. I do, however, have a game to play and the announcer's about to call my name." She kissed her mother on the cheek. "I do love you, though. Always will." Then she returned to her teammates and waited for her name and number to be called.

The crowd began cheering and the announcer came on over the loudspeakers, introducing the two teams. Zé watched each player as she came out to cheers and love from the audience but, at least for the Butchers, Nelle was one of the true stars. Especially among the males of the audience. But no one on the team was truly slighted.

When Max ran out, her sisters jumped up on either side of Zé, cheering almost as loudly as the crowd around them.

Max and her five friends didn't start the game, though. Instead, the teams began with more equally sized players.

The longer Zé watched the game, the more he became concerned about Max's safety. These two teams didn't play like the WNBA. Hell, they didn't play like the NBA. He wasn't talking about skill. Their skills were on par with those of any pro team. Maybe even better. But the brutality . . .

Bears hit cats, sending them flying down the court. Cats slashed bears, leaving blood on the court that "cleaners" came out to wipe up. There was blood on the uniforms. Scabbed-over wounds on the players.

He'd never seen anything quite like it. And if the woman he'd deigned to care for weren't about to jump in, he'd have enjoyed it much more.

At the beginning of the second quarter, Max and her four teammates took the floor and Zé's mouth dropped open. Because there Max stood, in front of a six-foot, seven-inch female who stared down at her with such withering contempt that he wanted nothing more than to go out there, scoop Max up, and make a run for it.

He had to give it to Max, though. She was putting in a lot of effort. Jumping around, moving her arms a lot. Trying to distract the other player. It didn't work, but it was a nice attempt.

The player threw the ball way over Max's head and the opposition easily caught it. But when that player turned to dribble down the court, Nelle stole the ball and went between the taller woman's incredibly long legs. She passed it off to Mads, who immediately passed it to Tock. Tock tried to make the shot, but the other team was all over her, so she passed it to Streep who head-faked to her left before passing it to Max, who bounced it under another set of insanely long legs, allowing Nelle to catch it, spin, and take the shot. She made the basket without even breaking a sweat.

"Holy shit."

He didn't say that, though. That was Charlie. But he totally agreed with her.

Freddy tossed what few clothes he had in his bag and threw that into the trunk of the car he'd stolen two days ago.

"Come on, come on!" he yelled. Then remembered. She couldn't hear him. "Fuck."

He started back to the motel room when a fist slammed into his stomach. He doubled over and a strike to the back of the neck dropped him hard. His entire body went numb, nerves sending out confused messages to the rest of him. He wasn't sure he could walk, much less fight.

Still, he tried to get up but a foot against his spine kept him pinned.

"Uncle Freddy. So good to meet you at long last."

He recognized that Scottish accent but not the voice.

"I promised Uncle Will I'd bring you in and that's what I'm going to do. Maybe those daughters of yours will care when you're dead and skinned and staked to the front of their house."

The only things his treacherous, unfeeling daughters would care about was that they would have to clean up the mess. He would have said that, too, but he couldn't speak.

Christ, what had the bitch done to him?

His arms were pulled back and rope wrapped around his wrists. Then his legs, ankles tied to the wrists. Hogtied, he was dragged to another car, his body pulled and pushed into the trunk.

He landed on his back, so he could look up into his assailant's face.

"Yeah. I found ya, didn't I, Uncle? I never should have focused on you in the first place. But the girl. She's been in contact with one of her brothers. I found her that way. Pretty disgusting, by the way, what you're doing. She ain't even eighteen. Even Uncle Will would never sink so low." She leaned in.

"I hope he lets me have some fun with you before he finishes ya off." She took a bandana out of her back pocket and shoved it into his mouth. "Now you keep quiet . . . or I'll start cuttin' off important bits before we even get to Uncle Wills. Underst—" She stopped speaking and swung around, catching the hand about to shove a blade into her back.

"Hello, little girl," his niece said. "You must be me Uncle Freddy's dirty little secret."

Charlie had never been so into a game before. She hated sports. Hated them! Always had. But watching not only her sister kick ass, but those weird friends of hers working together as a well-oiled machine was totally worth the price of admission.

Not only that, but who knew her sister was so damn good! She didn't even get that many points. Of the five, the ones who earned the most points were Nelle and Tock, with Streep and Mads coming in second. Max got baskets but she seemed to really enjoy stealing the ball away from the other team and passing it off to her girls.

"I never thought she was a team player," she admitted to Zé. "I was wrong."

"I know. She's amazing."

Charlie leaned closer to him and said loudly, over the roaring crowd as the timer counted down, "Can I start introducing you as 'my sister's boyfriend'?"

"Only if it annoys her greatly."

"It will."

It was the final minutes and Streep was shoved aside by a player on the opposite team. She didn't just fall, though. She did a very long stumble for several feet, until she stretched out on the ground, grabbing her knee and wailing. Loudly. Her teammates ran to her, then Mads threw the first punch at the other team. That led to a small fistfight and, of course, Max was right in the middle of it.

When the dust had settled and everyone had calmed down, the ref called a hard foul and Streep limped her way over to the free-throw line.

Wiping tears, she threw the first shot and bam! Nothing but net. The ball was passed to her again and she took a big, deep, shaky breath and boom! Same as the first.

After waving at the crowd, Streep headed back down the court . . . with no limp.

At this point, the two teams were neck and neck, but the Butchers fell behind when a cheetah for the other team leaped into the air, spun, and reverse dunked the ball over her shoulders. The move brought the crowd to its feet, screaming. Especially when she hung there, her tongue hanging out, her fangs flashing. If she hadn't been up against her sister's team, Charlie would have loved it even more.

The ball was passed to Nelle and she took it back down the court. From there, the ball was stolen, going back and forth between the teams until there were only four seconds on the clock. The dunking cheetah had the ball again and was racing down the court to the Butchers' basket.

That's when Max got it, dashing in front of the cheetah and stealing it from her. She headed back the other way but the rest of the cheetah's team was coming right for her. She had no time to reach that basket.

Charlie assumed Max would pass the ball to Nelle, who was closer. She probably wouldn't make the basket either but it was worth a try. But when Max realized she was blocked, she made a jump shot, that lateral leap coming into play again. The ball flew over the heads and hands of extremely tall women and whoosh! Went into that basket just as the final buzzer blasted, signaling the end of the game.

Charlie only had a second to see Max's hilarious expression before her teammates tackled her to the floor. Her grin wide, her tongue out, and her hands thrown out like, "Of *course* I made that fucking shot!" Then she was gone under a pile of cheering teammates.

She grabbed the girl's throat and began to squeeze. She smelled weird. A cat scent Mairi didn't quite recognize. Then she noticed the girl had something in her ears. Hearing aids.

"You sick fuck!" she laughed, looking back at her uncle. "She's fucking deaf? How do you live with yourself? And now you're making me kill her!"

She looked back at the girl and yelled, "You've gotta die! Sorry about that!"

Mairi decided to make this quick. No use torturing the kid for no reason. But just as she started to squeeze that skinny little cat neck, her uncle began to completely lose his shit, which seemed strange. He was a bastard. She'd expect him to try to use the distraction to make a run for it. He was badger, after all, and with just a little effort, he could get out of that binding. That's why she was planning to shoot out both his knees before she drove off.

Still holding the girl, she leaned down and used her free hand to yank the bandana out of his mouth.

"What are you trying to say to me?"

"You kill her," he said, "Will won't get his money."

"You think you can hold out, do ya? No matter what Will does to you? All for this piece of ass?"

"No, you dumb twat, she's the only one who knows where the money is."

"Really?"

"Yeah. Really. You kill her . . . Will gets nothing. The *family* gets nothing."

"All right, then." She dropped her and the girl bent over at the waist, coughing and taking in big gulps of air. "But then we don't need you . . . now do we?"

Freddy's eyes grew big when she pulled the .45 from the holster attached to the back of her jeans and pointed it at him. But just as she pulled the trigger, her arm jerked. Because her body jerked.

Two more shots went through her chest and she stumbled forward, then spun around.

She stared up at the buildings in the distance, trying to see who it was. Who had shot her?

"Come out, Max! You and your sisters! Show yourselves!"

It hurt to breathe, but the shots to the chest hadn't hit the right spot.

She glanced down and thought it again: *The shots hadn't hit the right spot.*

Whoever had shot her, it wasn't one of the sisters. They knew how to take down a badger better than anyone.

Then who—

The blade slid into the back of her neck. Right where the spine and the skull attached. Blood poured from her mouth and her body began to convulse.

Mairi turned and faced the deaf girl. She held the bloody blade in her hand; Freddy was still hog-tied in the boot.

Two more rifle shots hit Mairi in the chest, right through the heart. And she knew where the next shot would be coming. But it didn't matter. Not anymore.

The last shot went through Mairi MacKilligan's head and Dee-Ann nodded at Cella Malone. "Not bad."

"What do you mean, 'not bad'?" Malone asked. "I nailed that bitch with each shot. Center mass and head."

"But she still didn't go down."

"Not my fault. Bitch is a honey badger."

"What about your cousin? Should we go get her?"

Malone began carefully taking her rifle apart. "No way. I get near her and there will be another civil war between the Malones."

"I don't understand you cats. Smiths never have these problems. Someone gets out of hand, the Pack just turns on 'em, then we go about our day."

"It's always fascinating when you tell your family stories."

"Now, now. Don't be jealous, darlin'. Not everyone can be lucky enough to be a Smith."

Natalie waited to see if there would be any more shots. There weren't. Apparently, all they'd wanted was Mairi MacKilligan.

She stared down at her body. Could still feel the honey badger's hand around her neck. It had been risky, taking her on. But she hadn't had a choice.

She reached down and searched the body. She took some cash and the car keys.

Once she had what she needed, she looked down at Freddy MacKilligan. The biggest mistake of her life.

But she was ready to rectify that, too.

She took the bandana she now held and shoved it into his open mouth. He was probably screaming at her. He always thought if he screamed loudly enough, she could hear him. He didn't seem to understand what the word "deaf" actually meant.

Once she knew she'd made him quiet, she retied his bindings so that he couldn't slip out of them for a few hours.

Then she closed the trunk, grabbed her bags and laptop, and got in the car.

It was a Mercedes, which was a very nice car. She started it up and moved on to the last phase of this huge fuck-up.

chapter THIRTY

Their games—playoffs, finals, or otherwise—didn't end like the ones people watched on TV. There was no media, no interviews, no discussions about gameplay with anyone beyond the coaches. Instead, players just returned to the locker room, showered, changed clothes, and sometimes went to an after-game party or dinner.

Zé waited with Max's sisters and friends for her to make her way down the gauntlet of fans. She and the others signed autographs, hair wet from the shower, game bags slung over their shoulders. Looking at Max and the rest of the Butchers' "Badger Force"—which was what the triplets now called her four honey badger teammates—he couldn't tell that they'd just taken down a shifter-run kidnapping ring. Quickly, efficiently, and—according to his chat with Charlie during an interesting halftime show with giant panda rappers directly from Hong Kong—without any loss of victims or serious harm to her team.

That was huge, considering the number of victims they'd had to deal with.

Because the team had only won their first playoff game—they had quite a few games to go before they made it to the finals—their celebration consisted of a dinner at a shifter restaurant in Chinatown. Although Shen pointed out that this particular restaurant was not run by giant pandas but a South China tiger family, Zé noted that the menu still catered to the pandas. He'd never seen bamboo combined with so many things before. And Shen ordered at least half of them.

As the team and their friends and family enjoyed the night and their win, Max was surprisingly quiet. She didn't smile as much as she usually did either.

"Are you okay?" he finally asked her when she rested her head on his arm.

"We should have been better. Our timing tighter."

"During the game? Are you kidding?"

"No. We did pretty well at the game. I'm talking about . . . before. We were off before."

"You got yourselves and the vics out without any losses. That's impressive. You guys didn't even train together. And Charlie was a new element."

"Charlie and I have worked together most of our lives and I have worked with my teammates since we were all around eleven or twelve. Putting everyone together should have worked just fine, and it did. But still . . . we need better timing."

"Does this mean you're going to keep doing this?"

"I don't know. It was nice to help others . . . while still getting to kill assholes. That was very enjoyable."

Zé shook his head. "How about we not talk about this? You do your thing. I'll do mine."

"What does that mean?"

"I got an offer from the Group. And then I got an offer from Katzenhaus."

"That's cool."

"Yes."

"Do you know where you'll be stationed? Because both those organizations have offices around the world."

Zé put his arm around Max's shoulders. "Don't worry. I'm not leaving you."

"That was not what I was—"

He put his forefinger over her mouth. "Shhhhh, my love. We'll talk about your obsession with me later."

"I hate you."

"You wish."

★ ★ ★

When Max woke up the next morning, Zé had already gone downstairs. He was probably hanging out in that damn tree. He loved to lie around in that tree!

She showered, dressed, and walked downstairs. When she stepped into the living room, Max turned toward the kitchen. But she stopped and looked over her shoulder. Confused, she walked toward the front of the house until she reached the sunroom.

"Can I help you?" she asked the stranger sitting on the love seat that faced into the house.

The female frowned and stared at Max hard but didn't reply.

The front door opened and Stevie walked in. She smiled at Max and the woman on the love seat but kept going.

"Stevie?"

"Uh-huh?" She came back into the room. "What's up?"

"I don't know who this is. Do you know who this is?"

"No. I assumed you did." She smiled at the female. "Hello."

The female gave a wave.

"Can we help you with something?" Stevie asked. "Are you lost?"

The female shook her head. "I'm waiting."

Her voice sounded . . . odd. Muffled. Like she had a head cold. But nothing about that set off alarm bells. Her sister, however, reacted as if she'd been struck, stepping back and gawking at the woman.

"What's wrong with you?"

Stevie didn't answer. Instead, she stepped closer to the female and asked, "Are . . . are you Natalie?"

Now Max felt as if she'd been struck. She looked the female over. She did look young. And pretty. Big brown eyes, dark brown hair with red ends.

Stevie tapped her left ear with her finger. "Deaf?"

The girl smiled, nodded.

"You can read lips?" Max asked.

"Well," Stevie interrupted, "even those who can read lips only get about twenty percent of what people are saying."

"I didn't ask you. I asked her."

"I'm trying to help. It's better if we use ASL—American Sign Language." She looked at Natalie. "You do know sign language, yes?" And while Stevie asked the question verbally, she also did things with her hands and fingers that suggested she was asking it in ASL as well.

Max didn't know what she expected from the girl who'd been kidnapped by their father, but "I have known you five minutes and you have annoyed me" was definitely not it.

Max laughed but Stevie was just insulted.

"I'm trying to help you."

"Help me do what? I'm deaf, *not* disabled. And your ASL is weak."

"*Burn*," Max snickered.

"Well, you don't have to be *bitchy*." Stevie pointed at her mouth. "Can you read that?"

Max put her hand on Stevie's shoulder to calm her down. "Where's Freddy?" she asked Natalie.

"In the trunk."

The sisters exchanged glances.

"In the trunk of what?" Max asked.

"In the trunk of the car I stole from Mairi MacKilligan before I killed her."

Max cringed a little. "Sweetie, you only think you killed her."

Natalie stood and stretched her arm around Max's neck, pressed her fingers between the spot that connected the spine and skull. "I slipped the blade there. She's definitely dead."

When she stepped back, Max could only ask, "Wait . . . who are you again?"

Zé was relaxing in what he now considered his tree, the feral cat on a branch above, when a hand reached up and yanked him down.

He landed on his feet, his gun pressed against someone's throat before he realized what was going on.

"Nice reflexes, house cat."

He lowered his weapon. The Malone brothers. Just great. And he was having such a very nice morning, too.

"What are you doing here?"

"My sister's here. We want to see her now."

"Well, thank you for not taking down the door this time."

Keane Malone's snarl was disturbing but Zé ignored it and led him and his brothers into the house.

Kyle was eating breakfast at the kitchen table. "What's going on?" he asked.

When he didn't get an answer, he grabbed a piece of buttered toast and followed the group through the house.

As soon as they were near the sunroom, Keane shoved Zé out of the way and charged in. He picked up the young girl standing with Max and Stevie and hugged her so tightly, Zé was afraid he'd crush her.

The hug lasted a bit and then he lowered his sister to the ground. That's when they started talking to each other using ASL.

Zé had to admit . . . he was shocked. Shocked that someone like Keane Malone knew goddamn American Sign Language. And, from what Zé could see, knew it really well.

The pair were just chatting away, the other Malone brothers interjecting occasionally, when they heard yelling coming from out in the street.

Max and Stevie looked through the window and then both sisters were running out of the house.

"What's going on?" one of the brothers asked.

"Nothing good," Zé admitted.

Charlie was walking back to her house from Ruth's. She'd dropped off six large honey-pineapple upside-down cakes for Ruth Barton and her husband. If her kids had been home, she would have made the family at least a dozen cakes because Ruth's grizzly family could pack it away. She normally didn't just give the bears baked goods. She waited until they asked . . . or demanded. But Ruth had helped her. Had been kind to her when she didn't have to be. The *least* Charlie could do was bake the woman and her husband their favorite "Charlie Cake," as they named her nonexistent baking company.

Passing her garage, Charlie looked up ahead and saw the trunk of a car burst open and someone scramble out, tossing rope off his arms.

"Dad?" She hadn't said it loudly, but her father heard her anyway. They looked at each other, eyes locking . . . and that's when her father made a run for it.

"Motherfucker!" Charlie growled before taking off after him. When she caught up to him, she tackled him from behind, dropping him to the ground.

Before she knew it, she was kicking him across the street. A moment later, her bear neighbors came out of their houses. Soon the triplets reached her. And a few seconds after that came her own sisters.

Berg wrapped his arms around her body and carried her away from Freddy. She never wanted to hurt Berg, so she didn't fight him. But that didn't stop her from yelling.

She yelled a lot.

"*Youmotherfuckingcocksuckingspunkbubblebastardcuntwhoreofa-motherfucker!*"

Trying not to laugh—because hearing her sister use "spunk bubble" as part of one long diatribe of profanity was too perfect—Max grabbed her father by his hair and dragged him to his feet.

"Going somewhere, Dad?" she asked.

Freddy pulled away but he lost a hunk of hair in the process since Max refused to let it go on her own.

"I paid it back," he immediately told them. "I paid everything back."

"*Dad*," Stevie sighed. "Come on."

"It's true! Call your uncle. Call Bernice. They'll both tell you."

"Yeahhhhh," Max dramatically rolled out, "the thing is, Dad, we don't care if you paid them back."

"She's right," Stevie agreed. "We don't care."

"We do care, however, that you kidnapped a seventeen-year-old girl." Max pulled out her phone. "That reminds me . . . her oh-so-pleasant brothers are at the house right now. I'm sure they'd love to say 'hi' to you. Don't you think, Stevie?"

"They'd love it."

"Wait!" her father begged. "Just let me explain."

"Explain what?" Max asked as she texted the eldest Malone on his phone so he could come down and slap her father around. "How you're going to be arrested for statutory rape?"

Her father, for the first time she could ever remember, actually looked honestly stunned by her words. Not one of his fake expressions either, but as if she'd really caught him off-guard.

"Why the hell would I be arrested for statutory rape?"

"Because when one kidnaps a seventeen-year-old girl, the assumption is kind of made whether you did it or not."

"I didn't kidnap anyone."

"Riiiiiiiiiight."

"I didn't. I just . . ."

"You just . . . what, Dad? What did you just?"

"I just spent time with my daughter."

Max didn't really understand her father's words. She continued to stare at him, her mind trying to wrap itself around this new lie. But then Stevie tackled him to the ground and began pummeling him in the face.

Acting on instinct, Max wrapped her arms around her sister and carried her away from their father while Stevie continued to kick and scream and basically lose her mind.

"*Youmotherfuckingcocksuckingspunkbubblebastardcuntwhoreofa-motherfucker!*"

As she moved, praying her sister didn't take this moment to shift into her two-ton self, Max didn't even look at their father. There was no point.

She got Stevie back to the house but was unable to open the security door. She kicked the door with her foot and Zé opened it.

"What the hell's going on?" he asked, taking a still hysterical Stevie from her arms.

"Just hold her," Max ordered as Charlie returned to the sunroom.

"What's going on?" she asked, staring at Max.

"If I tell you," Max explained, relieved that Stevie had finally calmed down enough for Zé to put her on the ground, "it's just going to make you mad."

"Are you fucking kidding right now?" Charlie snapped.

Max looked at Natalie. "You already know, don't you?"

One side of her mouth lifted and all Max could say to her was, "I'm so sorry, kid. I'm so sorry."

She shrugged. "It's okay. It's not your fault."

"You're so sorry about what?" Charlie looked around the room. No one would look at her except Max. Even the Malones had their gazes fixed on the floor. "Tell me. So sorry about what?"

Her rage gone, Stevie simply burst into tears at Charlie's questions.

That's when understanding sank into Charlie's brain and she slowly faced Natalie. Gently, she asked, "You're our sister, aren't you?"

Natalie nodded.

Charlie moved closer, stood over her. Max doubted her big sister knew how terrifying she must have appeared to the kid. When she was thinking and concerned, Charlie got such a look. To this day, just the *thought* of that expression still freaked out her teammates.

Max could tell that everyone was waiting to see Charlie's reaction. What she would say to Natalie. What she'd say to everyone. But Max knew her sister really well. Maybe too well.

So she wasn't surprised when Charlie spun around and walked out of the sunroom, pushed past the triplets, and kept going until they heard the back door slam open.

Then the scream came. Just one long, anguished scream. A scream Charlie only seemed to use when her father had done something particularly fucked up.

It went on for a long time and shook the house windows.

It was such a strong scream that eventually their deaf sister tapped Max's arm and asked, "Is she screaming?"

Max nodded. "Yes."

"So I'm not the only one he makes do that?"

Max laughed. "Nah, kid. You're not the only one."

chapter THIRTY-ONE

They all stood in the sunroom, staring through the big windows. Together, they watched Charlie sit on the porch and seethe. No one seethed quite like Max's big sister. She did it silently but Charlie didn't need words when the very air around her pulsed with her anger.

"She hates me, doesn't she?"

Before Max could reply to Natalie Malone's question, Stevie did.

"No! Of course not. She just feels *so* bad for you."

"Why?"

Max finally looked away from Charlie to see Stevie give the saddest shrug. "Because you're a MacKilligan," Stevie said, wiping a tear. "That's so horrible for you."

"She's a Malone," Keane growled, still glaring out the window.

"Oh, of course! Of course!" Stevie nodded, but then she scrunched up her face and asked, "But is she? Really? Because your mother's not a Malone, right? It was your father."

Damn! Max couldn't believe her sister had gone *there.*

The Malone brothers faced her, and the triplets quickly moved behind Stevie while Shen stepped in front of her; all of them were ready to protect her with their very lives.

"Cool," Zé whispered to Max. "Fight."

"No, no, no!" Stevie jumped in front of Shen. "There's no need to fight. We can all get along."

Max studied the bears and the cats before asking her sister, "Are you fucking kidding?"

Stevie's little hands balled into fists. "I am trying to do something," she growled.

"What, exactly?" Max asked, laughing. "Because so far you've managed to fuck this up *spectacularly!*"

Stevie didn't reply; instead her eyes narrowed.

"What?" Max pushed. "What are you going to do?"

Britta shook her head and ordered, "You two, don't start this—"

But it was already too late. They were in mutual headlocks, both of them screaming at each other. Max could feel hands on her, attempting to pry her away from Stevie as they battled each other across the room. It wasn't until they were right in front of the windows that Max felt something in the air change. So did Stevie. At the same moment, they released each other and looked up to see Charlie standing in front of the window, fangs peeking out from under her gums, eyes a bright wolf gold. Then she snarled and Stevie yelled what they were all thinking but would never say out loud, *"Run for your lives!"*

Charlie watched an entire group of predators disappear deep into the house. The only one still standing there was Berg. But he was laughing so hard, she simply turned away and returned to her spot on the porch steps.

As she rested her elbows on her raised knees and her chin on her fist, she wondered how much more damage one man could do. How could Freddy MacKilligan be *that* much of a fuck-up? How was it possible?

"And that poor girl," she sighed out, thinking of Natalie Malone. She rubbed her eyes with both her fists, wishing she could wipe away all of it.

"Excuse me?"

Charlie lowered her fists but didn't open her eyes. "Sorry. I'm not baking today."

"Pardon?"

That didn't sound like the voice of any local bear. It was too polite. So Charlie opened her eyes and spotted a slight older man standing on the other side of her fence. He held a paper-back book in his hand and watched her with great caution.

"I'm sorry," she said. "I thought you were someone else. Can I help you?"

"I'm looking for Zé Vargas. I was told he was staying here."

Charlie leaned back a bit, letting her gaze look the man over. "You're his grandfather."

He nodded and Charlie smiled, getting to her feet. She walked over to the gate and unlocked it.

"Hi, Mr. Vargas," she greeted. "Come on in."

"Wait . . . why did *we* run?" Keane Malone asked.

"Because you're weak and pathetic?" Zé asked.

Dag gawked at him. "Wow. You went full-cat fast."

He really had. What was wrong with him? He was the quiet, observant one. That's how he'd always been described, whether it was playing football in high school or dealing with insurgents in a battle zone. Zé was always "quiet and observant."

What he'd never really been was snarky and mean. Until now. Until he'd become part of this world.

Even worse . . . he was really enjoying it.

"We should just get Natalie out of here," Shay said to his brothers.

"You're not taking our sister anywhere," Max said and she suddenly had the full attention of the Malone brothers. They locked on her the way those lions locked on that gazelle in the documentary he'd watched.

"She's *not* your sister," Keane snarled.

"She is now. She's already been through the gauntlet."

"The gauntlet?" Finn asked.

"Yeah. The Dad-gauntlet. Where he does something so ruthless and shitty that you realize you're stuck being his child. At least this time he didn't sell her."

"Sell her?"

"Yeah. Once he sold me to a family. Indentured servitude, I think it's called."

Stevie nodded sadly. "He sold me to lots of people. The most infamous, though, was the Peruvian drug lord."

"Yeah. Charlie and I dealt with that situation." That's when Max smiled. The smile said it all, and Zé knew he was in real trouble with this girl. He was no longer falling . . . he'd fallen. Because she was a nut. And he liked it. He liked her lethal nuttiness.

"Whatever," Keane finally snapped. "You're not keeping our sister."

"You can't raise her," Max argued. "You giant house cats don't know what to do with a honey badger."

As the two families bickered, Zé saw Natalie roll her eyes and wander off. She studied the trees and the house, then looked into the glass door of the garage and disappeared inside.

Kyle heard someone come into his studio. He didn't bother looking to see who it was. If it was Charlie, then food would be left on his desk. The woman constantly worried about his health. If it was Max, she would take a couple of basketballs from the shelves on the far side of the space and go outside to play. And if it was Stevie, she would simply look over his current work, nod her approval, and leave.

He appreciated that the MacKilligan sisters didn't really bother him while he was working and only occasionally got in his way. Like when he was going to destroy his worst work. He didn't see what the big deal had been but Charlie and Stevie were adamant. If he pulled out the sledgehammer again, they were going right to Toni. Just the thought of his sister's lecture had him tossing the hammer aside and simply moving his least favorite sculptures to the back of the garage so he didn't have to see them whenever he walked in.

So far that plan had worked just as well as hitting them with the hammer.

Kyle rubbed his nose, then lifted his head. He sniffed the air, surprised by the strange scent filling the garage. That's when he saw her standing in front of his work. She was in a long black skirt, a black T-shirt with some no-name band on it, and bright yellow Doc Martens boots. Her black hair was long and separated into three pony tails, one of them hanging in front of her face.

The "lost" MacKilligan sister, as he'd started calling her when he'd discovered who she was. When Charlie had let out that scream of rage at her father, Kyle simply went into the garage and got to work. He didn't want to get in the middle of his own family's drama, much less someone else's. But now he had the lost sister roaming around his workspace. Uninvited. Badgers and cats . . . they had absolutely no respect for other people's boundaries, did they?

Although he did have questions. For instance, would Natalie turn into a giant tiger-striped honey badger like Stevie? Or would she simply be a honey badger? Or maybe shift into a tiny tiger? Or . . . would she shift into something even more interesting than any of those options?

Yeah, see? He had so many questions!

Natalie was impressed by the work she was seeing. Not only the statues that took up so much space, but the rough drawings tacked to the wall.

She wasn't an artist herself. She could doodle a bit, but only when her computer was doing something that required her to wait until it finished. Otherwise, she was all about computers and games. She *loved* games! Of course, she'd have to convince her brothers that she should go to college to get a degree in game engineering, rather than just engineering. She was already dreading that conversation. Her mother knew what she wanted but her mother left almost all decisions about her only daughter to her eldest sons. Especially Keane.

Natalie loved Keane more than seemed possible, but he tended to drown her in concern. He was convinced she was this weak kitten he'd found dying under his house. He had no idea what Natalie and her friends got up to when he wasn't around. What had happened with Freddy MacKilligan was nothing, really. And she'd only gone off with him so she could spend some time with the man who was her father.

Ech! What a mistake. He was such an idiot. She could deal with almost anything, even pure evil. But pure stupidity? Who had time for that?

About to move over to another statue, Natalie abruptly realized that someone was right next to her. She looked over the kid standing at her side. She'd seen him in the house earlier, before he'd slipped away. He smelled like dog.

"What?" she finally asked.

"What do you look like when you shift?"

Natalie blinked. She had her hearing aids on and she could kind of read his lips, too. But the question was so bizarre that she immediately assumed she'd misread and misheard him.

"What?"

"Oh," he said. "That's right. You're deaf." That didn't stop him from talking, though. Only he spoke a little slower and used his hands a lot more. Not to speak in ASL, but to gesture.

"When you shift . . . are you all honey badger? Or all cat? Are you a giant"—he lifted his arms in the air—"tiger? Or a giant honey badger?" He brought his arms down and spread his hands a couple of feet apart. "Or a tiny tiger? Do you have fangs? Or are you fangless? Do you have a snaggle-fang?"

A snaggle-fang? Oh, boy.

"Um . . . who are you?"

"I'm Kyle. I'm a genius. Literally . . . a genius."

"I'm walking away now."

"Can't you answer any of my questions?"

"I don't want to answer any of your questions."

"Is it because you're shy?"

"No. It's because you're weird."

"I am weird. But that's because I'm a genius."

"Of *course* it is."

After a much-deserved eye roll, Natalie walked away from the kid, but he caught up to her at the door. He took her hand so that she had to look up at him.

"Do you date?" he asked.

"Not you."

"Because I'm a genius?"

She pulled her hand from his grasp. "If that makes you feel better . . . sure."

"Are you positive you don't want to go out and—"

The glass door swung open, slamming right into the kid's face. Natalie covered her mouth with her hands, shocked when she saw blood smeared on the glass from his broken nose.

Keane stood in the doorway. "What are you doing?"

She just shook her head.

Keane pointed at the glass. "Blood?"

She pointed at the kid. He was still behind the door, two bloody hands covering his nose. But Nat knew she didn't need to point him out; her brother could see him through the clear glass. She knew Keane had seen Kyle before he'd even opened the door! That's *why* he'd opened the door. He'd seen a boy talking to his baby sister. Once again, her psychotic brother was attempting to ruin her social life!

"Oh." Keane nodded at Kyle. "Hey." He jerked his thumb at Nat. "Let's go."

Keane walked out and she began to follow, but she did stop long enough to shrug at the kid and mouth, *Sorry.*

He'd needed a few minutes, so she'd let him sit down next to her on the porch stairs. His name was Xavier Vargas and he was a very nice man. He also missed his grandson. That was obvious without his even saying it.

"How long have you lived here?" he asked, continuing the small talk of the last few minutes.

"Not long actually. Just a few weeks."

"Do you like it?"

"It's nice. I wouldn't say the people are friendly . . ." Charlie thought long and hard about how to finish her sentence. After a good sixty seconds, she went with, "But I like that they're easily manipulated by food."

Mr. Vargas nodded, but then he began to rub his forehead with his fingers.

"This was a mistake," he finally said after blowing out a long breath.

"No. You guys need to talk."

"I don't know what to say."

"Tell him the truth. Tell him you did what you had to in order to keep him safe. He'll understand."

"You don't know my grandson."

"No. Not completely. But the more comfortable he becomes with himself . . . the more he'll understand. Just give him time."

Those words didn't seem to help and she worried that Mr. Vargas would leave before he had a chance to see Zé. So she quickly added, "But you know what? You've made the first move, which I'm sure he'll appreciate. And you've come to the perfect place to have this discussion. It's a nice, quiet house with quiet neighbors and—"

Her next words were abruptly cut off when the front security door was thrown open and Keane stalked out, dragging his baby sister behind him. Bears and cats and badgers followed.

"There's nothing left to talk about!" Keane barked, stepping over Mr. Vargas as if the man wasn't even there. "I'm taking her home!"

Stevie dashed around everyone, jumped over the porch steps—and Charlie and Mr. Vargas who were still sitting on them—and skittered to a stop in front of Keane and Natalie.

She rammed her hands into the tiger's chest and said, "You can't just take her away from us."

"Watch me."

"Natalie can stay if she wants to," Berg said. "Why don't we ask her what she wants?"

"Why don't *you* shut up?" Keane snapped back.

"Talk to my brother like that again . . ." Britta warned.

"Hold it!" Max stepped into the middle of the fray, right where she liked it. "Before this gets ugly, why don't we see if Charlie has anything to say."

That's when all those heads turned toward her. Even Mr. Vargas's. They all looked at her as if they expected her to say something that could help resolve the situation. But what did they expect her to say?

★ ★ ★

"Well," Charlie began, looking directly at Natalie, "let's face it. You're doomed. Your life is over. All your hopes and dreams are gone."

Oh, shit. Max hadn't realized that her sister was in one of her "moods" as the Pack used to call it. Of course, she should have realized. The only person who ever managed to make her like this was Freddy, but still . . . Max had never thought her sister was *this* far gone. Into the world of despair and misery.

Stevie tried to cut in. "Charlie, I'm sure you don't mean—"

"There's nothing you can do about it," Charlie continued, sounding sadder and sadder by the second. Even if Natalie couldn't hear it, she could read it all over Charlie. Like a misery shroud.

"And why?" Charlie asked. "Because you have a disability. The worst disability anyone could ever have."

Max quickly caught Keane's arm before he could storm over to Charlie and slap the crap out of her. "Let her finish."

"You have the painful, cruel disability . . . of being the daughter of Freddy MacKilligan."

"There it is!" Max announced.

"So, you might as well go back to your home," Charlie said to Natalie. "Go back. Pretend you're a Malone. And pray that being a MacKilligan won't catch up to you . . . but it will. It will catch up to you. And when that day arrives, come back here. Because if there's one thing the three of us can do, it's help you through the nightmare of your bloodline."

With that, Charlie sadly looked off across the street, placed her left hand over her heart, and let out a long, pathetic sigh of despair and misery.

See? It was always despair and misery.

After a few seconds, though, Charlie suddenly announced, "Now I must bake."

She disappeared into the house, and that's when Max finally noticed the older man who had been sitting on the stoop with her sister.

"Mr. Vargas?" she asked.

He gave her a faint smile and held up the paperback book she'd written her address in.

Zé came to the top of the stairs and glared down at his grandfather. "What are you doing here?"

Nope. Max didn't like that at all, but she knew she couldn't be the one to interfere. Zé knew her too well. He'd never take her seriously.

"Stevie," she said, motioning her sister over. "That's Zé's grandfather and Zé is being rude to him."

"He's your grandfather?" Stevie shook her head. "Zé, don't be rude to your grandfather! Grandfathers are the best! Well . . . not all. But most! And you should be nice. Whatever he did or didn't do, he did for *you*."

"Stevie," Zé said kindly but firmly, "stay out of it."

Stevie gasped and Max cringed.

"Not smooth, dude," Max warned.

"I will *not* stay out of it!" Stevie told Zé. "You will be nice to your grandfather! In fact," she added, looking around at everyone, "all of you will be nice! Do you know why? Because we're all family now! Whether we like it or not! So here's how this is going to roll!" She turned and pointed her finger at Natalie. "You're our sister and we do care about you. I have no idea if we like you, we may not, but we won't know until we get to know each other. We *will* get to know each other." Her finger moved to Keane. "You will *not* keep your sister away from us. Do you know why? Because we're all family! All of us. So if she wants to come see us, you'll let her. If she wants to call, you'll let her. But you guys are welcome here, too. Because you're family."

Stevie spun again and now that finger was pointed at Zé. "Now *you* will take your grandfather into the house. You will invite him to dinner. The triplets will arrange for the meal. While we're waiting for food, you two will talk. It *will be* a nice conversation because it will be between a grandfather and grandson *who love each other!*"

Max winced because that last bit was screamed quite close to her ear.

Stevie took in a calming breath and let it out before asking, "Have I made myself perfectly clear to everyone?"

When no one answered, Stevie's face turned a bright red and her hands curled into those tiny fists again.

That's when everyone quickly agreed that yes, she'd made herself clear.

She relaxed and the redness left her face. "Now, if you'll excuse me," she said before going back into the house. Shen and the triplets followed behind her.

Max looked over her shoulder at Natalie. They smiled at each other and Max winked. Then Keane and his brothers stepped between them.

Turning toward the tigers, Max threw out her arms in direct challenge and asked, "What? Ya got a problem?"

With growls and snarls, the tigers led their sister away, and Max really hoped she'd see the kid again. Then she remembered that "kid" had taken out their cousin Mairi, and she wondered if seeing her again would actually be a good idea.

"Eh," she said with a dismissive shrug. She wasn't going to sit around worrying about her murderous little sister right now. She had more important things to deal with!

"Would you gentlemen like a couple of beers?"

"That would be nice," Mr. Vargas said. "As long as it's American beer."

"We always have Coors for my friend Dutch."

She carefully stepped around the full-human. When she was next to Zé, she pointed at the old man and mouthed, *Talk to him!* Zé rolled his eyes, so she added with a vicious frown, *Be nice!*

Confident she'd gotten her point across, Max changed her frown to the smile she was much more comfortable with and went up on her toes to kiss Zé on the cheek. But before she could, he brushed his head against her cheek, her chin, her throat. She felt his purr moving across her flesh.

When he pulled away, Max walked to the door and went into the house. Once she was inside, she bent over at the waist, put her hands on her knees, and let out a long, shuddering breath.

There wasn't a lot in the world that rocked Max to her toes, but those feline moves . . . ?

Damn.

When Max disappeared into the house, Zé looked down at his grandfather. "Are you coming or what?"

"Are you going to help me up?" he snapped back.

"Why are you sitting down there anyway?"

"Just help me up."

Zé held out his hands and with a simple heave, he easily brought Xavier to his feet. They stared at each other.

They were silent for a long time until Zé said, "You should have told me."

Xavier nodded. "I know. But after your mother and grand-mother . . . I couldn't risk losing you, too."

"You couldn't lose me. Apparently once cats find people they like, they stick with them."

A small smile curled Xavier's lips. "You learn that from those badgers?"

"I'm learning all sorts of things from those badgers." He motioned to the house. "Let's go inside. We'll talk."

"Anything to keep that little blonde from yelling at us again," Xavier complained as he moved to the front door. "She's terri-fying." He stopped, looked up at Zé. "The one with the purple hair, though? Max? She seems really sweet."

Zé laughed so hard that Xavier had to ask, "What the hell's so funny?"

"Don't worry," Zé promised, putting his hands on his grandfather's shoulders and gently leading him into the house. "Just like me . . . you'll figure it out."

Connect with Us

Visit us online at
KensingtonBooks.com
to read more from your favorite authors, see books
by series, view reading group guides, and more.

Join us on social media

for sneak peeks, chances to win books and prize packs,
and to share your thoughts with other readers.

facebook.com/kensingtonpublishing
twitter.com/kensingtonbooks

Tell us what you think!

To share your thoughts, submit a review,
or sign up for our eNewsletters, please visit:
KensingtonBooks.com/TellUs.